THE F*I*NAL PROCLAMATI*O*N

CARLTON JAMES

Black Rose Writing | Texas

First printing

This is a work of fiction. Names, characters, businesses, places, events, and
incidents are either the products of the author's imagination or used in a
fictitious manner. Any resemblance to actual persons, living or dead, or
actual events is purely coincidental.

ISBN: 978-1-68433-724-8
PUBLISHED BY BLACK ROSE WRITING
www.blackrosewriting.com

Printed in the United States of America
Suggested Retail Price (SRP) $20.95

The Final Proclamation is printed in Garamond

*As a planet-friendly publisher, Black Rose Writing does its best to eliminate
unnecessary waste to reduce paper usage and energy costs, while never
compromising the reading experience. As a result, the final word count vs. page count
may not meet common expectations.

PRAISE FOR

THE F{NAL PROCLAMATI⚕N

"President Katherine Fontaine with her power-hungry coldness and harsh leadership has made the country vulnerable to a drastic shift in world domination prompting her to enact martial law in order to maintain the control she craves, her followers to falter, and citizens to prepare for disaster. A realistic story of corruption and terrorism, James's second novel in this series reflects well his thirty-one years in intelligence work."

–Penny Woods, Freelance Book Reviewer
for *Kentucky Living magazine*

"Although clearly fiction, certain passages bare striking similarities to recent events and readers will want to prepare for what may soon come."

–Arlynn McMahon, author of *Train Like You Fly*
and several other publications

"Interwoven stories, spell-binding intrigue, and characters who drew me into their world ... impossible to put down."

–Richard Warner, Ph.D., Emeritus Professor and author.

THE FINAL PROCLAMATION

ACKNOWLEDGEMENTS

Writing *An American Reborn Thriller* series, including this second installment, is my attempt to use an entertaining novel to begin the story of how America could easily slip into the abyss of communism in its many forms, causing us to climb back out through the faith and efforts of a few, strong, patriotic Americans. If you will, it can be viewed as a modern-day re-enactment of our nation's founding. In approaching such a broad topic, numerous friends and co-workers from my past and present provided examples, guidance and support making these novels possible. I continue to get outstanding support from several trusted friends including Richard and Arlynn, without whom there would be no series. Richard believed in me and this story from the beginning and I agree, my friend, it will make a great movie. Arlynn proved invaluable from reading and editing each chapter to coming up with, and refining some of the best ideas, many of which were incredibly entertaining. I could go on about how much support I received from my family, all of which is appreciated more than they know. I am truly blessed by God.

CHAPTER 1
CHRISTMAS DAY

Washington, DC
John Levy's Apartment
0900 Hours EST

John Levy was a tall, rangy Secret Service Special Agent with black hair who had served in the United States Secret Service for over eighteen years. When he was assigned to lead President Katherine Fontaine's husband, Walter Fontaine's, protection detail, he figured it was because he was recently divorced, had no kids, and probably needed the money such duty brought with it, including all of the overtime.

At the moment, John was incredibly pissed off. He had been dragged back from a well-deserved mini-vacation to babysit the First Man once again. The bastard was supposed to be spending his Christmas in California. Late yesterday afternoon John had received the call that Walter was on his way back to Washington, D.C. with plans to find somewhere to party late Christmas Eve. Instead of Walter's normal bootie call, he went to the condominium of a lesser-known Washington socialite with his detail in tow. After a quick search of the condo, the detail set up a perimeter while Walter was "entertained." It had happened before, but not very often. Usually he completely disappeared.

Unknown to John and the team, Walter was quietly furious that he could not get Mr. Sung on the phone. Mr. Sung was the Chinese lobbyist who gave him access to the spectacular Su Ling. Mr. Sung would not answer his phone so Walter reluctantly went through his little red address book and found the socialite's number. He told her how nice it was of her to delay spending Christmas with her parents and siblings just to keep him company.

John was exhausted when he stumbled back to his apartment at 9:00 a.m. Christmas Day. Just as he began to put the key into the door lock, he heard a man behind him say, "Hey, Johnny boy! How they hanging?"

To his absolute dismay, John turned to see three men, including his old college roommate, Bobby Waite. Shocked as he was to see Bobby, he was even more so to recognize the second man as W. Allen Kidd, the Director of the Federal Bureau of Investigation.

Bobby then said, "Hey, we're sorry to drop in on you like this, but it's *really* important that we talk to you. Can you give us a few minutes?"

John's fatigue seemed to have temporarily disappeared. "Uh, yeah. Sure. Come on in." He opened his door to a world crazier than usual, even by Washington, D.C. standards.

When the visitors sat down at John's kitchen table, one brought out a couple of large paper bags containing thermoses of steaming coffee and day-old donuts.

John was now fully alert and extremely curious. "Okay, what the hell brings the FBI Director and two other bureau types to my door on Christmas Day?"

Director Kidd motioned to Bobby and said, "Well, you know this guy and obviously know who I am. This other guy is Hugh McIntyre, one of my Unit Chiefs at FBIHQ, and a man with a tiger by the tail. It's our hope that you can figure out what kind of tiger it is and just maybe how we're supposed to let go of the tail."

At the confused expression on John's face, the Director continued, "John, the reason I'm here is that we're dealing with something at the highest levels of national security. I'm here to impress upon you that what we're going to go into today is legit. I also need to know if we can talk to you without your needing to share it with your supervisor or anyone else. I do mean anyone else. Quite frankly, if you don't think you can, our talk is finished and other steps will have to be taken. I'm sorry you won't have much time to think about it, but I need an answer now."

One of the traits of a Secret Service agent on a protection detail is the ability to make instant decisions that often involve life or death. Those that can't make those types of decisions find other work in the Treasury Department. John had no problem making decisions, but he made those based upon data. He wanted more data, so he looked directly at Bobby. "Should I do this?"

Bobby didn't hesitate. "I was just read in on this yesterday. Yes, John you really need to do this."

After a deep breath, John said, "I'm in. What do you need?"

The Director waved to Hugh. "You're up."

Hugh, with his graying hair and open face, gave John a smile that conveyed John could trust him and that he would always have John's best interest in mind. It was both disarming and reassuring. "John, you've been placed in a completely impossible situation, and I hope you know how much we appreciate the way you've handled it. I've already gotten the okay that should you decide you need to move on from the Secret Service after this, you will be granted a lateral transfer to the bureau." The Director nodded at this statement.

At the statement from Hugh, John's eyes widened and he instantly wondered how bad it could get.

Hugh continued, "Up to now, you've been screwed. I give you my word that ultimately you will not be left flapping in the breeze."

Seeing the growing confusion written on John's face, Hugh said, "Let me fill you in on what I know, or at least part of it. Your protectee, Walter Fontaine, has been regularly ditching his protection detail for several years. We know this and presume you have been threatened with professional suicide if you don't go along with his forays outside of your protection. Am I correct?"

John immediately felt his defenses going up. Using a conscious effort, he forced himself to lower them again. "Yeah, but I can only speak to what I know since I was brought on the team a little over a year ago. I did kind of figure he had been doing the same thing, even dating back to when he was Vice President."

"That would be correct," Hugh said with regret. "We need to know everything you can tell us about these forays and everything you have observed."

Had the question come from anyone but someone in the company of the FBI Director, John's response would have been to clam up completely. With the Director listening intently across the table, John told them about what the protection detail thought of as Walter's bootie calls, to include his look of complete sexual satisfaction every time he returned. He even told them about one of his detail getting a partial plate from a rented car that picked Walter up at a restaurant.

Pausing to let what he'd said sink in, John advised of the burner cell phone Walter thought was a secret and where he hid it in the First Lady's bedroom in the White House residence, now renamed the Gold Room.

Softly, Hugh asked, "Do you think you might be able to get the phone at an opportune time and carry it out of the White House for two hours?"

"Look, guys," John said with a slight tremble in his voice. "I'm already betraying the highest level of trust just by talking with you. I'm going to need more to justify doing something like committing espionage against the husband of the President."

With a nod from the Director, Hugh said, "John, you've trusted us so now it's time to trust you. You probably know in almost any other investigation we don't share the details. Everything is on a strict need-to-know basis. With the Director's approval, I'm breaking that policy and want to lay the cards on the table. Walter Fontaine has been meeting with a known Chinese intelligence officer, who sets him up with a well-trained Chinese girl for exotic sex. You do the math as to how many secrets he has given over to her and them."

John felt like he had been hit by a brick. His mind immediately leapt to the level of secrets that would be known by Walter, knowing he would give up everything for a pretty girl. It was a few moments before he caught up with Hugh's words.

"…we haven't been able to determine is, what Walter is saying to her and what he has access to in the White House. We're presuming he and the President don't exactly engage in pillow talk." An ironic chuckle was shared around the room at the notion that Walter would share anything intimate with Katherine.

"John," Hugh continued, "we don't even think Mr. Fontaine knows the Chinese businessman is a spy. He probably just thinks he's a lobbyist trying to garner influence. It really doesn't matter since they're gaining critical intelligence. Please tell us what you know about Walter's access to information, particularly whether he has either received briefings or has an active relationship with Cabinet Members or anyone with high levels of classified information."

John thought for a moment before beginning to list Walter's political cronies in descending order of their classified access.

After ten minutes of deep thought and over fifty names, Hugh asked, "Does this mean he has not met with or been briefed by the CIA Director, Homeland Security Director, or the like?"

John said, "No, I don't think so. He could easily run into those guys and others in the hallways of the White House, but that's one of the hundreds of odd things I see every day. They don't treat him like the Vice President with a presumed need to know. In fact, they would pretty much blow him off if he were to try to go fishing. But you may want to look at the secretaries, interns, and other support people that are in the middle of White House decision making. Walter charms any female, and many of the guys, like a proverbial snake charmer. If he wanted to learn about what was going on, he'd just strike up a conversation with the President's speechwriters or the acting Press Secretary, Towanda Jefferson. I heard Towanda wistfully say once, 'For a white guy, he does have a way with us girls of color.'"

The Director then asked, "Is there anyone inside the White House inner circle that you think we could trust with this investigation?" The Director's reputation for being direct was clearly demonstrated by the question. Unfortunately, that was what broke the camel's back.

"Hey, hey, hey," John said with hands up. "I will *not* spy on my Protectee or help you find a spy in the White House. I'm frankly surprised that you would even suggest such a thing!" John's temper and emotions were rising at the thought of violating every oath he had taken with the Secret Service. The look in his eyes told Hugh and the Director that their interview was over.

The Director paused to see if John had anything else to get off his chest. John only stared with a growing distaste at each of the three men.

"Okay, John," said the Director, "I'm sorry we even had to ask. But I am going to request you take a deep breath and just listen to what I have to say for a moment. Can you do that for me?" At John's cautious nod, he continued.

"Here is the way I see things. We have the husband of the President that has been knowingly or unknowingly lured into a classic honey trap by a Chinese intelligence officer. Walter has free run of the White House and has developed a large number of contacts over many years in Washington, D.C. Since before the election, Walter has most likely been telling his Chinese girlfriend virtually everything the President is planning in terms of foreign policy towards China, military readiness capabilities, economic strategies and even what the President will or won't do should China take further aggressive actions throughout the Pacific Rim." The Director decided not to tell John that he had read detailed debriefings of Su Ling that demonstrated Walter had given up that and much more.

John merely sat in his chair and mouthed the words, "My God." He then refocused and said, "We have to tell the President immediately!" John had even begun to rise off his seat.

"John," the Director said, "please sit back down for at least another few minutes." At the soft, but commanding request John slumped back into his chair.

"Before I go to the President, and I will be going to the President with this one, I want to make sure the evidence I present is not just *beyond a reasonable doubt*, but is incontrovertible. We need to have at least two more meetings by Walter and the Chinese girl, and those meetings cannot take place without you being willing to sit on what you have heard today. I'm sure you know how much the President will want to bury this and maybe everyone involved in it." The Director was displaying the kind of leadership presence that made him one of the few people in the current administration that could command nearly universal respect.

"I know your head is spinning on all of this, and we've given you a hell of a lot to take on faith. I would not be here having this conversation if I hadn't seen the evidence. I refuse to be personally involved in anything political and everyone here and the few others at the bureau that know about this feel the same way. Now the question is: What do we do about it? When I do walk into the President's office, I want to have everything that is possible in hand. All of us must think about what is best for the country, and Lord knows this country is in a world of hurt. Like in 1775, 1812, and 1941 'these are the times that try men's souls.' Thomas Payne said that during the Revolutionary War. John, I believe what we're facing in our country right now is every bit as desperate as it was then, with the potential to be a whole lot worse."

"John," the Director said, "we're going to leave you now. We didn't want to put you in the position of lying to your own agency, and I wouldn't wish it on anyone. But it is what it is, and we all have to deal with it. Hugh has brought along a simple transmitter that is activated by pressing the button. I'd like to leave it with you and ask you to think about pressing the button the next time Walter takes off for his unofficial liaison meeting. You can do so or not as you think is best for you and this country. I also ask that you sit on this information until after the next two outings by Mr. Fontaine. Can you do that for me?"

John looked into the Director's eyes for a full minute before saying, "I'll keep quiet about this visit, but I won't guarantee to help you going forward, you know, like pushing the button."

The Director nodded. "Last comment, John. Unless you decide to say something, no one in my shop will ever reveal this meeting took place. Should you decide you have to tell someone, I will back up your story, so long as it is accurate." With that last phrase, the Director even smiled. He laid the signaling device on the table along with a card bearing a phone number identified only with the word, "Hugh."

The Director stood up and offered his hand to John. His handshake was both warm and firm without being a vice grip. John's old college roommate and Hugh both got up, shook John's hand and walked out of his apartment without another word.

John watched them go. His brain felt like a drag-racing engine going at full speed, only to run out of fuel. Walking into his bedroom, he lay down on his bed, but was unable to sleep.

. . .

Alexandria, Virginia
1700 Hours EST

Lisa McIntyre sat on her bed in her parent's home in Alexandria, Virginia. Her father had, uncharacteristically, been out doing some type of FBI work all morning on Christmas Day. He finally returned late in the afternoon and Lisa's mother gathered the family to sit down to an abbreviated Christmas dinner. She could tell that Hugh was mentally somewhere other than at their home. What was worse, Lisa seemed to be off on some other planet herself.

"All right, you two," Lisa's mom said with authority. "It's high time you put aside whatever you have on your minds and spend a little family time sharing the love of the Christmas season."

The family had opened presents on Christmas Eve, so Christmas Day was traditionally just a gathering around the dinner table to give thanks for the birth of Christ and to celebrate their love for each other. This was to be followed by watching the NBA basketball game.

"I'm sorry, honey. I have something very pressing going on at work. Nothing to do about it now, so let me first thank my lovely bride for giving me a tremendous daughter and, most recently, a wonderful dinner!" Both ladies at the table smiled with appreciation at Hugh's comment.

Almost immediately, Lisa excused herself, got up from the table, and ran to her room. Her mother began to get up to follow her until Hugh stopped her. "I've got this one, honey." He patted her hand as he got up to follow Lisa.

Knocking on Lisa's door twice, Hugh entered without invitation. Lisa was lying on her bed crying in great sobs. He immediately went to her and gathered her up in his arms as he had done when she was a little girl. For several minutes he didn't say anything. He just stroked her hair and held her close until her sobs stopped, to be replaced by a serious case of the sniffles.

"Dad?" Lisa asked in a little girl voice. "Is Su going to get out of this alive?" Already the tears had begun to stream down her face again.

"Sweetheart, I've never lied to either your mother or you, so I won't say there is no danger. But she is an extremely resourceful young woman, so I expect she will be okay for now." He paused before going on. "When are you going to see her again?"

"We're supposed to have lunch at my apartment day after tomorrow. Why?"

"Tell her that her ordeal will be over soon, but I don't know exactly when. When that time comes, I will come for her, and she will need to leave without taking anything with her."

"But when, Daddy?" Lisa asked, somehow knowing her father wouldn't tell her.

In his mind, Hugh screamed at himself for not telling Lisa that after two meetings with the President's husband, he would be coming to end her torment. His only answer was a gentle kiss on her forehead.

CHAPTER 2
CHRISTMAS DAY - PLUS TWO DAYS

The White House
0900 Hours EST

"What is wrong with you assholes?" President Katherine Fontaine exploded at her Cabinet and staff with another of her tantrums. Returning early from her Christmas holiday coupled with her frequent migraines had caused her tirade to be shorter than usual. Recently, she followed these outbursts with clipped edicts to be carried out by her minions. Her Chief of Staff, former Senator Burt Combs, had heard from attendees Katherine was now known as "ES" or evil stepmother – a direct reference to the cartoon movie *Cinderella*. Wisely, Burt chose not to share this information with his President. Nor did he share with her the extreme annoyance of everyone, including himself, at being called to a Cabinet meeting during what was traditionally a holiday vacation period.

Peering through his thick horn-rimmed glasses, Treasury Secretary Seth Goldberg had just advised that another economic stimulus on the heels of the successful one initiated by the administration months earlier would not be successful.

His brief explanation was cut short by Katherine's low, threatening command. "Enough! Anyone else feel strongly that a second stimulus package would fail?" Like a snake waiting to strike, she looked around the room for any obvious sign of support for Goldberg. Stand-ins for CIA Director Bradley Pittson and Joint Chiefs of Staff Chairman General Steven K. Taylor were under strict instructions to only observe and report.

Most of the rest had previously taken their turn in opposing one of Katherine's ideas only to become the object of her personal ridicule. Seated at the table were men and women with over two hundred years of experience who had been relegated to being yes-men. That had caused their own levels of frustration to balloon to the point two cabinet members had stepped down for "personal reasons." Considering the egos in the room, it was amazing any had chosen to remain.

Katherine knew that her glares and steamrolling management style cut short any attempt to garner support from the rest of the cabinet in opposing her agenda. Also, it squashed discussion, which would add to the immense pain she experienced on nearly a daily basis from her migraine headaches. She reminded herself that a worsening economic crisis would soon create the need for her to take charge beyond what those present in the room imagined.

"Are we finished here, Burt?" Katherine asked her Chief of Staff in a tone that meant they were in fact, done.

"Yes, Madam President, the remainder will wait until the next meeting." Burt had to swallow the frustrated words he wanted to say. Only a few months earlier he had told Katherine that she could really count on his loyalty, no matter what. He had begun to have second thoughts. In true political fashion, he began to spin that promise in his mind.

Without another word, Katherine walked from the room toward the Oval Office. On the way, she was met by her assistant, Susan Cassel. Susan was an attractive woman in her mid-40's who kept Katherine's life organized and provided critically needed stress relief on a more personal level.

"Madam President," said Susan in a quiet voice, "Eli Fredericks is in your office."

Everyone in the White House staff, including Susan, was aware that Katherine's largest and most influential campaign donor was to be granted complete access and scheduling precedence over anyone else. He hadn't donated to her personally, although he did ensure individual hefty donations flowed to her campaign. Through shell companies and even certain foreign governments, he had arranged for donations to the Fontaine Foundation totaling in excess of $450 million.

Katherine could not help drawing in a deep breath as she walked in the office. She had been willing to deal with the devil himself in order to attain a position of power like no other in the world. In many ways, she had done so several times with different power brokers. Eli, however, was in a league of his own. The several hundred billion dollars he had made working hedge funds and other more unusual investment strategies had allowed him to expand his tentacles all over the globe. His multiple Political Action Committees were responsible for getting her elected. He had also covertly ensured she would never have to rely on anyone else for money again.

Waiting in Katherine's office was a clean-shaven, light-skinned black man in his late 50's, sitting patiently on her couch working diligently on his smart phone. Such devices were strictly forbidden in most of the White House complex, but then rules did not apply to Eli or to Katherine.

"Eli, to what do I owe the pleasure of your company this morning?" Katherine used the super-sweet tone of voice she reserved for those of color to convince them of her sincere respect. Her intent failed miserably in that regard.

Eli's tone and choice of words had lost their courtesy over the past several months. Previously, he had asked questions and guided Katherine to what he wanted in a respectful voice. Now, his voice was frequently laced with contained anger and a staccato, machine-gun like cadence.

"Katherine, rumors have been flying everywhere that your administration plans to roll out another stimulus plan." Eli stopped and waited for her response, adding the elevation of a questioning eyebrow.

"How big do the rumors say the stimulus package will be?" Katherine asked the question with genuine curiosity.

Eli did not like questions, far preferring to be the one doing the asking. "Well, Katherine, the numbers blow around like leaves, but most lean on the high side at two trillion."

"Hmm, Goldberg is certain that a second stimulus plan won't work, since it is too soon after the last one. Not to mention, it would drive up the debt above $30 trillion." After a pause, Katherine continued, "Tell me, Eli, would another stimulus package of, say, two trillion have any effect on this broken capitalist economy?"

Eli's cold, pale green eyes looked levelly at Katherine for a full five-second count before he responded, "Yes, Katherine, I think it just might work. After all, the whole situation is unprecedented. Nobody really knows what will work and what won't." After another pause for effect, Eli said in his most diplomatic and reasonable voice, "We're in uncharted waters here, but there is a chance the plan could drive things down into the economic toilet even faster. Are you willing to take that risk?"

The look on Katherine's face was different than Eli expected, although he really couldn't have said exactly what he expected. Regardless, he did not expect the appearance of determination and even carefully controlled excitement that he saw. "Yes, Eli, I think I am. Oh, I meant to ask. How is your new investment portfolio going?" Eli knew this question was code for, "How are my personal, off shore investments going?" Early in her campaign for President, Eli had shown her a printout for what he called a "new investment portfolio." It was understood between them that come what may; this portfolio was completely confidential and would always be considered hers. It was a covert backup to the Fontaine Foundation funds. She was obviously concerned about what the crumbling economy was doing to these funds.

"Since I have been managing these funds myself the past year, they have seen a percentage increase." As he said this he raised his hand and put up his index finger, followed by his middle finger and then his ring finger. He then balled his hand into a fist, signifying a three hundred percent increase.

With some relief, Katherine responded, "I suspected you would have funds you personally managed." She then let it drop.

Within the Oval Office, the recording equipment was supposed to be going at all times that the President was there. President Nixon found out the hard way how damning those tapes could be. One of Katherine's first moves was, by TOP SECRET executive order with a fifty-year expiration date, to ensure there was a switch that she could personally turn off. It was off now, but neither she nor Eli had any illusions of absolute privacy.

Eli stood up with purpose. "I have pressing matters, but thank you for taking the time to see me, Katherine." His smile was cold with just a hint of contempt.

Katherine watched Eli leave the Oval Office. She thought again about whether she should use the worsening economic situation to push through another stimulus package. If the package plunged the country into further depression, it would be easier for the public to accept a declaration of emergency. Riots and any actions that could be spun to the media as an armed insurrection would allow for gun seizures. Once the guns were off the streets, troublemakers could be easily arrested. Get rid of them and the sheep would follow her without question. This thought made her almost giddy, easing her throbbing migraine.

CHAPTER 3
CHRISTMAS - PLUS TWO DAYS

The Pentagon
930 Hours EST

The meeting had been called by the tall, willowy-framed man with short, steel-grey hair holding the title of Chairman of the Joint Chiefs of Staff. General Steven K. Taylor had endured many distasteful duties in his illustrious career and counted this one to be among the worst. In attendance were the Commanders for the U.S. Army and U.S. Air National Guard for all fifty states. The briefing was at the TOP SECRET level so all cell phones and any other transmitting or recording devices had been banned from the area. It was scheduled two days after Christmas in an attempt to avoid the press and make an impression on the National Guard commanders.

The National Guard Commanding Officers generally held the rank of one or two star General or the naval equivalent. A few "full bird" Colonels were also in the group. They had all expressed consternation when told their aids could not join them for the meeting. In front of each Commander was a yellow folder. Each was marked at the top and bottom with TOP SECRET and several other initials denoting the information was only given on a need-to-know basis. Virtually all had ignored the post-it note on each folder instructing them to refrain from opening until told to do so. No one in the room was used to this type of instruction. Each was busily leafing through the folder with a mixture of surprise and skepticism.

"Gentlemen, ahem, and ladies, thank you for coming here on such short notice. Without further ado, let me introduce a man you all recognize and many of you know personally, the Secretary of Defense." The applause was made up of a couple of dozen officers, clapping their hands unenthusiastically.

After twenty minutes of the second in command of all U.S. military forces spouting generalities about the bad situation in the country and world, it was clear he believed things were going to hell in a hand basket. "As Commanders of our National Guard, you are primarily tasked with protecting the people of your state. If things continue to deteriorate, you may be called upon to place those priorities on hold and protect the United States as a whole. Now this is classified 'TOP SECRET,'" but I wanted you to know the President is considering federalizing all National Guard units for the duration of this crisis. If she chooses to do so, I will expect you to provide the same level of professionalism and loyalty that you give to your respective Governors."

The Secretary of Defense's statement was met by complete silence as each commander in the room contemplated what the Secretary of Defense, known as the 'SecDef,' really meant by the statement.

"Now," the SecDef continued, "there is a number on the folder in front of you. Locate the staff officer near the exit holding your corresponding number and follow him to a smaller meeting room for further instructions."

Questions began immediately from the group, but were cut off quickly by the SecDef shouting over the sound system, "No questions will be entertained at this time. You will learn everything you need to know when you get to your next briefing."

The SecDef quickly left the stage, disappearing out a side door. The Commanders were professionals and kept their outrage under control, but the mood was a barely contained boil. Each Commander left the room to follow the group guide as instructed. Even though each state had two Commanders, one for the Army and one for the Air Wing, no two from a state were assigned to the same briefing.

• • •

The White House
2200 Hours EST

Burt Combs met with Marc Baxter and Don Stetson at his office conference table. Things had quieted down now that it was after 10:00 p.m. The support staff had almost all gone home. The Chief of Staff couldn't help but notice how much Marc Baxter had aged. Marc had joined Katherine Fontaine's campaign in the press liaison area a year before her election and had worked closely with campaign manager Don Stetson. At Katherine's insistence, Marc had been brought into the White House Press Secretary's office. When the appointed Press Secretary was stricken with Lyme disease, her deputy, Towanda Jefferson, was called to replace her. Towanda turned out to be incompetent, overwhelmed, and constantly used the "race card" to cover for her inadequacies. Columbia University Journalism School grad Marc Baxter was called on to handle any special public relations campaigns desired by Katherine, as well as to sit in on all staff briefings.

Don Stetson had been Katherine's campaign manager and had literally disappeared right after the election. With difficulty, Marc had tracked him down and enticed him to return to Washington using gun control as bait. A stray bullet had killed Don's daughter in Chicago years earlier, and this was the only project that could have brought him back.

"How's the campaign developing?" Burt asked the question knowing full well both men knew he really wanted to know about successes in the Administration's march to a gun-free America.

Don immediately responded, "Another two kids were killed outside of a high school in L.A. yesterday." Saying this, his voice was mixed with disgust and excitement.

Marc bit his tongue as he considered the incident Don mentioned involved a 16- and 17-year-old who had shot each other during a drug buy gone wrong. Both weapons involved had been obtained "on the street," and no amount of gun control would have prevented their deaths.

"So are you going to work that into the campaign?" Burt couldn't help but show his interest and guarded happiness at something actually going his way.

Don glanced at Marc before telling Burt, "Yeah, Marc has already written the press release showing the Administration's concerns about the continued mounting gun violence throughout the country. Did you see his piece on all the gun deaths last year? He highlighted a dozen or so, but quoted Centers for Disease Control and Prevention statistics showing over thirty thousand deaths involving guns in this country!"

Marc's feelings of guilt continued to grow. Over twenty-one thousand of the gun deaths had involved suicide, making the number of non-suicide gun deaths miniscule compared to auto traffic deaths, smoking related deaths, and even accidental deaths.

"Well, keep working on it, and keep me informed." After a pause for thought, Burt continued in a softer voice, "Marc, do we actually know how many guns are currently in the hands of private citizens."

Marc looked at Burt sharply, but quickly covered the shock in his eyes. "Burt, according to CNN, the number of guns is a gross estimate at best, but the number significantly exceeds the entire population of the United States. During the former administration, the numbers of firearms sold was out of this world."

"Yeah," Stetson said with disgust. "A huge reaction blossomed from the people that actually admired Charlton Heston when he said the government would have to pry his guns, 'from my cold, dead fingers.' People were so afraid the government would start confiscations that guns and ammunition were literally flying off the shelves. For a couple of years there was even a severe shortage on three-eight hundred ammunition…."

"Three eighty," Marc added helpfully.

"OK, point three-eight-zero caliber ammunition," Stetson said.

"CNN also said the Northeast part of the U.S. had the lowest percentage of households owning guns at twenty-four percent." Marc rattled off this and other statistics for Burt's edification.

Burt nodded his head and began to turn toward the door. Stopping, he said, "Katherine wants the vast majority of the public outraged at the carnage, with the prime focus being on the guns as the culprit. Assault weapons are at the top of the list, but be sure to keep drilling on how many people are killed by handguns as well. OK?"

Stetson nodded enthusiastically while Marc just nodded and smiled, feeling the growing knot in his stomach.

• • •

The Mountains of Southeastern Afghanistan
2200 Hours Local Time

Ahmed was furious as he nearly beat his older, first wife into unconsciousness. She endured his wrath as only one who understands that he was the one thing standing between her and starvation. In disgust at her stoic, uncomplaining attitude, he left the tent and walked to the nearby cave where his second wife, Jasmine, was sleeping on a thin mat. She awakened to find her husband on top of her and striving to passionately enter her. She immediately opened her legs and accepted her husband, moving with fake passion until he shouted with joy at his climax. It was not her turn, but she took pride in her husband coming to her. Unlike with his other two wives, he began to talk to Jasmine as he lay panting next to her on the mat.

"Two of the martyrs had to be disciplined when they broke orders and had their way with the aid girl." Ahmed's fighters kidnapped the aid girl bringing her to the mountains for the express purpose of training his twenty-four martyrs in how to travel successfully about the West. With Jasmine's personal training, the aid girl had done well in teaching his martyrs English and teaching them how to move through Western airports and various Customs authorities. For several months they learned from this Western girl, who looked directly into the eyes of these men. She also managed to show ample breasts and shapely butt through her hajib. Two of the fighters couldn't restrain themselves and had taken her by force. One at a time, Ahmed had been forced to get into their face, insult their families, and had slammed a knife into each man's heart. They met Allah with at least some kind of honor.

A week earlier, three of his martyrs had died in a tunnel cave-in. With the martyr that had died two months earlier, it left only eighteen to fulfill the mission set forth by Allah by way of the Chinese spy, Cho. A year earlier, after providing several truckloads of explosives and weapons, Cho had asked how many of the infidels Ahmed wanted to kill. He had replied passionately, "All of them."

Cho had nodded and described to him a plan involving a virus and the need for dedicated martyrs. Cho had asked for twelve, but Ahmed had chosen and trained twenty-four. Ahmed also arranged for Jasmine's brother, Ali al-Hadiz to come to Afghanistan to set up a secret laboratory. Ali held a Ph.D. in pharmacy and claimed to be able to manipulate viruses by way of something called nanotechnology. Ahmed thought it likely that Cho's virus would not affect the Chinese people, but Ali assured him that the virus could be altered, allowing it to kill all the infidels, even if they were Chinese.

Ahmed rose from Jasmine's bed and called for Hadi, his chief lieutenant. He met Hadi just outside of the cave entrance.

"Yes, great leader," Hadi said breathlessly.

"Tell me, Hadi, are the martyrs ready to travel in the West?"

Hadi paused for several moments after hearing the question. He knew the success or failure of the entire plan might hinge on his answer.

"Great leader," Hadi finally responded, "they are ready, but untested. I think we should send a few to Europe for three days and if all goes well, the rest should be sent. Once they have all returned, they will be ready to do Allah's work."

Ahmed contemplated his answer and said, "Send them to Macedonia in Greece, but only three at a time. Have each group spend two days there. Also, give them enough money to sample the infidel pleasures so that they will look forward to teaching their virgins when they have completed their task."

Ali's smile could not have been bigger. "Of course, Great Leader. It will be done."

CHAPTER 4
CHRISTMAS - PLUS THREE DAYS

Beijing, China
1030 Hours Local Time

Chinese Premier and General Secretary of the Communist Party, Song Ren, practiced his meditation ritual after having just received a briefing from Minister Lao Tung of the Ministry of State Security (MSS). Lao was in charge of the Chinese equivalent of the CIA, FBI, and part of the NSA. One of his many responsibilities was to keep a close eye on the People's Liberation Army (PLA), its leaders and capabilities. Song was annoyed. He had been forced to delay another important meeting with the lovely and exquisitely trained young woman from the MSS "Charm School" due to reports just given to him by Lao. Although Song had his own intelligence sources separate from the MSS, he had most recently learned to appreciate Lao's abnormal ability to glean actual truth from all the information provided by the PLA, especially relating to their readiness and knowledge of the American military.

Lao's briefing had shown the PLA to be far from ready for a planned invasion of Formosa, known in the West as Taiwan. This contradicted the PLA's own after-action reports of readiness. Song previously ordered his Secretary and de Facto Chief of Staff, Wong Jie, to warn the top PLA Generals and Admirals to provide only accurate information relating to readiness for the invasion of Formosa. PLA general's lies almost resulted in Song reacting violently in Lao's presence. Maximum restraint succeeded in stopping the outburst.

Lao departed and Song's rage continued to boil. With meditation, he would not shout or lose control. The meditation calmed him. He decided some rough, even brutal, sexual gratification with the Charm School girl would help to dispel his rage. Girls from that school had exquisite training, including how to placate a dominating master.

Song called Wong into his office. "Wong," Song said with no emotion in his voice. "You are to inform Lao that the three most expendable Generals involved with the PLA readiness exercises are to be arrested and charged with treason against the state. They are to be taken immediately to the special prison outside of Beijing and are to have no contact with anyone. You will next placate the three members of the Politburo, you know the ones, by moving an appropriate amount of financial resources to their favorite pet projects. They are, of course, to receive a greater than usual thirty percent for themselves. Also, have Lao let the word trickle out to the PLA commanders that the arrested generals have stolen money that was supposed to have gone to new equipment and that they have lied to their superiors concerning important tactical planning. I leave the details to you and Lao. Questions?"

"None, General Secretary." Wong bowed and began to leave the room. "Oh, and Wong? Have my car prepared to take me to my next meeting. Have the meeting after that rescheduled."

Wong responded with another bow. Song began to feel the stirrings of an erection as he contemplated which whips he would use on the china-like white skin of his Charm School girl.

CHAPTER 5
CHRISTMAS - PLUS THREE DAYS

The Callahan Residence
Outside of Cronin, Kentucky
1100 Hours EST

Sean Callahan was breathing deeply, but regularly after having just completed his fourth set of isometric exercises while lying in his bed. He was a light skinned black man with Asian features and green/hazel eyes like his Irish grandfather. His body may have been torn, but his spirit had developed even more resolve. Arriving at his childhood home in Kentucky a couple of months earlier, he had begun a modified work-out regimen, avoiding use of the leg he had lost to the improvised explosive device, or IED, on a covert mission in Afghanistan. This resulted in his being immediately chastised by both his local doctor and his physical therapist for busting out the sutures in three places. The doctor had inserted the sutures ahead of schedule after what they called "minor adjustment surgery" three days earlier. The ones on his stump he thought might give him trouble, but he hadn't anticipated popping the ones holding the gash closed on his left triceps or the one across his stomach. Infections had delayed healing for both wounds. He was under orders not to try any form of exertion without the strict guidance of his physical therapist. The only problem was they thought an hour, three days per week was enough therapy. Out of frustration, his doctor enlisted help from his mom. It is said that an Asian mother has a will of iron when it comes to her children, and Mrs. Callahan proved this to be true. Doctor's orders would be followed.

Continuing to breathe deeply, he couldn't help but both curse and thank "The Bitch in the White House." This wasn't the way a United States Army

Major should think of his Commander in Chief. Almost everyone who had sworn to uphold the U.S. Constitution and having spent more than his fair share in harm's way, known as combat, had less than fond things to say about President Katherine Fontaine. In addition to what she had done to the country, "The Bitch" had ordered, through the SecDef and the Inspector General, or IG all military units were to be assessed for their loyalty to the civilian chain of command. She apparently had less trust in the military than she did in her own Secret Service.

When The Bitch ordered the reliability check, specific emphasis had been placed on the Special Operations Forces, for which Major Sean Callahan commanded a Green Beret company. Sean was ordered to accompany and observe one of his A-teams, or operations team, on a mission in Afghanistan searching for intelligence on a new terrorist group called the Jihadist of the Prophet (JOTP). The commander of the A-team was First Lieutenant Linda Sharpe, an Olympic caliber athlete who had gained respect from the tough bunch of operators making up her A-team.

Had it not been for "The Bitch," Sean thought with some bitterness, he wouldn't have been in Afghanistan and wouldn't have had his leg blown off by the IED. On the other hand, if he hadn't been there, he might not have been able to save Linda Sharpe when a group of twenty terrorists captured her and another female operator. Both Green Berets had been successful in gathering significant intelligence from the wives and mothers of men recruited by the JOTP. During the last meeting they had been betrayed and captured. Sean had taken command of the A-team, called in armed Predator drone support, and had attacked and killed the JOTP terrorists before they could disappear into the mountains with their hostages. The female sergeant accompanying Lieutenant Sharpe had been killed during the operation along with another A-team member who had stepped on the IED during the team's extraction. For his actions, Sean was proclaimed a hero.

Sean had been quite impressed with not only Lieutenant Sharpe's professionalism, but had also noticed she was very attractive, a trait she worked hard to mask. She had hardly left his side at Walter Reed Army Medical Center, where he received comprehensive medical treatment. Her own injuries had mostly healed following the ordeal, but combining the bond of combat with knowing he had come for her seemed to have captured both her mind and her heart. To his surprise, the feeling was mutual. Two weeks earlier she had decided to begin out-processing from the Army to start a new chapter in her life, which included caring for him.

Contemplating how a man with one leg could hope to be worthy of a quality lady like Linda, Sean heard the doorbell ring downstairs. His mom, Penny, answered the door. He could hear her slight Korean accent as she greeted the visitor. Unexpectedly, it was apparent the visitor was not someone she knew. In only a few seconds, she knocked on the frame of his open door and said, "Sean, someone with a great deal of fruit salad on his chest is here to see you." Her smile was quizzical, but friendly, letting him know she approved of the man's character. She was a very shrewd judge of character as shown by her marrying his dad. Her own father was a wealthy Republic of Korea investor and businessman who initially did not want to see his only daughter marry an American police officer, even if he had helped her with a stalker while she was in college in the United States. In the Korean culture, his father being black didn't help, either. Fortunately, his grandfather had overcome his own racial prejudice and came to respect his son-in-law and deeply loved his grandson.

Standing in the door in Class A uniform was Command Sergeant-Major (CSM) Harold Walker of the U.S. military's Special Operations Command, or SOCOM. He was slender and just over six feet tall with close-cropped silver hair and a face with multiple scars haphazardly crisscrossing it. He came to attention and saluted Sean after stepping in the room. Seeing his mom beaming with pride, Sean returned the salute from his bed, dropped his voice into its command mode, and said, "At ease, Command Sergeant-Major. To what do I owe this great honor?"

Sean knew the CSM had responsibilities that exceeded his own on his worst day. Not only that the experience and level of professionalism embodied in a man holding that position was of the highest possible caliber. He was the senior enlisted man in all of SOCOM.

"The General asked me to come see how you were doing, Major. I think he wants to know when you'll be up to adding to your own fruit salad." The CSM pointed to the large number of commendation ribbons on his chest to add emphasis.

Sean noticed there was a Purple Heart with four oak leaf clusters included on his chest, plus a Silver Star ribbon. "Oh, I guess I'm doing as well as could be expected. That is, if a staph infection is expected. You know, they were actually going to take my arm, too, until Linda, I mean Lieutenant Sharpe, stepped in and told them to fuck off."

"Yes, sir, I heard about that." With a big smile the CSM said, "I don't think I'd EVER want that 'L.T.' pissed at me. Know what I mean, Major?"

Sean broke out with a deep chuckle of his own. "Guess it's pretty obvious that she's staked out her territory, huh?"

"Just within most of SOCOM and among virtually every doctor and nurse working at Walter Reed. By the way and off the record," the CSM lowered his voice, "the General approves. He also wants to keep you both, even though she seems insistent on out-processing. Anything you can do about that?"

Sean shook his head sadly. "No, Sergeant Major, I don't think I'm going to change her mind on this one. I'm not sure what she'll be doing going forward, but being an Army officer is not going to be part of it."

The CSM turned to Penny Callahan and politely asked, "Ma'am, is there any way we could have some privacy? I need to get into some classified things with your son, and although I know I can trust you…"

Penny waved the CSM off with a smile. "No need to ask more than once. I've got some after-Christmas cookies to put into the oven. Will thirty minutes be enough time for you boys?" Penny's conspiratorial smile showed an instinct about how to get a man's attention.

"Oh, yes, ma'am. Thirty should do just fine," said the grizzled CSM.

"One last important question, gentlemen," she said with authority. "Milk or coffee?"

"Milk for me, Mom. Thanks!"

"I think I'll go that way myself. Thank you, Mrs. Callahan."

"Oh, call me Penny, please." She left and could be heard quietly walking downstairs.

After a moment to collect his thoughts, the CSM said, "Major, do you know what your plans are after you complete your convalescent leave?"

"What do you mean? We both know the regs, and one leg doesn't let a man stay in Special Forces. Maybe someplace in the regular Army would take me, but I really don't have any interest in doing that."

"Well, Major, if you want it, the General does want you to stay in SOCOM and wants you to take over a newly created Battalion with a very covert mission. I can't go into it with you until you first say yes, and then the offer will be presuming you are able to pass the physical fitness test with your new bionic leg.

I'm sure you will since I'm giving it to you myself. You also get a promotion out of it as well. Is that something that might interest you?"

Sean sat quietly in his bed for a full ten count. Going through his head were several questions. Chief among them was what kind of shit-sandwich did the General think he could possibly handle better than all the other available competent officers that were physically healthy. In fact, it was astounding that the offer was being made when he still had at least three months, and probably more like six months, of intensive physical therapy to complete before he would be anywhere near ready to take a fitness test.

"Sergeant-Major? I'll give you a conditional 'yes,' but the answer will be 'no' unless you give me a hell of a lot more details about what this battalion will be doing. Let's just say I'm not particularly trusting when it comes to the current administration."

Nodding his head in agreement, the CSM said, "The General said you'd need to know. So here it is. And this is classified TS-plus. Capiche?"

Sean nodded.

"The President has ordered the SecDef to start standing up a battalion sized unit of Special Forces trained troops for a possible insurrection within the United States. The Bitch thinks as the economy continues to tank, and with potential loss of such things as power and water, there will be those that won't want to follow her emergency mandates." The CSM paused to let that sink in for Sean.

Continuing, the CSM said, "The General initially didn't want anything to do with this. His thinking was, why wouldn't she use National Guard or regular Army troops? Then it occurred to him, she knows SF had extensive training in convincing people to do things they don't want to do. They are also used to getting orders that are, shall we say, a bit outside of the norm." This put a slight smile on the CSM's face.

"Sergeant-Major, why would the General even consider this? He knows the Posse Comitatus Act doesn't allow the use of U.S. troops in the U.S for police actions. What's he really up to?" Sean had a healthy respect for the Commanding General and thought like all Special Operators do, looking behind the obvious.

"Major, the General thinks if he takes on this mission willingly, he will be in the position to mitigate the worst of the potential abuses and prevent some other knuckle draggers from stepping in and destroying the country from within. It's going to be frustrating, ugly work, but he thinks you are the best man for the job. It'll take at least four months to organize and gather all the necessary equipment. If you can talk Lieutenant Sharpe out of out-processing, you can have her run one of your companies."

"You know that's not going to happen, Sergeant-Major. Nor should it for a number of reasons, including I should not be in her chain of command. More importantly, does the General know that I lost a leg and have a long way to go before I will be physically able to assume command? Presuming, of course, that I can even pass the physical." Sean's head was still spinning from suddenly being offered a command again, despite everything that had happened.

"Major," the CSM said kindly, "the physical won't be a problem and the General knows exactly what your status is. He plans to make use of it to delay actually getting the unit up and running. That info, like everything I'm telling you today, should not go past this room. Understand?"

At Sean's nod, the CSM continued, "You're an honest-to-God war hero now, so you probably ought to start wrapping your head around that idea. What we're gonna do is get you set up, in this very room, with a full communications suite, including secure safe and the works. The General also thought you might not be able to prevail upon the good Lieutenant to stick around in the Army, so there is a company that specializes in providing specialists with security clearances to the government. She can be hired and placed here as a civilian contractor to handle your security and communications gear. I presume you'd prefer that to having a four-man security detail assigned out of MacDill Air Force Base."

Sean nodded his head again, with a look of spreading amazement.

"Just so that you know, sir, the troops and your subordinate officers will all be told that you are at an undisclosed location receiving briefings and continuing to recover from your wounds. You being located here, at your parent's home in Kentucky, will hereafter be officially buried. Although the NSA always has a record of where their highest level of classified equipment is located, in this case it is simply 'on assignment in the field' to SOCOM. I have to say, sir, that day before yesterday was one of my more enjoyable encounters when I looked the NSA liaison in the eye and informed him that, by direction of the President, they were not to be informed where the equipment was located, and that the tracking capability had been digitally removed from the signal. Something to do with the way it is bounced around the Internet, satellites or something. I don't frankly understand it, but the geek back at SOCOM assured me that was the case. The General received blanket authority from the President through the SecDef, so that's all he needed." The huge grin on the CSM's face confirmed the truth of his enjoyment at the encounter.

The CSM continued, "Now, sir, I know this is a lot to take in, especially in light of your injuries. With your permission, what I'll do next is, number one, talk to your mom and tell her just enough to get her permission to turn this bedroom into a secure work environment, or SWE. That'll let us bring in and store the safe and other equipment."

"Hmm," the CSM paused for more thought, "that will require that it be manned 24/7, so maybe I had best detail eight men to provide that security and coverage; will also have to make sure they bring a full kit of equipment, weapons, and ammo. Any suggestions of who should get the duty?"

With his mind still reeling, Sean gave the CSM eight names of men from his company in Colorado that did not have families and could be trusted. "Sergeant-Major? How long do you anticipate this arrangement to be necessary?"

"Sir, let's look at six to ten months and reassess as we go along. And by the way, you will have a direct line to me twenty-four seven through a secure phone should any issues arise that you can't handle. If I can't handle it, the General can. Also, the men chosen to fill out the officer corps for the new battalion do not include anyone that you know. That was done by design, and I think you can probably figure out why. You'll essentially be commanding and getting reports from them via secure video conference."

The CSM went on, "The second thing I will be arranging is a small team from MacDill to come here and physically set up the SWE. That is currently scheduled to begin in two days. You'll have to handle any questions that arise here locally. As soon as the SWE is established, you will get your official orders and a call from the General. In the meantime, Lieutenant Sharpe's out-processing has been delayed and she has received classified orders to come here without telling a soul where she is going. I understand she will be arriving later this afternoon. And, sir, think carefully before you answer. Did you get notification from her that she was on her way?"

"Relax, Harold," Sean said, using the CSM's first name to show the kind of confidential relationship those in SOCOM enjoyed the most. "She hasn't said a word to me about her coming. She's up there with the best I've ever seen and completely professional."

The CSM visibly relaxed and gratefully nodded at Sean. "Sir, that's going to be up to you how you recruit her, but I'd love to be a fly on the wall when she walks in here later today." Both men chuckled at the thought.

CHAPTER 6
CHRISTMAS - PLUS THREE DAYS

The Pen and Ink Saloon
Frankfort, Kentucky
2000 Hours EST

Kerry DuBois sat in his chair in the private room above the Pen and Ink Saloon in Kentucky's state capital. The room looked like an attempt was made to create a high class boardroom, but with a lumberjack as the designer. Lots of stained wood and brass, but with a total lack of class. Kerry's job in the Kentucky Transportation Cabinet didn't pay enough to be able to afford even this setting, but through various dealings and acquaintances, he was able to live well above his means. Kerry had just slurped down his second double scotch and was lamenting the fact the cute bar girl, whose nice, tight ass he had been blatantly admiring, had been sent away when the meeting got started.

In a rough circle of overstuffed chairs sat men he thought of privately as his minions, but could more accurately be described as his cronies. Jerry "The Tank" Monahan was a convicted felon who owned the saloon through a shell company. He had gone mostly legitimate after his release from prison for illegal drug sales, preferring to use the money obtained earlier through those sales and other ill-gotten gains to buy political favors. This, of course, added to his fortune by opening doors to government contracts. A large, grizzled man in his mid-60s with reddening jowls, Tank gave the impression of being the Kentucky version of a Mafia don.

Freddy Dobson, sitting with an extremely bored expression to go with his pale face, was the antithesis of Tank. Freddy came from an East Coast family with a great deal of money. His father had worked very hard to accumulate his fortune, but those genes apparently didn't pass on to Freddy. In disgust at his son's irresponsible, partying ways, his father had sent the 27-year-old Freddy to the family horse farm in Central Kentucky two years earlier, where the hard-nosed Irish farm manager was supposed to teach the boy how to operate a business and help him grow up. The manager's gambling habit had insured Freddy's father received good reports and had cost only an initial sixty thousand dollars to pay off his gambling debt. Other periodic costs of an additional five or ten thousand dollars from Freddy's trust funds continued to bail the manager out of more trouble. Freddy considered the farm manager one of his better investments. After meeting Kerry at a political fund raiser, life had gotten much more interesting for Freddy, but was still barely enough to tear him away from the girls provided by the local escort service.

Mickey Blondiac, known as Blondi, was the only man in the room, besides Kerry, that held a regular job. Blondi, with his trademark blond hair, published a weekly newspaper column dealing with political issues in Kentucky. During the campaign season, his column ran daily. Blondi had known Kerry in college at the University of California, Berkley and had taken Kerry's suggestion to move to Kentucky after he was caught in bed with his editor's boyfriend. Blondi had developed excellent sources throughout the area for all things involving politics and the dirt associated with state and local governments.

John Chapman had been the Lieutenant Governor in the previous administration and had contacts in almost all of state government. This included those parts that he deemed important due to their significant budgets, like the National Guard and Transportation Cabinet. John had been a community organizer in Louisville before being discovered and catapulted into office by the quiet support of Tank Monahan. John's brother-in-law was General Steven Thompson, the Commander of the Kentucky Army National Guard.

"Well, John, what's the word from your special source?" Knowing John made it a point to meet with his brother-in-law regularly, Kerry asked the question to start the official part of the meeting. Up until then, Blondi and Kerry had been joking with Tank about how often he enjoyed the services of the cute bar girl that had just left.

"He's at the Pentagon right now, having some sort of super-secret meeting that he won't even talk about with his wife. From some friends in the Fontaine administration, I'm hearing that as the economy keeps getting worse, there's talk about another stimulus package coming down the pike. There are also moves in the Department of Homeland Security to start preparin' for a declaration of emergency. The way they're talking now is Homeland Security is going to set up regions and expect the National Guard to support anything they think they need to do." With this comment, John couldn't help but smile. "Normally, if there were some sort of emergency in the state, the Governor would have to request federal assistance, and he would run things through the state government. Now, it looks like federal aid is probably going to run separately. And you know who is in charge of the region covering Kentucky, West Virginia, and Tennessee? None other than our own state democratic party chairman."

The surprised looks came from each of the others present. Even Freddy sat up before asking, "You mean that ol' Coyote Collins you guys keep talking about is really going to be running things?"

Everyone had heard the story about how Coyote had gotten his name. One day in high school he brought in a coyote he had run over in his ancient pickup truck. He wanted to put the carcass in the cafeteria refrigerator until he could skin it and mount it later. His friends began calling him Coyote, and from that day on, he wouldn't answer to anything else.

"Yep, that's the one," John said grinning ear to ear. "Coyote is going to not only be in charge of everything in his three states, but he'll have the National Guard to order around in support of his Homeland Security officials."

John said the word, 'officials' with the kind of emphasis an organized crime figure would use to describe his thugs or enforcers. "Should learn a lot more when my special source gets back."

All around the room each man was calculating how he would be able to take advantage of the new situation for personal power, influence and profit.

• • •

Washington, DC
2100 Hours EST

President Katherine Fontaine's husband, Walter, had just finished a meeting with three of his closest friends. He had wanted to discuss the terrible economic situation and how he could continue to insure his own investments didn't slide down the chute like the rest of the economy. Just over six feet tall and a pudgy 250 pounds, Walter's power came from his suave demeanor that could charm the socks off a snake, if a snake had socks. Two of the three men were with a prominent Wall Street brokerage house. The third, like the other two, had steered several donations, including a few that could be counted in eight figures, to the Fontaine Foundation. Much of the foundation's assets were located offshore, helping to prevent federal investigators discovering that less than ten percent of the foundation contributions actually went to charitable causes. Instead, it was essentially a private slush fund used by Walter and Katherine for political and personal expenses. It had also provided a big chunk of seed money to Walter's retirement fund. All three of Walter's friends had assured him that the retirement funds were as close to recession/depression proof as possible.

Before leaving the private club where the meeting had taken place, Walter stepped into the men's room. After taking care of business there, he gave the signal, by brushing the side of his nose with his index finger just like a scam artist from the roaring 1920s, and signaled his security team leader that he was going off on his own.

After Walter walked out of the back door, the team set up around the club and waited patiently for his return, expecting it to be in two to three hours if all followed the usual pattern.

John Levy walked into the restroom and into a stall. Closing his eyes, he bumped his head against the tile wall before carefully pulling out the small device from his pocket and pushing the button.

• • •

Walter entered the private automobile with the blacked-out windows and was greeted by Mr. Sung Hong, who Walter believed was a high level lobbyist. Because Sung provided access to the spectacular Su Ling, Walter was willing deal with him without asking too many questions.

A fifteen-minute drive through Washington, D.C. traffic, took them to a small luxury hotel located on a quiet side street. Sung provided a hat and tinted glasses for Walter along with a hotel key. While Walter exited the car, Sung simply said, "Four hundred." Walter understood that the key would open the door to suite number 400.

Walter tried and missed sliding the door key card into the door's key slot. A quick glance revealed the tent that had formed in the front of his pants. His anticipation appeared to be even more than usual this evening. It had been over a month since he had last seen Su. He had tried to wean himself from her pleasures, especially in light of what the Chinese government had done to the U.S. and world economy. When the Chinese government had stopped importing all foreign oil, except for oil from Russia, the rest of the world had learned immediately how important the oil industry was. An economic downward spiral had ensued. The stock market lost over one third of its value in less than fifteen days. The decline continued at a slow, but depressingly steady rate. The hate for the PRC government had reached an all-time high, making visits to see Su even more difficult. Unfortunately, after having enjoyed Su Ling's talents, the other two girls he had tried in the interim were like trying to drink a cheap whiskey after an initial glass of the finest scotch. One's taste buds, or your sexual nervous system (Walter began to giggle softly at his own clever phrase), simply wouldn't tolerate the inferior product.

Finally, he managed to get the key into the slot and entered the brightly lit room. Standing at the side bar was the most beautiful China doll he had ever seen or experienced. Of medium height with black hair and elf-like features, Su set the standard for sensuality. He loved her hair, which had given him exquisite sexual pleasure. His attention focused on her full, round breasts and the view of her pubis, clearly visible through her nearly sheer light blue silk robe. She was in the process of making his favorite expensive single-malt scotch on the rocks.

Before Su could hand him his drink, he gathered her up in his arms for a sloppy kiss. It wasn't an affectionate or intimate kiss, but the kind of kiss meant to hold her in place while his hands roamed over her body. Walter's fingers began to pinch her left nipple. She deftly scooped up his drink and her wine glass and moved over to the couch. Walter, with his tented trousers, followed as if he was on a leash.

"Oh, Walter," Su cooed softly in her accented China doll voice. "You too ready now. Tonight I want three times you scale the mountain." Her smile promised an incredible adventure to come. "You so tense. Tell me what trouble you." She had left the couch and had gone behind Walter to begin massaging his shoulders.

"Ahhhhh," Walter sighed with contentment, knowing he would get what he wanted soon enough. "The damned Chinese government..." Walter continued to complain about the Chinese-caused economic crisis and the details of what the Fontaine administration intended to do about it.

It took over twenty minutes before Walter began to repeat himself, under her soft but effective elicitation techniques. Su then moved her hands from his shoulders and began to slide them down his chest to his crotch while her breasts fell from her robe to encircle his head. Next, she moved around the couch to take up his feet, practicing her well-trained art of reflexology to first relax his body, and then to stimulate him. Within seconds, he achieved his first climax, all from her massaging his feet and brushing him with her hair. With her intelligence job done for this visit, she concentrated on simply getting him off.

After Walter left, she showered to wash off the whole experience and then gathered her things to leave. In the back of her mind, she hoped fervently that this was the last time she would have to endure the fat, ugly man.

CHAPTER 7
CHRISTMAS - PLUS FOUR DAYS

FBI Headquarters
Washington, DC
1800 Hours EST

Hugh McIntyre met with the Director in his office, located on the top floor of the Hoover building. When Hugh entered the office, Director Kidd thought of the day, over two months earlier, when Hugh had brought a fantastic story that included a Chinese intelligence operation targeting the First Man. Hugh's daughter, Lisa, had come to her father and told him about meeting a Chinese graduate student that was a virtual sex slave of the Chinese MSS. Hugh worked in the Counterterrorism Division, but was heavily skeptical of his daughter's story until he met Su Ling. He had then learned of a long-term Chinese intelligence operation that targeted Walter Fontaine. Su Ling was to provide exotic sex to Walter while skillfully and covertly interrogating him for the cameras of the MSS.

Hugh, like his daughter Lisa, had been particularly aghast at the description of the MSS's "Charm School," located outside of Shanghai. It was designed to prepare girls, and a few boys, for espionage penetration operations. The training involved brutally teaching them to use sex and other techniques to extract information. Each student either learned to be effective, or they were killed. Until he actually saw Walter taken to a luxury Washington, D.C. hotel by a known MSS Officer where Su was waiting for him, he had doubted the story. With photographic evidence and some very covert computer research in hand, he met with Director Kidd to ask what he should do.

Coming back to the present, Hugh blinked as Allen said, "Hugh, it's good to see you." Hugh could tell from the look in his intelligent eyes that he genuinely meant what he said. "What have you got for me?"

Hugh dove right into the briefing, without the usually expected fawning over the Director. With this man, it was both unnecessary and unwanted.

"The target and our source had another meeting last night." Allen nodded and appreciated Hugh's discretion in the matter.

"And I don't mind telling you, allowing this to go on seems very morally wrong to me, Sir. We're essentially allowing him to rape her with our knowledge and acquiescence."

Allen nodded gravely. "Hugh, we both know it's wrong, but she has been trained – for years – to do just that. Remember, you will be her ticket out of slavery to the Chinese government."

Hugh bowed his head forward, acknowledging the Director's point. "I'm sorry Sir, it just bothers me."

"I would worry about you if it didn't," Allen said. After a pause, he continued, "Did you receive a heads up from our new friend?"

"Yes, sir, I did. Fortunately our surveillance team was not detected by his team. I knew our guys were good, but I must admit I am surprised how good." Hugh was still amazed that the Director insisted on Hugh being his point of contact involving the super-secret task force, which was headed up by a Deputy Assistant Director. Hugh was at least three steps below a Deputy Assistant Director in the pecking order.

"Anything else?" Allen's question was light and casual, but his eyes were probing deeply into Hugh's own eyes.

"Yes, sir." Hugh said this with an equally light sounding response. "I was able to get some recordings of my own and will hand carry a report of the results to your office tomorrow. A quick review confirmed everything we have suspected so far. We could wrap things up with what we have, but one more meeting between them would, shall we say, ice the cake. I am, however, concerned the other side might discover what we are doing from the technical aspect."

Hugh had prevailed upon Su Ling to hide a tiny, passive recorder in the hotel room the previous evening. The NSA contact had assured Hugh it would not be found by a normal room sweep for bugs, but it was not their life that depended upon it.

After a deep breath Allen said, "One more meeting with recordings and I'll go to the President. Agreed?"

"Yes, sir. I think that would be best." As an afterthought, Hugh said, "It may take me forty-eight hours to get the next report properly written, sir. Will that be soon enough for you to brief the President?"

The Director sagely looked at Hugh, nodded, and then said, "Yes, that will be fine. I expect you to take any other appropriate steps as we previously discussed."

"Will do, sir. Anything else?"

"No, Hugh. Thank you for your time and for everything you're doing. We may not be able to talk much when this wraps up so I also want you to know how much I really appreciate everything you've done, even knowing the probable cost."

"Just doing my duty." Hugh said this as he rose to leave the Director's office. "Good night, sir."

• • •

Northern Virginia
2000 Hours EST

"Daddy, you CAN'T stop me from meeting Su! She needs me!" Lisa was nearly in tears after her father, Hugh, had asked his daughter to refrain from meeting Su Ling again for the time being.

"Sweetheart, it's too dangerous for you to meet her. If they catch her meeting you, they'll probably arrest her!"

"I know you said that, but you know how sharp she is, and I'm no slouch when it comes to analysis and acting." She couldn't help but let a little smile cross her face. She was in the process of getting two Ph.D.'s at George Washington University in Chemistry and Biology, along with mentoring a grad student and working on a school-funded project.

Hugh grudgingly acknowledged his daughter's amazing capabilities and had taken her word that Su Ling was just as smart as she was. This made it logical that Lisa and Su would become either great friends or dangerous enemies. These traits that had started their friendship in the Washington, D.C. coffee shop several months earlier.

Lisa continued in her, this-should-be-obvious-to-you voice, "And really, Dad, if Su is caught meeting me, it would be a whole lot easier on her than being caught meeting you!"

Hugh should be used to his daughter manipulating him with logic instead of the emotion that most fathers battle.

"Most importantly, Dad, I think she needs me - me and my friendship. You know, emotionally. That thing that girls have, that guys have too, but keep it buried too deep to keep them sane."

Handling his most difficult confidential source in the past was nothing compared to verbally sparring with his daughter.

"Okay, honey. Okay. Keep it to a minimum and I want you to let me know personally when you have the meetings. Agreed?"

He suddenly found his daughter giving him a big hug and sniffling into his shoulder. "Honey, what's wrong?"

"Daddy, how long is she going to have to continue doing those terrible things? I woke up last night with his picture in my head, and I almost threw up!"

Hugh thought about placating his daughter's fears, but instantly knew it wouldn't fly with her. "Pumpkin, I don't really know. As I said before, it will be soon. And when it does roll up, you know she'll have to disappear, right?"

Lisa nodded.

"I'm also thinking," Hugh said quietly, "you will have to do so as well. I can't say where, yet, but I do have a place in mind."

Lisa immediately started forming her most mischievous grin. "It wouldn't be Kentucky, would it?" The look on Hugh's face pretty much gave it away.

"I, I really can't say right now, Pumpkin."

Lisa let it pass. "That will work out just fine, Daddy. With everything that is happening, I think I'd rather be off the East Coast anyway. Something tells me things are going to get a whole lot worse before they get better. Am I right?"

"I wish I could say otherwise," Hugh said with feeling. "Unfortunately, I can't. I will really feel a lot better if you were out of here. Your mother, too, but she won't go, so at least I'll have one less McIntyre to worry about." With that he got another hug.

CHAPTER 8
NEW YEAR'S EVE

The Broehm Residence
Outside Cronin, Kentucky
1900 Hours EST

Mike Broehm usually felt each one of his forty-eight years, but today was an exception. He enjoyed the controlled chaos going on in his house as his closest friends and their families gathered for New Year's Eve dinner. He loved when his two small grandchildren chased the neighbor kids around the house while the wonderful aroma of food wafted out from the kitchen.

When he thought about it, Mike knew his life was blessed. After all, with so many bad things happening in the country, he had a growing number of close friends and neighbors he could count on. On top of that, he dropped thirty-five pounds over the last six months and no longer needed to take blood pressure medicine. This was the time of year to appreciate the good things in his life.

"Hey, Mike." Rollie McDermott called from the area of the small bar in the corner. "Looks like you could use a beverage."

Rollie, with his bright red hair, was probably watching as Mike had removed the empty bottle from its insulated cozy.

"Yeah, thanks, Rollie. How about some of that spiced cider?" Mike replied as he walked over to the bar. The atmosphere was permeated by a feeling of love and even leftover holiday spirit that continued after the neighborhood meeting and tree lighting event held a week before Christmas.

In a neighborhood of over two-hundred fifty homes surrounded by farmland, more than three hundred people had attended the meeting. The tree lighting ceremony was accompanied by the singing of carols. In addition to the holiday celebration, Mike wanted everyone to know the status of the neighborhood's emergency preparations. The association secretary had made up a list of their accomplishments. These included over one hundred eighty families reported having at least two weeks of emergency supplies. This included bottled water and prescription medications for their families. One hundred twenty-one families reported having over two months of supplies.

Mike had asked the secretary to poll the entire neighborhood, assuring everyone no record would be kept of what any individual family had. If no record was made of what any individual family had, then folks would be more likely to share the information with her. Most were honest, with the probable exception of Kerry DuBois. Kerry had told her he had only three days of supplies. Behind him, his long-suffering wife had bowed and shaken her head, confirming the fact that her husband was lying. Mike privately thought it was divine providence that Kerry did not have children to learn to be a socialist without morals like him.

Many of the neighbors had lost their jobs over the past few months as the economy continued to nosedive. This had made the Christmas celebration even more important for the neighborhood. Everyone had thoroughly enjoyed the potluck dinner, with the leftovers designated for those families out of work. By design, Mike and other neighbors insured several trays of leftovers were available so that each struggling family would have at least two extra cafeteria-sized trays of food.

From a banker in the neighborhood, Mike had learned about a procedure for dramatically lowering, or even postponing, required mortgage payments. After spreading this information around, no one was going to lose their home in these terrible economic times, at least for now. Mike's efforts in this regard had not gone unnoticed within the neighborhood, either.

At the tree lighting, Mike gave a heartfelt prayer of thanks for everyone's hard work and how they had pulled together in this time of need. When he was about to speak, he felt the all-too-familiar rising rush of anxiety that came when others looked to him for leadership. A feeling of panic seemed to flood into his brain whenever he was put in charge of anything.

He had been a fourteen-year-old Boy Scout on an overnight hike and campout in the Red River Gorge. After dark, a park ranger tracked down the Scoutmaster, causing him to leave to take an emergency telephone call. In those days before cell telephones, a hike to the nearest telephone was required. With no Assistant Scoutmaster present Mike was placed in charge of the eighteen-member troop of Boy Scouts.

No sooner was the Scoutmaster out of sight, the two most mischievous boys in the troop decided to sneak off to smoke smuggled cigarettes. Twenty minutes later, Mike thought to do a head count and found the boys missing. He then sent two trusted senior Scouts to find the smokers and bring them back. They found them, but the two smokers had climbed over a fence at a seventy-five-foot high overlook and had jumped out to a freestanding rock shelf. They refused to come back, so one of the senior scouts had tried to jump over to their rock shelf with disastrous results. By the time the Scoutmaster returned, he found Mike nearly delirious with grief and beginning his second continuous hour of CPR on the lifeless scout.

Mike never forgot the feeling of having failed as a leader, costing a boy his life.

Coming back to the present, a shudder went up Mike's spine with the memory of performing CPR on the cold body. Fortunately, it was replaced by one of joy as two of Peter Worthington's granddaughters flung themselves onto his lap. They were just what Mike needed to bring back the holiday spirit.

Mike's wife, Lauren, couldn't help but smile as she watched her husband being assaulted with New Year's kisses from Peter's granddaughters. She was very proud of the man her husband was becoming. That wasn't to say he didn't have more than a few rough edges. Nobody was perfect, but he seemed to have really grown lately.

Mike began to laugh uncontrollably with the two little girls, when suddenly Sean Callahan and Linda Sharpe both walked in the front door and into the family room. For a couple of seconds, all talk ceased and everyone turned to stare. The pregnant pause lasted only a moment before the applause started.

When the noise began to die down, both Sean and Linda could be seen blushing.

Rollie McDermott chimed in, "Welcome, you two! My God, Sean! You can walk!" Rollie's comment brought laughter, breaking the ice for everyone.

Sean's father, Fred Callahan, was the Chief of Police in the nearby town of Cronin. He was also on the Governor's Emergency Management Task Force. Fred and his wife, Penny, were seated nearby looking like the cats that ate the canary. They obviously knew Sean would be coming over to Mike's for his first social visit out of his home since the injury.

It was Lauren who noticed it first. "Okay, you two. I want to hear the details. Right now!"

Everyone who had begun to wander off came back to gather around Sean and Linda. The murmur, and even a few gasps from the ladies, could be heard as Linda shoved out her left hand to display a beautiful engagement ring with an enormous diamond.

"Honey, why don't you tell them," Linda said, smiling and looking deeply into Sean's eyes.

Sean had to clear his throat before saying, "You all probably know Linda and I have been very close since I was blown up."

This comment earned an affectionate, but painful, swat from Linda and a few chuckles from the onlookers. Everyone knew he had been seriously injured during a classified mission in Afghanistan.

"When I found this rocket scientist, athlete, military leader, and the most beautiful woman in the world, it looked like I'd have no chance with her. To make it worse, I was her commanding officer, making her doubly off limits. That explosion must have knocked some sense into me, though, and maybe the concussion knocked some sense out of her. I woke up enough to see that…"

"Honey," Linda said with a big smile. "They don't care about that. All anyone wants to hear about is how you did the deed." The look on her face made it impossible to take offense at her interruption.

"Ahem, well, that is…" Sean, the man of steel who was never caught off guard or out of sorts, stumbled over his words.

"Okay. Looking around the room, I see only people I can trust. Except for the popping the question part, please don't repeat any of the rest of it. Okay?"

Everyone in the room nodded their heads, thrilled at the concept of entering a conspiracy. Fortunately, the kids had wandered down to the basement rec room to avoid the "yucky stuff."

Sean continued, "Linda has taken some time off after leaving the Army and came to help me recuperate from my injuries. You may or may not have seen some unsavory characters wandering in and out of my mom and dad's house."

"It's your house, too," Penny said to her son with annoyance.

"Yeah, Mom, I know, but thanks for reminding me." Sean followed the comment with one of those mischievous little boy grins.

"Anyway, while I'm convalescing at home, the Army has asked me to work from home on some things I can't talk about. So if you see any of the guys sent to help me handle this stuff, please treat them like regular guys and don't mention to anyone that you've seen them. Not on social media, not even on the phone. Please try to ignore that we are even here. If it should get out, it could be dangerous for us on future missions."

Everyone nodded solemnly in agreement. "I was able to hand pick all the guys so I know they're all good men. Now, as to the pretty daughters in town, I can assure you that they'll all be gentlemen. They are, however, still all young men far from home, if you catch my drift." He said this last with a twinkle in his eye.

"Seaaann." His mom seemed to draw his name out into a five-second sound of exasperation. "The *ring* story!"

"Oh, yes. During these last few months of being in the hospital and then rehab, Linda has been there almost every day. My interest was there since the first time I saw her. That a beautiful woman like her could still love part of a man…"

"Honey, stop!" The command from Linda was short and full of barbs. She would not tolerate this topic.

"All right, Sweetheart," Sean said with a look of true contrition. "Since she believed in me even when I didn't, I decided nothing ventured, nothing gained. This afternoon while learning to walk on this new, bionic leg I seemed to stumble and ended up on my good knee. When she came over to help, I took her hands in mine, told her that I love her and asked if she would be my wife." Penny's eyes teared up as had several of the people listening. "When she didn't tell me what a fool I was…"

Linda chimed in, "Of course I said yes, you big ox!" Everyone broke into a cheer without any further discussion.

CHAPTER 9
NEW YEAR'S EVE

Lexington, Kentucky
2000 Hours EST

Kerry DuBois was slightly pudgy man, with slick-back hair that everyone associates with a slimy used car or snake oil salesman. It was New Year's Eve, and his wife had insisted that she had to go care for her mother in West Virginia. Having no real friends, Kerry had decided to make a rare trip to see his own mother at her Section 8, low-income row house in Lexington, Kentucky.

Since Kerry had been taking care of her finances for several years, it didn't surprise him to learn she qualified for Section 8 housing. Five years earlier, this wasn't the case. She had far too much money to qualify for low-income housing. From his viewpoint, she was just throwing it away on the nice little apartment where she lived. Through his diligent assistance, that was no longer a problem. Kerry's wife hadn't even questioned where the money for his new car, trip to Las Vegas, and the occasional expensive dinner originated. With Kerry's help, his mom no longer had too much money. She owed him, after all. Now she was paying peanuts for a place to live!

Since he had not seen her since long before Christmas, Kerry stopped at Walgreens on the way to get a box of chocolates. It was even in a gift box and on sale after Christmas! She loved chocolate, which he knew had been forbidden by her doctor due to her diabetes. Maybe with the gift, she would quit asking how much was left in her late husband's 401K account. The man he viciously thought of as his bastard stepfather had been a hard working over-the-road truck driver. He had taught Kerry about the Teamsters Union, but with those lessons came strict discipline that was enforced whenever he was in town. Kerry always felt that the bastard had driven him to the University of California – Berkley and the American Socialist Party platform. Like Saul Alinsky[1], Kerry felt that hard work was for the people too stupid to play the angles.

Walking to the door of his mother's apartment, Kerry dreaded the next two hours of listening to her complaints about her late disability checks and all of her ailments. In the back of his mind, he also realized that his mother wouldn't be on the list to receive re-distributed food if that became necessary.

"Hi, Mother," Kerry said as he entered her apartment. "Belated Merry Christmas and Happy New Year! I got these chocolates for you. I know how much you enjoy them, and they're sugar free!" Kerry said this with his most winning smile. It had been pretty simple to peel the sugar-free label off another box in the store aisle and stick it onto the box for his mother, directly over the nutritional information.

• • •

The Mountains in Southeast Afghanistan
1300 Hours Local Time

Snow was softly falling in the cold, clear air, only to be whipped around by the occasional mountain breeze. Ahmed had just praised Allah for the third time that day. A week earlier, he had spoken to the eighteen remaining martyrs. He applauded their dedication and reminded each one how much Allah and their families were depending upon them. Each family would receive money equivalent to over three years' wages after they had completed their mission. In addition, the martyrs would be rewarded by the services of many virgins when they went to heaven.

After Ahmed addressed his martyrs, the first three had flown off to Athens, Greece for practice in traveling and functioning in the West. They had been replaced by three more, a routine that continued every two days. All would complete their travels before the middle of January and should be ready to fulfill their mission.

Ahmed lamented that he was unable to smite the Christian Infidels a week ago, on their most holy day. But it was the will of Allah. He could not hide his

---

[1] See Appendix B

delight that everything seemed to be coming together. Jasmine's brother, Ali, would soon arrive to set up his laboratory in the most secret cave. When the opportunity came, he would be ready if it was Allah's will.

. . .

The Fontaine Estate
Outside of San Francisco, California
2200 Hours PST

Katherine Fontaine sat in her silk robe on her perfectly restored 17th century divan. Her office in the Fontaine Estate outside San Francisco had been designed to have a beautifully appointed space available for public meetings. Through sliding double doors, she could access her adjoining, very private sitting room. Those Secret Service knuckle-draggers were only allowed into that room once per day, only after receiving explicit permission to enter. This was a compromise. Susan had convinced her that they had to have some access in order to sweep for bugs. Since Katherine had an almost insane fear of all bugs, electronic and insect, she grudgingly agreed, but only once daily. The household staff knew to avoid the room whenever she was in town unless instructed otherwise.

"Madam President, your usual white wine?" Susan asked the question in a soft voice as she stood by the fully stocked bar, which was normally hidden behind closed doors.

It was Susan's job to keep Katherine's life in order. When Katherine had been elected, her choice for Press Secretary, Marjorie Klein, had been the one to provide emotional and other, more personal, support. Marjorie's health declined dramatically right after Katherine had taken office, making her unavailable. Without Marjorie, Katherine's more intimate needs fell upon the shoulders of Susan.

Susan did not consider herself a lesbian, but during the campaign for President, she had been swept up with the whole process of change for the country. Long ago she decided she would do anything to be a part of it. That level of power was intoxicating. When Katherine first maneuvered her into bed a few months before the election, it was a new, but not totally unpleasant experience. Since then, Susan observed the immense levels of stress placed upon the President and decided to do whatever she could to help manage that stress.

"No, dear," Katherine said in a husky voice. "I think a double tequila. You know the really good stuff provided by that Mexican donor to the Foundation? And make yourself two of those. It's New Year's Eve, and I think we need to let our hair down."

While saying this, Katherine pulled the elastic band from her hair to let it spill over her partially bare shoulder.

Susan smiled her patient, almost motherly smile to acknowledge her understanding of Katherine's meaning. She was wearing a cream-colored silk blouse Katherine had given her for Christmas, along with a luxurious red velour skirt that came just below her knees. At Katherine's request, she wore no bra, and although she had tried on the weird thong novelty underwear Katherine had given her, she opted for no underwear at all.

Susan swallowed her first double tequila in one gulp before bringing her second and Katherine's first over to the divan. It was going to be a long night of work.

CHAPTER 10
NEW YEAR'S EVE

The Great Wall of China
0900 Hours Local Time

General Secretary Song walked slowly down the section of the *Ten-Thousand Mile Long Wall*, known in the West as the Great Wall of China. Entering one of the watchtowers, he saw MSS Minister Lao standing at an open window. Lao was alone. Song's protection detail had insured there was no one else in that particular tower.

"Your family is doing well?"

Song asked after having stood next to Lao for a few seconds. Lao, for his part, had patiently waited for Song to speak first. That was one of many things Song respected about Lao. Simple courtesy to a superior was dying in the People's Republic.

"Yes, General Secretary. My wife and children are all faring well. And your family?" Lao was particularly impressed at Song's ability to recall the names and occupations of each of Lao's family, going back three generations.

Social convention having been met, Song asked his usual question. "Lao, when will our renegade province be returned to the People's Republic?"

Formosa, known in the West as Taiwan, was considered a mere renegade province of the People's Republic of China.

Lao knew Song's real question was how invasion preparations progressed.

"General Secretary," Lao said with respect and a level of confidence. "The three Generals involved with the sea-assault exercise were arrested, tried, and executed quietly, but with the full knowledge of the PLA General Staff. Two members of the Politburo have retired to their private estates outside of Vienna,

Austria after having learned of the failure of their latest plot to assassinate you. I fear they may not survive to see the Chinese New Year."

Lao's smile would have terrified a lesser man, but Song just nodded with his own satisfaction. The intrigues he had used to become Premier and General Secretary had given Song a fatalistic approach to life.

"How close are we to being able to launch a successful attack on Formosa?" Song asked the question in a voice that was barely audible to Lao.

"General Secretary, short of using nuclear weapons, with great losses we could take the island today. That is presuming American battle groups are within striking distance. Many of our casualties will come from the fight to neutralize that threat. Use of our tactical EMP[2] weapons on both the Americans and the Formosa forces will enhance our probability of success. There is new intelligence, however that indicates the Formosa military has secretly hardened their military command and control and some weapons systems against an EMP attack. The American Navy is somewhat hardened against an EMP strike, but such a strike would severely weaken their capabilities. Of course, if you choose to utilize the capabilities that just became available, their shields might prove useless."

Lao continued, "It is yet undetermined whether the island government would launch a counterattack against the Chinese mainland. They have the capability to do so in a limited way, even to strike Beijing and Shanghai with a few missiles. Their government, however, has an ongoing debate as to whether such a strike would remove their status as a victim of Chinese aggression among the world community. In reality, General Secretary, considering how we have crushed the Western economy by discontinuing oil purchases; the world community opinion should not be a factor at this time. There will be time to adjust that opinion after we have repositioned ourselves in the world power structure.

On another related topic, intelligence has just come to me indicating several members of the Politburo[3] were most unhappy at the prospect of a possible invasion, fearing war with the U.S. These men will have to be placated."

---

[2] Electro-magnetic Pulse – A nuclear device generated surge of energy that burns and destroys electronics

[3] The ruling body of the Communist Party and defacto, rulers of the PRC.

Lao decided to balance the bad news with his first smile. "Special Project 'Frozen Lilly' has been tested successfully and is ready for an appropriate real world test."

Frozen Lilly was the code name for a super-secret capability allowing a tactical EMP device to be directed at very small targets, such as a ship or small naval battle group. Unlike previous similar weapons, improvements in technology would allow it to overcome most military EMP shielding. The prospect of being able to temporarily disable an American naval battle group, without it being obvious that China was responsible, provided almost endless opportunities. Song continued to be amazed at Lao's ability to protect the program from leaking to the West.

"What needs to be done?" Song asked the open-ended question with more force than he had used in previous questions.

Lao responded thoughtfully, "With each passing week I believe the PLA General Command will adjust the level of corruption to provide funding for troop training and equipment upgrades. Realistically, it will be another six months to a year before there is a large improvement in the PLA casualty rate. Of greater importance is the continued weakening of the American economy and its effect on their Navy. Their President has already ordered much of the Pacific Fleet back to Pearl Harbor and San Diego, over the objections of both the Joint Chiefs of Staff and the Secretary of the Navy. I learned from our most confidential source that President Fontaine is planning to remove the Secretary of the Navy and replace him with a political creature that will reduce funding for the Navy across the board."

"This is important, Lao. When will these reductions reach the point where their President will forbid a response to our attack on Formosa?" Song had turned to Lao and intently bored into Lao's eyes.

"General Secretary," Lao said with unusual hesitation, "you have shown to have the best feel for timing of any leader I have ever known, including Chairman Mao. I can only give you the facts that are available."

Lao gave a pause for effect. "That said, it will be at least four months before the PLA can make meaningful changes in their strategy and training. If the American Congress goes through with passing veto-proof legislation forbidding payment on all foreign debts, a true weakening of the American military may take another four to six months. The Americans continue to print money while their real inflation rate has reached over two hundred percent. Your enemies in the PLA and the Politburo may gather their strength before then."

Lao had bowed his head slightly and then continued, "General Secretary, you are aware of the food riots and Muslim attacks in the western provinces?" At Song's nod, Lao continued, "Crippling the West's economies through our temporary discontinuance to purchase oil on the world market and the resulting trade war has, to a lesser extent, negatively impacted our own economy. Industrialists have begun to call in favors from their pets in the Politburo. Government contractor white-collar workers have staged an unofficial and illegal slowdown along the entire coast of China. They are protesting government restrictions and seizures of private and corporate property on trumped up charges.

Song paused within the inner calm he had enforced upon himself. In a faraway voice, he said to Lao, "I will meditate on these matters." He then made no move to either continue the discussion or dismiss Lao.

Lao waited patiently for over ten minutes.

Suddenly, Song's head snapped up and he said in his normal voice, "Lao, what is the status of Black Orchid?"

Lao moved closer to Song to speak softly in his ear. "Hu tells me that he is convinced the vaccine will work effectively. It has completed the production run and will soon be fully distributed to essential people. My best covert officer advised the cell in Afghanistan will be ready to perform their duties within the next few weeks." General Hu Sengai was the Director of the Special Warfare arsenal, including nuclear, biological, and chemical weapons.

"That will be all, Lao. Keep me informed." With that, Song left Lao standing at the window and walked out to continue his tour.

Lao looked out the window and wondered if his trust in Song was justified. Every time he thought about Black Orchid, he felt somewhat like the apostle, Judas, in the Christian mythology found in their Bible. This time, it wasn't just the mythical son of God that would die.

CHAPTER 11
THE NEW YEAR - PLUS TWO DAYS

Washington, DC
1600 Hours EST

Wu Chin waited patiently in the diner six blocks from Eli Fredericks' office in Washington, D.C. The slightly built Chinese man wore a dark, $4,000 Armani suit. He appeared to be of indeterminate age despite being well over sixty. Wu was the manager and clandestine mouthpiece in America for Chinese industrialist and billionaire Chen Wen, the second wealthiest man in the People's Republic of China. In this position, Wu held a great deal of power and moved in the highest circles of the most powerful men in the world. Wu was highly paid but knew his fortunes, status, and his life balanced on the thin thread of insuring Chen's interests in the United States were well managed. With the current relations between the People's Republic of China and the U.S., Wu's balancing act had become even more difficult.

Seated in the back of the diner, Wu recognized the advance security man for Eli Fredericks who entered the diner and conducted a quick survey. Wu was pleased to note Eli's security man did not appear to identify his own security man, who was seated with a young professional woman at a booth by the wall.

A few moments later, Eli walked into the diner and received an almost imperceptible nod from his security man. The nod indicated there were no known threats, from either the criminal element or domestic or foreign intelligence officers, and only the normal electromagnetic traffic was in the air from cell phones and computers. Eli ordered regular coffee at the counter and then walked to the back of the diner to take a seat at the table next to Wu's.

After a moment, Wu commented, "It may snow later today." The comment made no sense if one had listened to the clear and cold weather forecast for the next two days.

Eli responded, "I've had enough of snow, even this early in the season."

Both Wu's comment and Eli's response were part of a clandestine verbal dance known as a parole. Wu's comment meant there was no known threat and a normal meeting could take place. Eli's response merely confirmed this was the case. Eli had strenuously objected to the several days of training given to him by Chen's security people in such matters. He finally relented after it occurred to him the alternative was death or imprisonment should he be caught. Eli was acutely aware that Chen had the resources to have him killed should that become necessary. This was acceptable since Chen was aware the same was potentially true for Eli as well.

Wu launched into the meat of the meeting while there were no people within earshot. "You requested the meeting. Please share with me what our friend or I can do for you."

"I think it is time our friend and I should meet again." After a pause, Eli continued. "I'm planning a two–day trip to Singapore a week from now and hoped our friend might find time to enjoy the sights there."

Eli would have preferred to have simply picked up the phone and called Chen. Capabilities of the American National Security Agency, the Russians, Israelis, and the Chinese in intercepting such communications – even supposedly secure ones, prevented this.

Wu was mildly surprised to hear the invitation, but understood Eli and Chen had orchestrated many tide-turning events in the world and had profited handsomely each time. "I will pass on your request but cannot say right now if it is possible."

"I understand," Eli said softly. "You will let me know within twenty-four hours?"

"But of course," Wu replied. "My friend will want to know, have you been successful in weathering the economic storm?"

This was one of the tightest ropes Wu had ever walked. A few months earlier he had given Eli a mere twenty-four hour notice of the impending Chinese move to stop buying oil on the world market. With no time to make any moves based upon the information Eli had responded with a veiled threat to Chen for this breach of trust. Wu interpreted Eli's threat to mean a tortured death for himself and his family just to send a message to Chen. His price to avoid taking these actions was to make sure Eli had seventy-two hours to act before the Chinese government announced the move. The announcement came seventy-two hours later, thereby allowing Eli to protect his investments.

"I'm sure your friend already knows I was able to take appropriate steps and am secure, at least for now." Eli's response indicated he knew Chen's intelligence sources knew a great deal about his financial situation and thereby knew the answer to Wu's question already. Eli had the same level of intelligence, so he presumed Chen would have done his homework.

Wu nodded with appreciation. "My friend appreciates your understanding in the matter. I anticipate no problem in obtaining a response for you by tomorrow morning at the latest. Is there anything else I can do for you today?"

Eli merely shook his head no, got up, and walked out.

CHAPTER 12
THE NEW YEAR - PLUS FOUR DAYS

Washington, DC
1445 Hours EST

When Walter turned off the power to his covert, burner cell phone he was already feeling the stirrings of anticipation. It had been only a little over a week, but he didn't know how many more times he would be able to savor his little China doll. The day after tomorrow would be another wonderful day. With an effort he tried to clear his head. He had to get ready for a meeting with the representative of a Saudi royal to discuss another sizable donation to the Fontaine Foundation.

Walter knew his fortunes were determined by how effectively he utilized his wife's office to obtain donations for "favors." He didn't think of them as bribes so much as payment for the favors that could be dispensed at the discretion of those in power. Throughout history, wealthy patrons had financed the good works of favored politicians. Of course, payback was expected. No politician ever admitted the payback aspect, but it was always there. Some fools even called the arrangement "pay to play." Walter, and of course Katherine, simply knew it was the cost of being able to do what was needed for the people. Hell, even Robin Hood had robbed from the rich to give to the poor.

Considering his next meeting with Su Ling, Walter couldn't decide whether he wanted her to be the dominant one, or if he should plan to use something from her bag of toys. Just the thought of that bag brought an immediate physical response.

• • •

The Broehm Residence
Outside of Cronin, Kentucky
1930 Hours EDT

Mike Broehm sat out by his fire pit with a fine glass of bourbon on the rocks, looking into the fire. Peter Worthington, the slightly built Professor of Mechanical and Environmental Engineering had walked over from his adjacent property to visit. Mike's offered beer was readily accepted. Peter's two hundred acres of land backed up to Mike's place. He was Mike's biggest supporter and one of his best friends. He had become independently wealthy through non-university consulting that helped mining companies save literally millions of dollars in meeting environmental requirements efficiently. He also had a specially constructed home which included an armored bunker containing arms and a large amount of long-term storage food. Even before the last Presidential election, Peter had begun to nudge Mike into a leadership role in the neighborhood.

"Peter," Mike said over the crackling fire. "Almost a third of the neighborhood is laid off from work, and the economy keeps going down. That stupid bitch in the White House seems to be doing everything she can to make it worse. Do you think she really intends to drive the economy down to justify declaring martial law?"

Peter considered the question before saying, "Well, it sure looks that way."

After a moment he continued, "It was my financial guru Scott Shelby that told me Wall Street actually backed her over Donnelson because they thought she would continue the fiscally irresponsible policies that were making them all rich. But for the Chinese oil move, they would be right. It wasn't just the dirty tricks used by Fontaine's campaign that got her elected. Wall Street bet their continued fortunes on her being in the White House and financed a lot of her campaign through donations to the Fontaine Foundation. Donnelson had promised to clean up the government and quit paying for stuff that wasn't needed, including large-ticket social programs."

Both men sat contemplating the fire and the country for several minutes.

Finally, Mike said, "Peter, you keep pushing for me to head up the neighborhood as things continue to go in the toilet. Why are you doing that? Don't you like me?" Mike's question was followed by a wan smile.

Peter cocked his head a little as he considered his answer. "Mike, as you probably picked up on, I think a great deal of you and your abilities. You've got a lot more leadership talent than you ever imagined. In fact, you've got more ability than anyone I've ever met. Hell, people *like* you! They can't help themselves. You are who you are, and it comes through more clearly than you could ever imagine. If you're looking for a leader, you want someone that really doesn't want to seize control, but someone that is reluctantly drafted. Well, son, consider yourself drafted."

Peter's words were more than a little shocking to Mike. He had always thought of himself as someone that just had no problem making decisions.

"I don't *want* the job, Peter, and you know why." Peter knew the horrible fate of the Boy Scout and how it haunted Mike.

"Just the reason you should have it." Peter didn't hesitant, despite Mike's obvious reluctance. "Do you know of anyone else around here that can get the job done as well as you?"

That one stumped Mike for a moment. "How about you?"

Looking at Peter, Mike found he actually enjoyed seeing the hint of anguish that flashed across the older man's face. Somehow, it felt good and was at least a little bit of payback for Peter having pushed Mike to the forefront.

"OK, asshole," Peter said with a smile coming to his lips. "Yes, you know I love to be in control of things, but in business I also learned that usually the most powerful people are the ones in the shadows that," he paused for a two count, before continuing, "…exert influence over those in the public light."

Peter had hesitated as he was about to say either 'manipulate or control,' before deciding to change it to 'exert influence.' He could see understanding in Mike's eyes as well as the building of a stubborn resolve.

"Mike, we've known each other a long time, and I think I really do know you."

When Peter tried to look down, Mike's eyes held his and seemed to bore all the way into his soul.

Peter continued, "I know you're going to do what you see is right. Period. That's why you will always have my full support – even if it goes against what I want." Peter said this with some reluctance.

"All I ask of you, Mike, is what you already do. Just give me a listen and then do what you need to do. That's all. Just a listen."

Mike continued to stare intently into Peter's eyes for a few moments before saying, "Peter, if things really do get dicey, I'm going to need to know I can count on you in a crunch even if there's no time to listen. Are you OK with that?"

Both men sat quietly while Peter worked everything out in his head. "Yes, Mike, I am OK with that."

Mike silently let out his breath, which he had been holding while he waited for Peter's answer. He knew that in any crisis Peter's backing was critical. He also knew Peter was a man of his word and nothing more need be said.

CHAPTER 13
THE NEW YEAR - PLUS FIVE DAYS

Beijing, China
0900 Hours Local Time

General Secretary Song waited in silence for the military aid to complete his report, while a near blinding rage began to build within him. The staffer was a mid-ranking officer that brought daily reports from the General Staff of the People's Liberation Army (PLA) to the General Secretary's office. The plans to improve training and equipment for the invasion had been scrapped by the General Staff and required an additional twenty-one days to be re-worked. Two additional generals had been arrested for treasonous plans targeting government leadership, and overall morale in the invasion forces was low. The aid tried to add some good news by advising speculation by the General Staff that costs for the re-worked training and equipment could be reduced by twenty-five percent.

After the aid closed the door, Song turned his back on Wong and instructed him to leave. Right after the door had closed with Wong's departure; Song picked up the steel model of a Mig-25 fighter and hurled it into the glass doors of a display case, shattering them. He then began to curse in a deep, guttural way, bringing intense shame on the ancestors of every member of the PLA's General Staff.

Suddenly Song froze and looked at the door leading into his private lavatory.

When he had been denied the time to properly use his delightfully trained girl from the MSS's Charm School earlier that day, he had indulged her pleas to come to his office in Beijing. Before the briefing he had instructed her to go into the lavatory and remain absolutely silent. She had, of course, done exactly what he had told her to do.

With a purposeful step, Song walked to the door and opened it. Inside was the girl, standing against the wall across from the sink with a terrified expression on her face. It was obvious she had heard his explosion of temper and feared he would inflict his wrath on her.

Song placed a small smile upon his face and approached her with open arms while saying, "Calm yourself my dear. There is nothing to fear."

Gathering up the girl in his arms, he asked, "What has frightened you so?"

She was trembling with fear and through a sniffle, she said, "I heard something breaking and didn't know what was happening."

Song silently nodded to himself. He then said, "Well, it is time you cleaned up your tears."

With that he turned her away from his arms as if to push her toward the sink. He then quickly and efficiently moved his arm around her neck to crush her trachea, holding her against him until she stopped convulsing. When she slumped to the floor he stepped away and walked out into his office. Picking up his phone, he pushed a button.

"Wong?" He said softly into the phone. "Clean up the mess in my office lavatory. You will see that it is discreetly done. You will also contact Lao and have him arrange for a replacement for the Charm School girl."

He hung up the phone without waiting for a response.

Song took his desk chair and moved it to the corner window, where he sat and began to meditate. He did not hear Wong as he quietly came in with a large, plastic bag and cleaning materials. Ten minutes later Song's meditation was only slightly disturbed when Wong accidentally thumped the girl's head on a table leg as he dragged the bagged corpse out of the room.

• • •

Ronald Reagan National Airport
0900 Hours EST

Eli Fredericks sat in the back of his black Cadillac Escalade limo that had just picked him up from the airport. Per instructions, his assistant had handed him a one-page synopsis of his most important investment positions as he entered the Escalade, which was driven by a former Navy Seal.

A cursory review of the daily brief sheet showed him that the U.S. economy continued a steady decline rivaling, and possibly worse than that seen during the Great Depression. Any additional jolts could seriously affect his financial positions. Moves made just before the two trillion dollar stimulus package was announced yesterday had appeared to have the potential for profits of over twenty percent. A quick in-and-out of the green companies would also ensure he was able to get out with those profits before they went belly-up.

At least Katherine had arranged to have only half of the stimulus money steered into areas benefiting her radical left base. The other half she had directed toward infrastructure projects such as roads and bridges. For the first time since the Chinese had initiated the crisis, a significant number of Americans would be going back to work, albeit being paid with borrowed money. Printing money had continued to drive up interest rates to the point inflation was exceeding two hundred percent, despite what the government claimed.

Eli began thinking of his upcoming meeting with Chen. With his influence in the White House and Chen's influence with the Chinese Politburo and General Secretary Song, they could run the world – at least for a few years. The simple meeting with Chen in Singapore the second week of January could make it happen.

．．．

Washington, D.C. hotel
After-New Year's Eve Party Fundraiser
2015 Hours EST

Don Stetson sat down on the loveseat in stunned silence watching the President depart the fundraiser. Before leaving, she had jovially shaken his hand and whispered in his ear, "I know everything that you did to get me elected Don, and soon you'll see what true power can do. None of this better see the light of day, or your future might be quite short and maybe even painful. Do you understand me, Don?"

Don had nodded his head. She gave his eyes one last glare and then departed. He had no idea why she found the need to address the subject. In his slightly inebriated state, it was all he could do to refrain from wetting himself.

Taking a few minutes and multiple deep breaths, Don ordered two double scotches from the bartender before grabbing his phone and calling Marc Baxter. This was his third and fourth round, and he could tell that he would not be stopping until he lost consciousness. Don rarely drank alcohol anymore, but today was an exception.

The party was organized at the behest of the President for the highest-level staff to hobnob with the party's largest donors. The banquet hall was only a few blocks from the White House at the International Hotel in what was affectionately called the Old Post Office. Even with the country going to hell in a hand basket, Katherine continued to court donors. It was a command performance for all White House staff personnel, who were to 'make nice' with party money people who just might continue to give the Fontaine Foundation money.

Drinking had sufficed to dull Don's annoyance and pain.

Marc answered his cell phone on the second ring, seeing that it was from Don.

"Hey, buddy," Marc said cheerfully.

Don slurred his voice into the phone. "The Chief of Staff is asking about you. The President her-own-self even noticed you, I mean, you not here. If you don't want to catch a load of, well, ya' know, better get over here. No tellin' what I may say."

"I'm about to walk in the door now. And Don, please don't talk to anyone."

The line was dead for several seconds before Don noticed. Ten minutes after arriving, greeting and sharing brief words with a few of the donors Marc went in search of Don.

Marc found Don sitting on the loveseat against a wall near the corner of an out-of-the-way room. Five highball glasses sat on the coffee table, one of which contained a double bourbon for Marc. Don held another half-empty glass while staring at the ceiling above the crowd. Marc took the chair next to and very near the loveseat and reached to touch Don's arm, causing him to start and nearly spill his drink. The party noise made it possible to have a private conversation, just out of earshot of the nearest guests.

"Don, old buddy, what have you done to yourself?" Marc asked the question with true concern on his face.

Don slowly focused on Marc before answering, "God almighty, this is why I don't drink much. Don't have trouble with morals, except when Mr. Scotch gets 'a hold of me."

After a quick look around, Don grabbed Marc's wrist and in an almost sober voice said, "I took a lot of money from a lot of shitheads over the years, Marc, but none of them holds a candle to, well, you know."

Marc knew he was talking about Katherine Fontaine.

"Damn, the money was good, and with young punks like you around, it was easy."

Seeing the look that flashed momentarily over Marc's face, Don blurted, "Marc you know what I mean. The campaign wrote itself."

"You mean the lies we put out about the Afghan widows watching Donnelson's[4] men massacre their husbands?"

Marc let just a little emotion seep into the question. Being personally involved in that one still pissed him off, even if he didn't know it was a lie at the time. The lie, coming out as it did just before the election, had been sufficient to tip the scales to elect Katherine to the Presidency.

"Awwww, come on, Marc. Getting her elected was our job. She couldn't do all the great stuff we just knew she would do if she didn't get in. That's what they hired us to do."

Don's voice softened even more as he said, "They hired me to do even more. I laid hands on a lot, and I mean a LOT, of money to spread around to get her elected, to the tune of a couple or three hundred million!"

These last words were hissed in a hoarse, suppressed voice to add emphasis. "I never told you, or anyone for that matter, but we paid organizers in every single swing state, at least those without voter ID laws, to take thousands of busloads of illegals around to vote in multiple precincts. Nobody knew where the money came from, but I knew."

Looking around, Don said, "And you know most of the money came from that black devil or his flunkies."

Before the words were completely out of Don's mouth, Marc began to stand up and said, "Okay, Don. I think you've had enough."

Don caught Marc's arm and pulled him down.

---

[4] Katherine Fontaine defeated former U.S. Army officer James Donnelson in the Presidential election.

"Marc, Katherine musta' found out what I did. A few minutes ago, she whispered in my ear that I better keep quiet or bad, painful things would happen."

He looked pleadingly into Marc's eyes. "You need to see what really happened." Don's eyes seemed to lose focus briefly before he continued, "In every major city across this great land, *my operatives* made sure the votes got out. Without me, Katherine woulda' got three, maybe four million less votes. Don't ya see? The end justifies the means."

With that last statement, Don seemed lose all the wind in his sails before passing out on the loveseat. A quick look around found that everyone in the vicinity had discretely distanced themselves from the obvious drunk while his friend handled it.

Marc flagged down one of the servers and arranged for Don to be taken to his hotel room by private car. Such things were not unusual at these parties, and the staff took it all in stride.

· · ·

Two hours later Marc lay in his bed next to Susan Cassel, who usually crashed at his place to save the forty-five minute commute to her own apartment. They had a friends-with-benefits arrangement and enjoyed being able to talk to each other freely, without violating classification laws.

Susan had made love without the usual passion typically brought on by her always extreme stress. She lay in the bed with exhaustion showing on her face, but was not able to close her eyes.

"I know we're both exhausted," Marc said with just a tinge of humor in his voice, "but was I really that bad?"

After a deep breath, Susan rolled over on her side to look Marc in the eyes across the pillow. Over the past few months Marc had literally been her lifeline. He was the only person she could completely trust.

After a few seconds, she said with growing fear, "I think she's really trying to drive the country further into depression." The shock on Marc's face surprised her. "Marc, haven't you been listening to me? I mentioned this before."

"I know, but I really thought you were either joking or just plain wrong."

After a pause, "Why would she do something like that?" The exasperation was apparent in his voice.

"I really think she wants to declare a State of Emergency, so in her own mind she can do what needs to be done by issuing Executive Orders."

The words came out in almost a whisper. "She hasn't been able to get anything through Congress, and she seems to be hell-bent on disarming the public. Food riots keep reoccurring in Detroit and Philly, and I think she wants more. Anything for an excuse to impose a State of Emergency so she can start issuing edicts."

The enormity of what Susan was saying was not lost on Marc. His anti-gun campaign was all part of her plan.

Finally, Marc and Susan fell asleep as exhaustion took them away from everything.

CHAPTER 14
THE NEW YEAR - PLUS FIVE DAYS

Lisa McIntyre's Apartment
Washington, D.C.
2130 Hours EST

Su Ling had gotten lost in the college crowd outside of the diner where she had eaten dinner and appeared to finish up on some homework. Within a few minutes, she slipped into the apartment building where Lisa McIntyre lived and knocked quietly on the door. Lisa opened the door quickly and nodded as Su walked noiselessly through the door.

As the door closed, both young women immediately hugged with relief. Lisa even began to cry softly, which surprised Su enough for her to break the embrace.

"Why you cry, Lisa? Su asked the question with empathy and suspicion in her eyes as she looked at the only true friend she ever had. It was a testament to how comfortable Su was that she let her normal command of the English language slip.

"Oh, I'm just being silly," Lisa said while walking toward the small apartment kitchen. Music was playing from Lisa's MP-3 player to mask their conversation, just as her father had taught her.

Lisa turned and tried to be casual as she said, "Truth is, I'm scared to death for you and really upset that you have to do the things you have to do."

The words came tumbling out in a very untypical manner for Lisa.

Su surprised Lisa with a hesitant smile. "I have never had anyone care for me like that before."

The awkwardness lasted for only a couple of seconds before Lisa turned and poured two glasses of wine from a bottle on her kitchen counter.

They both settled into Lisa's couch and Lisa couldn't help but ask, "Considering all of your training, how could you possibly trust anyone at all?"

"When I was in school," Su always used this opening when she was about to talk about the horrific experience that was the MSS's Charm School, "I could convince anyone of anything. However, when I took my mind out of it and only listened to my heart, I could always tell when someone was lying to me, even those trained to lie. I don't know how, but at that, I am never wrong."

After a pause, "And when I met you for the first time, I knew I could trust you with anything. I have survived by trusting that skill, and it has never failed me."

To change the subject, Lisa began to tell Su about growing up in Central Kentucky outside of the small town of Cronin. When her dad wasn't around, she had the benefit of having been protected and taught many practical things by her godfather, Peter. Falling into her Kentucky drawl, she said, "Peter was partial to us young'uns and seemed to like me special, you know?" She drew out the word "like" for almost a full second.

At Su's questioning look, Lisa said, "Partial to, you know, like, he really liked me." This explanation gained a dubious nod. Lisa launched into describing three rapid thoughts using a thick Kentucky drawl that Su barely recognized as being related to American English. "Y'all, I ain't nuthin' but a hick girl from Kaintuck. Shoot girl, should have me a passel of young'uns and only a few good teeth by now. Billy Bob would run shine and smokes in his ole beater pick-em'-up truck." It brought an immediate round of chuckles from both.

"I would like to see Kentucky someday," Su said while looking closely at Lisa.

Lisa broke the look between them and quietly said, "Maybe someday you will be able to."

Lisa turned away and walked toward the wine bottle on the counter.

"Maybe someday soon?"

Su's question elicited only the barest quick shake of Lisa's head before she changed the subject.

"Here, did you see what Dwight wrote on Facebook?" Lisa approached Su again with the wine bottle in one hand and her smart phone in the other.

Lisa sat down next to Su and whispered into her ear, "Dad said you should be ready to leave at a moment's notice with only what you have with you. Is this okay?"

Su's normally blank look changed to cover a variety of emotions, all in the space of two seconds. She couldn't believe this was really going to happen.

Su gave Lisa only the briefest of a nod and silently mouthed, "Okay." She then switched to a soft laughter at partially reading what poor Dwight had said about Lisa on Facebook. Professionally putting on a false feeling of 'girl time' talk was easy for Su. All the while, her mind spun with the very real possibility she might escape from slavery with her life, and possibly even a best friend.

· · ·

Mountains of Southeast Afghanistan
0600 Hours The Next Morning

Ahmed reveled in the crisp, early morning hours. It was before dawn and very cold, but mercifully the wind had temporarily stopped blowing, and the stars were shining brightly. He had completed his pre-dawn routine. When he had awakened, a premonition had come to him that all of the planning with the Chinese demon Cho would actually work. He had been staying in the second-most secret cave complex for the past several days and decided it would be his home for the next year or more. It would soon be stocked with food, water, and communications equipment for at least eighteen months. A year after the martyrs do their work, he would stick his head up out of his hole and decide if it was time to bring the word of Allah to the survivors.

The most secret cave complex, only a few kilometers away, had been turned into a laboratory equipped with everything needed for this divine mission.

Many items had proven difficult to acquire, but with several months and much money, all was now ready. In three days Jasmine's brother, Ali al-Hadiz, would arrive in Kabul and would get the facility functioning. He said he was bringing two others who were trustworthy. Ahmed would determine whether that was, in fact, true.

• • •

Covert FBI Location
Washington, D.C.
2215 Hours EST

The Director of the FBI walked into the off-site[5] on the heels of his protection detail. Over twenty-five FBI personnel were packed into the small office space. All but two of the total number of people aware of the Walter Fontaine espionage case were present. The two missing men would be briefed by the Director the following morning.

"Good evening, everyone," the Director said. "Thank you for coming in at such a late hour. Also, I want to thank each one of you for your participation in this investigation, especially in light of the very unusual level of secrecy it demands. And," he paused for a moment to choose his words carefully, "and frankly to be involved in this level of risk."

Hugh, the two specially detailed surveillance teams, and the two administrative secretaries briefly glanced at each other before refocusing their attention on the Director.

"Yes, I said there was a level of risk involved in what you are doing and, unfortunately, that risk could come from within our own government. I'll get into exactly what that is in a moment. First, I want to share some intelligence with you. In a report squirreled away in a back paragraph of my daily briefing this morning, was a note from both the CIA and NSA liaison officers. In passing, they mentioned some highly classified chatter that Walter Fontaine might, in some way, be compromised. There were no additional details. At this time, I have no way of knowing if this information is related to your work, however, we cannot take the chance."

He gave everyone a few moments to digest the intelligence.

---

[5] Location outside of official FBI space used to conduct covert activities.

"Because of this information," the Director continued, "and because I have decided this thing has progressed as long as it should, tomorrow night's scheduled meeting with the Chinese girl will be the last. I don't know that I'll be able to provide answers, but what questions do you have?"

One of the team leaders raised his hand and asked, "Sir, you mentioned there was some danger to us?"

"Oh, yes," said the Director. "It is not finally decided, but until I have given it a lot more thought, my inclination is to bring the Deputy Assistant Director and go see the President within a day or two after tomorrow night's activities. That is anticipated to be a very unpleasant meeting. Doing so will allow me to better protect each of you from being identified as knowledgeable in what amounts to the former Vice President's treasonous behavior." The silence in the room was only broken by the soft hum of the computers.

"Now, I'm not big on conspiracy theories," the Director continued, "but it cannot be discounted that enemies of the Fontaine machine have seemed to die with unusual regularity. I am aware the safest way to handle this would be to call a highly classified briefing of multiple intelligence agency heads and as many of their people as could be gathered. This is under the theory that the more people that know a secret, the less likely someone in power will try to, shall we say, kill the messenger. Although this decision has not yet been made, I must also consider what is best for our country. Wide dissemination of this information would surely come out in the press and would likely bring down the Fontaine administration abruptly. In the country's current economic state, that could be disastrous."

"What I am going to ask of all of you is that after tomorrow evening, I want you to fade back into your former assignment before it was turned upside down by this one. In addition, you will need to remain completely silent about this operation. I'm also going to ask you to trust me."

Chuckling, the Director continued, "Yeah, I know, trust me is mob speak for F-you, but in this case I mean it. And if she presses too far in trying to identify you, I'll be out in front of the TV cameras."

Director Kidd fielded several questions from the Special Agents on the surveillance teams, many of which he didn't know the answer. When the questions dried up, he took his leave and asked Hugh to come with him.

In the car, the Director said, "Hugh, when she's done tomorrow night, I want you to take the Chinese girl and drop out of sight. Take her somewhere safe and debrief her for everything you can get on the Charm School program. You know operations security better than I, so do whatever you need to, to ensure you can't be found, even by our own people. Use the Deputy Assistant Director as a covert contact point. I will be in touch with you, through the DAD, within three days after you pick her up. Here's a personal burner phone number for one I will have available to receive your call tomorrow night. After the call, I'll turn it off and remove the battery, only to turn it on for ten minutes at 11:11 p.m. each night. Have you arranged for a place to take the girl after the interrogation?"

"Sir, yes I have, but I won't need to interrogate her. I'll literally have her write up everything she knows on a laptop that can't connect to the Internet. It is truly amazing how incredibly astute and intelligent she is. Puts Mensa's [6] to shame. Oh, and what can be done to help her parents in China?"

The Director looked Hugh in the eye and said slowly, "I will, ah, make sure to ask the CIA Director when I speak with him tomorrow about what could be done on short notice if I were to come to him with a personal request along those lines. I wouldn't hold my breath."

With that, the Director looked away, making it obvious he didn't think there was any chance at all to help Su's parents.

---

[6] Mensa is an organization whose members are required to have very high IQs.

CHAPTER 15
THE NEW YEAR - PLUS SIX DAYS

The White House
1300 Hours EST

Katherine rubbed her temples as she fought another head pounding migraine though her pain threshold had increased to almost tolerate them. Thinking coherently was painful, but necessary. When Susan knocked softly at the door and entered from her office side entrance, she saw the pain etched on the President's face and immediately walked over to take up a position behind her. Susan's firm fingers began to rub deeply into the President's temples while she softly sang a soothing children's song her mother used to sing to her when she was sick.

After a few minutes, Susan said, "Madam President, I've rescheduled your appointments for the next ninety minutes. Would you like to relax for a while?"

"Thank you, my dear." The President said the words in a dreamlike voice, although they did sound like unfamiliar words coming from Katherine's lips.

After a few moments, Katherine continued, "That's good, my dear. Please take a break yourself and come back in an hour."

Susan left to find coffee and possibly Marc Baxter in the White House canteen.

Katherine barely heard the door close behind Susan. Over the Christmas holiday and the first few days of the New Year, the U.S. economy continued to spiral downward unabated. Unemployment had spiked upward dramatically, even though her Labor Department had followed instructions to report only a twenty-five percent rate. The mainstream press refrained from asking too many questions, but the conservative press unsuccessfully tried to press the issue.

The energy sector had also plummeted resulting in over half of the government–financed green energy companies shutting their doors. Not before company management and many of her donors had escaped with a healthy profit. The conservative media also hammered daily on those former CEO's and their connections to the Fontaine Foundation. FBI investigations had been announced targeting the offices of the Secretary of Energy, Agriculture, Health and Human Services, and the Department of Defense.

Katherine was heartened by a respite from media scrutiny caused by the death of the most conservative member of the Supreme Court. He died while he was alone, on vacation. Curiously, once the local coroner determined the death was from "natural causes," the Justice's family had demanded that no autopsy be performed. It lessened the pain in her head to think the Court was now evenly split between conservatives and liberals. His replacement would be loyal to her. How the man had died at such a fortuitous time never entered her mind. She had others that took care of that sort of thing.

Turning her thoughts toward Eli Fredericks, she saw the country continue to devolve toward collapse, as he had predicted. When she chose to declare a State of Emergency, she would be in position to assert complete dominance over the country. Eli had told her this would be the case, and so it was playing out.

"When I make the declaration," she thought with a clarity not always present in her mind, "I need to arrange for the removal of Eli and his whole organization. But how?"

This would definitely require further thought, she knew, and would not be an easy task. She also needed to find the right minion, or, ah, she mentally corrected herself, the right tool for the job. Several options are available.

Out loud, Katherine whispered to herself, "Yes, that will require quite a lot more thought."

. . .

Frankfort, Kentucky
1830 Hours EST

The political rally was held in the downtown Frankfort hotel instead of the Pen and Ink Saloon. The hotel would both accommodate the greater numbers and be removed from the obvious influence of Tank Monahan, even though he was paying for it. All of the liberal movers and shakers in Kentucky were invited, along with a few people of influence in state government including General Steven Thompson of the Army National Guard, who arrived quite late.

Throughout the evening, alcohol and illegal prescription pills flowed freely through many of the revelers as they discussed the tough times and how the conservative state government had destroyed the state's economy. Never mind that the entire country was in an economic tailspin.

When General Thompson arrived, his brother-in-law John Chapman had asked Kerry DuBois to escort him around the room and introduce him to people Kerry felt were important. For his part, the General was the consummate professional, showing no indication of his contempt for Kerry and instead took his introductions as an opportunity to identify those in government who appeared to share Kerry's mindset.

"General, if you don't mind, we're holding a very special meeting at a suite just upstairs. Everyone is dying to hear how things are going in Washington."

Kerry's statements had been delivered with the intent of complimenting the General's importance and to further stroke him into sharing what he had learned during his trip to the Pentagon. For his part, the General resisted the inclination to tell Kerry and his cronies to buzz off. Curiosity kept him quiet as he followed Kerry to the elevator.

The suite featured a bar setup far superior to that offered in the party room downstairs. Five men were present as Kerry and the General walked in. Upon their arrival, Tank Monahan shooed the buxom bartender and waitress out of the room and gave his own booming welcome to them both.

John Chapman got up from the couch and walked to shake the General's hand. "Steven, I'm very happy you could join us tonight. I was delighted when my sister let me know you could attend. I think you know Mr. Monahan and of course, Kerry. You may even know Blondie here, but rest assured everything happening this evening is strictly off the record."

John's smile, as he said this, made the General want to reach to insure his wallet was still in his pocket.

"Freddie Dobson, there, is a prominent businessman and good friend of the party," John said.

Turning toward a man standing off by himself, John made the grand introduction with a flourish, with a short, grizzled man with longer gray hair. "Now, this man is someone you definitely want to meet. General, let me introduce you to our state party Chairman, Coyote Collins."

Coyote stood up and shook the General's hand while looking down at the handshake instead of looking the General in the eyes. "Good to meet you, General. Looks like we may be working together pretty soon."

"Oh, ah, Coyote, is it? How is that?" The General's question showed more surprise than he had intended.

"Well, General. Like you, I've been in contact with some people in Washington. In particular, I've been talking to folks with the Fontaine administration and with Homeland Security. For whatever reason, they have decided I'm the man to govern the three state region including Tennessee, West Virginia, and Kentucky if a State of Emergency is declared. The President seems to think these tough times are only going to get worse, and emergency measures may well be necessary. But then I understand you've already been briefed on all of that, haven't you?"

The General recalled his briefings had all been classified TOP SECRET. "Gentlemen, I'm not sure what you have heard, but anything I learned in Washington, D.C. is classified and not for public discussion."

Kerry couldn't stop himself from blurting out, "Awww, c'mon General. These are all trusted friends here."

The General ignored him and looked directly at Coyote. "I'm not sure what instructions or clearances you have, but we can discuss that some other time in a different environment."

The General turned and marched purposefully from the room.

When the door closed, Tank nearly shouted, "Why that arrogant cock su…" only to be cut off by Coyote.

"Now, Tank, we've all worked with people that didn't see the light right away. Like them, the General can be, as we say, edjumicated." Coyote said that with a smile spreading across his lips as he continued, "And by the way, I'm going to have authority to hire potentially thousands of security folks to enforce necessary directives. Might you happen to know some folks who will do what they are told without getting stupid about it?"

Effectively sidetracked, Tank asked, "Now how much will you be paying these security folks?" He was genuinely interested with the prospect of getting a cut of whatever they would be making.

"Oh, it'll be the federal government scale, somewhere around a GS 8 or 9 pay grade, probably. Hell, with no jobs available, anything with benefits should be enough."

Tank thought about this for a moment before asking, "How about a contract to supply X number of trained security personnel? And how about weapons and equipment. Is that included, too? They'll need vehicles, unlimited fuel vouchers, that sort of thing."

"Yeah," Coyote said with some resignation, "that should be no problem. Especially the weapons and ammo. Homeland has been stockpiling those for quite a while now and can get priority to buy whatever they need. But I want these men trained and reliable. Emphasis on reliability. They have to be willing to follow orders, period."

Coyote looked around the room. Everyone but Freddy nodded slowly, the wheels in their heads turning at a tremendous pace.

. . .

Frankfort, Kentucky
2000 Hours EST

General Thompson was internally fuming as he walked away from the meeting with Kerry and his cronies. After a quick look around to ensure he was not being followed, he pulled out his phone and dialed a number.

"Yeah, David? I'm sorry to call so late, but it's important. Is the Governor in his residence? Yes, I know I'm scheduled to meet with him in the morning, but something else has come up. Think he could spare me a few minutes? Okay, I can be there in twenty. And a quiet entrance would be best. And I need a completely private conversation. Is that doable? Thanks."

After disconnecting the phone, the General quickly drove to his home where he dropped his official government vehicle and jumped into his old beater pickup truck. He drove to the Governor's mansion where he was checked in before being directed to the back door.

The Governor's state police security detail head met General Thompson at the door. "David, thanks for setting this up. If you would, please stay close while I'm meeting with him. He may want to bring you in on this." David remained attentive, but expressionless.

The Governor received the General in a special room just off of his mansion office. The room was cramped and had the feel of a closet interrogation room.

"General, I was looking forward to hearing about your Washington trip in the morning. Is this about something else?"

"Governor, I've been trying to figure out how to brief you efficiently. Unfortunately, this just may take a little while to be able to give you a full picture. If you'll bear with me, I think the urgency will be apparent when I get toward the end."

The General gave a description of the Fontaine administration plan for a declared State of Emergency. It was a testament to the Governor's personal control that he contained the obvious outrage he felt. Decades of emergency response plans were going to be thrown out the window. All National Guard troops were to be nationalized and given orders to fully support the Department of Homeland Security and federally appointed infrastructure. State rule would effectively be subordinated to Regional Governors, who would be appointed by the President to maintain order and see to the needs of the people.

"They plan to convert the National Guard into the goons for Homeland Security, ignoring state and local government officials except to use them to pacify the populous. The Bitch has gone off the deep end, and her so-called right-thinking people want the military to enforce their agenda." The General paused to catch his breath.

"General, where do you stand on all of this?"

"If I defy the President's order, they'll simply replace me. The press has been in her pocket from the beginning, and I presume she'll use the emergency powers to muzzle conservative outlets and even social media, you know, 'for the duration of the emergency.' I think stall tactics would be best here, but, what I really want to know is what you would want. Only you need to hear the rest of it."

After a short pause to think, the General said, "This evening my brother-in-law, John Chapman, made a big deal of inviting me to a liberal party gathering. That split off into a private meeting with a few men including Kerry DuBois and Coyote Collins. Coyote told me he looked forward to working with me because the Fontaine administration would be appointing him Rgional Governor over a three state region to include Kentucky. His Homeland Security contacts expected the State of Emergency to be declared sometime soon. The worst part is that none of this is legal or even constitutional. But, with the Supreme Court divided and Fontaine's party holding half of Congress, she seems to be willing to go ahead with it anyway. Hell, it's like there are no adults to tell these idiots that what they're doing is wrong."

"General, give me a minute to process all of this." The Governor bowed his head and began to pray. After a few minutes he looked at the General with a nod of his head as if he had just received divine inspiration.

"General, at 4:00 p.m. tomorrow afternoon, please gather all of your senior people that you believe you can absolutely trust in a secure location. Just let David know where, and he'll see that I and possibly two to three more people will meet you there."

"Yes, Sir." The General felt relieved to have shared the burden.

"And, Governor? I'll mention this to David, but please understand that with what seems to be coming, you might be viewed as a liability around here. Under a declared emergency, they could do anything from authorizing your arrest to making you disappear, should they think you threaten their power. Please take precautions."

The Governor gave the General a thoughtful nod as he left the room.

CHAPTER 16
THE NEW YEAR - PLUS SIX DAYS

Covert Motel Room
Washington, D.C.
2130 Hours EST

When Walter entered the hotel room his mind was not very focused. His lust for Su Ling, the strange look on John Levy's face after he had given the signal, and the crazy things going on in the White House all seemed to throw him off balance.

Su was standing at the mini bar pouring his favorite scotch into a tumbler with two small cubes of ice. When she turned, displaying a sexy smile and the contours of her body through the thin, silk robe, his tough resolve and hate for the Chinese people seemed to float away like smoke on an errant breeze.

"Oh, Walter," Su said with her cute China doll accent, "you walk in like you rushed. You not want my company?"

Whatever Walter was going to say changed in the moment. "My Dear, um."

With that he grabbed the drink and gulped it down before shoving it toward her for a refill. After drinking the second just as quickly as the first, Walter roughly grabbed her for a sloppy kiss and the usual fondling of her body. He also tried to grind himself into her without regard to there being clothing in the way.

Shaking his head as if to clear it, Walter said, "I want you to bring out your bag of tricks. I, uh, I mean, I've been a very bad boy." He let the phrase drift off as he looked down at the floor.

Su immediately recognized the need to go into her dominatrix persona and barked at him, "You very bad. On your knees, you bad boy, and drop your pants. Bare bottom when I return. DO IT!"

Su shouted the last two words, allowing a small shower of spittle to escape her lips. She walked to the bedroom of the suite and came back with a wooden paddle and a short, nine-tailed whip. She wore knee high black leather boots, a leather cap and her other "whips and chains" garb. Walter had only wanted the rough treatment once before, but she was ready just the same.

Mr. Sung had told her several times that if Walter wanted the rough stuff, she could dispense with the usual debriefing before sex was initiated. She presumed that such film would be more valuable as a bribery tool.

After only seventy-five minutes, Walter bowed his way out of the room while saying, "Thank you, Mistress. Yes, Mistress. Thank you, Mistress." Sweat was still pouring off his head, accompanied by fire coming off of his tortured bottom, back, and the backs of his legs.

Five minutes later, after Su had changed to street clothing and packed the last of her toys, Mr. Sung and two technical-type men entered the room without knocking. Mr. Sung walked directly to Su and smacked her across the face with his open palm.

Having seen the blow coming, Su had pulled away as it was falling and staggered backward. This left the appearance the blow had been more devastating than it was.

In rough Mandarin Chinese spoken in a conversational tone, Mr. Sung said, "You were supposed to milk him for information before you milked his dick, you whore."

Su knew better than to remind Mr. Sung of his previous instructions. She bowed her head and said, "So sorry. It will never happen again."

"If it does, you beautiful pig, I will take it upon myself to show you the true meaning of pain and being a whore." He glared at her to insure she was appropriately cowed.

"You two, search this room. Search it well. I will search this pig." Turning toward Su, he uttered only one word. "Strip."

Su walked away from the hotel feeling more violated than she had since her first week at Charm School. Mr. Sung had probed everywhere on her body that could conceivably hide a recorder, including the tiny micro-dot size that could be purchased at local electronics stores. Despite their search, they had not discovered the passive recorder given to her by Hugh. A special extension stick had been disguised as a toilet plunger that allowed the recorder to be hidden well up inside of the ventilation system. She could not retrieve it before she left, but did not think that would be a problem for Hugh.

Still shaken from Mr. Sung's rough treatment, she didn't even notice the white van double parked just outside of her apartment building. As she drew abreast, a familiar voice said, "You're not gonna believe what Dwight wrote on Facebook."

Turning to look, Su saw the sliding door on the van standing half way open and Lisa sitting in a lawn chair inside next to her dad. Hugh motioned to her and said only, "It's time."

Su could never recall how she traversed the ten feet to the van, whether it was on shaky legs, a confident stride, or an all-out sprint. She just found herself sitting on the carpeted floor crying like a baby with her head in Lisa's lap.

CHAPTER 17
THE NEW YEAR - PLUS SEVEN DAYS

The Peter Worthington Residence
Outside of Cronin, Kentucky
0950 Hours EST

Mike stood up from his chair in his family room while Peter Worthington, along with Sean and Fred Callahan and Linda Sharpe, came in to join him. Lauren sat just inside the kitchen, listening from across the counter.

"Thanks for setting this up on such short notice, Mike." Fred had emotion in his voice, which was highly unusual for the Police Chief. "After the call I got last night, I wanted to get your take on it."

Both Sean and Linda were as mystified as were Mike and Lauren. Sean said, "Dad, what's up?"

With a deep breath, Fred said, "Last night, after midnight, I got a call from the Army National Guard Commander for Kentucky, General Steven Thompson."

Looking at Sean and Linda, he continued, "No, not his aid or anyone else in his chain of command. He called me himself. He wouldn't say much, but did ask me to join a select group this afternoon at 4:00 p.m. to meet with the Governor and a few others. He only said it was about emergency preparedness."

Saying the last two words, Fred managed to make them sound extremely ominous. Everyone sat quietly contemplating what it might mean for a few moments.

"Dad?" Sean asked in a soft but commanding voice, "the General just got back from Washington, didn't he?"

"Yes, son, I think he did."

Sean continued, "Now I'm just speculating here." Sean told the lie that everyone present recognized as such. "Has anyone heard about the Bitch declaring martial law? Anything?"

Surprising everyone, Peter spoke up. "I've got some pretty good sources in Washington, and all of them seem to say she will be declaring a State of Emergency any time now."

After a pause, he continued, "Friends in the EPA[7] and Bureau of Surface Mining all tell me that's the case. Scott Shelby even got a heads up from his money friends, who just happen to be major contributors to the Fontaine Foundation, that it was coming, and probably soon. Hell, they're all hopeful that the Queen's edicts will make sure the greenies are well protected. The Department of Agriculture has even been assuring farmers the government will be buying up most of their wheat, corn, and bean crops for next season. The inference is that it will go to supply soup kitchens likely to be opening throughout the country."

Peter seemed to have run out of revelations. Mike said, "Fred, I'm going to presume that whatever you hear at this meeting later, you'll be sworn to secrecy. How about if we plan on meeting back here later this evening and you can tell us whatever you think you can?"

Fred nodded with a guarded smile. "If I can't trust my Army hero son, my soon to be daughter-in-law, and my two best friends, we might as well give up anyway."

. . .

The White House
1030 Hours EST

Marc Baxter tried to keep a calm, interested look on his face as he listened to Don Stetson in the small conference room. "How are we going to ensure all this goes through, Marc?"

Marc said, "Don, I'm not sure the time is quite right to push for this gun registration law. Congress simply won't go for it, especially with all the acts of anarchy breaking out in the urban centers on both coasts and places like Chicago

---

[7] Environmental Protection Agency

and Detroit. Murder rates have gone through the roof! Although with the Supreme Court now evenly divided it might be just the time to try."

Don was convinced that with the two school shootings that had occurred the previous day, now was the time. In California, a fifteen year old boy had executed three boys at his school after they had accidentally shot his sister during a botched gang initiation rape. Both the shooter and the gang-member victims were wards of the state after their parents lost jobs and could not take care of them.

It was a mystery where the boy obtained the 9 millimeter pistol used in the killings. The second shooting involved a mentally disturbed fourteen year old girl in Raleigh, North Carolina. She heard voices in her head telling her to take her older brother's hunting rifle and shoot at the school windows. Fortunately, only three students suffered minor injuries from broken glass.

Don didn't care about the details. He, like Katherine, only wanted all guns removed from private hands. "Marc, we need to identify which Senators need their arms twisted by the President. You know, the ones who won't vote for the bill but are up for re-election and are vulnerable."

"I can only think of one off hand, Don. It's that junior Senator from Virginia. But even if we were to get him, it wouldn't be nearly enough."

"Marc, am I missing something here, or is your heart just not in this? Don't you agree that all guns should be taken off the streets?" Don began to focus closely on Marc.

Just before Marc blurted out his true feelings on the matter, he recalled that Don might just need someone else to throw under the bus should Katherine appear to view Don as expendable.

"Oh, hell, Don. Of course I'm looking to stop the killing. You haven't seen it, but between attending every staff meeting, doing this plus two other projects for the President and doing more than half of Towanda's job, I'm just totally fried."

Marc looked down at the table with what he hoped would appear to be placating submission. "I just hate to complain since almost everyone else is running just as ragged as I am. I'm sorry, man. Guess I've been letting you down."

Don immediately reacted as Marc had hoped. "Hey, kid, I'm not trying to bust your chops. It's kinda' easy for me to forget you've got more than just this one project to do. I'm just no good at crunching the computer shit, ya know? All the data on everyone in government is now only accessible on a friggin' computer. My thumbs get lost while my fingers try to find the right keys."

With a resolute voice, Don said, "What the hell, Marc, none of this will matter if she declares an emergency anyway, you know? At least that's what I'm hearing."

For a long two count, Marc didn't trust himself to look up. Then he asked, 'What do you think, Don? Is that a good thing if she does declare the emergency?"

"Sure!" Don said this with even more enthusiasm than Marc expected. "Then the shackles will come off, and we can just go out and take the guns. And people will have to give them up with the military backing up those dudes in Homeland Security. Finally, we can actually get something done! Best of all, we're on the winning team." Don's big smile was genuine.

Just then, Chief of Staff Burt Combs poked his head into the conference room door. "How are my two gun confiscation experts doing today?"

"Well, Burt. You're beating this poor boy to death here lately, but would you mind stepping in here for a minute?"

Burt was intrigued by Don's conspiratorial tone, so he stepped in and closed the conference room door. "Okay, Don. What's up?"

"We've gotten at least the mainstream media on our side on this one, pushing the idea that the Second Amendment is old and out of date with the times, but we still haven't been able to get enough Senators to roll over and play ball. Can the President do some serious arm twisting, or are my sources right and none of this will matter soon?"

Burt kept his cool, but as Don had pointed out to Marc in the past, Burt tended to stop talking and would look up, as if for heavenly inspiration, when he was about to lie. In this case, Burt looked up to the heavens and said, "Boys, let's get as much press as possible talking about how guns are what's making things so much worse. Okay? Just focus on that for a while. Let the President handle the Senate. Can you do that?"

Both Marc and Don nodded, keeping their faces serious but non-committal. After

After Burt left the conference room, all Don would say was, "See? Told you."

• • •

Outside of Shanghai, China
Noon Local Time

General Hu Sengai of the Special Weapons branch of the PLA had steered General Lao Tung, toward a table in the lunchroom. Lao unexpectedly arrived at Hu's offices outside of the highly restricted "medical research building" fifteen minutes earlier. Hu had ordered his personal orderly to find tea and sweets for Lao. Another assistant had cleared the lunchroom of staff, ensuring privacy for their meeting.

"Hu," Lao said calmly, "might it be possible to see the manufacturing facility where the flu vaccine is being made?"

Hu covered his shock quickly before using a wall phone to call for his driver. Thirty minutes later, they entered a non-descript manufacturing building which lost much of its anonymity by the two electrified fences and multiple guards with dogs patrolling the perimeter. The ride over in the back seat of an older model American Lincoln Town Car had been made with minimal conversation.

Entering the working part of the facility, the noise of whirring centrifuges and other equipment was quite loud. Lao pulled Hu aside and, while pointing at a random piece of equipment, leaned near Hu's ear and asked, "Tell me the status of the virus."

Hu responded, "Testing on the virus is complete and has a mortality rate of over eighty percent."

Lao pulled away and shouted, "How effective?"

Hu held up eight fingers and then a closed fist before mouthing "percent," followed by a smile.

Moving to Lao's ear again, he said, "The vaccine has also been thoroughly tested and is over ninety percent effective. Vaccine doses continue to be made and distributed. All desirables will be vaccinated by the end of the month."

Lao asked Hu, "What are your projections for the population of China?"

"Two thirds, made up of mostly undesirables, will die. Not all from the virus, but also from mass starvation that will result from the temporary crumbling of the infrastructure servicing those affected. Those that remain will be all that is necessary to rebuild China into the most powerful country in the world. There may, however, be the need for significant reeducation like Chairman Mao did previously."

The look on Hu's face was excited, but calculating. Hu referred to the Cultural Revolution in the 1950's and 1960's when Communist Party Chairman Mao Tse-tung sent millions of Chinese people needing "reeducation" to the collective farms in the countryside.

"Is your tactical team ready to travel for the operation?" Lao watched Hu's eyes carefully, assessing his truthfulness. Even though Hu had been threatened before to ensure only accurate estimates, Lao was not one to take anyone's word on faith.

Hu said, "All equipment and vials of serum-agent are ready. The medical team is now training with their Special Forces escorts to be able to pass through Customs wherever they need to go. They will travel under the auspices of the World Health Organization. It should take no more than a week before they can effectively travel."

Hu's pride at this accomplishment was clearly written on his face. Despite being a General in the PLA, he remained a scientist at heart. The world devastation that would be released did not impact Hu in the slightest. For him, the people affected were all merely laboratory animals.

"Good," Lao said with a nod. After a short pause, Lao continued, "Hu, after we complete our business here, you will be accompanied by my assistant, who is waiting outside of this complex, to get a vial of the vaccine and three syringes to administer it. My assistant is a medical doctor. You will accompany him in his waiting vehicle to a location where you will personally administer a single dose of the vaccine. Is there any reason why you cannot do as I instruct?"

Hu's eyes became larger than normal before he drew a deep breath and shrugged. "I will instruct that your man be brought in immediately. Presumably you will remain until he arrives?" Hu was not surprised to see Lao nod and smile. Both men knew what was happening.

After returning from Beijing Hu experienced an unusual feeling of satisfaction. He usually didn't feel anything when going about his business. He had given the vaccine from the same bottle to General Secretary Song, Lao and himself. He, of course had already been vaccinated, but did not believe a second vaccination would be harmful. It might even be beneficial.

CHAPTER 18
THE NEW YEAR - PLUS EIGHT DAYS

Mountains of Southeast Afghanistan
1015 Hours Local Time

Ahmed was both annoyed and worried. Despite his earlier premonition that the operation would soon be underway, he had not heard from Cho.

"Hadi," Ahmed said as his lieutenant walked past. "Have you heard anything from the Chinese Infidel?"

"I have not," Hadi said with reluctance. "My usual contacts told me he is not in Kabul. He is believed to have flown away to the East over a week ago. Shall I ask around again?"

"No. Just let me know if you hear anything."

Ahmed walked back into the cave where Jasmine and his first wife were preparing his meal. He said to his first wife, "Go outside and collect wood and dung for the fire." She nodded while staring her frustration into the ground at being tasked with duties typically handled by children or slaves. She wisely did not voice any of these frustrations as she walked out of the cave.

Jasmine observed this exchange and prepared herself mentally for whatever her husband would demand of her.

"The aid girl," Ahmed said with less demand in his voice and more curiosity. "Is she still of value?"

Ahmed understood that some women functioned better than others after being assaulted as the aid girl had been.

"My husband," Jasmine said carefully. "She was almost useless for the first two days after your fighters succumbed to her subtle enticements. I don't understand how she could hold them responsible when she looked directly into their eyes and let them see too much of her shape through her robe, while teaching them. I finally explained to her that if she wanted to live, she should strive to become a Muslim woman, and she should be glad that there are no family members that would stone her for having brought out the beast in your fighters. I think now she is being useful again."

Jasmine was quiet for a few moments before saying, "But, her usefulness will be done when your fighters are sent to kill the Infidels."

Ahmed looked sharply at her, only to find that she had dropped her eyes and bowed her head. He was aware that now Jasmine felt the aid girl might even tempt him, and before that should happen, Jasmine hoped the girl would be used as a slave by many men before being killed. It pleased him to see some jealousy in his favorite wife.

• • •

A classified facility outside of Lexington, Kentucky
1630 Hours EST

The Governor of Kentucky entered the room with the head of his security detail, the Lieutenant Governor, and the state Senate majority leader. "Please accept my apologies, gentlemen. We were unavoidably delayed."

He could see General Thompson, six of his officers, and two civilians.

The Commanding General introduced his officers first, followed by the Commissioner of the Kentucky State Police, who the Governor already knew, and Fred Callahan. The Governor nodded with understanding during the initial introductions until the General came to Fred, which caused him to glance at the General with one eyebrow raised.

"Governor, Fred, here, is the Chief of Police in Cronin. He's also the father of Sean Callahan, one of our most recent war heroes. He's been assisting with the emergency preparedness folks for several years now and may have contributions to make to our meeting."

Listening, the Governor saw the General give him a slight nod of his head, indicating that Fred was completely trustworthy.

"Thank you, Fred," the Governor said warmly. "Glad to have you with us. And you, too, Commissioner. General, is there any problem with classification level? I know this facility can handle almost anything, but do the Commissioner and Chief Callahan have clearances?"

"That shouldn't be a problem, Sir. Both the Chief and Commissioner have SECRET clearances, and I'll make sure to avoid any information with a higher classification."

The General referred to the common practice of removing items from highly classified information, such as sources and methods that would drive its sensitivity above the SECRET level.

The Governor continued, "Thanks, General. Ladies and gentlemen, let's take just a moment before we get started and pray for our Commonwealth, our nation, and even our world."

What followed for another few minutes was a prayer worthy of being given in one of the world's great cathedrals. It was heartfelt, articulate, and yet another example of why this Governor had been elected. Everyone in the room would later recollect the feeling that God was, in fact, watching over them during the meeting.

"General, would you please fill everyone in on what we discussed last evening?" The Governor wanted to hear what everyone else had to say before coming out with his own ideas.

The General gave a summary of both the probability of the President soon declaring a State of Emergency and what he had learned from Coyote Collins.

"The bottom line appears to be the President will soon declare what amounts to Martial Law in the United States, but without the restrictions of being required to follow the Uniform Code of Military Justice.[8] She will also ignore most of the previously planned emergency operations procedures to establish her own appointed governing system. Must have been her friends at UC Berkley who came up with that one. I suspect the various National Guard units may be less than fully supportive of these regional Governors and the Homeland Security group that will be organizing and ordering people around."

The questions came fast and furiously from the General's officers and even the Commissioner. Both the Governor and Fred merely observed with keen interest. More often than not, the General's answer to a question was, "I don't know."

---

[8] When Martial Law is declared, the Uniform Code of Military Justice (UCMJ) typically becomes the law in the affected area.

When asked if the President could actually do these things, the General said, "The State of Emergency and existing Presidential Executive Orders do have the force of law. With the Supreme Court evenly divided and the recent death of the conservative Justice, it's likely any legal challenges would be quickly swept away."

The air in the room hung heavy with the weight of what was to come. After the fifth consecutive, "I don't know" uttered by the General, everyone turned to look to the Governor for his comments. Instead of sharing those thoughts, the Governor looked at Fred.

"Mr. Callahan," the Governor asked softly. "Would you care to share your thoughts on this situation?"

"Governor, I appreciate the level of trust you have shown by having me here. In the spirit of that trust, I'm going to share a few things that I'd appreciate not leave this room. Please refrain from sharing it even with those with higher security clearances and the apparent need to know. Can each of you do that for me?"

Fred had the focused and somewhat surprised attention of everyone in the room as each man voiced their agreement. "You may or may not know that my son Sean is with the Army Special Forces and had his leg blown off during a covert operation in Afghanistan. It's not known to many, including a lot of Special Ops folks that he's here at home recuperating from his wounds. He has also been tagged to do some super-secret stuff inside the borders of the United States and has a small staff at my home answering to him. I don't know exactly what they are doing, but let me just say that everything you have mentioned here today seems to be confirmed."

Fred paused before saying, "That's all I will say on that subject. On the subject of what we in Kentucky should do about it, I'll just make a few observations that did not originate with my son. It seems to me that the President is preparing to seize control of this country and will immediately institute all of the policies that she hasn't been able to get through Congress. One of the more frightening things I think she'll do is to void the Second Amendment and start to seize guns from citizens, like what was done to a limited extent in New Orleans during hurricane Katrina. Once the guns have been seized, or the process to do so has been started, she will send out her Homeland Security Department people to collect resources such as fuel and food to gain control over the American people. Face it, folks, if you control the food and other resources, those of her mindset think they can control the people. It didn't work out very well with Venezuela or dozens of other socialist countries in recent years, but I don't think she either knows or cares much about history."

Each person in the room contemplated the enormity of it all. Fred said, "We can also figure that she will try to use the military to enforce her will. Her Martial Law or Emergency Declaration will temporarily put even the Posse Comitatus[9] Act on hold. You probably know that's the law that makes it illegal to use the military to enforce civil law on the American people."

"My question for you, General, and you, Governor, is what will you do when Coyote Collins comes to you and demands you provide soldiers and resources to begin seizing guns and other necessities smart people have stored away for emergencies?"

All eyes fell on the Governor. "Fred, thank you for that information and I ask everyone here to think about what Fred has been able to share, but then forget that he was even here. In addition, no covert military people are in Kentucky outside of Ft. Knox and Ft. Campbell. Understood?" Everyone nodded agreement.

"Good. I think Fred has accurately summed up what we're facing. Here's what comes to my mind. General, no matter what the Homeland Security people or even the duly appointed regional Governor has to say, you are in command of the Kentucky National Guard. I suggest you make sure your commanders become quietly aware that you and I and the people of this Commonwealth don't think their services should be used for other than their intended purpose. General, how can you do that without being summarily replaced by the Pentagon?"

The General looked to his Adjutant, who he knew was an extremely bright and competent attorney well versed in the law.

The Adjutant said, "General, what I would recommend is that you have very private 'off the record' meetings with individual Guard Commanders. You can explain the situation, including your thoughts that the Constitution is not suspended even under a State of Emergency or Martial Law. Also, reasonable men can interpret orders within that framework. If any Commander has doubts about an ordered action, he is required by the Constitution and the Uniform Code of Military Justice to delay action until he has checked with higher

---

9 ¹18 U.S.C. § 1385, original at 20 Stat. 152) signed on June 18, 1878 by President Rutherford B. Hayes.

authority. You might even suggest, Sir, that they should contact me for legal advice. Should I be unavailable for, say, a day or two or longer, then they can reasonably inform whoever gave them the inappropriate order that they are waiting for confirmation by higher headquarters. As you can see, Sir, this can effectively delay any demand for action for at least several days and potentially indefinitely. Sir, I agree with most everyone in this room that the National Guard should not be placed in the position of becoming thugs for this or any administration."

A fast look around the table confirmed universal agreement.

The Governor looked at Fred before asking, "Chief, would your son be amenable to a very quiet and unofficial visit from me? If it puts you in a position of betraying a confidence, it doesn't need to happen."

"Chief Callahan," the General said quickly, "so that you know, I had heard from a member of my staff that your son was recuperating at home with you and your wife. I think word leaked out from someone in your neighborhood. Regardless, we were in the process of working on some way to honor him as a Kentucky war hero just last week. That will, of course, be postponed indefinitely."

After a moment's thought, Fred said, "Governor, I'll ask him, but I think it can be arranged. It would probably be better if you met him someplace secure. I know of an abandoned farm outside of Cronin that's up a hollow and protected by a locked gate. He's starting to move around pretty well on his new store-bought leg, so if you don't mind meeting in a vehicle, that would be pretty secure."

"Sounds good to me," said the Governor. "David, would you work with the Chief and set it up? The sooner the better, if you please. "

The Governor's security chief responded with, "Yes, Sir."

"Chief Callahan" the Governor said, "You have my authority to brief your son on anything we have discussed here today."

"Oh, and General?" The Governor asked as an afterthought, "All the food and medical supplies we have been stockpiling for emergencies are those subject to seizure by Homeland Security or by Coyote?"

The General glanced at his Adjutant, who sadly nodded in the affirmative.

The Governor slammed his open palm down on the table in frustration and said, "That simply won't do. Won't do at all." All present nodded agreement.

CHAPTER 19
THE NEW YEAR - PLUS EIGHT DAYS

The Broehm Residence
Outside of Cronin, Kentucky
2100 Hours EST

Mike Broehm had to dry the tears from his eyes. While they waited for the arrival of Fred Callahan, Peter Worthington had given a rendition of Kerry DuBois' wife henpecking him for not doing his chores. In a different time or setting it might not have been nearly as funny. Now, however, everyone was on edge and needed the comic relief.

Sean Callahan was seated comfortably next to Linda Sharpe on the couch with his artificial leg propped up on a padded chair. All had gathered at Mike's place after Mike had received the call from Fred Callahan that he was on his way. Sean's mom, Penny Callahan, had come over with Sean and Linda. When Mike heard the driveway alarm sound, he poured a generous helping of fine Kentucky bourbon in a glass with one large ice cube and handed it to Fred as he walked in the door.

"Thanks, Mike. Just what the doctor ordered," Fred said, as he walked over to the chair by the fireplace, drink in hand. He didn't sit down, but instead took a long pull on his drink before jumping right into his briefing.

"Normally, I would want to start off with small talk and even a funny story or two. But how about I just jump right into what I can tell you?"

All nodded at Fred without comment. "I received the okay from the Governor to brief you, Sean, so I'm going to figure that's enough authority for me to brief everyone here."

"First, Sean, the Commanding General of the Army National Guard, Steven Thompson, was aware you were convalescing at my house and had planned to arrange for a presentation in the near future. Yes, I know, that wouldn't have happened anyway. You'll understand better in a few minutes. Also, the Governor has requested that you meet with him confidentially in the very near future. I'll let you think about your answer to that request as I explain what I learned."

Fred described the bazar meeting with the Governor and National Guardsmen. "Official word has been received that the President will be declaring a State of Emergency very soon. When she does, Coyote Collins will be appointed Regional Governor for a three state region including Kentucky. General Thompson was introduced to Coyote at a fundraiser, along with, of all people, our very own Kerry DuBois."

Looking at Sean and Linda, Fred said, "Coyote is our State Democratic Party Chairman and political hack. He's also a man without any honor or scruples. Kerry is one of our neighbors who believes himself to be a political mover and shaker. A real slimy weasel, that one. It is anticipated that the National Guard will be ordered to support the Department of Homeland Security goons in whatever socialistic actions they deem desirable."

Sean interrupted his father, "Dad? Will the National Guard follow those orders?"

"That's the thing, son," Fred said. "The National Guard will drag their feet and make excuses to the point where the DHS people will have to do whatever they have in mind themselves. In fact, I can imagine there's going to be a whole lot of very frustrated DHS managers running around Kentucky. When they can't get the Guard to do their dirty work, they'll hire thugs and send them out. Unfortunately, the Governor's not going to be able to do much to stop them."

Sean interrupted again to say, "Dad, does the Governor know that he'll be a target for them?"

"Yes, he does. In fact, at my recommendation, his State Police security detail is being tripled and a detachment of National Guard MPs are going to be assigned to support them."

A smile appeared on Fred's face. "I saw a slide show highlighting the capabilities of Combat Military Police units. The MP's will consist of one of those units who just returned from Afghanistan. Those guys have some very serious hardware!"

Mike interjected a question for the first time. "Fred, what about our county and even our neighborhood? Do you foresee trouble coming our way?"

"Yes, Mike, I do, especially when Kerry thinks he has acquired some power." Fred looked troubled as he added, "And despite my new relationship with the Governor and General Thompson, I don't think they'll be able to do anything about it should a band of DHS goons decide to come pillaging our way."

After a moment for this to sink in, Fred looked to Sean and asked, "Son, I suspect you've got a lot more experience at this sort of thing than I do. What do you suggest?"

It took only a second for Sean to think about the question before he said, "Dad, technically I could even be part of the problem. That being said, and I cannot explain further, here's what we're going to need to do."

Sean continued for the next forty-five minutes detailing preparations, actions, and training the neighborhood and its inhabitants needed to begin immediately.

"Fortunately," said Sean, "many of the items on the list were already in progress, thanks to Mike's gentle prodding."

A chuckle was heard around the room because everyone recalled Mike's prodding wasn't particularly gentle, but was very effective. Considering the group with whom he was working, it was somewhat amazing how well everyone worked together and especially how they seemed to accept his leadership.

Linda had thanked Lauren for the notepad and pen she had provided earlier and took professional notes that laid out the plan. Sean also mentioned he would ask some of the guys he had working with him if they would like to volunteer to help with training, on their own time, of course.

At the end of Sean's suggestions, Mike said, "Well, the county Judge Executive[10] has invited me to speak at the next Fiscal Court[16] meeting tomorrow evening. Apparently, they're expecting quite a crowd of county voters to attend. I won't go into any of these specifics, but at least I can nudge them toward beginning preparations themselves. Oh, and let's get the word out an important neighborhood meeting will be held in three days. I want to start putting Sean's ideas into motion. Before that happens, even after further discussion, I want us to be able to sleep on this. Can we plan on meeting around 7:00 p.m. day after

---

[10] The chief administrative officer in a county and the county's equivalent to a city's Mayor. [16] Governing body of a Kentucky county, headed by the Judge Executive.

tomorrow to lay out our plan for refinements? Also, Fred would you invite Matt Gibson to attend that meeting at 7:00 p.m.? His trucking company hauls most of the propane, fuel oil and even some gasoline for customers in the county. I think he's a good man to get involved."

Rather than break up, the group began to discuss a lot of different considerations this new reality had forced upon them. It was after midnight before all decided they had nearly reached data overload and needed sleep.

CHAPTER 20
THE NEW YEAR - PLUS NINE DAYS

Singapore Changi Airport
1230 Hours Local Time

Eli Fredericks walked down the ramp to his private jet parked at the last public terminal gate. He had been escorted by a Singapore police Colonel to the gate, where gate personnel seemed to have paused their usually busy day. Private aircraft always suffered long delays and difficult parking arrangements at this busy, international airport. However, since his arrival, everything had worked smoothly, almost too smoothly. Chen's power base here was broad and obviously very strong.

Entering the plane, Eli allowed himself to shiver and draw a deep breath in a combination of terror and exhilaration. His meeting with Chen had gone well but was haunting nonetheless. Chen chose to use a beautiful Chinese girl in her mid-twenties as his interpreter. He had explained that the interpreter spoke ten languages and was completely trustworthy. Although he did speak English, he said, "I would not wish there to be any misunderstanding due to some misinterpretation of my inexact choice of words."

The meeting had lasted over three hours. Through Chen's skillful direction, the men had come to an agreement on what was essentially a splitting of the world into spheres of influence. All of the Pacific Rim was to be under Chen's control, as well as Africa and most of Asia, to include the Middle East. If Australia, New Zealand, The Philippines, or any other parts of Asia or the former

British Empire didn't want to kowtow[11] to China, they would be brought into line harshly.

When Eli commented that Chen didn't appear to need his help, Chen stared at him for five full seconds before saying, "Both your President and my Premier are wild cards in this very dangerous game. I believe I can control Premier Song and the most powerful members of the Politburo. I cannot control your President. That is your job." Chen thought to himself about whispered reports that Song did have some type influence over the American President.

Chen said, "What Song did by discontinuing oil purchases was not in my original plans and could have been considered an act of war. I see that you have arranged for your President to react, ahhh, shall we say, cautiously? We should each be sure to continue building control and pressure points over key parts of our governments. Do you agree?"

Eli nodded his agreement. After all, Eli was to control all of North and South America and to have substantial mineral rights in Africa. This would include all of South Africa and its unmined diamond reserves.

"And the North Koreans and Russians," Eli asked quietly, "who will control them?"

Chen responded with a cold, emotionless smile at the question. "The fool in North Korea has nearly fulfilled his usefulness. I anticipate a military coup may occur in the very near future, before anything stupid can be done with their nuclear weapons." Chen didn't even notice that he had stopped using his interpreter, instead using correct English with a slight British accent. "As to Russia, negotiations are underway to deal with the decadent Europeans. Russia may have, shall we say, significant sway over the European Union governments. With all of their Muslim refugee problems, Europe may welcome the Russians with open arms if only they can stop the rioting and prevent institution of Sharia law. The Russians have had some success using their brutal methods in the past. We will see."

"Great Britain, on the other hand," Chen continued, "could present a problem. That is where your influence may be needed to prevent any attempt to aid the countries they abandoned under Brexit. You can do this?" Chen asked the question casually, however, Eli was aware it was another critical item in both of their calculations.

---

[11] Kowtow is to show deep respect by kneeling so low as to touch one's head to the ground.

"That should not be a problem," Eli said softly. "The Brits have been less than supportive of the President, and she was strongly against Brexit anyway."

"You can do this?" Chen asked the question again, while looking into Eli's eyes carefully. Eli had to remind himself that he was every bit as ruthless as Chen and that he had people in a position to kill Chen if he did not leave the meeting alive.

Returning Chen's stare and with a return to his black radical college roots, he said, "Yeah, muthafucka, I can."

A short pause later Chen looked away and nodded his head. "Good. We are concluded here?"

"Yeah, sure. We be done here." Eli didn't even try to hide his annoyance at the implied threat by Chen. Chen understood this and accepted it.

"One more thing," Chen said in conclusion. "Song is obsessed with retaking the renegade province of Formosa that you in the West call Taiwan. He may decide to take the losses an invasion would involve within the next few weeks. It will be better for us both if the American Navy is not in the vicinity when this happens. He plans to deal with them if they try to come to the aid of Formosan forces. You understand?"

Eli looked probingly at Chen for a moment before saying, "Yes, I can see that. I think protecting the United States from a major war may become the most important priority for the President."

With one more nod and without a handshake or other acknowledgement, Chen turned and walked from the room.

On the way to his plane, Eli picked up his secure satellite phone and immediately called to order several dramatic shifts in his investments.

CHAPTER 21
THE NEW YEAR - PLUS NINE DAYS

Cronin, Kentucky
1800 Hours EST

Mike tried to calm the butterflies floating around in his stomach. For several minutes, he had felt nearly paralyzed with stage fright, even in light of recent events. Not even the two shots of vodka he drank a short while ago seemed to help. Though he wasn't in charge of those present, his fears involving leadership created nearly overwhelming anxiety. Deep breaths seemed to diminish his trembling slightly as he looked out over the audience at the county Fiscal Court meeting. He saw only friendly and concerned people.

When the Judge Executive called Mike to invite him to speak at the meeting, he had first declined before calling him back and agreeing to come. It occurred to him that if he didn't start speaking out, at least a little, then the only thing people would hear was the kind of socialist drivel being spouted by the administration and mainstream media. It was still an effort to keep his voice from cracking.

"Hi, folks. And thanks for that grand introduction, Judge." Mike nodded to the Judge Executive as he said this, drawing a smile in return. "I guess what I'm doing up here this evening is sharing a little of what we've been doing in my neighborhood to help each other, and, really, reminding everyone what it means to be an American."

Mike's words were humbly delivered without great polish, but they connected with almost everyone present.

"First off, let me say the state has really done a good job listing all the things folks should be doing, if they can, to prepare for emergencies. Gathering together as a neighborhood and talking about the 'what ifs' of an emergency is a really good start. To me, being an American doesn't mean I'll sit back and wait for the government to help me and everyone else out. Shoot, we've all seen what the government has done with health care, and I defy anyone to tell me anything the government does efficiently. The military is an exception, of course. Rather than wait for the government to do it for you, I suggest you begin today to do it for yourself and your loved ones."

"Isn't that why we pay taxes, for the government to give us a safety net?" The question came from a man in the second row. He was one of the few unhappy with what Mike was saying.

"Yes, and through FEMA and both state and local emergency managers there is somewhat of a safety net. We've all appreciated the shelters being set up for the homeless and some of the other things available for folks in need. But let me ask you, is the government feeding more people or are church volunteers? Judge, what do you think?"

The Judge Executive was caught off guard, but stepped up and said, "You're right, Mike. Most of the hungry and out of work folks are being fed by donations and volunteers."

Mike nodded and said, "That goes right to my point, Judge. The more anyone looks to the government for help, the less help there will be. We can take care of our own, if we only decide to do it.

"Sure, that's what all you rich people say," said the man in the second row. "Maybe if you paid your fair share there'd be enough to go around."

"At least I pay my taxes," Mike fired back with rising anger. "Seems to me those that whine the most don't even pay taxes. How about you? How much did you pay in taxes last year?"

The man was startled and sheepish as he sat without answering. The audience was somewhat taken aback by Mike's temper. It was only with great effort that Mike took a deep breath, shook his head, and thought about what he had been saying.

"Folks, I'm not elected, and I'm just here to say what I think. Politically correct and other bull talk is, in my opinion, one of the reasons we're in this fix. The first question I have for anyone that whines about others not doing enough is to ask what they have done themselves. Were they one of the rioters in masks protesting and busting up things for fun? Are they someone that always asks for help but never even tries to help someone else? Is that the kind of people you want leading you? Leading you to what?" Again, Mike had to stop himself as he saw the small smile forming on the face of the man in the second row.

Mike said, "Let me get a show of hands. How many of you here think there's been too much political correctness and slamming of what should be plain ol' American values?" Almost every hand in the room rose while people glared at the man in the second row. His smile had been erased. With apprehension clearly showing on his face, the man settled in his chair and didn't say another word.

In his mind, Mike chided himself for letting the asshole get his goat. It was, however, a good lesson for him. The stress kept building over the past several weeks so he found it more difficult to control the rising frustration, especially when he watched the way the news twisted things and apportioned blame to the people working the hardest for themselves and their families.

"Ahem, where was I? Oh, yes, talking about what everyone can do to help. How many farmers in this community need help getting their fields ready for spring and don't have the money to hire help? Cash money is becoming hard to come by. Maybe some of those out of work could help out those farmers for a meal and a small share of the coming crop? Maybe many of the things we think of as necessities are only in the 'nice to have' category. I know I cut my cell phone bill in half by getting rid of the features I don't absolutely need."

After another deep, calming breath Mike continued, "Now I can only speak for myself, but I've had a cut in pay at the college and expect many of you folks have, too. Last fall, I decided to turn most of my yard into a garden, which will be planted with the kind of food and herbs that can get my family through next winter, if need be. Quite frankly, I used to buy an awful lot of things I figured out simply weren't needed."

Mike continued with several other suggestions of what he and his neighbors were doing to become more self-sufficient.

"On another topic, Judge, it looks to me like this economic situation is going to get a whole lot worse before it gets better. But let me say we can and will get through it if we all stick together and watch out for each other. I suggest the county start using any available money to start buying up some food and medicines. Especially focus on those things that are critical and won't be available in an emergency."

Mikes words seemed to have much more sway than could be attributed to the content. He was beginning to demonstrate that intangible known in some circles as 'presence.'

Mike concluded his talk with, "I probably don't even need to mention this here in Central Kentucky, but I also think it's a good idea for each family to have the means to protect itself and what you've worked for and saved. Most of us have the firearms and ammo to do just that, but if you're behind the eight ball, you may very soon be out of time to get what you need."

Mike looked directly at the man in the second row. "And should any of you think you'll just take what others have if you need it; remember they probably have the means to protect it."

After Mike's talk, the Fiscal Court voted to place all available money and half of the county's reserve funds into the hands of the well-respected county director of emergency preparedness. Mike made a mental note to himself to tell the Judge those supplies should be stored in a secret location to avoid being seized by the soon-to-be-appointed regional Governor.

The Judge shook Mike's hand afterward and said, "Thanks, Mike. I've been trying to tell the Court and anyone else that would listen what we needed to do, but I was just ignored."

On his way home, Mike detoured to the big sporting goods store and bought all of the .300 Winchester Magnum ammunition they had in the store. Expensive, but he had put off the purchase far too long. It was for his semi-automatic heavy caliber hunting rifle that, in a pinch, would serve as a sniper rifle.

It didn't surprise Mike to see the gist of what he had said in the meeting was published in the local newspaper the next day. The article included a recommendation for folks to acquire six months of everything they might need should an emergency or natural disaster cut off supplies.

CHAPTER 22
THE NEW YEAR - PLUS TEN DAYS

Beijing, China
0900 Hours Local Time

Lao met General Secretary Song along the walkway between Song's office and a nearby garden. The walkway was lined with latticework that was thickly covered by vines, leafless this time of year, but still effectively screening the area from view. Both men's security teams kept the area cleared of all foot traffic.

After Lao's initial bow and the bare-minimum formal pleasantries, Lao gave Song the information he had just obtained from General Hu. Like Lao, Song was pleasantly surprised to learn of the high effectiveness of the virus despite having been told early on of the initial ninety percent effectiveness.

Song said, "Lao, how secure is the Black Orchid operation?"

"General Secretary, it is as secure as I can make it. My top agent has been sent on a solitary vacation with instructions to see no one until contacted by my deputy. He can be recalled with a twelve-hour notice. Hu's team of medical people is equipped and will be ready to travel to anywhere, with their special forces escorts, by the end of this week. My best "wet group"[12] is being kept available to remove the handful of personnel that are aware of this operation, including the team dispensing the virus. Hu and his people will be effectively quarantined for the next year with a guard force to insure their privacy. None of the guard force is aware of who or what they are guarding, only that their testicles and families will be removed should they fail in their protective mission. Hu's

---

[12] Group of spies specializing in covert killing.

scientists will remain alive in case their services are needed for something unforeseen."

Song listened quietly to Lao before asking, "Anything else I should know?"

Lao replied, "No, General Secretary."

"Good. Lao…"

Suddenly a series of gunshots rang out with Song's shirt collar rapidly becoming bloody from the bullet that had just gone through it, nicking his neck as it passed. Lao reacted immediately by jumping on Song, bringing him to the ground to shield his body. Another bullet sprayed chips of concrete from the pathway into Lao's leg. Shouts rang out from both the General Secretary's protection detail and Lao's. Suddenly a deafening round of gunshots was heard as one of Song's bodyguards was cut down by a combination of Lao's and Song's security details. He had been standing about twenty meters away to shoot at Song with no intention of trying to escape.

Lao shouted, "No, no, don't kill him," several times, however, the assassin was riddled with bullets before anyone heard him. Lao was unable to rush to the assassin's body because he was pressing a cloth to Song's neck to stem the flow of blood. Within seconds, Song's medically trained technician on his detail took over to immediately apply a blood clotting agent and then a cloth bandage. He glanced quickly at Lao and said simply, "Not serious." Lao nodded before limping over to the bloody carcass of the assassin.

CHAPTER 23
THE NEW YEAR - PLUS TEN DAYS

A Deserted Farm Outside of Cronin, Kentucky
1520 Hours EST

Fred and Sean Callahan rolled through the gate toward the old, run-down farm house along two strips of gravel with brown grass sticking up between them. The grass had been bush-hogged at the end of the season by a tractor and mower but it had grown almost a foot before being stunted by the first frost. Fred muttered a soft expletive as the tire of his truck ran right over a fresh pile of steaming cow manure. He could smell its pungent aroma through his open window. Obviously cattle still grazed on the old farm. He had hoped to find a frozen mud puddle to run through, but was disappointed. Ice was present here and there, but nothing deep enough to wash off his tire.

At the farm house, with faded white paint and what used to be a red metal roof stretching over a broken-down front porch, Fred rolled to a stop. Within a few minutes he could see a black limousine coming up the driveway. It stopped beside Fred's truck and the driver's window rolled down to reveal David behind the wheel.

"Hi, Fred," David said cheerfully. "Would you and Sean be able to join the Governor in back? I think there's more room."

After a glance at Sean and receiving his nod, Fred said, "Sure." He and Sean got out of his truck and walked to the passenger door of the limo. Sean used a cane, but was able to slide into the large interior with relative ease.

"Gentlemen," the Governor said as he offered both men a firm handshake and a wry smile. "Thank you for agreeing to meet with me. Especially you, Sean.

I can see you got your mom's good looks," he said with a smile, drawing a collective chuckle.

David was listening intently from the front seat with the separating window rolled down. David then said, "In case you're wondering where the rest of the detail is, I've got two other cars with seven troopers staged out of sight near the road. Two of my former Marines are moving into an over-watch position right about now. The Combat MP Detachment is split and watching the road from whatever cover they could find. Fred, your warning along with the General's was heard loud and clear."

The Governor quickly changed the subject. "Sean, please accept my personal thanks for your service and my sympathy for your loss. I also want to thank all of the men and women in Special Ops. The work you have done, which likely will never see the light of day, is very much appreciated by those of us who know. Don't know if you were aware, but I served in the U.S. Army Reserve as a Captain and Transportation officer. Don't talk about it much, but spent eleven months in the sandbox of Afghanistan running convoys from Kabul to Kandahar for a lot of that time. It was before the IEDs [13] really got popular, but we did take fire regularly. Stupid bastards learned quickly that if they took the time to put their AK-47 sights on target, our boys would shoot their heads off, and so they just stuck their rifles around the side of their rock and fired off a magazine at a time without even aiming. We really liked to haul fuel cause then we had an Apache helicopter or other air support watching over us. Now those guys usually made short work of the fool."

The Governor had a look of satisfied contemplation on his face. "Hell, none of them had any education and were told by their Imams that we were invaders sent by the devil. Tough, but we had our mission and didn't like it when bullets were sent our way."

Sean showed open surprise at the Governor's story. "Governor, why hasn't this been out in the news, or at least been used for your campaign?"

"Truth be told," the Governor said, "that was a long time ago, and I'd usually prefer to leave it in the past. My wife has finally stopped complaining about me thrashing around in bed at night or waking in a cold sweat with the vision of an RPG[14] pointed at me. My political campaign was based on cleaning up the state and putting its fiscal house in order. That was what I did in business so

---

[13] IED – Improvised Explosive Devices.

[14] RPG – Rocket Propelled Grenade, a Soviet made type of bazooka.

campaigning on bringing jobs to Kentucky seemed to be a more likely winner. Guess it turned out to be the case."

"Anyway," the Governor said, "I mentioned these things because I wanted you to know I understand, at least somewhat, the position you're in when talking about what's currently happening in the country. That being said, General Thompson, the Commander of the Kentucky National Guard Army, informed me the crazy Bitch in the White House is planning on declaring a State of Emergency and totally trashing the Emergency Preparedness plans we have had in place since right after 9/11. I don't know if you can say anything at all, but whatever you feel you can share by way of information would be greatly appreciated. I may have specific questions later, but everything is going to be based upon you only telling me, I should say us, what you're comfortable sharing. Kind of long and convoluted, but I think you get my drift. Guess this is my way of reaching my hand out for help, without pressure. Son, what can you tell us?"

Sean could see how such a man could be elected. He wasn't flashy, but when he spoke, it definitely seemed to be from the heart. "Governor, all of my work is highly classified and placed in that category of "need to know.""

The Governor bowed his head in resignation. Sean continued, "But I have a pretty good feel for what my Commanding General of SOCOM thinks about this issue, so let me begin by imploring you both that what is said here does not get repeated. Okay?"

Both the Governor and David solemnly agreed. "And Dad, if a word of this gets repeated by you, there'll be no invitation to my wedding. Agreed?" A snort of humor followed by a grunt was all Fred had to respond.

With a deep breath, Sean said, "What you've heard from General Thompson is right on track with what is being sent to everyone. On top of that, the inside word is that she won't even try to declare Martial Law. If she did, she would be bound by the Uniform Code of Military Justice. Her own military would insist on that being the case. No, the thinking is that she will try to keep everything under the declared emergency umbrella. When any Executive Orders wander outside of her Constitutional authority, she'll just continue on and depend on the divided Supreme Court to do nothing. She may even try to order the National Guard to go out and seize guns, but my guess is that's not going to fly very far or fast."

Sean said, "Now, if she can spin any situation into what will be described by her pet press as an insurrection, she will be able to order out the military to keep the peace. Like everything in politics, a farmer refusing to let DHS officers take his pigs could be spun as a traitorous uprising."

The disgust on the Governor's face was rising rapidly.

"Realistically, Governor, I wouldn't think many military units will be part of that sort of thievery. The bigger question is, what will your National Guard do when citizens start shooting at those DHS people?"

The Governor reacted thoughtfully. "I don't really know. Usually Standard Operating Procedures (SOPs) are in place to provide guidance. Putting down on paper what we really intend might not be a good idea. What do you suggest?"

For the next hour and a half, Sean gave the Governor an outline of possibilities for a handful of likely scenarios he may be facing from the administration, along with his own ideas on how to address them without appearing to be directly contradicting the administration's authority.

"Governor," Sean said as the meeting was wrapping up, "in my gut it just feels like some other world event or events will make a lot of these concerns seem pretty moot. Between the idiot in North Korea and those crazy Iranians, up to half a dozen other things could come up to take everyone's focus away from the country's heartland. I just hope whatever it is; the President doesn't push us all over the edge."

"I'm with you there, soldier," the Governor said with more than a bit of reverence in his voice and his eyes. "Do you know if you and your people will be operating in Kentucky?"

That question was troubling for Sean, but like everything, he met it head-on. "At this point I don't know. Sir, this conversation has helped a lot in my understanding of how things will work here, and really, in a large part of the country. You can have my word that whatever operations me or my people undertake, they will be in the best interest of my country. I swore an oath to the Constitution which includes following duly assigned senior officers all the way to the Commander in Chief. If given a choice between following Constitutional mandates or a contradicting order, I learned as a brand new lieutenant that no one can or should make me violate the Constitution."

"Son," the Governor said softly, "I'm proud to know you and would serve with you anytime, anywhere."

CHAPTER 24
THE NEW YEAR - PLUS ELEVEN DAYS

Outside of Beijing, China
0600 Hours Local Time

In a Spartan bunker located on a secret military base Premier Song Ren rested uncomfortably on a hard bed inside of a well-stocked infirmary designed to handle the Premier and other heads of state in case of a nuclear attack. He had arrived the day before, after his security detail had transported him from the scene of the assassination attempt. He chose to remain pending a report from both Lao and his own assistant security detail chief, with a determination of his current vulnerability to another attack. His injuries, including a bloody but superficial wound to his neck and concrete shrapnel wounds to one leg. They had been dressed and sutured where needed. He refused all pain killers stronger than aspirin, even when the sutures were inserted.

Wong had arrived during the night and had been dispatched to implement Song's few orders that were possible while waiting for information. Throughout the night, Song had slept fitfully, being awakened by both discomfort and periodic updates of how the very quiet investigation progressed. No indication of the attack had been released to the public or even within the government. It was expected not even a rumor of it would leak. Unlike in the West where the news media had sources everywhere and would disseminate whatever they chose, in China, such information was carefully regulated by Lao's propaganda people. Lao had a vested interest in preventing any dissemination.

Wong came to Song right after lunch to advise that Lao had arrived with a report.

"Have him come in," Song said with a hard voice.

Lao entered the infirmary, limped to Song's bedside, and bowed his head without a word. It was apparent that Lao's leg was heavily bandaged and gave him much pain to walk.

Song glared at the top of Lao's head for several moments before barking out the command, "Report."

"General Secretary," Lao said without emotion, "the fool on your detail was visited two days earlier, late in the evening, by two unknown men at his home. His family had not been seen for at least twenty-four hours before that. He had a wife and ten year old son. In his home was a small box containing what appeared to be the severed finger of a woman and a note from his son pleading that these evil men be stopped from hurting his mother. A low-level MSS source had observed the visit and recorded the license plate number from their vehicle. Both men's bodies were found behind an opium den in a bad section of Beijing, dead from an apparent overdose. Neither man had the telltale needle tracks usually found on the arms or legs of a drug addict. They do belong to a Tong[15] that has strong ties with, and has been used by, the three Politburo members I have described to you previously as being backers of the three PLA Generals that were arrested and executed. On the way here, I was informed this Politburo power block has substantial financial interests in Formosa and stands to lose a great deal should your planned invasion go forward. They have already lost significant resources from your oil import policies."

Song waited for additional information when Lao fell silent. He asked, "What is the level of accuracy of your report?"

"General Secretary, I assess the probability of the identified Politburo block being responsible for this assassination attempt to be seventy percent. All other possibilities, however, rank below five percent in probability, to include rogue PLA Generals and other enemies you have developed over the years." Again Lao fell silent.

"Lao," Song said with a much softer voice, "what moves have you made with my security detail?

"I have arrested your security leader, and he is currently being subjected to physical and chemical interrogation. So far, there is no indication of any knowledge on his part and I do not expect to find any. Your assistant security leader has reminded all members of your security apparatus that should anyone

---

[15] Tong is a criminal Chinese gang, used in this context.

fail in his duties, not only will they and their families be tortured and killed, their families stretching across all generations will suffer the same fate. All members understood this before, however, they have just seen photos and video of what will happen should they fail."

Song only nodded to this information.

"General Secretary, it appears that your political enemies have determined use of criminal gangs or any other means to remove the threat to their prosperity are warranted. With your permission, I will institute a war-time footing for your security to include staggered travel times, multiple identical convoys departing from your location, and other measures."

Again Song only nodded his head.

"Lao, why did you risk yourself to protect me yesterday?" Song's most penetrating gaze met Lao's eyes as he asked this question.

After a polite bow of his head, Lao looked into Song's eyes and said, "General Secretary, you represent the best way forward for China. It is not personal for me, only logical."

This answer surprised and satisfied Song.

"General Secretary," Lao said very softly, "have you suffered any ill effects from the flu vaccine we received two days ago?"

"I felt a mild fever after four hours. However, that passed with no after affects." Song discussed this in a tone like both men were discussing the flowers in Song's favorite garden.

Lao replied, "I, too, had a similar reaction. Fortunately, it was quick in passing. It is most comforting to know the flu will pass me by, should it come my way this year."

Song made no response. After another moment, Song said, "Have your agent in Afghanistan return there and determine if and when the contingency plan can be launched. No date is to be suggested, only determine the earliest timeframe for readiness."

"Also, Lao, bring me a proposal for a test of the Frozen Lilly EMP technology on an American Naval ship. It must be a lone ship cruising somewhere other than the South China Sea and probably at night, although I will not presume to tell you your business. Any chance of detection or identification must be very small. You have my authority to use one of our new stealth submarines."

"Is there a preferred timeframe for this test?"

"Yes," replied Song, "it should occur within the next few days, if possible."

"I will advise you of the proposal within twenty-four hours, General Secretary," Lao said softly.

At Song's nod, Lao hobbled out of the infirmary.

CHAPTER 25
THE NEW YEAR - PLUS ELEVEN DAYS

The Broehm Residence
Outside of Cronin, Kentucky
2000 Hours EST

Mike welcomed Peter and Matt Gibson into his family room to join Sean and Fred Callahan, Rollie McDermott, and Jim Carson. Linda had not accompanied Sean as she was working on training schedules for the neighborhood.

"Rollie, Jim, and Matt, thank you for coming over," Mike said with a smile. "I've talked to each of you a little off-line but wanted to bring everyone together tonight and make sure you guys have a clear picture of what we're facing. By the way, guys, Sean, Fred and Peter have been following along since day before yesterday."

"Oh, hell, Mike," said Rollie with a grin. "We figured you'd get around to cluing us in eventually. Like I always say, only the im-po-tent folk like yourselves really need to know this stuff up front. Of course it didn't help that we were out of town until today."

A general chuckle echoed around the room at Rollie's substitution of impotent for important.

"Now Rollie, you know since the 'ole snip, snip-vasectomy, Lauren hasn't had to worry about me being 'potent' anymore, anyway." Mike said this with a large smile. "After all, you all know what Lauren wants, Lauren gets."

"Now that we've gotten beyond my potency, let me bring you up to speed on some recent information. I'll give you the Reader's Digest version. Reliable information says President Fontaine will soon be using the devastating economic downturn to declare a State of Emergency, which will be similar in effect, and in some ways even more powerful than, a declaration of Martial Law. A Presidential Executive Order gives her the authority to essentially seize control of almost everything. Some folks a lot smarter than me think that she will treat it as though there is little or no state or local government, so the feds will try to run everything. With the recent death of the conservative Supreme Court Justice there is little likelihood she will be challenged by the Supreme Court."

Mike drew in a slow breath to let all this sink in.

"Coyote Collins is going to be the federal Regional Governor of a three-state region including Kentucky, Tennessee and West Virginia for the duration of the declared emergency. All previous emergency preparedness plans are being scrapped. The Department of Homeland Security will be tasked with providing support for Coyote, which will probably involve hiring thugs to enforce his directives."

Rollie interrupted by saying, "Now, Mike, is state and local law enforcement, along with, heck, the National Guard going to be ordered around by that dooffus?"

Mike chuckled wryly, "Yeah, well that's the thing. We have it on good authority that the National Guard will be finding lots of different reasons why they can't be ordered to do things they shouldn't. If Coyote decides to order law enforcement to do things like seize goods and property for redistribution, they will likely hear, 'Sure, I'll get back to you on that.' So we're thinking that the most likely play will be for Homeland to augment their agents with hired contractors, who will be thugs. Am I getting it right, Peter?"

"Yes, Mike. That just about sums it up."

Continuing, Mike said, "We're going to have a meeting of the neighborhood tomorrow and provide a version of what I've just told you. Working with Sean and Linda, we're going to present a plan of action to step up the training we've been doing and will be taking several other steps to get ready for what may come. I already talked to the Judge Executive and local Emergency Manager last night. They want to cooperate with us. It seems to me that the Governor is about to be cut out all together in favor of Coyote, but he does have quite a bit of loyalty in both the State Police and National Guard. Hell, listening to me talk, it sounds like we're planning on some type of revolution, but that is farthest from the truth. What we're going to do is just prepare to survive the coming upheaval. What do you guys think about this?"

Rollie and Jim were both short in their replies, "We're with you, Mike."

Matt, who had been very quiet as Mike laid out the situation, seemed particularly troubled. "Mike, do you really think all these things will happen?"

"Matt," Mike said, "you haven't had the benefit of hearing from Fred Callahan and his son, Sean. Both have access to information no one else in Kentucky has. I don't know if you are aware that Sean is in Special Forces. He's had training and experience around the world, the likes of which I can't even imagine. Fred is on the Governor's Emergency Management Task Force. Fred got confirmation from the National Guard itself they were about to be activated and will be ordered to support Homeland Security. Coyote Collins being appointed Regional Governor has been confirmed by two reliable sources. The rest is just a pooling of experience to interpret what all these revelations will bring. Does that help?"

"Well, shit," said Matt with disgust. "I was in the Marine's handling logistics in the sandbox[16] and thought that whole situation was "FUBAR"[23], but this is even worse! With things going downhill the way they are, sounds like the government people will be seizing everything of value including fuel and food. They may even seize my trucks!"

The situation dawning on Matt moved him from being troubled to becoming very angry.

Watching Matt's anger mount, Mike said, "I wanted you here tonight to talk about what help you might bring to our preparations. I didn't know you were a former Marine…"

With the beginning of a grin, Matt said, "We like to say once a Marine, always a Marine. You know, Semper Fidelis?"

Smiles from around the room definitely helped lighten the mood.

"Anyway," Mike continued, "it's a real bonus that you have a military background in materials and logistics. Do you think we could come up with a plan for our neighborhood?"

For the first time, Peter chimed in, "I've got some investment capital available if we want to immediately acquire, say, a lot of different types of fuels? But as you can see, we need to move quickly."

The next ninety minutes were spent discussing immediate actions and formulating logical next steps.

---

[16] Sandbox is used to refer to areas of the Middle East where U.S. military personnel were deployed in combat. [23] Fubar is a military term popularized during WW II loosely meaning, 'fouled up beyond all repair.'

• • •

Undisclosed safe house in Northern Virginia.
2200 Hours EST

Hugh McIntyre sat in the safe house feeling very tired as he looked across the coffee table at Su Ling and his daughter Lisa. Both young women were glaring at him with their arms crossed and feet planted squarely on the floor in front of the old, dusty couch. After three days of debriefings, they wanted answers. But for the circumstances, Su would not have had any ability to put pressure on Hugh, but she demanded Lisa remain for the debriefings. Lisa joined her in solidarity, causing Hugh great anguish until he gave in to the inevitable.

The safe house was, in fact, a house located in an older middle class neighborhood tucked away back in the hills outside of the Washington D.C. metro area. It was a small Cape Cod style house with a single stall, stand-alone garage. The local neighbors believed it was a summer house used only infrequently by a very old couple. It had been furnished over twenty years ago as someplace defectors could be taken for debriefing. The budget to do so resulted in acquisition of thrift store furniture and functional, but not any up-to-date kitchenware. It was dusty after having been cleaned only sporadically over the past twenty years, causing Hugh's allergies to flare up. Hugh had arranged for the safe house by calling in a favor from a colleague that was responsible for several of the covert safe houses. He had assured his buddy that it was official business and would only last a few days. Also, a sizable increase to his buddy's budget would be available for the next fiscal year.

Hugh thought about the Director's last instruction to him. After Hugh had brought Su to the safe house and called the Director on his private line using a burner phone, he said simply, "It's done."

After a pause, the Director said, "Give me three days to work on some things." He then hung up the phone.

Since that time, Hugh had debriefed Su, using encrypted recording equipment as well as his own notes. Although interesting, there were no new critical items of intelligence. Su had, however, repeatedly asked what was being done to get her family out of China. Hugh didn't have the heart to tell her absolutely nothing. Instead, he had said the FBI Director was supposed to be in contact with the CIA Director to arrange for that to happen. Although this was technically correct, in his heart Hugh knew the Director never made the call, and Su's family would be left hanging in the wind.

Hugh was also highly annoyed that at the Director's prior instruction, he would not have any support for the debriefing and security operation for Su. Typically, there would be an entire squad of Special Agents available for security and support with such a valuable defector. This case was different, but still frustrating. The sensitivity was completely unprecedented and if anyone else was involved leak chances rose exponentially.

"Daddy," Lisa said with exasperation, "Su typed up everything she can remember on the laptop you gave her two days ago. You even reviewed it, asked all of your questions, and got answers for all of them. She needs to know what's being done about her family, and what's to happen next."

Again, Hugh sighed when he considered the intellectual capacity of both Su and Lisa. In all but experience, they dwarfed his own. The groceries he and Lisa had brought with them in the van were beginning to run out. Hugh would not leave Su Ling and was not comfortable letting Lisa run out for anything, even though she had done so once already.

"Daddy, what aren't you telling us?"

Hugh wanted to lash out at his daughter to just shut up and let him do his job. Instead, he said, "Honey, I should know something tomorrow. At least by noon."

He didn't say the Director's call was already a day overdue. "Until then, we'll just have to be patient. And I'm sorry you girls are bored, with no Internet, TV, or communication with the outside world. You have to believe me that it's all necessary to keep you safe."

Both young women had almost burst into tears when he had smashed their cell phones with a hammer at the rest stop just outside of Fairfax, Virginia. His own phone and the burner phone had been turned off, with the battery and SIM card removed for the past three days to prevent it from being traced or covertly activated. It amazed Hugh that the girls had spent the past three days, in between his questioning, playing memory games and breaking into song. Su had even begun teaching Lisa Mandarin Chinese, the official language of China.

With the deadline of noon the next day, both girls seemed to relax and began another Mandarin lesson.

CHAPTER 26
THE NEW YEAR - PLUS TWELVE DAYS

The White House
1030 Hours EST

Katherine Fontaine sat at her desk in the Oval Office looking at the latest report from the Labor Department. Unemployment in the United States had continued to skyrocket and now stood at sixty percent. Many factories across the country had shut down, taking the supporting infrastructure with them. She made sure the Labor Department would release a simple statement that the unemployment rate remained high, but had not increased from the twenty-five percent announced several weeks earlier. Mark Baxter, in her press office, had already written a press release touting the benefits of her stimulus package at holding the line, which would be sent out on the heels of the Labor Department statement.

Just as she was about to pick up the phone, her secretary buzzed her. Eli Fredericks had been admitted by the Secret Service and would arrive momentarily. Katherine responded, "See him in when he arrives."

Three minutes later, Katherine surveyed Eli carefully as her secretary closed the door to the Oval Office behind her. "My God, Eli. You look like shit. Were you hit by a truck?"

Eli had walked to the couch as Katherine moved to a chair across from him. He was impeccably dressed, as usual, but his baggy eyes and worn expression were most unusual for him.

"No, Katherine," Eli said in a slow voice, "I've been taking care of some things on the other side of the world. But how badly is the economy crumbling?"

With raised eyebrows, the President checked her inclination to make a smart retort to the man who had ensured her election and watched over her retirement account, especially since he might soon disappear. She made a mental reminder to begin the covert contacts to make that happen. Even when Walter was Vice President, she was always the one who handled the delicate political 'fixes,' like making problems go away.

"Unemployment is much worse than published and the Commerce Department says the oil industry won't recover for at least a year, maybe more."

"Then you're considering taking full control and making things right?" Eli asked the question softly, while disguising his excitement concerning what was to come.

"I haven't decided yet, but there may be no other way." Katherine looked across the room and away from Eli's eyes as she said this. It was obvious to Eli that she was lying.

"On the other side of the world, I learned the Chinese are quite serious about taking Taiwan back, by force if necessary. Will the U.S. honor its treaties and go to war over Taiwan, Katherine?"

The change of topic checked Katherine's reverie about taking control of the country through a declaration of emergency. "Uh, what?"

"Will you go to war over Taiwan, should the PRC attack the island? It would be a very foolish move to start World War III over a small island off the Chinese coast, don't you think?" Again Eli used his soft, persuasive voice to give him the sound of reason.

"What? When will the Chinese attack? What have you heard, Eli?" There was both urgency and anxiety in her voice.

"I don't really know when," Eli said truthfully. "My information comes from extremely reliable sources that Premier Song is really contemplating retaking Taiwan by force. He knows it will be a short, but very bloody fight. When he will pull the proverbial trigger is anyone's guess at the moment. Haven't your intel people been briefing you on this?"

Katherine thought back to her last several morning briefings when she had cut everyone off after shouting about the economy and the threat posed by anarchists with guns. She hadn't even heard anything about China since before the holidays. Time to correct that little error.

"What I've heard isn't nearly as specific as what you just provided, Eli. For that, I thank you. Is there something else I can do for you today? My schedule really is insane."

Eli was taken aback by Katherine's tone and apparent dismissal of him, but could see that her mental wheels were turning in the direction he had pointed, so he chose to overlook the slight.

"I, too, need to be somewhere else. I'll just let myself out." With that, he rose, nodded in Katherine's direction, and left.

Katherine picked up her phone to call her Chief of Staff. "Burt?" she said curtly. "I need you in my office." Before he could respond, she hung up the phone.

Burt entered Katherine's office with a harried and annoyed look on his face. He was obviously involved in juggling numerous different crises and didn't appreciate being summoned in the middle of them, like he was a lowly minion.

"Yes, Madam President?" His words were respectful, but he couldn't keep the sickly sweet tone from his voice to further announce his displeasure.

Katherine glared at him for a moment before deciding he had become immune to her contempt.

"Burt, I want you to have a Presidential Declaration of Emergency drawn up immediately. It doesn't have to be pretty, just legally binding. Check with the lawyers, but make sure I have the power to circumvent normal Constitutional protections, particularly the Bill of Rights. Do you have any problem dealing with that Burt?" Her eyes bored into his as she asked the question.

"Madam President, I know you've been frustrated with …"

Katherine cut him off by saying, "The country is going to hell in a hand basket. Everything I want to do to stop it is stalled by those bastards in Congress. The people are suffering, including the children! I can't let that happen any longer. Didn't you tell me yourself that the polls were in my favor concerning the gun issue? We'll play it up that to protect the people of this country; we need to have the tools to handle the anarchists who threaten our very way of life." Her voice had steadily risen, and she took on a wild-eyed look.

Burt was inwardly horrified to hear what Katherine was proposing. On his face, he maintained a neutral expression. Deep inside he was thankful he had already begun a strategy to escape from Katherine and Washington, D.C. when things became untenable. That could come from either Katherine going completely insane or when the country crumbled to the point of no-return.

"I'll see that it is done, Madam President. A draft should be on your desk by the end of the day. Should I call an immediate Cabinet meeting?"

Katherine had been distracted with her own thoughts almost as soon as Burt began speaking. Coming back to the present, she said, "Cabinet meeting? No, not yet. I was going to simply sign it this evening without fanfare."

She glanced at Burt who displayed his shock.

"Madam President," Burt said quickly with feeling, "a great number of things should be done before you make the announcement to the American people. Line up Cabinet support, brief the Joint Chiefs, even notify Congressional leadership."

"Fuck all of them!" Katherine shouted at Burt. "Most of them have done nothing, *nothing* to support what I've been trying to do to keep this country afloat. Why should I consult with any of them?"

Of all the shocks Burt had suffered over the past year, this reaction to his advice was the greatest yet.

Taking a quick, but deep breath, Burt said, "If you do not at least explain to your Cabinet, military leadership, and Congress why you need to declare the emergency and what doing so will accomplish. If you do not..." Burt paused for effect. "You will certainly face *immediate impeachment* and, theoretically, even a *military coup*, Madam President. Without proper introduction of the reasons for the declaration, you will be portrayed by even the mainstream press as a dictator taking over the country."

Burt paused to let what he had said sink in, then said, "Your actual goals don't need to be included, but you must present everyone with where you think you will be leading the country by these actions. Even if you don't personally believe what you say. Please, Madam President, let me at least begin the process."

Burt's mention of Impeachment and a military coup had given Katherine pause. Neither had occurred to her as possibilities. Since her meeting with Eli, she had been drunk on the vision of having the absolute power needed to accomplish what she just knew had to be done.

In a calmer tone of voice, Katherine said, "Burt, how long will it take you to make a proper introduction, as you call it?"

"That's where it gets tricky, Madam President. There needs to be the right amount of notice to the smallest number of people, but we have to move very fast before Congress can make any meaningful move to stop it from happening. Can you give me twenty-four hours to develop the plan? It must be done quietly."

"All right, Burt. Twenty-four hours for a plan, but I expect to sign the document very soon. Do you understand me?"

"Yes, Madam President." With that, Burt quietly left the room and walked quickly to his office. He told his secretary that he did not want to be disturbed for the next thirty minutes unless war broke out. She had looked at him with surprise since the Chief of Staff's door was supposed to always be open in an emergency, even one short of war.

At his desk, he opened the bottom drawer and brought out a bottle of very expensive scotch whiskey. After pouring two fingers of the brown liquor into his coffee cup, he poured the entire amount into his mouth. Swallowing it in one gulp brought the expected burn and complaint from his mouth and throat. He poured a second, which he had intended to sip and try to savor. Instead he glanced down at the cup to find it empty again. He picked up the phone and ordered Marc Baxter to report to his office.

A few minutes later, Marc arrived to find Burt sitting at his desk with two crystal glasses containing scotch.

"Close the door, please, Marc."

"Are we celebrating something, Burt?" Marc asked the question cautiously, fearing the worst.

"You might say that," Burt said bluntly. "This single malt scotch runs over five thousand dollars a bottle, when you can get it. Before I get started, I suggest you slam that one down, and I'll refill it for you."

Marc was obviously surprised, but decided the best course was to knock down the scotch. After the brief shake of his body from the liquid burning its way down his throat, he allowed Burt to pour another two shots into his glass.

"Are you okay, Burt?"

"No, I'm not, Marc. And just so that you know, if a word of what I'm about to say ever sees the light of day, you will likely find yourself disappeared. Do you understand me?"

Marc accepted the threat thinking it was a bit melodramatic, but then looking into Burt's eyes, decided he was deadly serious.

"Burt, I don't know that I want to hear this." Saying this, Marc began to get out of his chair.

"Sit down, Marc. You don't have a choice, just like me." Marc slowly settled back into the chair.

After a pause, Burt continued, "The President just ordered me to have the legal staff draw up a Declaration of Emergency for her signature. She planned to sign it this evening before announcing her 'coup d'état' of Congress on national television. I convinced her to give me twenty-four hours to give her the plan for properly rolling out such a declaration."

Burt drained his scotch in one motion before pouring another.

Marc sipped his scotch, but his mind was racing. "My God, Burt. Doesn't she know, oh, I don't know, that maybe she would be impeached for trying that?"

"Yeah, she does now. I told her, which is what got me the twenty-four hour delay. This is the last one for both of us, by the way," Burt said, motioning to their glasses, "so you might want to really savor it. When they're done, we need to make a list of the bare minimum of people that will need to be informed and make sure they are available by secure telephone to receive the President's call. I'm thinking she can call the people on the list by secure phone between 8:00 p.m. and 9:00 p.m. day after tomorrow before signing the damned thing and then going on national television in a live address to the nation. Does this sound about right to you?"

Marc responded, "None of it sounds very right to me, but if it's going to happen, I can probably set it up with the major networks to be prepared to preempt programming for a major announcement from the White House. I presume I should tell them it is about the economic crisis? They'll get really pissed when I don't give them a preview outline of the speech, but they'll figure out why after she says whatever she's going to say. Speaking of which, what the hell is she going to say?"

"I've got to corral Danny and get him working on it," Burt said thoughtfully. "On second thought, maybe I'll just tell him to be in early tomorrow morning and tell him then. That will save the possibility of it getting out too soon. Speaking of which, I really did mean what I said about this getting out. Not even pillow talk with Susan tonight, Marc. Got it?"

Burt was rewarded by Marc's look of surprise.

"Oh, and Marc? Think I'll schedule a dinner meeting from 7:00 p.m. to 9:00 p.m. the day after tomorrow for the key staff and cabinet members. Make sure Towanda is there. The President can advise any other critical personnel by secure telephone."

CHAPTER 27
THE NEW YEAR - PLUS TWELVE DAYS

The White House
1145 Hours EST

"Madam President," Katherine's secretary said into the intercom phone, "Director Kidd is on his way over here and requests a meeting at your earliest convenience. He did not say what it was about, but advised that it was important that he see you right away."

In light of Eli's message earlier, Katherine wondered if the message was going to be intelligence that China was about to launch an attack on Taiwan.

"When he enters the building, let me know. I will call you when I'm ready to see him."

Katherine thought more about the possible reason for such a face to face meeting and she began to wonder if this might concern her invocation of the State of Emergency. "Whatever revelation the man brings," Katherine thought darkly, "it has doubled the pounding in my head."

Nearly fifteen minutes after her secretary announced the FBI Director and a Deputy Assistant Director (DAD) had entered the building, Katherine called and asked that they be shown into the Oval Office.

"Director," Katherine said with a stern look on her face. "You have something that could not be handled on the phone?"

"Madam President, no, this could not be handled on the phone. This is my Deputy Assistant Director in the Counterintelligence Division. With your permission, he will set up the laptop with information to supplement what I am about to tell you. And Madam President, it is not good news."

Katherine had come around the desk but had not offered her hand. She sat down in the chair across from her couch and motioned both men to be seated across from her. In anticipation of this arrangement, the Deputy Assistant Director had brought a special laptop computer with screens facing both towards him and the keyboard and one facing the President.

"Madam President, I've tried to think of the best way to approach this matter and decided bringing it directly to you, confidentially, with no one else in the loop, was the best way to handle it. To be blunt, we have strong evidence that your husband, Walter Fontaine, has been having an affair with a young Chinese girl."

W. Allen Kidd let the statement hang in the air for a moment to allow the President to digest it, wanting to ease into the espionage part.

Much to the Allen's surprise, Katherine broke out into almost giddy laughter.

After a moment to compose herself, she said, "Why in the hell should I care who Walter happens to be fucking this week?"

Through another giggle, Katherine said, "My God, man. He's been boinking some bimbo regularly for years." She became serious for a moment. "And that statement better not ever see the light of day. Do you understand me? I thought you were going to tell me something I didn't know." She continued to laugh softly as she shook her head.

Taken aback, Allen drew a deep breath and continued, "Madam President, the Chinese woman he has been seeing works closely with a Chinese intelligence officer. The Chinese intelligence service has been videotaping each encounter. Worse, she has been skillfully interrogating him for everything he knows about U.S. government actions relating to China or anything about which they have an interest."

Katherine's smile disappeared as her face turned first white, then ashen, and finally began to redden. "What?! Tapes?!" She shouted this across the coffee table.

At Allen's nod, the Deputy Assistant Director pushed a button and the laptop screen came alive. A video flashed on the screen depicting Walter walking down the sidewalk and getting into a gray vehicle with blacked out windows. The scene cut to a distant video, zoomed in to the point it was quite grainy, showing Walter getting out of the car and a Chinese man extending a plastic hotel key card to him.

"Madam President, the Chinese man is Sung Hong, a First Secretary in the PRC Embassy and a known Chinese intelligence officer. This was four days ago."

The screen then shows Walter entering a small, plush Washington, D.C. hotel. The screen is dark when sound can suddenly be heard over the laptop speaker.

"Oh, Walter," a woman said with a cute China doll accent, "you walk in like you rushed. You not want my company?"

"My Dear, um," Walter could be heard mumbling. This was followed by the sound of someone gulping down a drink followed by Walter's mumbling for the glass to be refilled. After the second round of slurping the sound of the woman giggling could be heard along with, "Oh, Walter," and sloppy kissing.

Walter then said, "I want you to bring out your bag of tricks. I, uh, I mean, I've been a very bad boy."

After a slight pause, the Chinese woman said, "You very bad. On your knees, you bad boy, and drop your pants. Bare bottom when I return. DO IT!"

Katherine's face had flashed between anger, embarrassment, and morbid fascination multiple times as the audio tape continued. After the first crack of a whip followed by Walter's voice saying, "Thank you mistress," Katherine reached across the table, grabbed the laptop and threw it off the coffee table toward the far wall. To add to her frustration, the sounds of whipping and Walter's pleas for more punishment continued from across the room until the Deputy Assistant Director could recover the laptop and turn it off.

"I'll kill the son-of-a-bitch," Katherine said in a short, staccato, and malevolent voice. She then looked up and glared at both the Director and Deputy Assistant Director. "You will both wait outside of this office until I call you back in. Do you understand me?" Her voice rose slightly as she displayed great effort in avoiding the shout she wanted to use.

Both men got up and left the Oval Office to take seats in the waiting room outside. Right after sitting down across from the President's secretary, her phone rang once. After she listened for a moment, she said, "Yes, Madam President," and hung up the phone. She looked at both men and smiled before asking if either would care for a cup of coffee. Both politely declined.

Hanging up the phone, Katherine's mind was in a whirlwind. At least she had the forethought to have her secretary call immediately should the Director and his assistant get up and leave.

• • •

FBI Headquarters
1830 Hours EST

Allen had just poured two fingers of fine bourbon into a tumbler without ice. He followed by pouring a similar drink, which he offered to his Deputy Assistant Director. He had pushed the button that created "white noise" or static on any device that might be trying to record what was said in the office. After both men had drained half of the contents of their glass, Allen asked, "Well, what do you make of that?"

The DAD responded, "I've been trying to understand what just happened all the way back, Sir. Quite frankly, I'm a bit afraid. Not just for me but for my family."

If he was expecting a surprised look from the Director, he didn't get one.

"I've been thinking the same thing for the first time in my life," said Allen. "I had expected her to let us cool our heels for a while as she considered what actions to take, but not for over four hours. And then to have her secretary do the throat clearing thing and shake her head no when we started to get up and leave. Well, it was shocking and insulting."

"Was it just me," the DAD said, "or after she called us back in, was every question she asked focused on identifying every single person, by name, that knew anything about the Chinese intel operation? If she had the power, I think she would have had you drawn and quartered when you refused to identify agents by name who were read into this. And, Sir, I was never more proud to work for you when she said, 'How dare you deny me those names.'"

The DAD actually smiled as he repeated what his Director had told the President of the United States, "Those men and women have trusted me with their lives and until you can provide me with a valid reason that anyone outside the FBI needs those names, I will protect them. Listen, Allen. I know D.C. is the center of conspiracy theories in this country, but her whole attitude was one of building a hit list. Did you notice how she made a point of reminding me that the whole thing was classified to the highest level? She was telling me about classification? What a flaming hypocrite!"

"Sir," said the DAD, "you promised Hugh McIntyre an update by noon yesterday."

With a nod of acknowledgement, Allen said, "Okay, here's what we'll do. You don't know where Hugh or the girl is now, do you?"

The Director knew the answer but wanted to insure that continued to be correct. He was also unaware that Hugh's daughter was now accompanying Su.

"No, Sir," said the DAD. "Per your instructions, they have been completely off the radar.

Allen considered the whole thing again and said, "I want you to use this burner phone from a non-bureau location and set up another secure communications plan, one that doesn't involve either you or me. And no, I don't want to know any details. I imagine he is prepared to disappear for an extended period, so have him do so for at least three months. Do I remember from his personnel file that he did some covert work several years ago?"

At the nod from the DAD, Allen continued, "Okay, then arrange for him to get an appropriate amount of covert cash. Make sure he includes his family and the girl in these instructions. He is to have no contact with anyone from the FBI or U.S. government. Did I leave anything out?"

"No, Sir. I can fill in any other details, but that should cover it."

"After you get that done," the Director continued, "I want you to do the same thing for yourself."

"Sir?" The confused look on the DAD's face showed a little of the insult that he felt.

"Listen to me carefully." Allen's voice had gotten very quiet and very serious. "Enemies of the Fontaine's have disappeared by the dozens over the years. I've got a protection detail, but my wife is going to be leaving the area by tomorrow morning. We've done everything we can do, considering the cat is already out of the bag, or out of Walter's lips and over in Beijing. With the economy, tensions with the Chinese, and everything else going on right now, arresting anyone at this point would have very negative effects on our country. Do you really think the President's State Department is going to throw out any Chinese spies at this point? Suddenly, the Internet will light up with a video in living color with the First Man being whipped by a Chinese girl, and asking for more."

"But, Sir? With this information, the Chinese own her! She should step down and have the Vice President take charge." The DAD's words were a mix of outrage with a plea for sanity.

With a resigned sigh, the Director said, "If an opportunity presents itself where she can be removed without plunging the country into complete chaos, I will do what is necessary. What I don't want is for anyone else to take the fall for doing what is right. You and I both know the press and her allies will protect her at all costs."

Looking the DAD directly in his eyes, the Director said gently, "Go protect your family. But before you go, make sure there are multiple copies of everything we've done to investigate this thing to include your recollection of the meeting with the President. Hard copies, thumb drives, whatever it takes to make sure a record of what has happened survives. Send me a copy with a TOP SECRET/EYES ONLY classification and a marking stating it is the only copy. Can you do this in twenty-four hours?"

"Sir, all but the White House meeting write up, it's already done."

CHAPTER 28
THE NEW YEAR - PLUS TWELVE DAYS

Undisclosed Safe House in Northern Virginia
2300 Hours EST

Hugh McIntyre arrived at the safe house to find his daughter, Lisa, and Su Ling sitting anxiously on the couch. Su was much calmer than Lisa.

"I have news." Hugh made the statement without any inflection that would indicate whether the girls would find it desirable or distasteful.

Looking directly at Su, Hugh said, "Lisa has told me that she trusts you completely. You'll have to understand that I've been doing this for a long time and with lives in the balance, so I really have a tough time trusting anyone. A case in point is what happened when the President was informed her husband had been videotaped in compromising positions while giving up our country's highest level of secrets. Instead of meeting the threat head-on, she is determined to bury the whole thing and anyone that is aware of it."

Su quickly said, "Beijing will own her. That was the plan from the beginning. You must get rid of her, or at least throw her out of the White House."

"Yes, I agree with you." Hugh said this with a heavy voice. "Unfortunately, there are too many moving parts for that to happen at this time."

"Then we are to be killed?" Su made the comment as both a question and a statement of fact.

"No, that will not happen." Hugh said this with firmness and conviction.

"Just like my family will be saved and smuggled out of China?" Su was allowing her emotions to come out for the first time in many years.

Lisa chose that moment to jump in and defuse the tension. "Su, I was there. Dad never said he could get your family out of China, only that he would do everything in his power to do so." Turning to her dad, Lisa asked, "And you did, didn't you daddy?"

Hugh felt momentarily trapped between telling his daughter the truth and revealing his having done something way outside the rules.

Finally, he nodded his head to the silent argument in his mind and said, "Yes, Sweetheart, I did. The Director had told me he would personally speak to the CIA Director about getting them out, but I didn't believe he would. I contacted a friend over there and asked if such a thing could be done. He told me that if the CIA Director ordered it, it might be possible, but realistically, if the PRC government were watching them, the risk to those making the attempt would be extremely high. He didn't think anyone would want to take that risk."

Turning to Su, he said, "Su, I'm sorry. Should I have told you this three days ago, when I found out? Would it have changed your mind in helping us further?"

Tears streamed down Su's face as she realized that her actions may have doomed her parents to possible torture and death. To her credit, even with her buried emotions leaking out onto her cheeks, her mind continued to hum along at a high rate of speed. "I chose to help you and take this chance to escape knowing what it might mean. The decision was made when I first agreed to speak with you and really, when I decided to become a friend of Lisa's." Looking at Lisa, she could see tears welling up in her eyes as well.

Su continued, "I can tell that what you say is the truth."

This statement resulted in a look of astonishment from Hugh.

"I can always tell," Su said. "It is a gift, or a curse, or both, but I'm always right. Since beginning Charm School, I always know when someone is lying. No, it would not have mattered if you had told me three days ago."

After another pause, Su said, "I just need to learn how to grieve." With this she bowed her head.

Hugh waited for several seconds before saying, "Su and Lisa, I can tell you from experience that grieving takes a lot longer than anyone logically believes it should. That being said, let's put that on the back burner for now and go into some additional news."

Both girls looked up quizzically.

"Because of what's happened and the President's reaction, I need to get both of you out of here to a safe place. There, you will have access to news and other information, but will still need to follow some strict rules to keep you safe. I'll get into those in a minute. Right now, I need to leave you both alone for a couple of hours." Looking again at Su, Hugh said, "Can I trust you to remain here until I get back?" Su nodded her head. Again, her instincts told her she could trust Hugh.

"Good. Now, Lisa, you've got your car here, and I acquired you an alternate license plate for it. I presume you still have the toolbox I gave to you in your car?"

"Yes, Daddy," Lisa said with a little exasperation.

"Good. If for any reason I am not back by morning, you need to load up your car and drive yourself and Su to Uncle Peter's in Kentucky. Can you do that? Oh, and here."

Hugh took five hundred dollars out of his wallet and handed it to her. "Make sure you do not use any credit cards and avoid any roadside conferences by driving the speed limit."

Su asked, "Roadside conferences?"

Lisa smiled and said, "Yes, that's what Dad calls it when a policeman pulls him over. He never gets a ticket and usually makes a friend of the policeman in the process."

Turning to her dad, Lisa asked, "Dad, what's this all about?"

"Honey, there is the possibility that some of our own people might be looking for you. I'm just being careful, okay? Anyway, I should be back in a couple of hours. Love you." Hugh picked up his briefcase and walked out of the door.

CHAPTER 29
THE NEW YEAR - PLUS THIRTEEN DAYS

The Mountains of Southeastern Afghanistan
0515 Hours Local Time

The cold, pre-dawn light had just begun to cause the eastern sky to glow when Hadi's steps could be heard softly crunching through the snow and ice up the path. Ahmed had been standing at the entrance for over an hour, staring out into the night.

At Hadi's arrival, Ahmed was not pleased at the disturbance. "Why have you disturbed my quiet time, Hadi? It had better be important."

Surprised at the brusque tone of voice, Hadi bowed deeply and said, "Great leader, I have additional news. The Chinese Infidel has arrived in Kabul and will be here by early afternoon. Also, your wife's brother, Ali al-Hadiz, has also arrived in Kabul with two friends. They will not be arriving until after darkness has fallen."

Ahmed's mood brightened instantly. "Inform me when the Infidel has arrived. Serve him tea."

Hadi said, "I will do as you command. He also comes alone this time. No assistant to carry his water."

Ahmed nodded and then motioned his dismissal to Hadi.

• • •

Forty minutes after Cho was led to the protected cliff overhang where he was to meet Ahmed, Hadi listened as one of his men whispered in his ear. He relayed to Cho, "He will be here in a few minutes."

For his part, Cho sat patiently on the rock. The tea had initially at least warmed his hands, even if he didn't drink it. Eventually, however, it had grown cold, so he set it aside. He responded to Hadi's statement with a slight nod.

Ahmed walked into the overhang area with a purposeful step, as if he had just come from an important meeting. In reality, he had been waiting impatiently, 100 meters away, to make his entrance. He did not wish to be seen as too eager to meet Cho.

"You are back." Ahmed's statement was given in a neutral, matter-of-fact tone.

"May Allah be merciful on you and your people." Cho gave this polite greeting with a slight bow as he had arisen when Cho approached.

"What brings you back, without useful materials or even your follower?" Ahmed was aware that Cho had brought neither his assistant nor any trucks filled with weapons or explosives.

Cho said, "I have been sent with an important message for your ears only." Cho glanced around at Hadi and four fighters acting as guards.

Ahmed ordered the four fighters to move out from under the overhang and out of earshot, but still within sight. He then motioned for Hadi to join him as he moved close to Cho. All three men were standing.

"Hadi will remain. What is your message?"

Cho stared at Hadi for a moment before choosing to ignore his presence and turned to Ahmed. "Are your fighters ready to take Jihad to the world and kill Infidels?"

Ahmed smiled broadly and said, "Yes, they are ready. Each man speaks English well enough to go through Customs. All have been to Europe for several days and returned on their own, as a test. All are committed to this cause and will glory in meeting Allah."

Cho nodded his head at the news. "The last time we spoke, you said your martyrs must receive the virus here, in the mountains. My superiors have told me to arrange for my medical people to be in Kabul, at a safe location near the airport. Your martyrs will go to the location with their tickets and luggage three hours before their scheduled departure. There they will be injected with the virus and taken directly to the airport to board their plane."

Ahmed was initially inclined to argue about everything to show that he was in charge. After further thought, he decided to appear to be reasonable. He asked Cho, "How long will it take from when the martyrs get the virus until they begin passing it to others? And how long before they will be obviously sick and then too sick to travel?"

Cho hesitated before saying, "The symptoms of the virus will not become obvious until about thirty-six hours after they receive the injections. I do not know how soon they will become contagious or when they will no longer be able to travel. I presume they will begin passing the virus at least several hours or more before they start showing symptoms."

"When will this happen?" Ahmed asked while failing in his attempt to mask his excitement.

"I do not know. I am led to believe it will be soon. Maybe within a month or two and maybe sooner. You must be ready. I will send my assistant the day before the medical team will arrive in Kabul. I am sorry, but that is as much advance notice as I can give. Once the decision is made to go forward, things will have to happen very quickly. Your security remains good? No one knows of our meetings?"

"If my security were not, an American cruise missile would have killed us long ago." Ahmed's fatalistic statement showed his true belief on the topic.

• • •

Undisclosed Safe House in Northern Virginia
0200 Hours EST

When Hugh returned he found both girls still up, although in pajamas. Su had even giggled like a little girl when Lisa pulled out a pair of PJ's for her four days earlier.

"See girls," Hugh said as he walked in the door. "Told you I'd be back. But I'm only here for a few minutes and have to leave again. Lisa, I have a number of items that might be useful in this bag," showing Lisa a large duffle bag he had just dropped in the corner. "My same instructions from before are in place. If you don't see me by 7:00 a.m., I want you to load your car and head for Uncle Peter's. Take this bag with you. Okay?"

"Daddy?" Lisa said this with annoyance.

"I love you, Sweetheart," Hugh said with a hurried smile, before giving her a big hug. Breaking the embrace, he reached over and brought Su in for a mini-hug with Lisa.

With that, he abruptly broke away from them and walked toward the door. "And I mean it. By 7:00 a.m., if I haven't come back, you two be on the road for Kentucky. Got it?"

"Okay, I've got it, Dad."

CHAPTER 30
THE NEW YEAR - PLUS THIRTEEN DAYS

The Callahan Residence
Outside of Cronin, Kentucky
0300 Hours EST

Sean woke with a start to find himself in his childhood bedroom in his parent's house outside of Cronin. The secure room was down the hallway. His start had awakened Linda, whose long blonde hair was scattered haphazardly across his chest. She peered at him through folds of hair to see what had caused him to wake.

"I'm sorry, beautiful. Just a little flashback," he said with a wan smile in the light of the moon peeking through the window. "Guess it's my turn, huh?"

Linda had recurring nightmares several times each night of her kidnapping and rescue by Sean during an operation in Afghanistan.

Linda kissed him and snuggled closer under his arm, feeling the reassurance brought by her soon-to-be husband. She made sure to sleep on the side opposite from his stump to avoid bumping it and causing Sean pain. Of course this was only after Sean's mom had moved her things from the guest bedroom into Sean's room. She had somehow gotten a wardrobe into the room as well just to hold it all. When Sean had asked his Mom who had done it, he had gotten a terse, "I did. Any problem?"

Being the intelligent son he was, he kept his mouth shut and merely shook his head no. Since both were wide awake, Sean asked, "How is the small unit training of your security force going?"

Sean remembered the large number of volunteers that showed up for the first neighborhood security meeting just after Christmas. Even better was almost twenty percent had prior military experience. Since that meeting Linda had taken them in small groups out to a nearby state park rifle and pistol range to familiarize them with their firearms. Accompanying these training sessions were lessons on small unit tactics. Once they had gotten over the fact that she was female, everything had flowed smoothly. It didn't hurt that word leaked that not only was she one of the rare female Special Forces (SF) operators, she had also been in command of an "A" Team. All of her "troops" were in awe of her.

"Amazingly well," Linda said with genuine surprise. "Especially when you let me borrow the guys in your SWE security detail to help. They were getting pretty bored anyway and appreciated being able to get out. These folks are very gung ho and with so many out of work, they have the time and are really motivated to do something productive. Most even have their own AR clone,[17] and at least a thousand rounds of ammunition. With the Fontaine administration pushing hard for an Australian-style gun confiscation, everyone stocked up. With what we have, we should be able to handle at least a few small skirmishes. Good thing, too. No ammunition is for sale anywhere."

Pausing to wipe away a drop of sweat from Sean's face, Linda said, "Fortunately, someone in the neighborhood, with deep pockets and a strong vision of the future, bought out an ammunition warehouse and had been stockpiling. Some of that ammo has been made available to us."

Linda continued, "I've got the volunteers broken into six, eight-man teams so we'll be able to have one team out patrolling round-the-clock if necessary, while another team will be split between the two neighborhood entrances. At least initially, all those teams will do is observe and report. I don't think it will be very easy for anyone to penetrate the perimeter of the neighborhood by vehicle, so the only reasonable access is by the two entrances. Someone trying to get in would have to cross the creek or traverse some pretty difficult farmland. In case of an attempt to do so, on foot or by some type of off-road vehicle, I'll have the roving patrol keep an eye out for those types of infiltrators."

Sean could only stroke Linda's hair and look at her in amazement.

"The security force has five single women and three, sixteen or seventeen year old girls, who volunteered," Linda said. "All play varsity women's sports in

---

[17] AR is an abbreviation for Armalite and is used to designate w semi-automatic version of a military M-16 rifle.

their high school and all have experience shooting, including two bona fide deer hunters. I think at least three of the females will be a good sniper."

Sean was smiling. "How about leadership on each team?"

That brought Linda back down to earth. "That's where we're weakest. Two of the team leaders are former non-coms,[18] so I think they'll do fine. The other four kind of make me nervous. They just don't seem to be very good at thinking on their feet. Like we always say, though, the best way to train someone to think on their feet is to drill them repetitively until they don't have to. At least not much." That last comment was what made every commander very nervous.

"Mike and your Dad have also been getting a lot done. They went around to all the surrounding cattle and horse farms and talked to the owners and their managers. All but a couple of these farms were pretty intelligent and have signed on to a verbal agreement to cooperate with the neighborhood if things get really bad. In exchange for protection and some manual labor we'll at least have access to beef and horse power. One of my security teams also happens to be made up of experienced horsemen and women, some with their own horses stabled nearby."

Sean rose up on one elbow and brought Linda's face up for a kiss. "My God, you're amazing!"

"Best Damned "A" team leader in the world you incredible man, you." It was quite a while before they managed to get back to sleep.

• • •

The White House
0835 Hours EST

Burt sat on the couch in the Oval Office facing his President with a very sour feeling in his stomach. It wasn't enough that the President wanted him to help her seize unprecedented power. Now he had to inform her that it would take an additional twenty-four hours before she could sign the Executive Order and announce to the world that things were so bad in the United States that she must essentially take control of the country and its economy herself. He hadn't felt

---

[18] Non-commission officers or sergeants.

this nervous since the time five years earlier while awaiting word of the paternity test for that young intern.

Burt had merely given a deep, but quiet sigh when twenty minutes earlier he had sent Katherine's favorite speech writer, Danny, to write the speech that would change America. At least there would be over a full day to refine and make small changes to the speech before Katherine delivered it the following evening. He'd have to insure Danny didn't leave the White House until after her speech.

Sitting across from Burt in her usual chair, Katherine had sat measuring her Chief of Staff for the past several minutes. She didn't want to contemplate how she should react if he told her the Declaration of Emergency could not be done. Finally, she said,

"All right, Burt. Out with it."

"Madam President, key members of your staff have been working almost nonstop since yesterday." Burt paused before continuing, "But unfortunately, it will take until tomorrow before the barest of the required formalities can be met. With your permission, I will ensure key members of Congress and the military will be available by secure telephone tomorrow evening between 8:00 and 9:00 p.m. You will need to call and inform fifteen individuals. I have placed them in descending order of likelihood that they will run immediately to the press. Before that, from 7:00 to 8:00 p.m. you can inform your staff and Cabinet. An emergency meeting will be called for that time later tomorrow morning under the ruse of an urgent need to discuss a possible wage and price freeze. Of course it really isn't a ruse, but only a small part of what will be announced on national television at 9:00 p.m. Baxter doesn't think there will be any problem pre-empting programming on the major networks, at least within the mainstream media. Does all of this sound all right to you, Madam President?"

"I don't like these delays." Katherine seemed to spit out the words with distaste. "It will have to do, though. Now, where's the first draft of my speech?"

"I have Danny working on it now," Burt said. "He's highlighting the need to cease all gun sales in the country and for the government to take steps to secure public order and ensure that everyone has what is needed to get by. Heavy emphasis is placed on making sure everyone gets enough to eat and the need for the government to manage critical resources. We'll cite Presidential Executive Order 13603 once for justification, but will mostly focus on all the bad things that have happened since the economic crisis began. Got to be careful not to turn the speech into a blame game against the Chinese, or we'll have too many people in Congress and elsewhere shouting for war with China. I asked him to write it to point the blame at past administrations that left us with so many trillions in debt that we were doomed for a very painful correction."

Throughout this explanation, the expression on Katherine's face went from near outrage to almost calm and thoughtful. Hardly missing a beat, she said, "Thank you, Burt. Get the first draft over to me when it's done, and I'll have a look at it."

CHAPTER 31
THE NEW YEAR - PLUS THIRTEEN DAYS

Southbound on Interstate 81 in Virginia
1055 Hours EST

Lisa McIntyre was very worried. Her dad had not come back before 7:00 a.m. Following instructions she and Su managed to switch out the license plate and had loaded their meager belongings, including her dad's duffle bag, into her car. When she opened the duffle bag, she was shocked to find several items, including more cash than she took time to count, as well as a handwritten letter from her dad. It gave her a very eerie feeling to recall his words.

"Lisa, Sweetheart, if you're reading this note, I didn't make it back with your Mom. I don't want you to worry, because as I write this, I haven't decided if I should come back, or if we should part ways for a while, for your safety. You know me and checklists, so here are a few instructions I really need you to follow to the letter.

Remove the battery from your GPS, laptop, and any other electronic devices I didn't already destroy and hide them under the brush pile in the back yard. You should not have a cell phone, but if you do, include that as well. Yes, it is very important that you leave anything with a GPS locator on it behind.

Take the duffle bag and its contents, along with all of your stuff, and load it into your car. Try to be heading toward Kentucky no later than 7:00 a.m.

Make sure you and your friend are very careful to avoid creating ANY electronic signature during your trip. Think of it as one of those TV shows where the bad guys have access to every computer and surveillance camera in the world.

Try to change your appearance and your friend's appearance to make it more difficult for facial recognition software to be able to identify you. Hats, sunglasses, haircuts, and some judicious makeup come to mind, but you two are very capable, so I leave that in your hands.

While traveling, use only cash. NO CREDIT CARDS! There is more than enough cash in the duffel bag to get you to Kentucky. Please store the rest of it at Peter's when you get there. To alleviate your curiosity, this is legitimate cash I was given for this specific purpose. Without writing it down, please try to keep receipts or recall approximately how much you spend and where it was spent.

While traveling, make sure you go the speed limit or with the flow of traffic. You need to avoid roadside conferences. Should you encounter any government officials, like police etc., DO NOT mention me or where I work. Needless to say, drive very safely and avoid having any accidents. You and your friend should come up with an appropriate story should you somehow end up in an accident to explain the cash and your friend's lack of identification. Claiming to be from Eastern Kentucky and not trusting banks might help explain the cash and your friend could be an exchange student who was robbed of her documents. You might also want to dust off your Southern drawl. I'm sure you two can come up with just the right story, just in case.

Do not call anyone unless it is the last possible option. Then, the only person you should call in an extreme emergency is Uncle Peter.

You should be able to get there in a long day's drive. Drive carefully and take no unnecessary detours. I know your friend would like to see as much as possible along the way, but do not deviate from the fastest route. Think speed and stealth.

You should have a paper map to use for your trip. If you don't have one, shame on you! Stop into somewhere without surveillance cameras and buy a road atlas.

I plan to go directly home, pack up your mother and the dog and head out myself. If we aren't there with you, we have gone someplace safe and will be laying low for a while. Please trust me when I tell you that I will do whatever is necessary to keep your mom safe. I don't know when we can come to you, but we will do so whenever it is possible. I love you with all of my heart. Be safe!

Love, Dad"

Even though she could see some logic in her dad's thinking, she felt more than a little alone and afraid. After only a moment's thought, she had passed the note to Su. She was surprised to see Su only nod her head with approval after finishing the note.

"Lisa," Su said softly, "do you have your father's note memorized?" With a start, Lisa nodded yes.

"Then I think we need to destroy this note. Would it be all right if I tore it up into small pieces and flushed it down the toilet?"

Again Lisa's eyes widened, but she nodded once again before following Su into the bathroom. After tearing the note into pieces the size of small confetti, Su flushed them down the toilet, then flushed again three more times. This took a few minutes for the water tank to fill between flushes.

Staring at Su throughout the process, Lisa finally said, "This type of thing was part of your training, wasn't it?"

Su nodded with a smile. "Flushing it down is much better than chewing it up and swallowing it."

This lightened the mood as both laughed softly at the thought of tasting paper and ink.

CHAPTER 32
THE NEW YEAR - PLUS THIRTEEN DAYS

Outside of Cronin, Kentucky
1800 Hours EST

Mike stood before his gathered neighbors at the outdoor pavilion in a cold, blowing wind but thankfully, with no snow or rain. Use of a PA sound system negated the need to shout to be heard. Despite the dark and cold, there was a cautiously positive buzz coming from the crowd. Every household in the neighborhood was represented along with several families from neighboring farms, but with everyone bundled up it was impossible to identify most attendees.

"Folks, can I have your attention?" Mike used his firm but friendly voice over the PA system and was surprised when everyone quickly quieted.

"First, thanks for coming out on a cold January night. I know most of us got together after Christmas and even beforehand to begin making some preparations, but I think you will all understand why we're here in just a moment."

Mike's voice settling over the crowd seemed to both calm and focus everyone's attention.

Mike then said, "To start out, I'm going to ask each of you to try and keep what you hear this evening between us. After you hear what we have to say, I think you'll agree that discretion is important to the safety of us all. Everyone knows the country is going through a real economic crisis brought on by the Chinese crushing the world-wide oil industry. Yes, I know the press would have you ignore what they did and want you to believe it is all because of those big-money corporations and wealthy people not paying their share. Based on my conversations with some finance people I trust a whole lot more than the press, and some inside information from sources I can't discuss, we know that when the Chinese stopped buying oil on the world market it literally screwed the entire petroleum industry and everyone else affected by it. Think of every company that is affected by petroleum and it includes almost all of them. Add to that, the President, in one year, has already brought the national debt to twenty-seven trillion, so things are really looking tough. Truth be told, we're in the middle of a full-scale depression."

Whatever optimism the crowd had before Mike began to speak had disappeared.

"Now for some good news," Mike said boldly. "In our neighborhood and throughout this county, I believe we have everything we need to get by and make it through this crisis. It won't be easy, but with the kind of people we have right here, we will, as Larry the Cable Guy says, 'get 'er done."

In just two sentences, almost everyone began to feed on Mike's energy and enthusiasm. "Now, who here agrees that we can get through this together?"

The crowd broke out into a cheer, with the muffled sound of gloved hands clapping and whistles adding their screech to the positive roar.

Everyone began to calm down a little and Mike held up his hands for quiet. "One thing I learned as a kid, and it has recently been reinforced by some very competent friends, is that nothing can be accomplished long-term without a plan. I have such a plan, and its well on its way. But before I get into the meat and potatoes of it, let me introduce a couple of people to you."

It seemed like everyone began talking at once.

Mike spoke softly into the microphone causing everyone to stop talking, as if there were a magic quality to his voice. "I think most everyone already knows Fred Callahan here. Most of you already know Fred is the Police Chief in Cronin and he's come by some important information." Mike handed the microphone over to Fred.

Fred looked out over the crowd and liked what he saw. Some fear was present, but with the majority there were looks of determination. Fred said, "Are there any of you here that don't have enough food and necessities to get by for at least two weeks?"

A hand went up in back briefly before being lowered. "Who was that in the back?" Almost as soon as he asked the question, the space where the hand had been raised was empty.

"Good. Now, for those who don't know, in addition to being Police Chief in Cronin, I'm on the Governor's Emergency Preparedness Task Force. I've learned from several sources that it appears the President will be declaring an emergency sometime very soon, maybe even during her speech this evening."

The crowd began to murmur softly. A moment later someone shouted, "Fred, what exactly does that mean?"

"That's just the thing," Fred said. "Under most situations, a declaration of an emergency would be for a short period of time and would allow for the federal government to send resources to affected states to help their state and local governments deal with the emergency. I'm told this one is different. This President is going to throw out all those procedures and appoint a Regional Governor to administer the states under his or her control. The Department of Homeland Security will be in charge of coordinating those efforts."

Again, someone shouted out from the crowd, "What's the Governor got to say about that?"

"The Governor is in charge of all state resources, but he'll have to defer to the appointed Regional Governor if there's a conflict."

"Awww, come on, Fred," said the questioner. "What does THAT mean?"

Fred stood quietly for a few moments before saying, "I don't know."

The crowd immediately began to show confused looks rapidly turning to deeply troubled ones.

"Hey, folks," said Mike, while stepping up and taking the microphone from Fred. "Just because we don't know what to expect from the unelected federal Regional Governor doesn't mean we don't have a plan to get through this. Let me introduce you to an impressive young lady. For those that don't know her, this here is Linda Sharpe. Until recently, she was First Lieutenant Linda Sharpe of the United States Army and a Green Beret "A" Team leader. She's been gracious enough to help me put together a plan and to get things organized. In fact, that's what she's already been doing with the new security teams who volunteered after our last meeting. Linda? Would you please tell these folks what you recommend for us to do in this situation?"

Linda took up the microphone with confidence and addressed the crowd.

"Thanks for that introduction, Mike. Just so that you know, I recently left the Army where one of my jobs in Special Forces was to go to foreign countries and organize groups and villages to be able to defend themselves. At Mike's request, I will work with you folks to do just that."

From the crowd someone shouted out, "Defend from what?"

Linda seized on the question and said, "Glad you asked. My intention is not to scare you, but the truth is nobody in this country has ever dealt with what is probably going to happen in the next few months. When an economy collapses, several things happen all at once. Things you have come to rely on suddenly are unavailable. How many people here are ready for the electricity to go out for an extended period of time? How will you do if the grocery stores suddenly have no food and the drug stores close?"

From up near the front, a man shouted, "I've got to go buy some food!" With that he turned to run away from the shelter.

"STOP!" Linda used her command voice and it had the desired effect.

"Mike said he had a plan and he does. The first item on that list is to avoid panic. Everyone here will have time to get what they need, but it's important that each of you has an individual plan to determine what, in fact, are your needs."

"None of that is going to happen!" The statement was made by Kerry DuBois from the back of the crowd. Several others also expressed their doubts.

Linda zeroed in on Kerry and asked, "And what is your name, sir?"

Kerry began to walk away, feeling he had sewn the necessary seeds of doubt when he found himself surrounded by four members of Linda's security team.

One security team member said, "This is Kerry DuBois. Come on, Kerry. Don't you want folks to know it's you that doesn't think the lady knows what she's talkin' about?" Everyone in the crowd parted as Kerry was politely, but firmly escorted up to the front.

Linda looked at Kerry with a penetrating stare. "You have some experience with economic crises, Mr. DuBois?"

"Young lady," said Kerry carefully, "I've been in state government for many years, and the Regional Governor and Homeland Security will take care of everyone!"

"Everyone? Is that what you said?" Linda asked the question softly in a voice that just happened to carry to all.

"Yeah, sure." Kerry was completely out of his element talking to this beautiful, young woman. "I mean, er, yeah, everyone that does what they're told! Maybe not hoarders and the rich that got us in this situation in the first place. I, uh, everyone should give up their fair share!" Kerry almost spit out the last sentence.

Linda continued to stare at him without saying a word. With a hand motion, she indicated the security team should release his arms. Kerry almost fell to the ground before gathering himself.

"You better watch yourself, young lady," Kerry was finally collecting himself enough to respond. "People like you are the problem." He seemed to realize everyone was looking at him with disgust. He tried, without success, to regain a little of his pride as he stooped his shoulders and slunk away from the shelter.

Linda watched patiently as Kerry walk from sight. She turned off the microphone and asked in a slightly above-normal voice, "Can everyone hear me? In the back there?" Several in the back of the crowd nodded affirmatively, Linda continued, "Let me be clear. The federal government will be more concerned with taking from you than giving to you. I've got some handouts that list the most important things for you to acquire as soon as possible. One thing you'll notice is that everything on the list is something you will need eventually anyway, so it won't go to waste. What I'm going to talk about for the next few minutes is to prepare you for what is likely to come. Not definitely, just likely. I've seen this happen all over the world, so think of it as being better safe than sorry. For those that don't have any space left on your credit cards, see Mike after this meeting."

Linda spent the next twenty minutes describing what should be done in the event of a societal collapse. She suggested those that could might make a run into town that evening and get every item on the list from the all-night stores. There were also clipboards for signing up to be on all the different committees. Linda was astounded to see that almost all of the committee sheets were filled by the time everyone left.

"Mike," Linda said as the last neighbor walked toward his garage before heading to the local Wal-Mart, "when you told me there would not be much problem getting participation for the committees, I have to admit I didn't believe you. How did you know?"

Mike smiled as his sigh came out of his mouth like fog in the cold, night air. "I know these folks, and with all the craziness that's been going on, I think almost everyone is thankful to be living in this community, among these people. You missed the Christmas tree lighting and meal afterward. It started way back last summer when me and some others began walking around the neighborhood and just talked to and listened to folks. So, in many ways, they've been preparing for a while now. Another thing, in times like this, I think most people just want to believe someone can lead them through the hard times. You being up there showing them what needs to be done, with confidence, made them want to jump in and help. Too many people, especially among the liberal elite, think we Americans are lazy and soft. Can't vouch for those in New York or Los Angeles, but what I know of people in Kentucky is that when things get tough, they can do what needs to be done. Hell, Linda. I'd follow you into battle anywhere. You've walked the walk to be able to talk the talk. Sean's a very lucky guy."

Linda looked a little pensive before saying, "I'm just glad nobody asked why I was here. At least a few probably know Sean is back and that I'm with him, but I certainly didn't want to announce it. And by the way, just so that you know, these folks are so cooperative because they know and trust you, Mister. They don't know me, yet, or at least not most of them. But, they do know you. That seems to be enough."

Looking at Mike, Linda said, "This not your typical neighborhood."

Mike blushed under his knit cap and looked at his feet for a moment before deciding to change the subject. "The best part of this evening," Mike said with a chuckle, "was the bumbling mess you made out of Kerry. That was worth the price of admission."

Mike's smile was short-lived when Linda said, "Unfortunately, now Kerry, and by extension Coyote Collins, will know the neighborhood won't be easy to pillage. That's a double edged sword. They may hesitate to send out their thugs, but when they do, they'll come in force."

The whole concept of what Linda said gave Mike a very restless night.

CHAPTER 33
THE NEW YEAR - PLUS THIRTEEN DAYS

Outside of Cronin, Kentucky
2130 Hours EST

After talking with Mike following the neighborhood meeting, Peter Worthington and his wife, Liz, walked through the woods on the path toward their own home when suddenly Peter grabbed Liz's arm and motioned for silence. Peering through the leafless trees Peter could just make out a small vehicle sitting in their driveway with the engine running. No lights were visible on the vehicle and the windows were beginning to fog up. Peter indicated Liz should wait behind a large tree trunk while he carefully approached the vehicle. He had removed his gloves and drawn his favorite .45 caliber automatic pistol. It felt very cold in his hands, but reassuring.

Peter approached the vehicle from the rear, he saw that the driver's window was rolled down a full inch. Through the window he could hear a woman talking to someone else in the car. Waiting patiently for a full two minutes, he was rewarded by finally recognizing one of the voices in the car.

"All right, young lady, what are you doing sneaking up to my house at this late hour?"

Peter used his command voice and still kept his pistol drawn, although it was now hanging by his side. From inside, he could hear a sharp intake of breath from more than one person.

"Uncle Peter!" The driver's door popped open and Lisa spilled out to give Peter a bear hug, made more than a bit awkward since Peter's pistol was trapped in between them. At the sounds of Lisa's voice, Liz moved quickly from her position behind the large tree trunk and came over to greet Lisa.

"Lisa!" Liz said loudly, "why are you sitting out here in the dark?"

Lisa's reaction was not what either Peter or Liz expected. Dropping her voice to just above a whisper, Lisa said, "Can we talk about it inside? Also, Uncle Peter, can I put my car into a garage or somewhere out of sight?"

Both Peter and Liz were mystified, but caught up quickly.

Peter said, "Okay." He drug out the word for a few seconds and then asked, "Are you going to be staying with us for a while?"

When Lisa nodded, he said, "Then why don't you drive into the attached garage right after Liz backs out, and we'll get everything sorted out. Is that all right?"

"Yes, thank you so much," said Lisa quietly. Peter was rewarded with another quick hug before she hopped into her car. Liz walked to the garage, raised the door and backed out her full sized SUV, leaving a nice big space for Lisa's car.

Both Peter and Liz stood by the door into the house as Lisa and a beautiful Asian girl exited the vehicle. Lisa walked to the girl and took her gently by the arm before leading her up the five stairs and into the house. From there, Liz took charge.

Because of Lisa's earlier warning tone of voice, Liz asked both girls to find the powder room and then get settled in the family room while she made some hot cocoa. Lisa and her friend mumbled their thanks and walked quickly to the restroom where Lisa waited while Su used the facilities. Both girls were almost ready to pop after their long drive. Peter made himself useful by putting together a small tray of snacks while Liz fixed the cocoa.

Finally, everyone was settled around the unlit fire pit in the overstuffed couch and chairs. Each held a mug of hot cocoa. The indirect lighting in the room gave just enough soft glow to see lots of wood, stone, and a few large animal heads hanging from the walls.

After a satisfied sigh of appreciation for the cocoa, Peter cleared his throat and said, "In the vernacular of today's youth, 'Sup?'"

Lisa giggled and Su smiled hesitantly. Lisa said, "Uncle Peter, Dad left a note for me last night before ordering us to load up and head here at 7:00 a.m. We destroyed it," she said while glancing conspiratorially at Su, "but it said, 'Lisa, Sweetheart.'" Lisa then recited the rest of her father's note.

After thinking about it for a few moments, Peter said, "Well, that certainly clears up all of my questions." Sarcasm dripped from his voice. "Oh, and are you going to introduce us to your friend, Lisa?"

"Oh, I'm sorry! This is Suzie. And let me apologize in advance, because I won't be able to answer most of your questions."

"Dear Lord, my dear!" Liz's comment was blurted out with more than a little exasperation. "What has your father gotten you into?"

Lisa took a deep breath and then launched into her rehearsed speech. "Suzie is my best friend and she has gotten wrapped up in the stuff that Dad told me not to talk about. Being my best friend means I trust her with anything. Except for my promise to Dad, I'd be telling you both everything, so hopefully he and Mom will get here soon and do that for me. Dad asked me to come here and insure that no one, and I mean no one, outside of this house, is aware that we are here. It is literally a life and death situation. He also said I should tell you that we should treat this as though the Russians, Chinese, FBI, CIA, NSA, space aliens, zombies and everyone else in the universe is looking for us and we must NOT be found. He knew he could trust you, Uncle Peter and asks that you help keep us safe. He also told me to assure you that none of this is illegal or wrong in any way. It involves the craziness going on in Washington and the rest of the world."

Lisa let what she had just said sink in a little before asking, "Will you help us? Please?" Tears of fear and stress began to drip down her cheeks.

Peter's response was immediate and heartfelt. "Of course, my dear. Your vouching for Suzie is good enough for us and let me assure you both, you are as safe here as you could be anywhere in the country. In fact, I'm sorry now that I drew my pistol on you, but damn it, I couldn't imagine why anyone would sit in a running car outside of my house with no lights on!"

Turning toward his wife, Peter asked, "Dear?" Liz again jumped right in and asked, "Would I be correct that you have been traveling constantly for at least the whole day? I can see you're both exhausted. Why don't you go to your car and get just what you'll need for tonight and set up shop in Junior's old room. There are two beds in the room. We can talk more tomorrow." With that she herded both girls out of the family room and soon had them bedded down in the spare bedroom.

Walking back into the great room Liz sat down across from her husband and softly, but firmly, asked, "Did you know this was coming, Peter?"

He looked his wife in the eyes and said, "No, Sweetie I did not. Hugh had asked me back in the fall if things got really bad, would it be all right for him to send Lisa and her mom here, but there was nothing about it involving bureau business or a Chinese girl. My guess is that this has to do with something else and probably the security of the country. Hugh would never endanger his family or us for something less." Peter motioned Liz to come over to his chair, where she plopped down into his lap. "Do you know how much I love you?"

"Of course I do."

"This time, my love, you know as much as I do about this. What I do know is that Hugh is neither melodramatic nor foolish, so if he sent the girls here that covertly, he had to. It also sounded like he and his bride will need to disappear themselves. I'm going to take him at his word and help the girls stay off the radar. Nobody needs to know they're here. Can you help me with that?"

"I have some ideas," Liz said softly.

. . .

The White House
2330 Hours EST

Once again, Susan Cassel found herself slipping out of the President's bedroom late at night while wondering what Marc Baxter thought about her trysts. She had no illusions that Marc didn't know. After all, she would be sliding into his bed within the next half hour in the vain hope to grab a few hours of sleep before returning to the pressure cooker again in the morning. Considering what she had just learned, it was a wonder that she could even sit down.

Susan had expected the President to be wound tight with stress when she appeared as instructed ninety minutes ago. Instead Katherine was sitting at her makeup table in a sheer gown sipping on a glass of wine when Susan entered. She had suggested Susan pour herself a glass, which turned out to be an incredible vintage of Chardonnay.

"Susan, dear, why don't you get comfortable?" Katherine had said after Susan had poured the wine and refilled hers. "Those straps must be about to cut into your shoulders by now."

Although Katherine was not flat chested, she was not nearly as busty as Susan. Katherine seemed to have somewhat of an infatuation with what she frequently called Susan's perfect breasts.

From past experience, Susan knew Katherine preferred that she remove everything before putting her blouse back on – unbuttoned of course. As Susan crossed the room toward Katherine, she regretted having worn a blouse that stopped just above her waist that day. It clearly showed where she had gone a bit wild with her razor down below, leaving only soft skin in its wake. Katherine's eyes seemed to focus directly on her crotch as she approached. Over the next several minutes, Susan was reminded of the groping she had received from her boyfriend in college. She already knew Katherine was incapable of gentle intimate subtleties. She was more into taking what she wanted by force. Although reluctant, Susan did not need to be taken by force as she still believed anything she could do to relieve Katherine's stress was, well, her patriotic duty. This evening she went above and beyond the call of duty.

Marc was awake and reading when Susan reached his apartment. All he did was smile when Susan walked into his bathroom and turned on the shower. She had never told him directly that she was sexually involved with the President, but he did have a nose for such things. A few minutes later, she came out of the bathroom wearing one of his work button-down shirts and crawled into bed, wet hair and all.

Susan looked at him with a troubled smile and asked, "Do you know what she's going to do tomorrow?"

Marc tried to look innocent, but failed miserably.

"You *do* know, don't you?" Susan's accusation was strong and surprised.

"Honey, whatever I know I've been threatened with not just removal of gonads, but that I'll literally permanently disappear if I tell anyone. Can you please let me leave it at that?"

"Oh, dear God. Well, I can believe Burt would say something like that. How about being a good guy and just listening? Can you do at least that?"

Marc grabbed her face and planted a gentle kiss on her forehead. "Yes, I can."

For the next twenty minutes, Susan poured out all of her fears and frustrations concerning Katherine's plans to declare the emergency. "I think she's already thinking that the Constitution no longer applies and that she'll be able to rule with absolute fiat. God, Marc. I'm scared to death."

Marc held her in his arms and whispered, "Me, too."

CHAPTER 34
THE NEW YEAR - PLUS FOURTEEN DAYS

The Mountains of Southeastern Afghanistan
0700 Hours Local Time

Ahmed met Hadi over a small campfire as both sipped on a cup of bitter tea. Although they could both see the clear winter sky up through the rocks above their heads, their campfire would only be visible to the devil Americans if they were to fly directly over the two meter wide and eight meter deep crack in the ground that made up the ravine.

"Hadi?" Ahmed asked, "What do you think about the two that came with Ali al-Hadiz yesterday?" Ahmed had barely had enough time to formally greet the three men before being called away for a briefing.

"At first I was concerned," Hadi began, "but both of his scientists seemed to be even more focused on doing the work of Allah than Ali himself. When Ali was here before, I spoke with him at length and am impressed with his devotion."

"Good," Ahmed said thoughtfully. "I will speak to them over tea later this morning, but expect that you can take them to the laboratory cave to let them begin setting up." As an afterthought Ahmed continued, "Did you have people assigned in Kabul to follow the Infidel Cho?"

"Yes, great leader." Hadi said this while bowing his head, but his voice was full of pride at having anticipated Ahmed's wishes.

"Three of our more dependable men grew up just outside of Kabul and know the city well. They will follow Cho as well as it can be done without being observed."

"Good," Ahmed said softly. "Also send them instructions to identify every hotel or other building the Infidel visits or passes that might be used to prepare for the great day. I want to know where they will plan to meet our martyrs. In this they cannot fail. Do you understand?"

"Completely, great leader."

"Also," Ahmed continued, "send an additional twenty men to Kabul and have them set themselves up to observe the logical choke points leading to and from the airport. If they need more men to do this, send whatever number they need even if it is everyone but the martyrs themselves."

"It will be done." Hadi hurried away to send the additional twenty men.

Ahmed then began to give thought on how best to test Ali's two friends to ensure they would prove to be entirely faithful to the cause.

. . .

Looking into the eyes of Ali and his two friends, Ahmed liked what he saw. A fire burned in all three. Also, they each had an advanced degree at a university in the land of the Great Satan-America. It was fitting that they should be trained there in skills that would lead directly to that country's downfall.

"Ali," Ahmed said softly, "you have explained that they will be working on a project that will do more to kill Infidels than anything else has throughout the ages?"

Ali nodded and smiled, "I have, Ahmed, without telling them too much. They have heard such claims before and have had their hopes crushed."

Ali glanced at each of his two assistants and found them glaring their anger at past lies, but showed fervent hopes for what they were told by Ali.

After a deep breath, Ahmed said, "None of you will leave here for at least a year. After I tell you how we are to do what no others have ever done, you cannot leave. Your possessions are being searched. There must be no chance you can communicate what I am about to tell you to anyone outside of this camp."

They each first showed alarm and then quickly quelled resentment.

Ahmed continued, "Now, you will each place your cell phones and anything else that can transmit a signal in this cloth bag. They will be destroyed. If you should need another, it will be provided for you."

Under Ahmed's intense glare, each man took out his cell phone to place in the bag. Ali and one assistant also pulled out tablet computers and did the same thing.

"Ahmed," Ali said quietly, "we will need the tablets and our laptop computers to accomplish the goals you have set."

Nodding twice, Ahmed said, "I have brought a man from Kabul that will respond to your requests for information and other things that you need from your equipment. He is very good with such things and will ensure that nothing is contained in the request that should not be. If he does find anything in your equipment that should not be there, you may find yourself meeting Allah in a very painful way. Understand?"

Each of the three men bowed and loudly proclaimed their faithfulness to both Allah and to Ahmed, as His instrument.

• • •

Beijing, China
1230 Hours Local Time

General Secretary Song walked calmly toward his office, in full view of several members of his staff. Although inside he felt extremely uncomfortable, it was important to appear that he was acting normally. Once inside his office behind a closed door, he immediately loosened his necktie and tall dress-shirt collar to reveal a thin red line on his neck where the bullet wound had been glued together. The slacks of his suit covered the sutures on his leg and some judiciously applied makeup covered up the discoloration on his hands and one cheek.

Wong had followed him into his office to help with the tie and collar. "General Secretary, Lao has requested an audience as soon as possible. I have scheduled him for thirty minutes from now, if that is convenient?"

"Wong, do you know the subject matter of his visit?" Song knew Lao could and, in fact, should have news on a number of areas of interest for him.

"No, General Secretary. However, Japanese and Australian news agencies are reporting that an American destroyer was struck overnight by a two hundred twenty two meter[19] container ship. Early reports indicate the destroyer may have been at a full stop in the ocean, off the coast of Australia."

Song waited for any additional information about the collision, but Wong remained silent. After a moment, he looked at his desk, Song asked Wong, "Those are the most recent economic reports?"

"Yes, General Secretary. There are also reports from Lao's people and your own sources regarding the growing unrest among the collective farms in the interior because of the necessary cuts in their food allotments. Government officials have disappeared, when they were not accompanied by armed police."

With a sigh, Song asked, "Is that all of the bad news?"

"Unfortunately not," said Wong, while bowing his head. "Real inflation has risen over seventy-five percent and Muslim insurgents have killed and beheaded over twenty police officers in the far Western provinces. Local officials are screaming for a PLA response to these atrocities."

"Enough, for now, Wong. Advise me when Lao arrives." Wong bowed, left the room and closed the door.

Twenty five minutes later Song's desk phone rang and Wong announced the arrival of Lao. Song had taken a strong, narcotic pain-killer twenty minutes earlier and was already feeling better, although slightly groggy and sleepy.

Lao's entry had all of the normal formality, except he still walked with a pronounced limp. He approached Song's desk, bowed and remained still, with his head down, waiting to be recognized.

In a soft and slightly airy voice, Song invited Lao to sit in the chair across from his desk and engaged Lao with the usual pleasantries. Once these formalities were completed, Song did not ask his usual question regarding when the renegade province of Formosa (Taiwan) would be returned to China. Instead he asked, "You have heard about the American destroyer being struck by a container ship?"

Lao's normal non-committal expression was not replaced by a smile, as Song expected. Instead, a combination of annoyance and outright anger showed clearly.

"Yes, General Secretary. I am quite aware of this incident. In fact, my team has arrested the Captain of the covert submarine on charges of treason. After the destroyer had floated motionless for about fifteen minutes, the Captain

---

[19] 222 meters equals 730 feet.

informed my team leader, 'Watch this.' When the team leader looked through the periscope he could see a brightly lit container ship bear down on the destroyer. It then struck the destroyer causing significant damage and probably, loss of life."

Song looked in wonder at Lao and his anger. "You believe the submarine Captain calculated the perfect moment to strike the destroyer so that it would be motionless, directly in the path of the container ship?"

"Yes, General Secretary, I do."

Looking at Lao carefully, Song said, "You don't believe the Captain should be commended on making such careful calculations that allowed this to happen?"

"General Secretary," Lao said, taking a deep, calming breath. "If the test of White Lilly had happened as planned, the American destroyer would have quietly sat out in the ocean until their crew managed to restart the engines without the electronics that had been burned out by our EMP. They were without communications, and generally without all electrical power on the destroyer. They would have limped back to Australia where all would have been kept quiet as they frantically tried to discover what had happened. Instead, now the world knows they were struck by a slow-moving container ship. Your instruction to insure that this test was done covertly has failed miserably."

Song waited for several moments before saying, "Lao, this may very well work to our advantage. The Americans will not want to admit that their destroyer could be struck dead in the water, with no mark to indicate how it was done. In fact, they will probably conduct an investigation and publically announce the crew was derelict in their duties, just to hide this new vulnerability. The U.S. Navy will also suffer a very public embarrassment. At the same time the Fontaine administration will have one more reason to ignore their mutual defense treaty with our wayward Province. Yes, this is good news. Now, arrange for me to meet this amazing submarine Captain and I will present him with the second highest covert services award."

Lao had not risen to head the MSS by being mentally slow. He quickly determined that Song was probably correct and that, despite stepping outside of his strict orders, the Captain had, indeed, provided China with a unique opportunity. In reality, what he had accomplished was truly amazing. Unfortunately, Lao was not able to capture those positive feelings for very long.

Song said, "Lao, why cannot your people handle the insurgency in the West by the Muslims?"

For the next 90 minutes both men discussed the many problems facing China including the massive economic fall due to the American's temporary trade freeze. Muslim attacks in the West, collective farm uprisings and minor riots occurring in cities throughout China, at least those cities away from the coast. The sporadic unofficial strikes being held by workers whose pay and hours had been dramatically cut by the economic downturn. The whole economy was spiraling upward. The country was becoming unstable. The instability and insurgency justified a mobilization of the rest of the reserves within the PLA, which had already been occurring. Only a small percentage of these reserves would be used to quell the insurgency; however most would be readied for the invasion of Formosa.

"General Secretary," Lao said softly, as the strategy session began to wind down, you're aware of the loss of a member of the Politburo?" At Song's silent nod, Lao continued, "He was killed by a prostitute, who used poison in his drink. He somehow managed to strangle the girl before he died. Very sad."

Lao's face remained neutral as he reported this event. Song had no response.

CHAPTER 35
THE NEW YEAR - PLUS FOURTEEN DAYS

The White House
1900 Hours EST

The conference room in the White House was jammed with Cabinet members and staff. Burt Combs ensured all of the Cabinet members located in Washington, D.C. attended by promising them advance details of the impending wage and price freeze the President was about to unveil, along with other, unspecified actions. Top staff members were present as ordered. There was a blend of emotions, including a buzz of cautious excitement in the room, which was muted by an unexplained uneasiness.

The Secret Service had set up equipment at the door that detected any electronic devices. Never before had such measures been taken. Everyone had to pass through the scrutiny as well as declare whether they carried any electronic devices. Flaunting the rules had been commonplace over the past year of this administration. Two Cabinet members were relieved of their cell phones, despite strenuous objections. Press Secretary Towanda Jefferson had been one of them. She had only closed her mouth when informed by Burt that she would leave her phone and enter or spend the evening in the Secret Service lock-up. Opening her mouth to fire off a new protest, Towanda saw Burt raise his hand toward a uniformed officer. With a look that would have soured milk, she shut her mouth, gave up her cell phone and stomped into the conference room.

Marc Baxter had come into the room thirty minutes early to miss the last-minute rush. He left what had become his normal chair at the main table open for Towanda and, instead, took a seat against the wall. The look on his face was pale. All who asked were told he had eaten something that didn't agree with him.

At 8:35 p.m. Katherine came into the conference room using a full ceremonial entrance, which included being announced and everyone standing as she walked in, while "Hail to the Chief" played in the background. This was more appropriate when the cameras were rolling for an address to the press, but she chose to do so with her Cabinet and staff. She walked quietly up to the podium set up at one end of the table. A neutral expression on her face ineffectively covered her growing excitement. Katherine blew on a small microphone at the podium. She had placed notes on the podium, but did not look down to read.

Katherine didn't begin with thanks, or any of the other normal words spoken to an august group summoned for something momentous. Instead, she began in a soft, dreamy voice, "Every President must make decisions that will affect her country and even the world. The world faces crises that demand firm control in order to prevent everything from falling into chaos. At this time only a firm hand will prevent total collapse of what we have all come to depend on."

Marc could feel the people present hanging on every word. Everyone could tell they were witnessing something that was momentous. None seemed to notice Katherine's continued referral to the world, instead of just the United States. Having far more knowledge of what was to come than most, Marc closed his eyes and forced himself to take deep breaths as one tear leaked from his left eye. Unlike the slowly building excitement growing within many in the room, Marc could almost feel the cry rise up from the Founding Fathers, protesting the seizure of power from the people into the hands of one.

Katherine continued, "Twenty minutes ago, I signed a Declaration of Emergency that not only invokes Presidential Executive Order 13603, but due to the looming economic crisis, rioting in our cities, and even the threat of war with China, the gridlock caused by Congress and those that I'll call haters, it grants authority for me to do what I must to save us all. The People cannot do for themselves, so it has become necessary for their government to do for them. In order to do that, we must have the tools. I have also signed a highly classified Presidential Executive Order granting this administration those tools. Both PEO's will be in effect for the duration of this crisis. Others will be issued as needed to meet the challenges that we face."

At the mention of possible war with China, a collective gasp could be heard. Katherine had received a briefing from CIA Director Brad Pittson earlier in the day that confirmed what Eli had told her about China's intention to invade

Taiwan. Pittson had also brought along the Secretary of the Navy, who had briefed her concerning the Navy destroyer that had been struck by the container ship off the coast of Australia. They had no explanation for the ship going dead in the water, however the potential for some type of new, and more powerful EMP weapon was discussed. Burt, Susan, Pittson and the Secretary of the Navy were not surprised.

"Burt, will you please pass out the information packet?" Katherine had finally looked down at her notes to see that instruction highlighted with a yellow star. "The entire contents of the packet is classified TOP SECRET, except for the first PEO. In addition to the PEO's they contain instructions for each Cabinet member and staff manager for what needs to be done going forward. I will not tolerate any leaks of this information, understand?" Katherine glared at all of those in the room. "Now, at this time, I will need to inform several members of Congress and others. Then I will go before the people of the World at 9 o'clock. I expect each of you to go through your packet, here in this room, over the next hour." With that statement, Katherine took up her notes and walked from the room.

Towanda was the first to blurt out, "What the fuck is that supposed to mean? We can't leave here? That's bullshit. I'm out of here." She got up and began walking to the door before being stopped by the Chief of Staff.

"Towanda," Burt said in a commanding voice that could be heard clearly throughout the conference room. "The President was quite specific. There will be no leaks and anyone that feels the need to leave will forfeit their security clearance and will be taken out of this room by the Secret Service to be out processed from government employment. Now, come on people, it's only for about an hour. Now is a very good time to go through your packets and begin deciding how you will implement those instructions. I'll be scheduling time to answer questions tomorrow, after everyone has had a chance to digest our new marching orders. The first thing you will notice is that most of your jobs will suddenly become easier, without so many of the roadblocks that existed before this evening. The opposing party in Congress will no longer be a problem."

Brad Pittson sat quietly in his chair, but with a glare at Burt that should have frightened him. NSA Director Donald Clayburn said, "Burt, really? She's really locking us in this room?"

"General, I'm just doing what I'm told." This was the first time Burt showed any of his own misgivings about Katherine's actions. "I also checked with the lawyers that drew up the Declaration, who are also sequestered, by the way, and they tell me that when she signed these PEO's, she assumed the power to do just about anything, for the duration of the emergency. The only body with the authority to challenge her is the Supreme Court and she's calling each of the four Justices likely to support her as we speak. Let's give her a chance to do what's best for the country, shall we?"

"Who else is she calling, Burt?" Clayburn's voice had dropped an octave and had added a gravelling tone that underlined the dangerous line that was being drawn.

"Fifteen in all, General. They include the four Justices I just mentioned, the House and Senate leadership, and the military leadership, beginning with the SECDEF Hathaway, the FBI Director and those Cabinet members not able to be here now."

Clayburn asked, "And, what, exactly are they being told?"

"General," said Burt with hesitation. "I don't know. The President tore up the script I had prepared for each of them."

The room fell almost quiet for the next ten minutes as everyone read through the packets. Being speed-readers and used to going through voluminous amounts of paperwork, most were able to get through the material quickly. Burt heard several conversations break out in soft voices, with none of them being happy.

Pittson finally asked Burt, conversationally, "Where do you stand on all of this Burt?" The question brought instant silence as everyone strained to hear Burt's response.

"Brad," Burt said before looking around the room at everyone present, "and everyone else, I swore an oath to this President. I believe in that oath and so long as she is working to fulfill her own oath of office, she will have my unwavering support. I expect nothing less from everyone in this administration. These are very tough and dangerous times. We elected her and it's now time to show the trust we placed when we cast our vote."

Most of the talk, within small, informal groups, then turned to how each part of the administration was going to most effectively use their newly acquired authority.

Marc sat quietly, rebuffing any attempts others made to get his take on events. His secretary had strict orders to contact him, via the Secret Service protection detail, if there were any issues with getting the President on TV. The

White House technical staff was setting up TV camera feeds from the Oval Office for her address. They too, could contact Marc if there were any problems. All staff working outside of the conference room was mystified as to why the administration leadership was not present for the President's address.

. . .

FBI Headquarters
Washington, D.C.
2052 Hours EST

Director Kidd at FBI headquarters stared at his secure phone, feeling stunned. The President had just finished informing him of her having signed a Declaration of Emergency that activated PEO 13603 and another, classified PEO that would be available to him on the TOP SECRET system by the following morning. Her reasons for the Declaration would be provided to the country, via all major television networks, in her address at 9:00 p.m. The call lasted less than one minute. He could expect a visit from the Attorney General in the morning with further instructions. She then broke the connection.

The Director turned on the television to await the President's address. He was feeling sick to his stomach. After her twelve minute address to the nation, he did not feel any better.

CHAPTER 36
THE NEW YEAR - PLUS FOURTEEN DAYS

The White House
2215 Hours EST

Susan brought the President a glass with high-quality tequila on the rocks in the President's sitting room outside of her bedroom. Unlike the evening before, both were fully dressed. Katherine was smiling broadly and appeared euphoric. For the past twenty minutes, Katherine had rambled on about all of the critically necessary things that would be accomplished, now that the Declaration had been signed.

Holding up her glass to Susan Katherine said, "A toast! To now having the power to do what needs to be done."

Susan clinked her glass into Katherine's and took a tentative sip of the drink. Her attempt to smile and project a celebratory mood, but was not successful.

"All right, my dear," Katherine said, "out with it. Why are you such a damned sour puss?"

"Madam President," Susan started.

"I've told you, my dear, call me Katherine when we're alone. Here, let me hear you say it." She gave the order to Susan with quite a bit of annoyance, although it was apparent she relished watching Susan follow her orders.

"Katherine. Yes, well, you know I am not comfortable calling you by your first name."

Katherine began to chuckle. "After where you've been, my dear, you have earned the right and I demand you recognize the intimacy we share."

Softening her tone a little, Katherine continued, "Besides, how can you be so formal in the room where you've given me so many orgasms? You know, after a rough start, you've really improved your technique. Of course, I'm a pretty good teacher." Katherine laughed softly at the whole conversation. "Now out with it. Don't you relish the chance to help me fix all those things that need our special touch?"

Susan was in a quandary. She could not tell Katherine how much it terrified her to see the President seize the reigns of a dictator. There simply was no right answer to Katherine's question and it was apparent she would keep probing until she received an answer she would accept.

Suddenly, inspiration struck. "Katherine, many of the things that need to be done will outrage some small but dangerous segments of our population. Some may even perceive that you are in some way violating the Constitution. Of course, the Supreme Court will settle that quickly, but some will feel that violence is the only answer. I'm afraid that even the Secret Service might not be able to protect you from assassins, especially if the unrest in the country continues or gets worse."

Katherine reacted immediately, by losing the happy face and showing her flashing anger. "Those cretins better not try and come for me. By God I'll have them all strung up and shot!" Her eyes burned with fire as she mentally contemplated several people jerking from the hangman's noose while bullets riddled their bodies.

Susan felt bad about driving Katherine into this mood, but it was effective in avoiding her own interrogation.

"In fact," Katherine began a new thought out loud, "one of the first things to do is to demand that all guns be turned into the Department of Homeland Security. No guns, no threats. Dear one, tomorrow, have an appropriate declaration drawn up."

"Yes, Madam President, only should we wait to sign the order until Homeland has a system in place to collect them?"

Katherine poured herself tequila on the rocks before answering, "Hmmm, yes, that makes sense. Have the Attorney General (AG) come to my office tomorrow afternoon. I'll need to goose him more than a little to get it done quickly. Oh, and speaking of something quickly, after last evening, I think it's time for you to experience something that is not done quickly. Maybe you should unlock my private trunk and retrieve the new item in the pink plastic bag. It's high time you got some appreciation for everything you do for me."

169

Katherine kept a private, steel trunk, padlocked with a lock that was supposed to be impervious to picking. Inside were certain personal items that no one, but Susan, could access.

Susan knew it was going to be another very short night of sleep for her. The newfound power was obviously a powerful aphrodisiac for the President.

• • •

Washington, D.C.
2330 Hours EST

Marc dragged into his apartment after walking the four blocks home from the White House. He was exhausted to the point he no longer cared what Katherine had done and would do, only numb to it all. All press inquiries had been put off until the scheduled press conference late the following morning. He didn't even want to think about the profanity-laced tongue lashing he had received from Towanda when she discovered that he had known of the announcement and had not told her. He had never heard so many uses for the phrase, "Dickless, white boy," and hoped to never have it repeated again. The last time she used it was when he had tried to refer her to the Chief of Staff, who had ordered the secrecy. It was obvious that she was afraid of Burt and believed his threat to have her removed and detained. Marc, on the other hand, had no such power, so he became her verbal whipping boy.

Don Stetson had been jubilant about Katherine's announcement, foreseeing the possible eradication of privately owned firearms in the United States. He kept saying that if he could do this one thing, his daughter's spirit might finally rest in peace.

Marc threw his winter coat toward the chair in the corner and walked into his small, efficiency kitchen. He knew the only thing he had to eat in the place was a jar of peanut butter and part of a sleeve of crackers. Susan complained about his Spartan existence and lack of groceries on many occasions. Of course, it didn't bother her enough to go to buy groceries herself. On the counter was an unopened bottle of very good bourbon. He had been saving it for a special occasion. After giving it minimal thought, tonight warranted not celebration, but the temporary forgetfulness only alcohol could bring him would have to do.

When Susan walked in an hour and a half later, she found him asleep on the couch with his glass spilled onto the carpet beside the coffee table. She didn't even shower before falling into bed. Despite being nearly as tired as she could ever recall, sleep did not come easily.

CHAPTER 37
THE NEW YEAR - PLUS FIFTEEN DAYS

FBI Headquarters
Washington, DC
1130 Hours EST

FBI Director, W. Allen Kidd, sat at his desk looking with near disbelief at the Presidential Order that had been hand-delivered to him, by the Attorney General, ten minutes earlier. The Order directed him to immediately seal all records involving the investigation of Walter Fontaine pursuant to PDD 13603 and the new, highly classified PEO that had not yet been numbered. Ten minutes after delivering the new PDD, the AG left his office. He was not a happy man.

The AG was technically the boss of the FBI Director, in the hierarchy of the Executive Branch. The AG had demanded all the now sealed Fontaine investigation documents be delivered to his office within forty-eight hours. In addition, he demanded the Director identify everyone involved in the investigation and to have their personnel files delivered to his office at the same time. The Director had refused the second order, with the admonition that should such a blatantly illegal demand happen again, he would personally stand before the press cameras and provide to them evidence of Walter's activities. Barring the implementation of that demand, he would seal and sit on the Walter Fontaine investigation at the order of the President.

Allen was further shaken when the AG's response had been to ask about how several of Allen's family members were doing, by name. His immediate response was to instruct his security detail to remove the AG from his office and the building. His follow-up call to the President went unanswered.

Two hours later twenty men and women of the Director's protection detail sat or stood in his office while Allen paced in front of the corner windows. The room had just been swept for electronic listening devices and all cell phones left outside. When the last members of his detail hastily arrived, the team leader advised him all were present.

"All right," Allen said with no preamble. "Since you folks have volunteered to lay down your lives for me, I want you to know what you're facing and give each one of you the opportunity to gracefully bow out. Less than three months ago I was informed Walter Fontaine, the First Man, had been meeting and having exotic sex with a well-trained Chinese girl, who was working for the MSS. These meetings were video-taped in living color by the MSS." A few under-their-breath curses could be heard in the room.

"During these sessions, the First Man not only got his rocks off, but he was also skillfully interrogated resulting in the PRC having extremely sensitive, up-to-date and reliable information concerning our country's intentions toward China and throughout the world."

All present waited to hear what Allen intended to do about such an obvious case of espionage. It is in the DNA of every FBI Special Agent to want to see justice done, no matter who committed the crime.

Allen said, "After an extremely covert, but thorough investigation was conducted, the DAD for Espionage and I took compelling evidence to the President. At first she literally laughed at the revelation that her husband was cheating on her, telling us that fact was well known to her. When we provided audio tape recordings of one of the trysts, along with advising her that the whole operation was video-taped by Chinese intelligence, she became understandably angry. No, that is an understatement. Furious would be an understatement. The DAD and I spent the next four hours sitting in chairs outside of her office like misbehaving school boys. When we were called back in, she demanded to know who knew about the investigation, to include the names of all of the agents involved." A look of horror began to appear on several faces in the room.

"When I refused to provide that information to her without a reasonable justification for her need to know, she threw us out of her office. Not before, of course, ordering us to maintain everything at the highest classification level and tell no one else about the investigation."

A muted chorus of, "That Bitch," "What the Hell!" and other expressions of outrage began to be heard throughout the room.

Allen continued over the outraged voices, "This morning…" Everyone quieted down allowing him to continue in a normal voice. "This morning I was visited by the Attorney General. He presented me with a Presidential order, a couple of them, actually, demanding all documents and evidence relating to the investigation of Walter Fontaine be sealed and delivered to the AG's office within forty-eight hours. He then demanded both the names and personnel files of everyone in the FBI who was knowledgeable about this investigation. When I refused and threatened to go to the press, the bastard began to ask me about the health and happiness of several of my family members. That's when a few of you were so kind as to show him out of the building."

Any outrage felt up to this point was minimal in comparison to that felt by every member of the protection detail now. Allen had to shout for quiet.

"You can imagine my first inclination was to make good on my threat to take it all to the press. I still have at least a decent reputation with the press and even both sides of the aisle in Congress. That is a card I do not want to play, if it can be avoided. My primary responsibility is to the Constitution and the people of our country. I believe that with all of the upheaval happening today, a change in leadership, or splashing the First Man's indiscretions in the media would result in nothing good, and would harm the United States greatly. What I do intend to do is send a carefully worded note to the President assuring her that so long as she does not succumb to blackmail by the Chinese, that for the good of the country this matter will remain sealed and she will continue to have my loyalty. I will also mention the veiled threat by her AG has caused me to take steps, should anything 'accidentally happen.' It is my earnest hope these actions will be enough."

"Sir," said head of the detail, "so you believe there is truth in what people say about the Fontaine machine being responsible for the death of over forty people, who could be considered their enemies?"

With a wry smile, Allen said, "Now that's a tough question. The FBI investigates the toughest drug and organized crime groups. Yet, we've only managed to arrest a few politicians, relatively speaking. You all know how we work; we follow the guidelines set out by the Attorney General. In political investigations, if the proverbial "smoking gun"[20] doesn't fall in our laps, the Department of Justice, or at least *this* Department of Justice, won't even allow us to open an investigation. They fear it would appear we were trying to influence elections. We all know that attitude is very one-sided. The public believes that we closely monitor election fraud, when, in fact, we can only investigate allegations after-the-fact. With this Attorney General, do you think there would be any chance at all the Department of Justice would authorize an investigation of the Fontaine Empire?"

Heads shook with either sadness or anger, while many sets of teeth clenched.

With a deep breath, Allen said, "I didn't answer your question, so here is what I personally think. Yes, I think there are those in the Fontaine administration and those who believe they have significant influence over that administration, with the resources and motivation to protect their power base, using whatever means they believe are necessary."

Allen paused to give everyone time to digest the new threat. He said, "My primary concern is that this information will get out and bring down this government at the worst time for all of us. Here's what I am going to do about it. The team who investigated the First Man has already been sent back to their original offices with instructions to remain silent on this. A number of people have been entrusted with a thumb drive containing all relevant evidence and a detailed video statement by me, which will be safely and covertly stored. Should it become necessary, meaning I am no longer able to act freely, they will make sure copies of this information reach Congressional leadership and the Supreme Court.

"I hope it doesn't come to that. These are very difficult times for our country and any President, including this one. She deserves our full loyalty to assist her in meeting these challenges. My oaths command that I give her every benefit of the doubt. By doing so, I realize that it may place each of you in much more danger. That's why I want to offer you the chance to take an immediate reassignment to the office you came from, no questions asked or judgments made by me."

---

[20] Smoking gun refers to nearly incontrovertible evidence

Allen paused and slowly moved his eyes to each person in the room, one at a time. After the team leader gave a simple 'thumbs up' gesture, everyone in the room followed.

Allen bowed his head and with a choked up voice, said, "All right, then. I will leave it to you professionals to determine how best to keep me safe." Looking at his team leader, he said, "Please give me a plan, as soon as possible, to keep my immediate family safe as well. I'm presuming they should take a trip, starting this afternoon, but I can't think of a safe place that isn't known by far too many people."

He felt better when his team leader told him there were several possibilities and choices would be presented to him within the hour. He also knew of some trustworthy people that could both help and keep their mouths shut.

CHAPTER 38
THE NEW YEAR - PLUS TWENTY-FIVE DAYS

Beijing, China
2200 Hours Local Time

General Secretary Song sat in his office waiting for his specially armored Mercedes limousine to arrive. Three identical vehicles along with similarly matching security vehicles made up motorcades for Song's movement. The times of departure varied.

Over the past several days, he moved every two to three hours to one secret location after another. Civil unrest continued to increase across China, particularly in the interior of the country. Song's previously ordered buildup of the PLA, by activation of all reserves, had drawn protests in the United Nations by the United States, Japan and Taiwan. The Chinese Representative to the UN had dismissed the protests by claiming the buildup was an internal matter. The military for the renegade province (Taiwan) had begun to mobilize as well.

When the first decoy convoy left his office parking lot, Song sat quietly in the back seat of his limousine. He had decided he needed to get away to his country house for a couple of days. When the invasion of Taiwan was ordered, such a break would not be possible. His new Charm School girl would be there, just to make his leisure and relaxation complete. He was not sorry to be leaving the intrigues of leadership in a communist country behind, at least for two days.

Two hours later Song found himself instructing his new girl in exactly how to prepare his favorite beverage. She had offered to prepare tea for him, using the full ceremony reserved for special occasions. Having taken one of the little blue pills from America that his physician had given him, he found the stirrings of passion leading him more toward alcohol and a faster route to a release of tension.

"And that, my beautiful creature, is how to make the perfect drink."

His description completed, as well as two glasses of the mixed drink containing expensive vodka, he drank half of his in one gulp before leading her by the hand to the couch. He didn't even become angry when she giggled at seeing his reaction below the belt of his black, silk robe. If anything, the giggle made him even more excited.

The soft sound of musical notes like a waterfall made a romantic setting. Song looked into her mischievous, smiling, eyes and returned the smile. His, of course, was without warmth. "Dance for me." She began to sway to the music in a sultry way. After an agonizing few minutes of dance, she spun around and pulled the pins from her very long hair, allowing it to flow down her shoulders to cover the front of her silk robe.

With one quick motion, her robe dropped from her shoulders and onto the floor, revealing tantalizing glimpses of her brown, standing nipples and well-coiffed pubis.

In a husky voice, Song said, "I want your tongue to taste me." Obediently, the girl dropped to her knees, spread open his robe and began to utilize her tongue in ways she had been taught at Charm School. Over the next five minutes she teased him, bringing him close to climax before cleverly cooling his passion. Several times she used different techniques before she buried him into her throat.

He did not hear the sound of the explosion, but did clearly see the flash and the partial wooden beam that nearly tore her body in half. He also felt the agony of her death convulsion as she bit deeply onto his nearly-exploding member. In that moment, he lost consciousness.

• • •

Outside of Beijing, China
0945 Hours Local Time the Next Day

Song came awake to the sound of hospital equipment. He found himself back in the secret military bunker where he been taken after the first assassination attempt. Since then, the primary medical suite had been completely remodeled, with all new equipment, beds and other modern hospital conveniences installed. It no longer looked like a military M.A.S.H unit, but instead looked like a modern hospital. Even the lights were bright, LED bulbs, causing his eyes to burn and water with pain. He could hear whispered voices nearby as a person ran away to notify someone that he was awake.

Song's mind began to focus and he could see that Lao was approaching his bed with his chief deputy right behind him. Even through the fog in his brain, Song could feel his anger begin to rise. Lao stopped by his bed and bowed his head. Song tried to bark, "Report." To his disappointment, he was only able to croak out the word.

"General Secretary," Lao said with deep deference, "this is my deputy, as you know. Since I have failed you twice, my shame will only be addressed by my death. Before taking care of that detail, I will brief my deputy and he will assume all of my responsibilities."

With that statement made, Lao bowed his head again and made motions to withdraw from the room.

"Lao," Song said in a stronger voice. "Dismiss your deputy and come here."

With near shock on his face, Lao motioned to his deputy to depart. He then walked over to Song's bed and bowed his head again.

In a normal, but stern voice, Song said, "I ordered you to report. Not your deputy. You. Do so now."

In an uncharacteristically husky voice, Lao said, "A missile battery twenty-four kilometers from your country house released two missiles that were targeted at your coordinates. It appears that one experienced a failure of its guidance system and struck a school building ten kilometers from your location. There were only two casualties. The second struck just outside of your country house and exploded with a high explosive charge. Your security detail found your companion dead and you severely injured. The missile battery detachment was found murdered at their battery, to include their officer. Early investigation appears to point to the same Tong that tried the last assassination attempt. You will recall that they were traced back to three Politburo members. The two that remain living have gone into hiding, but are believed to remain somewhere in the Shanghai area."

Song remained silent for several seconds before asking, "What is my condition?"

"General Secretary, you have suffered a mild concussion, a compound fracture of your arm, several broken ribs and severe lacerations to your penis, which has been surgically repaired. You have also received over two liters of blood, to replace that lost due to your injuries. You should be able to recover from your wounds." Lao discreetly left out the fact the lacerations would leave scars that looked very much like teeth marks.

"Tell me, Lao. Are there only the two Politburo members that are active threats?"

After a deep breath, Lao said, "No, General Secretary, I have four others under surveillance, as well as three members of the PLA General Staff."

Over the past several minutes, Song had formulated his decision. "Lao, how soon can you to initiate Black Orchid?"

Lao managed to keep his face placid as he responded, "In six hours a military plane can depart from Shanghai with Hu's two people and the security team. Two hours before that the clean-up team will depart for Kabul."

"See that it is done." Song's words were said without emotion, but with the cold calculation for which he was well known.

"Yes, General Secretary." Lao made no argument nor did he offer any resistance to unleashing the worst plague in world history.

"And Lao?" Song stopped Lao as he was about to walk away. "You have not outlived your usefulness to me. I expect you will not allow a third attack?"

The question did not receive a verbal response, but only a short bow of Lao's head, before he turned to leave the room.

When Lao entered his designated office in the bunker, he walked to the secure telephone and called General Hu. The General picked up the telephone on the second ring. "Hu? This line is secure."

Hu responded the same way and waited for Lao to continue. "Hu, my next call will be to the security detail. Black Orchid is activated in one hour. Clear?"

In a voice completely devoid of emotion, Hu responded, "Yes."

Lao hung up the telephone and called his chief aid and activated the security detail.

Hanging up the telephone Lao looked at the sole photograph sitting on his desk. It was an old Polaroid of his wife and daughter on the wooden dock at a beautiful, hidden lake. Both wore floppy hats and big grins as his daughter, who was twelve years old at the time, held up a tiny fish she had caught. His wife had died of cancer and his daughter rarely allowed him to see his grandson. He was overcome with emotion and buried his head in his hands as he sobbed without shame.

CHAPTER 39
THE NEW YEAR - PLUS TWENTY-EIGHT DAYS

Kabul, Afghanistan
0005 Hours Local Time

Cho met the two medical technicians and half of what should have been their twelve-man security team at the Kabul airport and transported them to the nearby safe house, where the technicians carefully plugged in the non-descript refrigerated container. Two thermite grenades[21] were placed on top of the container and could be ignited within seconds, thereby completely incinerating its contents. With a deep sigh, both technicians fell into bed and were almost immediately asleep. Travel to Kabul had been a nightmare. Cho had arranged to meet Ahmed and the martyrs at a small, two-story hotel only a block away, in the morning.

Cho had an uneasy feeling as he paced in the medium-sized hotel room. The room was on the top floor of the two story concrete building that had only twelve clean, but very simple rooms for rent. He didn't personally know the PLA Special Forces security detail team leader and had been pointedly ignored when he had asked for a briefing on security arrangements. He was infuriated to learn the security team had been cut to only six operators. The team leader was equally angered when Cho and the medical technicians would not tell him what was in the refrigerated case. He would become very disturbed when the technicians put on full hazardous materials suits in the morning. The portable refrigerated case containing the vials that would change the world hummed quietly in the corner.

---

[21] A thermite grenade is a non-explosive grenade that creates intense heat in a small area.

Early the next morning, everyone showed signs of being sleep deprived. They had been awake, with only a few catnaps, since departing China. Cho's assistant had confirmed by radio that Ahmed and his martyrs would be at the hotel within the hour. The three departing flights for the martyrs were scheduled for just after 10:00 a.m. The two technicians did not seem to know what to do with themselves.

Cho's assistant knocked at the door using the precise cadence and correct number of taps. When Cho opened the door, his assistant quickly entered, followed by Ahmed and Hadi. Guns appeared in the hands of the Special Forces team leader and his two operators when Ahmed refused to be searched.

In a commanding voice, Cho barked out in Mandarin, "Do not move, you fools!" Everyone in the room froze and glanced nervously at Cho. "Lower your weapons," Cho said sternly. The team leader merely aimed his pistol just off to the side of Ahmed's torso.

"Camel herders," said the team leader under his breath.

Cho continued to address the team leader in a conversational tone. "Holster your weapons now, or your families will have the opportunity to watch each other die slowly, painfully and without honor as they curse you for the fool that you are."

The look in Cho's black eyes was enough for the team leader, who, after a hesitation, holstered his pistol. He nodded to the two other operators standing off to the sides and they followed suit.

Ahmed looked at Cho for a few seconds before nodding and turning to signal Hadi. The technicians and all three Special Forces operators sucked in their breath when Hadi opened his robe to display the suicide vest packed with plastic explosive, ball bearings and other bits of metal. His hand was holding a spring-loaded triggering device and the look on his face was the serene look of a man about to meet his maker.

In Arabic, Cho said, "It is difficult to find good help these days, even for such an important mission."

Ahmed snorted with mild humor and nodded his agreement.

"Your martyrs are ready?" Cho asked the question out of formality.

Ahmed responded, "Yes. They await my order in two school buses outside."

Cho then handed a small briefcase containing passports and plane tickets for twelve of the martyrs, to Cho, for inspection.

After a careful inspection of the passports and tickets, Cho said to the two technicians, "Prepare the first two doses." Both nodded.

In a deferential tone, Cho said to Ahmed, "Please bring in the first two." Ahmed calmly left the room, while Hadi continued to stand against the wall, left hand displaying the vest detonator.

Two minutes later, Ahmed returned with the men. Both had the look of apprehension on their faces, mixed with what could only be described as religious fervor. At Ahmed's instruction, they lined up in front of the technicians standing at the table.

On cue, the first man pulled a revolver from under his robe and fired one round into the forehead of the nearest Special Forces operator. Hadi then killed the team leader and the third operator with two suppressed bursts from a modified AK-47.

Ahmed had fired two electric tasers into Cho, who fell to the floor in convulsions. Ahmed then calmly walked to the doctors and shot each one in the head. Hadi walked to the side wall of the hotel room and took off his vest. It was a disguised breaching charge. He quickly set the charge against the wall to the adjoining room.

When the firing had stopped, the second martyr rushed to secure the virus vials and return them to their refrigerated container. He wore protective gloves and quickly gathered four vials of blood from the technician's bodies. Ahmed had brought his brother-in-law Ali, as the second martyr to properly handle the virus.

Since the first shot, less than twenty seconds had elapsed. Over the ringing in their ears from the loud gunfire, they could hear several bursts of automatic fire outside of the hotel. A few seconds later the explosive punched a hole in the concrete wall leading into the room next door. Ahmed paused briefly to write a short message on the front wall of the room, using blood from the security team leader's leaking head. Ahmed and Ali then carefully carried the refrigerated case through the hole to discover another hole in the opposite wall into the next room. In this room there was a large hole in the floor leading into the room below. Through the back wall of this room was a hole leading to a small carpet shop that was connected to the hotel. Through a trap door in the floor of the carpet shop, Ahmed and Ali carefully carried the refrigerated case, followed by Hadi and the martyr, who were roughly dragging the semi-conscious Cho. They had wrapped him tightly in a carpet, securing it with nearly a roll of duct tape.

The trap door lead down into a narrow tunnel leading away from the direction of the airport. Two blocks later, the tunnel entered the basement of a home.

The refrigerated case and Cho were lifted into the waiting truck. A plume of smoke could be seen coming from the airport where a diversionary attack had taken place simultaneously. The attack had involved sending a rocket-propelled grenade into a fuel storage tank, which immediately drew all American "Advisors" in the area. This allowed Ahmed's truck to roll away from the area unnoticed.

• • • •

The White House
1610 Hours EST

Katherine glared at her National Security Team across the table. CIA Director Bradley Pittson and NSA Director Donald Clayborn and Chairman of the Joint Chiefs of Staff General Stephen K. Taylor and a total of four aids sat at the table, having just briefed the President on what was now called, "the destroyer incident." Each of the men present attempted to return the President's glare with confidence, however all but General Taylor could not help but allow embarrassment for their intelligence failure to creep onto their faces.

"So you're telling me, Bradley," Katherine said while dragging out the CIA Director's name, "that there's been no intelligence about anyone having the capability to defeat existing EMP shielding? You can't even hazard an educated guess as to who was responsible? What the hell *can* you tell me?"

"Madam President," Pittson began, "intelligence reports indicate, with high confidence, that two days ago, General Secretary Song was attacked by rogue Generals of the PLA, using a Tong as a surrogate."

"A what?"

"Madam President, a Tong is an organized crime enterprise in Asia," Pittson explained. "Members of the Tong murdered all soldiers of a PLA tactical missile battery, while they were conducting annual live fire exercises. They then launched two missiles at the General Secretary's summer house, located over twenty kilometers away. The General Secretary was severely injured, but not fatally so, and is expected to recover. The day after this attack, recently activated

Chinese reserve units were ordered to begin moving toward Fujian Province, located right across the Formosa Straight from Taiwan."

Pittson took a deep breath, before continuing, "Based upon the Chinese moves to cripple Western economies, moving their troops into potential attack position for an attack of Taiwan, and the complete void of intelligence regarding an enhanced EMP weapon, my people assess it most likely that China is responsible for crippling the destroyer's entire electrical system. By keeping the attack completely covert and maintaining plausible deniability, the Chinese have sent a veiled but explicit threat to us to stay out of what they view as their internal squabble with Taiwan."

Everyone in the room was silent as all eyes fixed on Katherine. Her glare had morphed into a look of deep concentration, which masked the intense migraine headache that threatened to rip her head wide open.

"General," she said while looking at General Taylor, "what naval forces do we have west of Hawaii?"

"Madam President, besides small naval forces based at several ports in the Far East, we have two small Naval Strike Forces consisting of eight ships or less. One is standing off the Korean Peninsula and one is in the South China Sea. The one off the Korean Peninsula has been on-station with anti-missile defenses since their President threatened to rain death, in the form of a nuclear EMP, upon the United States. To date, we have given no response to these threats beyond the presence of the Strike Force."

Through the pounding in her head, Katherine said, "Order the one in the South China Sea back to its home port. Where is that?"

"San Diego, Madam President." General Taylor could not believe the President was going to abandon the treaties with Taiwan that had been in place since the early 1950s. "Madam President, the USS Ronald Reagan carrier group that you ordered moved from Japan to Pearl Harbor has been re-provisioned and can replace the smaller flotilla."

Katherine's screeching response was immediate. "Goddammit, General! I will *not* tempt war with the Chinese. We've got our own civil war brewing in this country and I will not get into one that would go nuclear! When you have some useful intelligence," she emphasized the word useful, "make sure Burt hears it immediately. We're done here."

She then stormed out of the room, closely followed by her Chief of Staff's primary aid.

Each of the men looked at one another other across the table. Not a word was spoken, but expressions on faces ranged from stunned, to sad, to hints of fear. It was several seconds before first Pittson, and then the rest, rose and quietly walked from the room. From his car Pittson placed a secure phone call to the FBI Director.

CHAPTER 40
THE NEW YEAR - PLUS TWENTY-NINE DAYS

Secure Bunker for Chinese Leadership
Outside of Beijing, China
2100 Hours Local Time

General Secretary Song lay in a hospital bed in his office within the emergency bunker when Wong knocked on the open doorway. "Come," Song said in an annoyed voice.

"General Secretary, General Lao has arrived and would like to see you. He apologizes for the inconvenience and the late hour." Wong delivered the message without any emotion in his voice, like a robot.

When Lao entered the room, he placed a box on Song's desk and turned it on and closed the air-tight door. "Even though this place is supposed to be secure, now we can definitely speak freely, General Secretary."

Song asked, "Black Orchid?"

"General Secretary," Lao said softly, "it did not go as planned. The clean-up team observed an attack on the security team members outside the hotel room by Islamic fighters. Those fighters killed all security team members. An explosion was heard inside the room. When they made entry, they found three security team members dead, both medical technicians dead and an escape hole blown in the wall. On the wall, painted in blood, was a message in Arabic that said, "We have it now. Death to Infidels everywhere.""

Lao continued, "My best agent, who was in the room during the fight, was carried off by the terrorists. Two taser pistols, with expended shock probes, were found on the floor of the room. The team leader believes Cho was struck with the tasers and, while incapacitated, was carried off, along with the virus container. The terrorist group had also orchestrated a diversion at the airport, which drew off available American Special Forces trainers and Afghan forces, in that direction. My clean-up team removed the bodies of Hu's security team and erased the bloody message on the wall.

Song had been staring at Lao throughout the briefing. When Lao fell silent, Song said, "Do you believe they will release the virus as planned?"

Lao said, "Based upon my own analysis and gut feeling, yes, I do, General Secretary. Unfortunately, they will release it on their own timetable and not ours. Alternatively, the virus may kill them all and everyone around them, if they do not have the expertise to handle it properly."

Song asked, "How long before the military reserves are fully activated and moved to Fujian Province?"

"My agents tell me the vast majority of them will be in place in fourteen days. Attacking the renegade province after that time will ensure the best possibility of success. It is still important to confirm the U.S. President's intentions in this matter."

Lao had just been briefed on the PLA reserve status before walking into Song's office. "Lao, what is the status of the special source in Washington," after a short pause for thought, Song continued, "the Charm School girl?" They could speak openly about Black Orchid, so all topics were now suitable for discussion.

"General Secretary, she last met Walter Fontaine on January 6th. The video tapes showed a session in which he requested to be beaten for having been bad. Little intelligence was gained, however the embarrassment factor alone should prove devastating to the Fontaine Administration, if you choose to use it. The Charm School girl's handler did not attempt contact with her for the next two weeks. When he did try to contact her, she had disappeared. One of my most reliable deputies was sent to Washington three days ago to investigate. He took our top interrogation team with him. Initial interviews showed her handler, Sung Hong, had treated her brutally, directly after the January 6th meeting. Review of surveillance video from her apartment building did not show her returning to her apartment since that time. After twenty-four hours of appropriate questioning, Sung admitted having suspected she might be in contact with the Americans and causing him to carefully search her body and the hotel meeting room."

Lao briefly enjoyed the thought of a pig like Sung being subjected to what the Americans called "extreme interrogation techniques" in the basement of the

Chinese Embassy. He had personally approved their use, to include the mentally-damaging chemical substances.

"Nothing was found during the search of the hotel room. Curiously, there has been nothing to indicate the American intelligence community is aware of this operation. This shows that if the operation has, in fact, been discovered, they are compartmentalizing[22] it to the point that not even high-level gossip is being heard. Conversely, Walter Fontaine has traveled to California and has not been seen outside of their estate for several days, which may indicate the President is aware of the operation and has tied him securely to the family tree."

After a short pause, Lao continued, "Over the past few weeks, the American President has withdrawn all U.S. Navy carrier groups from the Pacific Rim and smaller naval task forces have been recalled, except for the anti-missile strike force off the Korean Peninsula and one small strike force in the South China Sea. Their actions and her State Department's diplomatic rhetoric also seem to indicate she is consciously avoiding conflicts with us. General Secretary, if the Charm School girl has been collected by the Americans, as presumed, their President must know that the video tapes of her husband will be widely released, in the event of war. We will continue to watch the situation closely, but at this time, it appears the Americans will not react in defense of the renegade province."

Lao allowed a smile to spread across his face, drawing a similar reaction from Song. Subtlety was definitely needed in handling of this information. With this information, if used properly, Song now owned the American President.

---

[22] Compartmentalization – Restricting access to information to only those with an immediate need to know.

CHAPTER 41
THE NEW YEAR - PLUS THIRTY DAYS

The White House
0800 Hours EST

Marc nodded to one of the Secret Service uniformed division men as he walked through the metal detector into the White House. Instead of the usual joke about how he didn't look anything like his ID photo, the officer merely grunted, "Okay," before allowing him to enter. The White House had changed since Katherine had signed what was covertly but universally called "The Proclamation." Instead of the loud, hustle and bustle of a normal, busy White House, it felt like pre-World War II German Gestapo Headquarters. Everyone walked the corridors speaking in hushed tones, as if waiting for the other shoe to drop.

Katherine's Presidential Executive Orders (PEOs), known behind her back as "edicts" to the staff in the White House, seemed to have increased to one or more every day since the Proclamation. When she had addressed the nation, she had not tried to appeal to patriotism, nor to the American people as a whole. In fact, she castigated the NRA and everyone that insisted on gun ownership, inferring they were responsible for most of the problems faced by the country and certainly all of the gun deaths. She then identified the problems as she saw them and declared the need for her to assume the power to fix them. The speech lasted twenty minutes, but seemed like it had lasted only ten. Her base of support heard the speech with wonder and hope. Finally, their agenda would be implemented without the stone walling House of Representatives.

Outside of her base, which included a majority of Americans, it was apparent that she had simply seized power. When the first Federal District Judge had ruled one of her edicts was unconstitutional, it was sent to the Supreme Court on emergency appeal by the Justice Department, the judge's ruling was overturned, after the court vote of five to four. Fortunately, Katherine's nomination had been confirmed by her party's slim majority in the Senate only days earlier.

POEs had directed National Guard units to support the missions of eight different federal agencies, all of which were tasked to enforce Katherine's unpopular policies. FEMA had established centers in each state where contractors delivered pre-stored food and medical supplies. Soup kitchens were established by FEMA, with little regard for state and local governments or religious organizations providing similar services. The National Guard's overt mission was to keep the peace while the hungry were fed and to secure available stores.

Under one carefully written POE the Guard was given full arrest authority on the federal level, without the need to show probable cause, for the duration of the emergency. Local congressmen were outraged when Katherine ordered the National Guard to establish prison camps in the different regions for those arrested on suspicion of sedition. The dictates of the POEs were generally followed on the East Coast, at least along the Northeast Corridor, and in most of the West Coast states. The heartland states were either ignoring federal authorities or, in egregious cases, were arresting Homeland Security and Fontaine administration managers on state corruption charges.

Marc walked into his office and noticed Don Stetson sitting at a side table talking on the phone. He was clearly under the influence of something, most likely either booze, pills or both. His words slurred as he spoke with someone about Katherine's latest Executive Order. He gleefully told the listener the President had just signed a PEO directing the FBI's NICS computer background check system records be turned over to the Department of Homeland Security. When the "gun clingers," as Katherine called them, showed their expected acts of defiance, Katherine would issue another PEO instituting a program for Homeland Security to begin collecting all guns that threaten national security. These would include all semi-automatic weapons, both pistols and rifles, with a particular focus on the so-called assault rifles. For the time being, bolt action rifles and shotguns would be excluded. When citizens turned in their guns, like had been done in Australia several years earlier, each would be given a government voucher for reimbursement.

Don became deliriously happy when he told the person on the other end of the line that collection centers would be established. Once they were opened, people would have thirty days to turn in their now-illegal firearms. After the thirty day period expired guns could be seized by the government without recompense. Press Secretary Towanda Jefferson had personally written the press release in anticipation of the PEO.

Hearing Don explain the program out loud terrified Marc. He envisioned his friends in Kentucky reacting violently to anyone that tried to take their firearms, or even their stored food. Very soon Americans were going to begin killing each other, all because of the woman in the Oval Office.

. . .

The Pen and Ink Saloon
Frankfort, Kentucky
1400 Hours EST

Kerry DuBois sat down at a table in the upstairs private meeting room at the Pen and Ink Saloon. Coyote Collins sat nursing a beer while a scowl deepened on his face. Both men were waiting for the arrival of Tank Monahan, Blondi, Freddie and John Chapman.

When Kerry tried to pump Coyote for information, in his high, squeaky voice, Coyote had glanced up and said, "Wait." Kerry wasn't happy, but decided shutting his mouth was probably the best course of action. When Tank and the rest had arrived, Coyote called the unofficial meeting to order.

"Who the hell does your Goddamned Governor think he is?" Coyote's question was delivered as a rhetorical question. "Homeland Security went to the National Guard for help in collecting food and fuel for redistribution."

He let the statement hang for a moment before continuing, "All of the Commanders of the units contacted had the exact-same-answer, "We must check with higher headquarters before we can help you." The word from Homeland seems to point to the Governor and Commanding General as being the people that sent down the word not to do what the President's order says they should do." He then raised his voice and said, "It's a Goddamned Presidential Order!"

"I've already talked to my contact in the White House and have the go-ahead to start hiring contractors. Out of all the regions, I guess seven of them have done the same. Tank? I want you to send a list of 300 reliable contractors, and I mean reliable. Understand?"

Tank nodded with a grin spreading over his face.

"I'll go ahead and suspend the need for background checks, but, you better not be sending me any with active warrants out on them. Got it?"

"Sure Coyote," Tank said. "How soon do you want 'em to start? I got a list made and ready on the computer."

Coyote looked at Tank and blinked slowly in mild surprise. "I want 'em yesterday, so you send your list over to my chief of staff after this meeting. He'll let you know where they should go tomorrow evening to get the paperwork done. They'll start officially day after tomorrow."

With an undertone of anger in his voice, Coyote said, "And you make sure you tell each and every one of 'em they better plan on following orders. Period. Understand?"

"No problem," Tank said solemnly, "I'll talk to each one myself."

Coyote then turned to Kerry and John Chapman. "When I hired you two as consultants, you were supposed to tell me what the Governor and his people were up to and how to get what we want. Why isn't he cooperating with my people?"

John smoothly turned to Kerry and motioned for him to respond to Coyote's question. Kerry's showed surprise and annoyance on his face before his whiny voice raised an octave, as he said, "Well, I mean, you know, uh the Governor has really circled the wagons in his administration. It ain't near as easy to talk to his people as it used to be. You know?" His voice trailed off as he looked pleadingly at John.

John nodded slowly and said, "Kerry's right about that, Coyote. Both the Governor and Lieutenant Governor have really put the clamps on their people about what they're doing. All my usual contacts have dried up and his State Police protection detail seems to have put the fear of God in everyone to keep their mouths shut, that is if they want to keep their job."

John believed it was the fear of losing their job that stopped the leaks of information. He never considered the possibility that loyalty to this Governor was the real reason.

• • •

Mike Broehm Residence
Outside of Cronin, Kentucky
1800 Hours EST

Snow was spitting outside of the windows at Mike's house as a bitter wind blew the light, puffy flakes around in circles and into wiggling lines in his driveway. They could be seen under the spotlights that illuminated the cars and trucks parked there.

Inside, a fire was blazing merrily in the fireplace and the small group of neighbors were scattered around the family room. Each held a glass that was being merely sipped. When Mike walked into the room, everyone stopped talking and waited expectantly.

Mike looked around for a moment before saying, "Geez, guys. It sounds like a morgue in here." He broke into a smile, melting the tension in the room.

"Didn't we just celebrate the birth of Christ a little while ago? Near as I can tell, he's still looking over each and every one of us. Agreed?"

Everyone in the room nodded their head, with some offering their glass in salute to that Christian truth.

"Okay, then," Mike said, "Let's focus on how thankful we are to live in this great country, even if the Bitch is bat-shit crazy, but we have the best friends and neighbors in the world. We will overcome and be stronger for it. Right?"

Mike's comments had drawn initial chuckles, followed by a chorus of, "yeah, you're right, Mike!'

Mike then looked to Sean and Linda, who were wedged together into the overstuffed chair. "What can you tell us, Sean?"

"Mike, let me defer to Linda. Honey?"

"Once a commander, always a commander. Is that it, my dear?"

Sean merely smiled, before saying, "Honey, I know who the real brains of this outfit is, so of course, I defer to you."

Linda gave him a playful swat across the arm, before saying, "Smooth, mister. Real smooth." She then turned to everyone in the room and launched into a concise situation report or sitrep. "The President's address and her executive orders have completely changed the landscape in America. The military has been placed on a footing designed to combat civil war. Despite what the mainstream media would have you believe, the President's address was received by everyone but her staunch followers to be a declaration of her intent to rule by fiat."

Most in the room reacted with horror. Rollie, on the other hand, asked in his Kentucky drawl, "Now hold on, little lady. What's a little I-talian car got to do with any of this?" His question caught everyone by surprise.

Mike jumped in by asking Rollie, "Are you trying to relive your first car accident, Rollie? That girl in the pickup nearly killed you when she blew the stop sign and crushed your Fiat Spider."[23] As I recall, you were so pissed about it, you married her!" The mood in the room went from horror and despair to a jovial one.

Mike looked back at Linda, who had just caught on to what he and Rollie were doing. "I'm sorry Linda. This knucklehead over here keeps wanting to relive the night he went from being nearly killed, to getting laid by a crazy lady. Now, what were you saying?"

Linda deftly changed the whole tenor of her sitrep. "With the political situation being what it is, we're very lucky here to have the kind of support that will see us through the coming troubles. Now this is all very hush, hush, but we've been working with contacts in the Governor's office and the state police and have been able to get some pretty good Intel on what Coyote intends to do, at least in the short term. The best part is that we should be able to get at least advance warning before the Homeland Security people start to target our neighborhood specifically. There are no guarantees, but we should be ready for most of what they can throw at us."

Linda went on to describe some of the tactical and strategic plans for keeping roving bands of thugs at bay. "There are many who aren't convinced such a thing can happen here, so to some extent, we'll just have to react when it does come to us."

---

[23] Fiat Spider – a small Italian sports car made and imported to the U.S. from 1966-1985.

CHAPTER 42
THE NEW YEAR - PLUS THIRTY DAYS

The Mountains of Southeast Afghanistan
1900 Hours Local Time

Ahmed received the evening report of activities from his assistant. "Hadi, has our unhappy guest said anything since waking up?"

"No, esteemed leader. He just glares at whoever brings him water and a plate of food. He may be even more uncomfortable when he learns of what his own people planned to do."

"Ahh, then it is time to go tell him." Ahmed got up and walked through the cave complex to the chamber where Cho was chained.

Ahmed stood in the doorway, looking at Cho through the dim candlelight. A candle was always burning in Cho's chamber and two armed men watching him constantly. Ahmed could see the metal shackles on his wrists and legs, beaten into place by a hammer. The dried blood on Cho's wrists showed where he had tried, unsuccessfully, to pull his hands free. He had learned the hard way that trying to attack his guards resulted in being beaten unconscious by a club. He now offered his shackles for inspection whenever asked to do so.

Cho's eyes did not betray any thoughts as he looked at Ahmed. This pleased Ahmed greatly.

After several minutes Ahmed asked, "Do you know why I chose to capture you instead of leaving your body for your so-called comrades?"

Cho slowly shook his head.

"You have honor, Infidel. I respect that. I also decided it was not your time to die. Did you know a Chinese team was waiting to kill all of you after you had prepared my martyrs for their mission? There were twenty-five of them surrounding the meeting site. Two were recorded quietly talking to each other by one of my fighters. Would you like to hear what they said? A friend just got me the translation."

Ahmed opened a flip phone and could just make out the soft voices of two men speaking Mandarin Chinese. "Why do they want Cho killed? I know him. He's one of us."

"I don't know and don't care. It came from the top. He must know something he shouldn't."

Ahmed was pleased to see a small amount of consternation come over Cho's face.

"That is why I trust no one, my friend. Why would they want to kill you, too? They came in and removed all of the bodies before the Afghans and their devil patrons, the Americans, could get there. They were *prepared* to haul away the bodies, including special bags for them, wrapped in carpets. What have you done to deserve this?" Ahmed did not try to hide his genuine curiosity.

After a long pause, Cho said, "This thing you have done for them, it will change the world." Cho then nodded to himself before continuing, "It is extremely important that when people of the world begin to die, it is someone like you that is to blame, with no possible link to China. From China it is an act of war. From you it is an act of terrorism."

Ahmed scoffed at the comment. "We have been at war with the Infidel for many centuries. Everything about this land is war."

"You will kill me now, in retribution for what my government intended to do to you?" Cho asked the question matter-of-factly.

Ahmed smiled and said with humor, "They do nothing more than I would do myself. No, if you behave yourself, I will not kill you now. When my martyrs have left to wipe out the Infidel, maybe I'll even let you go, to survive if you can. Now, tell me what I don't know about how the Infidels are destroying the world."

For the next two hours, and for at least an hour each day, in the days to come, Cho told Ahmed what was happening in the world outside of Afghanistan.

CHAPTER 43
THE NEW YEAR - PLUS THIRTY-FOUR DAYS

FBI Headquarters Building
Washington, D.C.
0900 Hours EST

W. Allen Kidd sat at his desk looking out the window of his corner office at the Hoover Building, but did not see the nearby buildings or the Washington Mall. Instead he was wrestling with the dilemma of what, in this most critical national security situation, was the right thing to do. Six days earlier the CIA Director had come to his office to demand to know why the FBI was not represented at the White House any longer. Allen had looked the man directly in the eye and had told him the President had made some demands of him that he could not do, in good conscience. When pressed, Allen refused to elaborate. When Pittson described the President's behavior and reactions to the destroyer incident and intelligence of an impending invasion, Allen had become particularly troubled.

"Listen, Brad. I'm trying to keep confidences made to the President here. You understand, I'm sure." A quick look showed Pittson did not understand nor did he think she was worthy of receiving any confidence. "Let me ask a favor of you, though. Please let me know if there are any other indications she may be influenced by the Chinese." Merely making the statement could be viewed by some to border on treason and both men knew it. Normally little love is lost between the FBI and CIA, however in this instance, both men literally felt the fate of the world on their shoulders. Allen did not say what he would do if such information became available.

"Brad, my analysts briefed me this morning on the assassination attempt against General Secretary Song, his moves toward an invasion of Taiwan, and their assessment he would probably pull the trigger within the next few weeks. They also tell me the President has pulled back virtually all naval forces from the area that might support the Nationalist Chinese in the event of an attack. Has she really thrown in the towel toward the PRC and given up on Taiwan, or does she have something up her sleeve?"

Following a deep breath with eyes closed, Pittson had told him, "Everything I know indicates she has decided to give up on Taiwan. Worse, she mentioned she was focused on addressing a brewing civil war here at home." After a pause, Pittson said, "If you know anything or can do anything to inspire her to change directions, you better consider it quickly."

Pittson left Allen's office without the customary handshake in parting. While Allen had stewed over the issue for the past six days, he kept thinking divine guidance would show him the correct path. He knew that any attempt to schedule a public, or even private statement to Congress could be met with violence. He could simply call a press conference at the small auditorium on the first floor and inform the press and the American people that the President had been compromised by Chinese intelligence, through her husband Walter. This would have to be followed by calling for her to immediately step down for the good of the country. Thinking this through, he could anticipate she would order his immediate arrest for treason that would likely throw the country into a real civil war, bordering on anarchy. Doing nothing would probably avoid having the country immediately falling apart, but would mean abandoning not just Taiwan, but most of the rest of the foreign interests of the U.S., along with the country's place as leader of the free world.

• • •

The Mountains of Southeastern Afghanistan
2300 Hours Local Time

Hadi gently called to Ahmed, who was sleeping in the alcove in the cave where second wife Jasmine kept her blankets. He had only been asleep a short time, but he was used to going from sleep to full wakefulness at need.

"Great leader," Hadi said softly, "Ali has news that you will want to hear."

Ahmed rose immediately, quickly dressed and walked beside Hadi toward the main entrance to the cave complex. It was very dangerous for anyone to walk outside, especially during the hours of darkness, due to the Great Satan's Predator Drones tendency to rain down missiles. Standing just inside of the cave entrance, next to a single candle, was Ali.

After making the appropriate greeting, Ali said, "Ahmed, our work has gone more quickly even than I had hoped. I won't bore you with the science details, but we initially took samples of the virus and separated them into twelve different groups. Each group was subjected to changes at their most basic level, using a different nanotechnology technique, for each of the twelve samples. I had planned to work through several thousand samples before finding the best one, a process that should take weeks or months. Instead, two days ago, I found that two of the first twelve had appeared to do what we want them to do." Ali fought the temptation to use the large, scientific description that would demonstrate his high level of ability and accomplishment. Instead, he dumbed down the description, for Ahmed's benefit.

"Ahmed, I took a sample of the virus from each of the promising test viruses, and injected two of the Infidels you had captured. They are each strapped to a table, with access to nutrient fluid tubes, in a cave with a controlled environment. I mean the infected air in the cave cannot escape. One of the Infidels began showing fever and skin blister symptoms within thirty-six hours. The other showed symptoms two hours later. Both worked!" Ali nearly shouted his excitement! "I even tested the breath coming out of their mouths and found the virus to be present. This means we have two strains of an airborne virus that will spread quickly. When I added the virus to the blood taken from the two Chinese medical people, the virus attacked their blood on the molecular level, so if they had antibodies created by a vaccine, those antibodies won't work against the newly created virus strains!"

Ahmed was not fully awake, nor did he understand much of what Ali was saying, but he was quickly caught up in Ali's excitement. "What do you need to do now?" Ali paused only for a moment, before saying, "I need at least three, and up to six more test subjects to place in the room with the two infected men strapped to the tables. In fact, they can take care of the two men and refill their water tubes. My assistants are reluctant to enter that cave again."

Ahmed thought for a moment, and then said, "We have four Afghan soldiers and the Infidel aid girl. She's no good to me anymore, especially since I allowed our martyrs to have their way with her.

Ahmed then turned to his assistant. "Hadi? See that all are taken to Ali's laboratory cave in the morning."

What Ahmed did not know was that when Ali had started with a weapons-grade virus, his changes through nanotechnology made the virus even more virulent. Ali had created the most devastating weapon ever created by man. In truth, Ahmed would not have cared.

. . .

SOCOM Headquarters
1600 Hours EST

The Colonel in charge of the Intelligence Section read over the report from Kabul concerning the attack at the airport. It was instantly clear that it had been a diversionary attack, with the most likely true target being in a neighborhood just over a kilometer away. The reaction team made up of Afghan soldiers and several Special Forces advisors had moved quickly from the airport to the other location, only to find a real puzzle. In the primary hotel room a significant amount of blood was found indicating the deaths of from four to five people, however all of the bodies had been removed just before the team's arrival. A quick search of the area near the hotel found the body of one Chinese male with the tattoo of a Chinese Special Forces operator. The tattoo its self was probably against PLA rules, but like many rules had simply been ignored. Blood stains found around the area showed where two other individuals had been killed. Their bodies had been removed. The best guess was that the remaining body's removal had been interrupted by the arrival of the reaction team.

The holes in the hotel room walls and floor, as well as the tunnel, told an even stranger story. Because of the odd nature of the whole scene, elements of an A-Team were dispatched to the area to discover what had happened. The preliminary report could only pinpoint involvement by the group JOTP or Jihadists of the Prophet. This was the same group that had taken two female Special Forces operators several months earlier, only to have them, or at least one of them, rescued and the kidnappers killed by a team which national hero Sean Callahan had commanded. Since then, no work had been done on the JOTP.

Sitting back in his chair, the Colonel called the SOCOM's chief analyst to his office. "Son," the Colonel said, "I want you to write up a request and begin broad aerial satellite and drone surveillance in this area here." He had circled a 700 kilometer square area making up the extension of the route being taken by the JOTP people that had taken the operators, months earlier. "I'm looking for this terrorist group called JOTP, who are probably hiding out in the mountains, somewhere in here. Let me know when you have something."

"Yes Sir," the analyst said, before turning to go back to his desk for the write-up.

• • •

The White House
2315 Hours EST

Susan held the most powerful woman in the world in her arms like a small child, stroking her hair. Katherine had asked her to come by the bedroom suite earlier in the evening, using a tone of voice that was unnatural for the President. It held sadness and a lack of confidence. The President was wearing only a silk robe. Susan was still fully clothed. Apparently it was not going to be one of those kinds of nights, Susan thought. Instead, Katherine had patted the couch in the sitting room beside her when Susan had arrived. When she was seated, Katherine had said only, "Hold me, please."

Although Susan was surprised by this first sign of vulnerability, she was shocked by the quaking tears being shed, by the older woman in her arms. After a few minutes, Katherine caught her breath and began to softly speak. "You know why I chose to declare the emergency and take charge of the country, don't you? Everything that I just know needs to be done in this country keeps getting stopped by Congress. Hell, those bastards on conservative talk radio, the NRA, you know they've driven their foolish sheep to violence just to stop me in doing what needs to be done!" Katherine was breathing deeply and emotionally.

"If they won't let me protect the American People and those cretins won't do what they should to protect everyone, then, for their own good, I just had to take charge."

Katherine rambled on until she managed to convince herself that all of her actions were not only reasonable, but that almost all of her problems were due to traitorous actions by her enemies. "Then, of all things, the FBI Director came to the White House to tell me Walter had been fucking a Chinese girl. Of course I laughed at him – like I didn't know Walter was a hound dog. Then the asshole told me the girl worked for Chinese intelligence and those fuckers had video tapes, in living color!"

Katherine's breathing had turned into panting. Although her mind continued to jump around, she seemed to calm down.

"God, but I did enjoy the look on Walter's face when I told him who his latest whore was and how pathetic he sounded begging for punishment from his mistress. The blood had drained from his face and probably, for the first time in his life, even from his penis!"

Susan couldn't help herself when she asked, "Katherine, what did you do?"

"That was the easy part. I ordered him home to California and called in the Secret Service Director to have his protection detail changed and their orders modified to prevent him from even whacking-off without me knowing about it. Had to write another TOP SECRET order to violate his so-called Constitutional Rights, but it's kind of nice to have that ability now."

Katherine lay in bed talking to herself aloud. "I don't think Director Kidd will blab about it, but I may have to take steps if that changes."

In just a few minutes the doubtful school girl was gone and back was the arrogant, driven Commander in Chief.

"Dear, thank you for helping me through that. Now, I can trust you, can't I?" Katherine bore deeply into her eyes.

Susan fought the temptation to look down into her lap and instead looked into Katherine's eyes and said, "Yes, Madam President. You can. Always." It was said simply and sincerely.

"Good," Katherine said. "In the morning, have the Director of Homeland Security come to the office. I want to push for complete confiscation of firearms as soon as possible. It's for the security of us all."

"Yes, Madam President." It took all of Susan's will to keep the determined and expectant expression on her face.

CHAPTER 44
THE NEW YEAR - PLUS THIRTY-SIX DAYS

Temporary Offices Regional Governor
Frankfort, Kentucky
1015 Hours EST

Kerry sat in Coyote's Kentucky headquarters conference room, along with Tank, Coyote's Kentucky Chief of Staff and four of Tanks contractor team leaders. Coyote wasn't in the state, however since his area of responsibility had been expanded by three states, he had hired a Chief of Staff in each of the states. The Chief of Staff was going through a simplistic PowerPoint presentation showing a map of Kentucky and the food distribution points located in the state.

"As you can see, we're okay in the Louisville, Lexington and Covington/Cincinnati areas, but the kitchens in Frankfort, Ashland, London, Bowling Green, Versailles, and smaller towns throughout the state are running low, fast."

Kerry couldn't help himself, when he corrected the man's pronunciation of "Versailles". Going into his thick, Kentucky accent, he said, "You ain't from around here, now is 'ya boy? 'Round here we say "Versailles," just like it's spelled, not the Frenchie "Versii," rhyming with high."

The man had been sent to Coyote by Fontaine administration people in Washington and he was from Northern Virginia. He looked directly at Kerry and said, "I don't give a shit if you call it Timbucktu. Fact is, you aren't collecting enough food to keep people fed. What the hell are you gonna' do about it?"

Tank spoke up, "I think that's where my contractors come in, isn't it?" The man gave Tank an appraising look, before saying, "Yeah, that's just what they're for. The boss has hired an administrator for each one of those towns, but local grocery stores and even gas stations don't seem to want to sell to them. Something about not trusting the vouchers they have for payment. How long would it take you to get a team to meet up with each administrator and help educate the local vendors?"

Tank looked at his four team leaders and said, "Boys, are your teams ready to saddle up?"

The largest of the four men said, "Sure, Tank. Only we're gonna need some kinda voucher or paper saying we got priority for gas for our new vehicles." He was smiling as he thought about the SUVs that had been essentially seized from dealerships by Coyote's people for use "during the duration" of the emergency. Vouchers had been given to the dealers, but the only paperwork provided was a handwritten notice, with the vehicle description and vehicle identification number or VIN. The normal government contracting and acquisition documentation had been "waived" by Coyote. For some reason, they seem to have favored black SUVs.

The Chief of Staff reluctantly nodded his head before saying, "All right. I've been passing out way too many of those certificates, but I can see where you're going to need them. See my Secretary. And only one for each team. You'll have to fill all of your team's vehicles up at one time."

The four team leaders rose and left the room. Kerry cleared his throat before mentioning, "I know where there's quite a bit of privately held stuff we might use. Only thing is, the folks storing it might take offense at anyone from the government coming around to get it." He waited for someone else to follow up on this line of thought.

Tank said, "You talking about the neighborhood where you live, Kerry? Aren't you kinda shooting your own-self in the foot?"

"Those asshole hoarders think they're too good to help out other folks. I don't know exactly what they have, but they're bragging about having over a year's worth of food for each family, and maybe more. Hell, their garages are loaded with cases and cases of food." As he said this, he imagined the fearful looks on their faces when Tank's armed security team rolled into the neighborhood. His wife had gone to her mother's house in West Virginia and he hadn't been home himself in over two weeks. His status with Coyote allowed him to stay at a luxury apartment in Frankfort, where he was closer to the money and power.

Coyote's Chief of Staff said, "Nawww, for now let's focus on distribution warehouses and normal grocery stores. We'll remember your neighborhood for later." Tank nodded, but began to think of possible opportunities outside of the watchful eyes of the Regional Governor.

Casually, Tank asked, "What are you and Coyote gonna do about the Governor, his National Guard and his State Police?"

The Chief of Staff instantly caught Tank's meaning. "Anything your people could do about that little problem?"

Tank's face lost some of its enthusiasm at the question. "I had a couple of guys watching the Governor's mansion and his office at the Capital the past few days. I was expecting they'd see only his normal State Police protection detail. Now, everywhere he goes, he's got some damned National Guard unit riding shotgun for 'em. That might be a tougher nut to crack. It'll be expensive, too."

The Chief of Staff thought for a moment, before saying, "The guys at the Homeland Security office have some pretty good toys that might prove useful." He then took out an index card and wrote down a name and telephone number. "Give this guy a call and see what he can do for you. The White House has told Homeland to start planning for a full-blown insurrection, so he should be able to help. There's also a slush fund available for important miscellaneous needs."

Tank took the card and left. With excitement in his eye, Kerry couldn't contain himself. Looking at the Chief of Staff, he said, "You done that without ever giving Tank any orders. I was sittin' right here and could swear you never told him to do anything."

The Chief of Staff looked closely at Kerry, smiled just a little, and walked away. He was humming some bars from the song, *Anticipation*, but mentally inserting the words, "plausible deniability."

• • •

The Peter Worthington Residence
Outside of Cronin, Kentucky
1300 Hours EST

Lisa's heart was, once again, being torn at the thought of what might have happened to Su Ling's parents. It had been nearly a month since arriving in Kentucky and there had been no word from her Dad or anyone else. Looking at

Su Ling's teared face, Lisa said, "Maybe we could figure out a way to contact someone from your village. Someone you can trust?"

Sadly, Su shook her head no. "Lisa, you don't understand. Every email or computer message of any kind in China is carefully reviewed by the MSS and PLA computer people. They have sweatshops of literally tens of thousands of hackers looking for everything. After I disappeared, they will task one or two hundred of them to sift every computer bit or bite of data going to anyone that has ever been in contact with me and everyone within fifty kilometers of my parent's village. Not only might it show the MSS where I am, but even the attempt would make sure my parents would end up being tortured, just to force me to return. Your father was right, we must remain completely hidden."

Fortunately, two days after their arrival "Uncle Peter" had told Lisa that he and Aunt Liz were always on their home computer searching for what is going on in the world. "If you stick to the sites listed in my computer history, and refrain from clicking on any of the click-bait articles floating around, you should be able to at least do some general computer searching." He had also said, "I'm also on the board of Hillsdale College. They have some great courses on the Constitution and American History. Feel free to delve into those areas if you have questions about how our capitalistic system works, maybe that would be fun for you two to explore."

Lisa had seen a new look on her friend's face for the first time. It was as if Su had suddenly discovered a meaningful focus for her life.

"Yes," Su almost shouted in response. "That is just what I will do." She walked into Peter's office, sat down at his desk and began to search for everything she could find on the United States Constitution.

After seeing that Su would be absorbed with her research for the near future, Lisa had gone to see "Aunt Liz."

"Lisa, honey? I found some books on the shelf in the basement that Peter had labeled 'good to know.' Would you like to have a look at them?" A quick perusal found the books to be mostly instruction manuals on how to make and grow all kinds of useful things, including food, medicines and the like, in an environment without electric power.

"Do you and Uncle Peter really think we'll be without power soon?"

Aunt Liz said, "Dear, we certainly hope not, but, let's just say that we're planning for the worst and praying for the best. One of Peter's favorite things to say is that with Murphy's Law, we'll more likely need these preparations if we haven't done them, than if we do. You've heard him say, 'The only time I'll ever need my gun on me is if I don't have it!' I have to agree with him. Once the prep is done, we just thank the Lord it is done and look around at all for which we are thankful. Seems the more we focus on being thankful, the more good things that happen. Wonderful how that works!" Aunt Liz's smile was radiant and infectious.

Lisa had given her a big hug and began to study the books.

Coming back to the present, it seemed that Su never tired of talking about how the American Founding Father's vision of the United States had been perverted over the years, but particularly in the last half century. Both agreed that the communist and socialist efforts to tear down what was previously a pretty good system had been very effective.

"What puzzles me the most," said Su, "is the communist means and methods for doing this were well known as early as the 1930s. How did they achieve so much success when Americans should have known exactly what they were doing?"

Further exploration and a few long discussions with Peter filled in what even the extensive library at Hillsdale College failed to explain. He explained Saul Alinsky's book *Rules for Radicals* was designed to prey upon natural human greed and laziness. This movement sought the removal of any moral responsibility to govern one's actions. It even pushed questioning of the most blatantly obvious truths, such as a person being either male or female. Religion had to be ridiculed, as it brought an undesirable moral certainty. By removing all of these certainties, any law or policy became open to question, making it easy for paid demonstrators to sway public opinion. Seeing the way it was orchestrated was both fascinating and frightening at the same time.

• • • •

Colonial Williamsburg, Virginia
2045 Hours EST

Marc and Susan sat in the historic Christiana Campbell's Tavern in colonial Williamsburg, Virginia sipping on their drinks. Marc had finished almost half of his IPA beer in two big gulps. Susan only sipped on her red wine. Surrounded by history in one of the country's oldest and finest places to get seafood (they say George Washington considered it to be his favorite seafood restaurant), they both managed to only look at the table and savor a day and a half away from the White House. Marc had tried to get Susan to open up a little about what was bothering her, without success.

"Heh, lady," Marc said softly, "I know it's tough, you know, to let things go for a little while. What say we get off the world, at least for this evening? Okay? After all, the boss is at Martha's Vineyard, so you really have gotten away for a day or two."

Susan looked at him with intensity and said, "Take me back to the room and make me forget everything. Now." She put an exclamation point on the statement by draining her wine glass. Marc didn't even finish his beer as he led her by the hand back to their room at the nearby motel.

Marc had pulled every trick he could think of to sexually distract Susan's mind away from work. Quite a while later, after coming up for air and to allow his aching neck and shoulder muscles to rest, he thought he had done it. At least her screams of pleasure sure seemed to indicate he had done it, but when he looked at her face, there were tears streaming down her cheeks.

"My God, sweetie," Marc said gently, "was I that good?" He couldn't help but follow the statement with a smile. His dark curly hair was well mussed and had nearly been yanked out by her fingers.

She didn't say a word, so after a few seconds, Marc walked to the bathroom for a two minute shower, and then climbed back into bed to hold Susan. She cried gently until she fell asleep.

When Marc woke in the morning, Susan was in the shower. When she walked out in a terry cloth bathrobe, he held his arms open for her to climb back into bed. She did so, but kept on the robe and the towel on her wet hair. He glanced at the nightstand for a moment and felt near panic as he noticed his phone was missing.

"Marc, don't worry. Our phones are in the bathroom with the water running. We can hear them if they ring, but we can't be overheard." Marc realized she was right and that everything that happened last night could have been monitored by any major state sponsored intelligence agency, including their own government.

"You are a wonderful friend, Marc." She said this while stroking his hair and looking vaguely toward the wall.

Marc enjoyed the delightful feeling of snuggling his head between her breasts. They were lovely, soft, but delightfully firm pair of breasts to bury one's head into. Softly, Susan said, "She expects there to be open rebellion in several parts of the country. When the NRA people and, well, a lot of loyal Americans refuse to turn in their guns, troops will be sent in to seize them and pacify the populous. Yes, you and I know that won't work, but she and some of the people whispering in her ear do truly believe it will. I wonder if Lincoln felt this threatened during the Civil War? Anyway, I don't know of anything to do about it, right now. I'm doing all I can just to keep her from going off the edge." Susan then pulled Marc even closer into her embrace.

In barely a whisper, Susan said into Marc's ear, "The FBI brought her evidence that Walter has been fucking a Chinese whore. She laughed at that, at least until they let her know the whore was being handled by Chinese intelligence and that they had everything recorded, in living color." Susan rocked Marc, while holding him in a near death-grip. "That's why Walter was banished to California. The Chinese can now do whatever they want, cause she won't see her country fall apart if those videos are released. I heard her talking to someone on a special cell phone about taking care of the problem two days ago. She snapped at me to get out when she noticed I had walked in. She never does that."

After a few seconds more of being squeezed and rocked, Susan said, "I think she was talking to someone about the FBI Director. There was something about the CIA Director being seen going to FBI headquarters right after a national security meeting and that they and others might need to be silenced. God, Marc, do you think she was talking about having them killed?"

Marc's brain was flying around in dizzying circles trying to understand it all. "Honey, at this point there's no way to know what she really meant. The sparking civil war part does seem likely. I know way too many people back in Kentucky that take the late Charlton Heston's words as gospel. 'They'll have to pry my gun from my cold, dead, fingers.' Almost all of them are really patriotic Americans. How can she, and Don for that matter, be so blind and stupid?"

This did nothing to brighten their already gloomy mood. By mutual consent they packed up and returned to the pressure cooker.

CHAPTER 45
THE NEW YEAR - PLUS THIRTY-SIX DAYS

Martha's Vineyard
One of Eli Frederick's Twelve Estates
2015 Hours EST

Katherine had just suffered through a long, boring dinner with half a dozen Fontaine Foundation donors at Eli Fredericks' Martha's Vineyard estate. Susan had not made the trip, so she was stuck with Susan's assistant and her Chief of Staff to try to keep from telling them all to go screw themselves. Burt was not happy about being drafted for this occasion, but did so when she suggested she really needed his presence.

Directly following a gourmet dinner, the guests wandered toward the indoor arboretum to admire the exotic plants and flowers Eli had flown in for the occasion. By mutual consent, she walked with Eli toward an alcove for a private conversation.

"When will the Chinese attack Taiwan?" Katherine asked the question, somehow fully expecting Eli to know the answer.

"Katherine, apparently, no one is sure when, only that it will happen soon. When it does, they are already planning to attack any American forces that try to support the Taiwanese. Will you go to war for this small island?"

It infuriated Katherine to be pumped for a decision like this. Katherine had to quell her anger and said, "We will not engage in nuclear war with the Chinese. That answer may change if they attack American vessels without provocation; including any attacks with secret weapons. Make sure you tell someone that. There better not be anymore, shall we say, odd incidents."

She was surprised to see the questioning look on his face. When she did not elaborate, Eli asked, "To what specific incidents do you refer?"

"Just deliver the message," she said cryptically. "And please forgive my early departure, but there are things that need my attention." She nodded to her Secret Service escort across the room and walked away toward her waiting helicopter.

Eli walked quickly to his office and placed a call to Wu, using one of the burner phones. When Wu picked up the phone, Eli said, "I need to speak to the owner, today. I am highly displeased with your service." No elaboration was needed. Wu's burner phone was registered to a Chinese laundry. Wu recognized Eli's voice and code phrase indicating he wanted to speak to Chen today. This was highly unusual and would involve some risk of interception of the contact by any of a half dozen different intelligence agencies, however it was not Wu's place to remind Eli of that.

"So sowry, no here," Wu said smoothly, using a heavily accent. "Can find and tell him, Okay?"

"Just tell him. I am very unhappy." Eli broke the connection, secure in the knowledge the urgency would be conveyed to Chen.

Twenty five minutes later the phone connected to his computer VOIP, or Voice over Internet Protocol, line gave a high-pitch twitter. When Eli picked it up, he waited for a few seconds until he saw a readout that said the line was secure. Chen's distorted voice said, "You called me?"

"Yes," Eli said into the receiver. "She said she would have no reaction if a fight broke out, so long as none of it involved her close friends."

In the soft, distorted tone, Chen asked "Is that all?"

Eli responded, "No, I have one curious item. She also said there better not be any attacks against her close friends with secret weapons, and a reference to odd incidents. She would not clarify what she meant."

"Anything else?"

Eli said, "No."

"It is good to hear your voice. You are a valuable friend." Chen then broke the connection.

Eli snorted to himself with amazement and some pleasure. Chen had just acknowledged the high value Eli added to their partnership. It was extremely rare for Chen to show appreciation to anyone, but he had felt compelled to do so to Eli. If the U.S. would avoid entering into war with China, he had also just become a prime backchannel for information between Katherine and General Secretary Song. Such a position would prove to be extremely valuable for both himself and Chen.

CHAPTER 46
THE NEW YEAR - PLUS THIRTY-SEVEN DAYS

Outside of Beijing, China
1025 Hours Local Time

Song had graduated from his hospital bed to a well-padded wheelchair, which allowed him to sit up at his desk in the emergency bunker. Over the past two days, he had increased his ability to concentrate, which allowed his unusually keen mind to absorb the stacks of papers on his desk marked, "Most Urgent." After over an hour of such work, he managed to move thirty centimeters of paper from one pile to another.

Wong walked into the room without knocking to stand in front of Song's desk, with head bowed. After another five minutes of work, Song looked up and uttered only one word. "Yes?"

"General Secretary," Wong said formally, "Ching Kai was brought here in a windowless van by your security force and requests an opportunity to speak with you." The polite version of a blindfold was to ensure the location of the secret bunker was not revealed.

After having Wong remove the wheelchair and replace it with a normal office chair, Song said, "See him in."

When Ching entered the room, he immediately dominated it with his two meter tall frame. Without invitation, he sat down in the chair opposite Song's desk and bowed his head with just the right amount of deference. "General Secretary, please accept my apologies at disturbing you at this time. My employer thought it important you receive certain information immediately."

Song was only mildly surprised at the lack of formal courtesies and his interest was piqued immediately.

"What information?"

Ching relayed the information Eli had given to Chen, including the warning to avoid firing upon American military personnel and to dispense with use of "secret weapons" that would result in "odd incidents," that had happened in the past. Doing so would avoid military action by the Americans in any upcoming small conflict.

"Is there anything else?" Song asked the question, while presuming what the answer was.

"No, General Secretary. Except, of course, to reaffirm my employer's admiration for what you do and represent, and to request, if possible, an approximate time-table for any anticipated hostilities with the renegade province to the east."

Song looked at Ching with something wavering between anger at the audacity of the request and respect for Ching's delivering it with a level of confidence that actually presumed he would provide an answer, patronage or no patronage. Song held Ching's eyes in a penetrating stare for over two minutes without speaking. Ching consciously blinked only two or three times each minute and refused to lower his eyes.

With a slight nod of his head, Song said, "There may be hostilities in one to two weeks, or not. That decision has not yet been made. Suggest to your employer that he should not pose such questions again."

Ching rose, bowed and left the room without another word.

Inwardly, Song fumed at Chen's demand. He understood the balance he walked when he had taken Chen's financial and other support, but after having survived two assassination attempts, he was in no mood to be threatened, nor was he anyone's puppet. The information he provided was enough and as much as he was willing to give to Chen.

. . .

The White House
Washington, D.C.
0830 Hours EST

Katherine turned off her burner cell phone, just as Susan had taught her to do all those months ago. Before she took office, she had ordered Susan to make quiet contact with the NSA to determine how she might call someone without fear of the call being intercepted. They had, of course, proposed an elaborate electronic scrambling situation that was far too cumbersome before mentioning clandestine purchase of a burner phone would accomplish much the same thing, but was much less secure. They had even offered to provide such a burner phone. The phone they had provided was carefully kept in a steel, soundproof container in Katherine's special footlocker in the President's bedroom. Unknown to her, however this phone had a voice scrambling system to disguise the sound of her voice, making it even more secure to anyone monitoring all the calls flowing through the nearest cell tower to the White House. Katherine also had Susan purchase two of the burner phones at a suburban discount department store (without the voice scrambling capability) and set them up for Katherine's exclusive use. They were also kept in another steel, soundproof box in the footlocker. She retrieved one of them now.

When the phone rang, her heart began to beat at least twenty beats per minutes faster than normal. That isn't to say her heart raced. No, after all, this was merely necessary housekeeping. Nothing that should overly bother her.

On the forth ring, a male voice answered. "Speak."

Katherine said softly into the phone, "There is a mess at my estate out West. You need to clean it up. Quietly. Let the state funeral grab all the headlines. It must be done discreetly and I don't care if it is painful. In fact, that would be a bonus. Any investigation can be squashed, if necessary. Ten times the normal donation. It can be done?"

She was surprised that she was actually holding her breath for the ten seconds before hearing the response, "Okay, but the donation will be twenty times, and in advance."

Her initial reaction was a flashing fury, before she calmed down and simply said, "Get it done." With that she hung up the phone.

On the other end of the line was a very close family friend that had spent a great deal of time at the Fontaine Estate. Overtly he knew Katherine only superficially, but he was considered one of Walter's minor drinking buddies and on the outer ring of his close acquaintances.

With that detail handled, Katherine replaced the burner phone and walked out of the Presidential bedroom to begin another day of ruling. She had decided to postpone any action regarding the FBI Director for the time being. He appeared to be willing to keep things under wraps and when Walter was no longer a problem, it all might just go away. Despite herself, she couldn't help but begin to hum a tune under her breath.

CHAPTER 47
THE NEW YEAR - PLUS FORTY DAYS

The Mountains of Southeastern Afghanistan
0600 Hours Local Time

Ali al-Hadiz put on his SCALP[24] suit, with protective gas mask, for the fourth time to enter the small, sealed, cavern. Even through the gas mask, the stench was noticeably bad. The two naked men strapped to the stainless steel table had died very painfully, two days after their symptoms began to show. Now the cadavers were decomposing rapidly, causing them to first inflate with internal gases, and then to erupt internal fluid and tissue from several places. All four of the Afghan soldiers had been stricken by the virus, along with the aid girl. Their symptoms had appeared about forty hours after having been locked in the cavern. The Afghan soldiers were all dead, but surprisingly the aid girl continued to breath. She sat on a bench against one wall and dully looked at Ali's covered form, as he entered the cavern. Beside her were three bottles of a food supplement drink from the U.S. called Ensure. They were empty and the girl was trying to open a forth.

Through his mask, in English, Ali said, "Aid girl, can you hear me?"

The girl looked up and seemed to focus on him for the first time. "What? You speak English?" Her arms, visible where she had rolled up the sleeves of her robe, had only a couple of slowly healing, open sores. Although very weak, her mind seemed to be clearing. Her clothing was soiled from an apparent attempt to help the dying Afghan soldiers in the cave.

---

[24] SCALP – Suit, Contamination Avoidance, Liquid Protection

Ali decided it might be interesting to study her further, possibly even using her to create a vaccine for the newly engineered virus.

"I will bring you a clean robe and soap and water to wash with, aid girl." He then walked out of the cavern to the door, made out of corrugated steel, and walked out of the horror chamber. He looked forward to observing the girl wash up through the cameras recording all activity in the cave.

Behind Ali, the girl just looked at the closing door and said softly, "My name is Julie. Someday, God will repay you all for what you have done and you will know my name."

. . .

The Pen and Ink Saloon
Frankfort, Kentucky
1915 Hours EST

Tank sat at the table in the small, upstairs meeting room. He tried to gauge the level of comprehension and competence of the man who would lead a team on a raid at 8:00 a.m. the next morning. The raid wasn't sanctioned by anyone in Coyote's chain of command, but would tell him whether Kerry had been blowing smoke about the riches to be had in his neighborhood. The team was equipped with raid jackets proclaiming them to be part of the U.S. Department of Homeland Security. The target was the first three houses inside the main entrance of Kerry's neighborhood. Their orders were to take two empty trailers and eight men to search the houses for contraband. This could be guns, stores of food or obvious valuables. The team leader would provide a voucher that would signify paying a low-ball estimate of the value for all the items seized. No itemized listing would be made. The voucher would list in ten words or less, the items taken. In a weird twist of Tank's personal sense of humor, the voucher itself was a forgery with the name "Oregano Julius" authorizing payment. Tank had grown up loving the cold, sugary, ice cream drinks available at the local Orange Julius in Lexington, Kentucky, at least whenever he was lucky enough to visit the town.

Tank dismissed his team leader and called in a man who was not officially on any team. The man was tall, with a long, gray beard. He had been a strike breaker back in the 1970s and 1980s, in the coal fields of Eastern Kentucky. He was getting older, but he knew how to do things discreetly, yet violently. He also didn't much care who felt the hammer, so long as he got paid. He had received five hundred dollars just to come to Frankfort and meet with Tank.

"It's been a long time," Tank said casually. "Have any trouble finding the place?"

In a deep, grizzled voice, the man said, "Nope."

"Okay, then," Tank said. "Got a little project for you, if it can be done with no splash back, you know, like you used to do back in the day. You picky about it maybe involving someone high-profile? Even with a security team?"

The man looked at Tank with a cold stare in his pale gray eyes. "How much do you want this?"

Tank said, "You will probably need some help, so let's just say fifty thousand to get the whole thing done, and I can even provide you with some pretty impressive firepower. Interested?"

The man thought for a moment, before saying, "Make it a hundred and give me more details."

For the next twenty minutes, Tank tiptoed around the whole project, giving the man details about what he would need to overcome, to including a military escort. He then offered up three weapons systems, including two 1980's era LAWS[25] rockets, a machine gun called a SAW,[26] and two Barrett .50 caliber sniper rifles.

The man finally asked, "So how soon do you want the Governor killed?" Tank had not mentioned the identity of the target.

"Well, what makes you think…"

The man cut him off. "Cut the bullshit, Tank. Who you think you're talkin' to? Has to be that asshole, but what's with the Guard soldiers in the mix?"

Tank dropped all pretenses and said, "Ever since the President set up the Regional Governors and quit working with the Governor, he's been operating like he's still in charge. Some of the fools in the National Guard even seem to want to help, so there are going to be a few of them around, helping out his Kentucky State Police security officers. To hell with them all."

---

[25] LAWS is a light anti-tank weapons system, like a disposable portable bazooka.

[26] SAW is a squad automatic weapon or belt fed machine gun shooting 5.56mm rounds similar to an M-16

"Now if he's such a pain in the ass to the President's people, why don't they just take care of it themselves?" The man seemed genuinely curious.

"They are. They sent me and I called you." Tank made the declarations softly, but the man understood immediately.

Twenty minutes later, the man agreed to take care of the problem within the next few days for a price of $250,000, half up front and half when the job was done. It also had to be paid in gold, based on gold values measured a year earlier. A very reluctant Tank shook his hand and decided he would charge Coyote's Chief of Staff a half a million, in year-old gold.

. . .

The Fontaine Estate
Outside of San Francisco, California
2355 Hours PST

Walter's eyes fluttered open as he lay draped over the flimsy, expensive divan Katherine had purchased at some antique auction, with Foundation money, of course. When he tried to roll off of it, he slid on the silk covering onto the floor. Not, however, before nearly tearing off one of the divan's now-rickety legs He was seriously drunk, with that cotton-mouth feeling that left his mouth sticky and tasting like something had crawled in there and died. He slowly looked around the room, searching for the bottle that must inevitably be there. His eyes focused on the bottle of fine brandy laying on its side on the floor, now at eye-level. He could tell there was at least a quarter of the expensive liquid left in the bottle, as he looked at the night light through the glass. A significant puddle of spilled brandy was pooled on the bamboo wood floor under the bottle. With an effort, he recalled this was the second bottle he opened later the previous evening after those Goddamned Secret Service pukes had refused to allow him to leave or even call anyone. He had desperately wanted a woman to run her hands and her lips over his body. Never again would he have the exquisite Su Ling. This thought sent him into depression again, so he reached for the bottle and took a long, slow pull on its contents. Maybe he'd have to take the estate housekeeper again, although it had been fifteen years since he had paid her last and she had not aged very well, even for an oriental woman. As he drifted out of consciousness, all he could think of was the phrase, "Any port in the storm....."

CHAPTER 48
THE NEW YEAR - PLUS FORTY-ONE DAYS

The Mountains of Southeastern Afghanistan
0800 Hours Local Time

Julie recalled having sipped on the lukewarm bottles of Ensure, days earlier, as she watched the four Afghan soldiers beginning to suffer strong symptoms from whatever disease these monsters had created. Now her mind was clear. She felt quite a bit better than she had the day before, when Ali had been so surprised that she was still alive. Her slight fever had broken completely, soon after he had brought her a bucket of water, soap and clean robes. Actually, it was Ali's two assistants who had brought the items. Both assistants bore frightened looks that were plainly visible through the gas masks they wore. Ali had then ordered them to bag up and drag out the dead bodies. Under his breath, one of the assistants told the other, in Arabic, not to worry because Ali said he would be able to make a vaccine from the blood of the "aid girl whore." The fear in his eyes belied his faith in the statement. He neither worried about nor cared that the girl might hear him, as she was nothing more than a laboratory animal to be used for experiments. They continued to talk freely as they went about their grim task.

While carrying out the last body, the talkative assistant also commented to the other, "Be sure to look around carefully, Ali wants to document everything onto that laptop he keeps locked up in his cave. I wonder how he convinced his sister to get it for him."

The other aid replied, "I don't know and I don't care. Have you ever seen Jasmine's eyes? I think I'm more frightened of her than of Ahmed."

"Shut up, you fool!" The first aid hissed this warning softly under his breath. "That kind of talk will get your throat slit, or worse!" Their conversation died as they passed outside the corrugated steel door with the last body and down the cave tunnel.

. . .

Mike Broehm was just rising from his breakfast table to begin his cold, winter day when a twelve year old named Randy came bursting through the back door of his kitchen without knocking. He was gasping with excitement and from running to Mike's house as he made the announcement. "Mr. Mike, come quick! LT said fetch you right now!"

The words tumbled from the boy's lips as he reached for Mike's arm, paused and thought better of it, and said, "Please, Sir! Come quick!"

Mike always had his pistol on his hip, so he grabbed his coat and followed Randy out of the door. He then followed the impatient boy toward the entrance of the neighborhood. He could see a small crowd of people gaping at the group of four security personnel standing over what appeared to be two men laying on the cold driveway of the second house inside the neighborhood entrance.

Approaching one of Linda's security people, the man motioned to Mike to enter the house. When he entered he could see a group of five men tied up on a bloody floor and three men were kicking them in the ribs with heavy boots. Mike barked out a loud, "Stop," causing the men to stop what they were doing. Glancing at him, the men lost some of their blood lust and assumed the hang-dog guilty look of boys caught with doing something wrong.

Just then Linda seemed to materialize out of nowhere, dragging a mean looking man with his elbow bent the wrong way and his hands tied behind his back. Linda threw the man down into the pile of men on the floor and motioned for Mike to follow her outside for a quick briefing.

Although out of earshot of the prisoners, two of Linda's security teams were listening by the open doorway. "Mike, these six criminals were captured after having kicked in the front door of this house and ransacking it. They also brutally beat the elderly homeowner and his wife and killed their little dog. After interrogation, the one I just finished with claimed they worked for Tank

Monahan, under the umbrella of Homeland Security. You probably recall Tank's name from my earlier briefings of the Frankfort situation. The overt purpose of their criminal acts was to seize foodstuffs and other items required for redistribution. Their real purpose was to steal whatever was of value and take it to Tank."

Linda finished her briefing and the security team dragged out the six captured goons from the house. Laying them beside their cohorts laying in the driveway, Mike could see most were being treated for injuries to their heads, faces, as well as their arms and legs. Linda had apparently brought along one of Sean's security team that was a trained Special Forces medic, to oversee the treatment. "What happened to them?"

Linda said, "They never knew we spotted them as they rolled into the neighborhood. The two left behind to watch their truck, trailer and SUV were obviously more interested in what their buddies were doing inside than in looking out for trouble. It usually gets smelly when they get choked out using the carotid method to put them down. You know the neck choke that cuts off blood to the brain without actually killing them? By the way, Mike, if you hadn't insisted, we would have simply killed them. Not sure why you want to take the moral high ground here, but my guys, especially the ones with no combat experience probably appreciate it. Anyway, the carotid technique usually ends in loss of bowel and bladder control. They went down quietly, so my two best men took their coats and hats and went inside, followed by two more of our men. Classic pincer move with myself and three others coming in quietly from the rear of the house. Not a shot was fired, although it did take a couple of well-placed rifle butt strokes to get their attention. When we walked in, we saw the bastards hitting and kicking the homeowner and his wife, who were bleeding on the floor. Well, let's just say these cretins were properly subdued. Somehow I doubt they will be kicking or hitting anyone else anytime soon. Tough to do with broken knees and elbows. I took the leader aside for a private chat and learned about their orders from Tank."

The smile on her lips made Mike very glad she was on his side.

Mike looked at Linda searchingly for a moment, before saying, "Make sure no more prisoners are abused. Period. Understand, LT?" Mike used the nickname Linda's security people had given her. Although the prisoners couldn't hear their conversation, several members of Linda's security team did.

Linda paused briefly before snapping to attention with a growing respect in her eyes. "Yes, Sir, Mike." That simple act and her three words were repeated throughout the neighborhood several times that day. Anyone who had doubted that Mike was in charge no longer had those doubts.

"Mike," Linda asked, "follow the SOP as we agreed?" Mike didn't respond except to nod his head. "We'll keep their guns, but you still want to leave their trucks and trailers with them when we drop them off?"

Mike nodded again before saying, "Yes, we're not thieves. Don't want their guns pointed at us again, but we will not take government trucks and equipment." After that comment Mike was amazed how incredibly easy it was to be a leader when you had top-notch people working for you. Pressure points, he just needed to make the right decision at critical times.

"All right, guys," Linda said, "just like we trained." Looking at two of her people, she said, "Let's do this in the vans, okay?"

With a short, "Yes, Ma'am," the two were off on foot to borrow two mini-vans staged nearby in their owner's driveway. In short order, the home invaders had received treatment for their broken bones and lacerations and placed, on a plastic tarp, in the floor of the vans. Linda had called someone at the National Guard Armory in the state capital to advise them to expect a quiet drop within the next hour. All the vehicles, including the ones brought by Tank's thugs, were driven to the Armory. Their winter coats, guns, and boots had been confiscated. Two envelopes had been left with the men. One was addressed to the Governor and one to the Commanding Officer. They contained a one page, unsigned letter describing what the men had done and that they were being turned over to the National Guard for appropriate law enforcement handling. It also stated such barbarous behavior would not be tolerated in a society run by laws. Also in each envelope were flash drives containing video evidence shot showing the thug's illegal entrance to the home and showing still photos of what they had done to the two, elderly, homeowners.

When both mini-vans returned with Linda's team, they were in a celebratory mood, before Linda sobered them by simply saying, "You know, it isn't over; not by a long shot." Although subdued, each man looked around at his friends knowing they had won their first victory.

Mike was highly annoyed when he discovered the next day that the story of what had happened, including photographs, had been put up on social media.

CHAPTER 49
THE NEW YEAR - PLUS FORTY-TWO DAYS

The Fontaine Estate
Outside of San Francisco, California
1610 Hours PST

Walter had awakened with only a minor hangover just after 3:00 p.m., and had spent the past forty-five minutes working up a minor sweat at the estate exercise room. He had gone from machine to machine before settling into the chair of the exercise bicycle for twenty minutes of slow spinning. A popular news channel was on trying valiantly to describe the necessary and brilliant things President Fontaine continued to do to bring America through the crisis. Mixed in was only the occasional mention of what the "opposition press" kept trying to do to divert the country's attention away from the real problems of gun violence and wealthy people that refused to pay their fair share. Compounding the problems were those that refused to give up to the government necessary supplies to help feed the American people. It had even been necessary to cut back on providing financial support to environmental companies struggling to produce energy in ways that will help stop global warming.

Walter had chuckled under his breath as he thought about what the news wasn't telling everyone. Over forty percent of the "green" companies had gone bankrupt, with U.S. Department of Justice declining prosecutions into what happened to taxpayer dollars. They had also used "prosecutorial discretion" to decline to follow up on complaints that the IRS, EPA and other federal agencies were using their administrative powers to harass, or in some cases, run anti-Fontaine organizations out of business. The discretion was augmented under the various PEOs brought on by Katherine's declared State of Emergency.

While riding on the exercise bike, Walter's mind began to clear and refocused away from the news and onto the maid. He thought to himself, "Her face isn't much to look at, but her tits do stretch out the uniform top and her lips are full and soft." He could already feel himself reacting to the thought of her lips sliding up and down. It shouldn't take much of the cash he had stashed in his bedroom to convince her to help him out.

Although there was an embarrassing bulge in his shorts, no one was present to see it except for the Secret Service asshole and to hell with him, Walter thought as he walked toward his room.

Once in his room, he dialed the house phone and asked for the maid to bring up a bucket of ice and a pitcher of ice water to his bedroom. He didn't notice the nervousness in her voice as she mumbled in her heavily accented voice, "Yes, Okay."

In preparation for her arrival, Walter toweled himself off before slipping out of his gym clothes and into a silk robe. As she arrived, she stared at the floor as she said,

"Where you want?"

Walter intentionally said nothing, but pointed his finger at a coffee table in front of the small loveseat, across the room from the big, king-sized, four-poster bed. This caused her to look up into his face where he presented what he believed was his most winning smile. He invited her to sit and enjoy a drink with him. She looked at the floor and attempted to decline, but he insisted.

Surprisingly, the maid took the scotch and downed it with a big gulp. Walter said, "Wow, little lady, I've really missed you all these years." He was even more surprised when she smiled and reached out her hand to stroke his crotch.

Walter didn't notice the slight tearing in her eyes or the tremble of her chin. If he had, he would have presumed they were excited reactions for what was to come. As she opened his robe and took his member in her hand she suddenly paused to reach into her uniform pocket and bring out a tube of red lipstick. Still smiling, she quickly put on the lipstick, which would have been a better color match for her ten years earlier, when she still had jet-black hair. She would never wear such a color now, with her salt and pepper colored hair.

Of course, Walter didn't notice nor did he care. All he saw were those bright, red lips. As her head bobbed up and down in his lap, he marveled at the tingle on his member, thinking there must have been some kind of menthol mixed into the lipstick. It took less than thirty seconds before he exploded into her mouth.

She tried to pull away then, but he grabbed her wrists and pulled her up onto him as he tried to regain his breath. Holding her against him, he could feel himself growing again, although it felt like it was almost on fire. He then tore off her clothes, not even bothering with her bra, before he pulled her over to his bed and threw her down, face-first. He then began to enter her prone form from the rear, pumping for a long time, until he again exploded into her.

Walter was shocked to wake up thirty minutes later to find himself lying on top of her still form. His crotch seemed to be on fire. Looking down, he could see the entire area grossly swollen and inflamed. He reached over to the maid's still form and turned her over. Her tongue was sticking way out of her mouth and it was black. Her lips were also black and much of her skin around her mouth was streaked with black lines. He could also tell she was quite dead. She did not breathe and a quick listen to her heart found no beat.

In a panic and nearly delirious with his own pain, all he could think about was that he needed to get her body out of the house. With his robe hanging open, he wrapped her up in a sheet and stumbled his way through his bathroom and out a seldom-used servant's door to a stairway that lead past the estate kitchen and down to his massive garage. Somehow he managed to negotiate the stairs without falling, knocking her head on the handrail several times. In his garage, he stumbled to the first vehicle he came to, a vintage Lincoln Limousine convertible dating back to his first campaign for Mayor of Sacramento, California. It was kept in pristine, running condition and still bore the hand-painted slogans, "Fontaine for Mayor" on the sides.

Walter's delirium and pain had increased to the point where he no longer consciously thought about, or cared what he was doing. He fired up the Lincoln, inched toward the door until it automatically opened, and picked up speed as he wound his way along the driveway to the front gate of the estate. Secret Service agents guarding the gate stood in the driveway with hands up as they saw their protectee approach at a high rate of speed. He never slowed down as he smashed his way through the wrought-iron gates, turning onto the four lane toward the shopping center. The older, heavier vehicle was able to crash through the gates, unlike any of his modern vehicles. The Secret Service agents dove out of the way as he sped by. Their security mission focused on threats from the street and not the First Man driving a veritable tank of a vehicle through the gates.

Within seconds, two Secret Service SUVs screamed down the driveway in pursuit. Less than one quarter mile down the road, they saw Walter's limo had crashed into the coffee shop on the corner of a busy intersection. Before they could get out of their vehicles, over a dozen patrons had pulled out their phones and were tape recording the whole scene. They could just hear Walter's delirious voice over the pandemonium, "I think the bitch had me killed!"

When the Secret Service Agents arrived, they immediately attempted to establish a perimeter. The agents also began to seize the video-taping cell phones of those closest to the crash. Seeing the phones being seized, several of the younger people decided to quickly run away and almost immediately posted their videos on social media.

· · ·

The White House
2035 Hours EST

Katherine had gone to bed early with a bad head cold when she was awakened out of a sound sleep by the annoying ring of the phone on her nightstand. She was instantly awake because for that phone to ring unexpectedly meant something extremely important, up to, and including nuclear war. Her response into the phone was, "What?"

The current head of her White House Secret Service detail's voice said, "Madam President, my Director is on his way over with an analyst. Madam President it is not good news concerning your husband. All available information will be available to you in ten minutes."

"I'll receive him in my sitting room." With that short comment, Katherine hung up the phone. She couldn't keep a small smile from her face as she considered the bastard had probably died painfully, and that the Goddamned Chinese bastards had just lost most of their clout over her. She decided to wear her dark robe over her nightgown to receive the Director. She then called the White House switchboard and asked them to locate and have Susan Cassel come there immediately.

Twenty five minutes later, with Susan Cassel standing by her side, Katherine asked the Secret Service Director and his analyst to come into her sitting room. Without ceremony, Katherine said in a soft voice, "Director, please tell me what happened."

"Madam President," he said with all the solemnity he could muster, "I'm sorry to inform you that your husband, Walter is dead."

He paused to allow the President to respond, but then continued when there was no reaction from her. "Madam President, the details are sketchy at best at this point, however we know that approximately two hours ago, Mr. Fontaine drove his old campaign Lincoln Limousine through the locked gates of your San Francisco estate and crashed it into a coffee house approximately one quarter mile down the road."

Katherine's demeanor went from concerned concentration to complete shock. "What did you say?! He drove *through* the gates? *Crashed?*"

The analyst continued, "Yes, Madam President. There are several other crucial details to report." He paused and then continued, "Your husband died from apparent poisoning and was wearing only a silk bathrobe that was hanging open. In addition, the dead, nearly-naked body of your Chinese born maid was partially covered by a sheet in the back seat of the convertible. Madam President, despite the best efforts of the security team, several civilians present were able to depart the area with cell phone video recordings of your husband and the naked maid in the crashed vehicle."

"*Best Efforts!*" Katherine screeched the words as loud as she could. "You people were supposed to watch the son-of-a-bitch! It was your *job*! What else could possibly go wrong?" Katherine was enraged to the point of reacting and not thinking when Susan's touch on her shoulder.

"Madam President," Susan said softly, "you may need some time to reflect on everything that has happened. Please give me twenty minutes and I will bring you all the details you will need at this time. Okay?"

Katherine looked into Susan's eyes with as close to relief and affection as was possible for her. Reaching up to Susan's face and stroking it, Katherine said, "Yes, dear, please do that. I need a few minutes to myself."

Susan rose and escorted the Director and his analyst to a small conference room, just outside of the Personal Quarters area of the White House. Although shocked herself, she had been able to compose herself during the minutes it took to get settled.

"All right, gentlemen, give it to me again. Slowly."

The analyst gave a full narrative of everything they had discovered in chronological order. This time, he added the blackening of Walter's crotch, the same for the maid's lips and the fact that her lipstick was being rushed to the

FBI laboratory as quickly as possible. Inferences were presented as just that, inferences without hard facts to back them up, yet. When they advised of the social media posts, they also mentioned Walter's last words, "The bitch had me killed."

The Director insisted they had locked Walter down with everything short of shackles. The maid had been part of the house staff for over twenty years and had been vetted as well as possible, considering the, "Presidential restrictions on our ability to vet the Fontaine staff."

"Was it the Chinese?" Susan asked the question while boring into the Director's eyes.

"Susan, at this point we don't know. I personally highly doubt it, but you may know more about that than I." The look in the Director's eye was both probing and offensive.

The comment caught Susan off guard. Under the circumstances, it would appear that the Secret Service Director was another that knew about Walter's dalliance with the Chinese whore.

Susan didn't relish the briefing she would have to give to Katherine.

CHAPTER 50
THE NEW YEAR - PLUS FORTY-THREE DAYS

Command Bunker
Outside of Beijing, China
0745 Hours Local Time

Song sat behind his desk watching the monitor he had ordered Wong to install in his bunker office. It gave him access to the entire security camera system in the bunker complex, including inside and outside. Watching the dawn break in the mountains was how he most often used the system. A few minutes later Wong announced the arrival of an officer from the PLA General Staff. The officer gave his briefing concerning the readiness for the upcoming invasion. The logistics of amassing an invasion force across the straight from Formosa were immense and Song had expected to find the list of critical issues extensive. He was pleased, however, that the officer appeared to be providing accurate information that conformed with what Lao had told him an hour earlier. He took some solace knowing the PLA was preparing for an invasion anticipated to take over a month to complete. In his estimation, the fight should take less than one week and possibly as little as a few days. It would be very bloody, but the Nationalists would finally capitulate or die. The General Staff did not know the Americans would be sitting on the sidelines while the invasion and occupation were launched and were, therefore, planning on being required to fight them as well.

After Song dismissed the officer, he took stock of the situation. Although it still burned to urinate through his re-attached penis, and his various cuts and bruises itched incessantly, he no longer needed any strong pain killers. His brain functioned at an acceptably high level and Lao's efforts had been effective in keeping his enemies off balance and, at least for the time being, slowed their assassination attempts. It did trouble him that he was not ruling from his seat of power in Beijing, but with secure teleconferencing, coupled with his own spies and those of the MSS. He was able to see most of the political moves and maintain a general level of control. In the back of his mind was also the belief that Black Orchid would manifest itself within the next few weeks, if not sooner. If he could be sure, there would be no need for the invasion. Lao had been correct. He did have an uncanny ability to intuit just the right action to better China's goals. If only it worked to warn him of personal attacks.

Three hours later Wong advised of an incoming secure telephone call from Lao. Once all the lights and beeps indicated the line was secure, Song said simply, "Speak."

"General Secretary," Lao's voice said with his computer encrypted voice sounding strange, "my computer people tell me that within the last hour, the American social media has exploded with homemade videos of the death of Walter Fontaine. He apparently died when an old convertible that had been used decades ago in one of his campaigns, crashed into a coffee shop down the road from the Fontaine estate in California. Claims on social media say the dead, naked body of a Chinese girl was in the back seat, partially wrapped in a sheet. The initial analysis of the videos appears to record Fontaine shouting out the phrase, "The Bitch had me killed," just before he died from what my analysts believe was poisoning. From the black swelling and markings in the vicinity of his crotch, and the swollen face and black lips of the unrecognizable Chinese girl, it appears at least possible the girl may have poisoned him using lipstick during oral sex."

"Lao," Song said with a strained voice, "do the Americans believe we have assassinated the husband of their President?"

"General Secretary, it is too early to determine what the American's think. That however, is a logical conclusion for them to draw. A lot depends upon who the Chinese girl is in the back seat of his vehicle and many other facts not currently available."

After a pause for thought, Song said, "Is it possible this is the missing girl we discussed?"

"General Secretary, at this point, I don't know." Lao's voice was low and tinged with regret.

• • •

The Mike Broehm House
Outside of Cronin, Kentucky
0745 Hours EST

Lauren called to Mike as he was coming out of the shower. "Honey, you might want to come see this."

While toweling himself off, with crazy salt and pepper hair sticking up in all directions, Mike walked into the bedroom to see what she wanted. Lauren was rooted, almost spellbound, in front of the TV. Glancing at the screen, Mike could see the caption, "Walter Fontaine dead at 66." The commentator of the only conservative national news channel said, "…and although details of his death have not been confirmed by the White House, initial reports from San Francisco seem to be in agreement that former Vice President Walter Fontaine was dying as he crashed his convertible limousine into a coffee shop less than one quarter mile from the Fontaine estate. Unconfirmed reports say the naked body of an oriental female was in the back seat and that Fontaine was babbling deliriously just before he died. Secret Service agents swarmed the scene within seconds and immediately began confiscating camera phones of several observers. We have exclusive video from a confidential source that took video at the scene and posted it almost immediately on social media."

The screen changed to a somewhat grainy and bouncing video tape showing Walter in the front seat of the limousine, bathrobe flung wide open with his private area blurred out. The body of a woman could be seen on the floor of the back seat, partially uncovered by a sheet. The back of Walter's head was pressed tightly against the headrest, eyes closed as he shouted, "I think the bitch had me killed!" Within seconds, his head slumped forward, he shuddered and appeared to die. The sound of car doors could be heard, footsteps running and the video blurred into scenes from a person running quickly from the scene.

Mike quickly pressed the record button and switched to one of the other major network news channels. Local morning program had been preempted and the morning show host scheduled to begin his broadcast at the top of the hour was seen speaking without his usual teleprompter. Across the bottom of the screen ran a tag-line similar to that seen on the conservative station. In a calm voice, the host said, "Former Vice President Fontaine had served with distinction, in public office, for over thirty years. In his role as Vice President, he was trusted by the President to work closely with the Senate and to cast the tie-breaking vote on over a dozen important pieces of legislation. There has not been any word from the White House yet concerning either the upcoming state funeral or how the President is enduring her grief."

Mike continued to watch for another thirty minutes before satisfying himself the host would not even acknowledge the sordid details of Walter Fontaine's death. Just to be sure, he changed the channel to another national news outlet and discovered the same somber and laudatory descriptions were being given concerning the former Vice President.

Just before Mike decided to turn to the conservative station's recorded programming, the talking head on the screen became even more serious as he said, "Through unofficial sources in the White House, it has just been discovered that some parties unknown were publishing one or more staged videos claiming to depict the fatal crash of the former Vice President. These false depictions are reported to be an attempt to harm the reputation of the deceased. FCC Enforcement actions are on-going to remove these false videos. White House sources also indicate that any media outlet that shows them are, under the state of emergency, in violation of FCC protocols and will be subject to being shut down in the interest of National Security. The White House is expected to make a special announcement at 1:00 p.m."

. . .

The White House
1332 Hours EST

Marc Baxter sat quietly in his office chair, having just turned off all of the televisions mounted on his wall. Press Secretary Towanda Jefferson had just given a fifteen minute press conference where she announced that by Presidential Executive Order, and in the interests of National Security, the Federal Communications Commission (FCC) was to insure that no false and libelous news concerning this tragic event was allowed to flow over the airwaves, through regulated cable or via cyberspace. Marc had feared the President would decide the Constitution no longer applied to her.

Towanda's canned speech at the press conference was the third shock of the morning. Having learned of Walter's death late the previous evening, he had spent the entire night at his desk in the White House. At 9:15 a.m. the TV that showed the conservative news channel had suddenly gone dark, before blinking back on to show only a test pattern with the message, "Temporarily off the air."

Ten minutes later Marc had received a call from one of that channel's Washington correspondents who he knew from journalism classes at Columbia University. Instead of asking Marc the expected questions, he claimed to have a personal emergency involving his wife and asked if Marc could spare him just a couple of minutes. Marc had agreed to meet him two blocks from the White House at a sidewalk coffee cart.

* * * *

When Marc arrived, he found his buddy standing near the cart. His buddy opened an opaque envelope, placed his own cell phone inside and motioned for Marc to do the same. With a sigh, Marc did so.

"Marc, were you aware the FCC just came over to our station and completely pulled the plug on us?"

The look on Marc's face was answer enough. His buddy continued, "Yeah, I thought not. Some goons from Homeland Security waltzed in with the FCC guys and slammed us with an Executive Order to shut us down. They justified it by saying we were broadcasting a false video depicting the death of Walter Fontaine, which threatened national security. Can you believe that shit? In America? What the hell, Marc?" The exasperation was plainly written on his face.

"I don't know what to tell you," Marc said honestly. "I mean, if the video is bogus, during this time of crisis it could be a threat to the stability of the gov...."

"Marc, buddy! Listen to yourself. Do you really believe that load of crap? Anyway, the truth is the video is absolutely authentic. I won't give details, but first, it was posted within five minutes after the crash, so there was no time for it to be staged. Second, it was taken by a very reliable source, and I won't even tell you any more about it. Just take it as gospel, it's legit. Third, did you see it? It sure sounds like the bastard is accusing the President of having him killed. Jesus, Marc!"

Stunned and mentally exhausted, Marc found a moment of clarity before looking his buddy in the eye, before responding, "Look, I wish there were something I could do to get you guys back on line, and if I can, I will. Beyond that, well that's all I can do. Listen, thanks for this. I mean it."

With a hint of fear in his eye, Marc's buddy said, "This is off the record and will be just between us, right?"

"Yes," Marc said, "and I mean that. Now can I have my phone back?"

Reluctantly, the man handed Marc his phone, turned and walked slowly away.

. . .

Marc now sat in his office contemplating the PEO shutting down the conservative station in light of his President's actions, what he knew about Walter as a liability and all the rest. It was no great leap to believe Walter had been killed at the order of the President.

He was startled from his thoughts by Burt sticking his head in the door. "Heh, Marc. Want you to sit in on a meeting at 6:00 p.m. Oh, and by the way, Towanda isn't invited, okay?"

Coming out of his reverie, Marc said, "Uh, okay. What's it about?"

"God, man. How long has it been since you slept? We need to decide if the Chinese are responsible for Walter's death. Get some coffee or something!" Burt shook his head and headed off down the hall.

Taking Burt's advice, he went to the canteen for coffee.

CHAPTER 51
THE NEW YEAR - PLUS FORTY-THREE DAYS

The White House
1813 Hours EST

For the past twenty minutes, Marc, Burt, CIA Director Brad Pittson, NSA Director Donald Clayborn, and Secretary of Defense Carlton Hathaway had learned all the known details about Walter's death from the Secret Service Director and the Homeland Security Director. For unexplained reasons, the FBI Director and had not been invited nor had his agency been involved in the investigation. All anyone present knew was that this was at the order of the President.

Katherine arrived soon after the briefing had been delivered. She looked terrible, with large bags under her eyes and fatigue written all over her face. Contrary to looking sad, an angry fire was flashing in her eyes.

Looking at Burt, she said, "Anything new that I don't already know?"

Burt took a deep breath, sighed and after another moment for thought, said, "No, Madam President. I believe you're aware of all the details that have been presented just now. May I say how sorry I am that you have to go through this?"

Her response was a look of near contempt. "Oh, can it, Burt." She forced herself to stop before she said how much the bastard deserved what he got. The only problem was how difficult he had made it for her on his way out.

"Gentlemen, I want to know what, if anything, the Chinese had to do with Walter's death." Looking at the Secret Service Director, she said, "You're sure it was our maid, Lu Lu in the car with him? Did he have sex with her?"

The bluntness of her questioning only mildly surprised those present.

"Madam President," said the Homeland Security Director, in a slightly embarrassed voice while looking at his hands on the table, "the preliminary autopsy of the maid found traces of semen in her mouth. Her lipstick container was found in Mr. Fontaine's bedroom and has been sent to the FBI Laboratory. They have informed us that it will be about twelve hours before they can provide a definite description of the presumed poison. The most experienced examiner I spoke with said there are several chemicals that can carry almost any liquid substance through the skin quickly, to be absorbed by the victim. His best guess was that one of those transfer chemicals had been used to inject the poison into Mr. Fontaine. My people are in the process of running down all of her relatives for interviews, along with pulling all available information from her phone records, E-mail and everything else we can think of. I have received no updated results from the investigation since entering this meeting. Oh and Madam President, the FBI is quite a bit better at this sort of thing than Homeland, and they have significant resources and primary jurisdiction. Shouldn't I turn the investigation over to them?"

Katherine rose and turned her back to hide her nearly incapacitating apprehension, before building into a rage and turning to him. "No! I ordered you to do it and I expect you to get the job done!"

Glaring around the table, she could see the faces laced with both concern and disbelief bordering on anger. After a deep breath, she said, "I won't go into it, but I don't trust the FBI at this time to do the investigation. Any problems with that decision?"

No one responded.

"Good," Katherine said. "I ask again, did the Chinese do it?"

Pittson responded first. "Madam President, I received a direct call from MSS Director Lao, who expressed his sympathies. In an unusual move, he also denied any involvement or knowledge by his government. He went so far as to say doing something so outrageous was counterproductive to China's goals. I have to say, Madam President, he made a convincing case for no involvement by his people. Also, the CIA did develop several poisons capable of doing this sort of thing. We even invented the felt-tipped pen to deliver it back in the 1960s, but in the last two decades, knowledge and ability to access these materials has devolved to the capabilities of almost anyone with an advanced chemistry degree. There are a few known cases where drug cartels and organized crime organizations have used this method of assassination. Of course, any one of dozens of countries have the ability to do this, but politically it would be suicide for them to do so. Madam President, I would start with extensive investigation of your known political enemies."

Each of those present echoed Pittson's conclusion. With something akin to relief, Katherine dropped her head and said to the Homeland Security Director, "Do that Director. Task the FBI if you must, but insure that your agency remains in charge of the investigation."

With a nod received from the Director, she turned to Marc.

"Whiz kid, what do we need to do to A) let the country know we don't think it was the Chinese that did this, and B) keep the country's attention off the sordid details that got the bastard killed in the first place?"

Marc had known the question was coming and he took a deep breath before responding. "Madam President, your PEO shutting down the conservative news station and stifling the entire Internet has been and will continue to be extremely counterproductive. Many people believe the order is both unconstitutional and an illegal seizure of power by the executive branch."

Marc stopped talking and waited for the anticipated explosion. The others around the table looked at Marc with new respect, considering he had just said what they were all thinking.

Instead of the expected explosion, Katherine said, "Okay, I see your point. What do I do about it?"

After a stunned moment of silence, Marc said, "Madam President, you should immediately lift the PEO and have the FCC remove all restrictions from all news organizations."

A quick glance showed Katherine looking at him with a thoughtful expression and not rage. "Next, Madam President, you should address the nation and apologize for the well-meaning but incorrect information about your husband's death. We can ignore any statements made by the government concerning the video being staged, but we will need to acknowledge the video is accurate and come up with our own narrative that fits the video. Maybe the maid was off her medications and hated Mr. Fontaine for rebuffing her perceived affections. Middle Eastern terrorists had been looking for a way to strike back at you and had blackmailed her into trying to poison Mr. Fontaine." Marc looked around the table for ideas or suggestions.

Katherine said, "That's why I hired you Whiz kid. You work with my professional Secret Service Director," she paused to let sarcasm drip from her voice, "and get a story that will fly. I will deliver it tomorrow evening. Oh, and Burt, have the FCC back off on all the censorship." She then rose from her chair and walked from the room.

Clayborn looked over at Marc and said, "Boy, don't know how you managed it, but you may have just saved her and us from making the worst mistake of our lives. Keep that up and you'll go far." Nods of agreement were made around the table.

. . .

Mike Broehm Residence
Outside Cronin, Kentucky
1900 Hours EST

Mike had gathered what he now considered his command staff at his house, including Sean and Linda, Peter, Fred Callahan, Rollie McDermott, Lauren and Mrs. Onie Lisle, whose husband, Jim, had died three years earlier. Over the past several weeks, Onie had stepped in to help Mike handle the day-to-day issues involving the neighborhood and would prove to be invaluable when the power was cut off. The purpose for this meeting was to discuss the death of the First Man and the Fontaine administration's reaction to it. Linda and Sean were the last to arrive.

"Mike," Linda said, "you might want to flip on your favorite news channel."

With a questioning look on his face, Mike walked to the TV and turned it on. Unlike thirty minutes earlier when all he had seen was a test pattern and short message, now he and all present watched with interest as the lead evening commentator for the news channel read his statement. A banner flashed at the bottom of the screen that said, "President rescinds illegal order."

"At 6:38 p.m. Eastern time the district manager for the FCC delivered a supplemental order to one received by this station earlier in the day. In the first order, this station was directed to terminate all broadcasts, for national security reasons, based upon the President's authority under the declared state of emergency. The order recently handed to us rescinds that order without explanation. Our contacts within the White House indicate the President will be making an address to the nation tomorrow evening concerning the death of her husband and explaining the White House reaction directly following that tragedy. Now let's turn to our White House correspondent, who can tell us what is known about this whole incident."

Mike pushed the record button and turned off the TV. "I've spent the last four hours scouring the web for information and unless there has been a major breakthrough, which they would have announced at the beginning, they're just speculating and rehashing what we already know. Peter, do you have any insight on this stuff?"

Everyone turned to Peter, who usually had excellent sources in Washington, D.C.

"I'm sorry, Mike. Everyone I know seems to be as baffled about it as we are."

Although uncomfortable about it, Peter kept to himself Lisa and Su Ling's opinions of what might have happened. They were speculating and to relay their thoughts might compromise the fact they had been hiding in his house for a month. Both were strongly of the opinion that the President had ordered Walter killed, but would not elaborate why they had that opinion, citing Lisa's promise to her father.

Peter continued, "I have no idea about who killed the First Man, but I kind of suspect that the President's reaction to publication of the video by denying it and trying to crush further publication was literally a knee jerk reaction. Seems like her staff was finally able to talk some sense into her and she's trying to do damage control. What is most frightening to me is the fact that she ordered a blatant violation of the First Amendment and won't be held accountable for it. We'll have to see what she says tomorrow evening, but if she keeps this stuff up, the country is going to revolt on her. It'll be Patriots versus King George, or Queen Katherine all over again."

Looking around the room, Mike saw only agreement. He asked Sean for his take. "Mike, I have to agree with Peter. Honestly, I'm just waiting for the other shoe to drop."

Just as he said this, power was cut off in the house. After about five seconds, Mike's automatic whole-house generator fired up and the lights came back on. Mike asked Lauren, "Honey, how many times has that happened this week? Four? Five?"

Lauren said, "I think it's the fifth time. So far an hour is the longest it has been out. I did hear the power company has been cutting employees and has been having trouble buying power from other regions." The whole concept of no power was depressing for everyone.

CHAPTER 52
THE NEW YEAR - PLUS FORTY FOUR DAYS

State highway
Outside of Shelbyville, KY
0830 Hours EST

Cruising down the two-lane highway between the state capitol and the small town of Shelbyville, Kentucky was the Governor's convoy consisting of ten vehicles. It included the Governor's limousine, two Kentucky State Police cruisers and seven military vehicles. The National Guard Captain in charge of the Kentucky Governor's protection motorcade was only a little concerned. He had complete confidence in his men and their equipment. It had been gained through two tours in "The Sandbox" of Afghanistan and Iraq, over the past four years as Combat MPs. These military policemen had literally been to war and returned to tell about it. He was confident that he would win any fight that might come their way, but he was less certain he could avoid casualties. This concern was heightened when he recalled the briefings identifying potential threats to the Governor. With less experienced troops, he would have been riding without any weapons "locked and loaded," or having shells in the chambers and capable of being fired by simply flicking off the safety switch. He now treated every movement of the Governor to be the same as a combat patrol in the Sandbox. For firepower, his people had everything available from individual M-4, fully automatic rifles to grenade launchers to the mounted, belt-fed M240 machine guns atop two of his armored HMMWVs, known as the Humvee.

The original plan was to drive to the Interstate for the short trip to Shelbyville, however, the leader of the Kentucky State Police protection detail for the Governor had been informed the Interstate was shut down by a bad tractor trailer accident just west of Frankfort. The motorcade approached a cut between two hills and the hair on the convoy commander's neck began to stand up. Automatically, he reached for his radio and announced for his men to go on high alert. He had trusted his instincts before and had always been right. Within seconds everything seemed to happen at once, but to the commander, it played out in slow motion.

A pickup truck roared out of a driveway off to one side, heading for the side of the lead armored Humvee. At the same time bullets began to bounce off the sides of several vehicles, coming from at least 4 directions. The turret gunner of the second armored Humvee brought his M240 machine gun that was mounted on the roof, to bear on the pickup and riddled the front seat area of the vehicle. At the same time the third Humvee opened up with its MK19 automatic grenade launcher, causing the pickup to explode. None of the vehicles in the convoy had slowed and all maintained their assigned distances from the vehicle in front.

The Governor's armored limousine passed the middle of the cut through the small hills when two men could be seen standing on top of the hill to the right, each with a LAWS rocket on his shoulder. The first fired at the limousine, with the rocket passing several feet over the roof. Just as the second man fired his rocket, he was blasted backward by bullets striking him from at least three different sources. His rocket struck the limousine in the passenger compartment, causing the vehicle to lose control and crash into the rock wall making up the side of the hill.

With the limousine disabled, the Combat MP's that were not manning mounted weapons dismounted, and immediately set out to secure the perimeter. A loud crack was heard and the MP manning one of the machine guns felt a bullet tear through the cloth on the side of his shirt. He immediately shouted, "Sniper!" He then pointed in the approximate direction from which the bullet had come. Four of the MPs began to quickly and stealthily make their way toward the sniper position. It took them less than a minute to cover most of the distance. Twice more shots were fired from that position, but it was obvious the sniper was focused on the convoy. When the MPs were within eighty yards of the sniper one of them launched a 40mm grenade, ending the threat. It had landed eight feet from the old bearded man, but he had suffered several shrapnel wounds and lay crying in pain.

The sergeant in charge of the four approached the bleeding man, who was doubled over, holding his gut. Conversationally, the sergeant said, "If you don't roll over and show me your hands, I'm just going to put a bullet right between your legs and then through both knees."

After a moment, the man rolled over, pulled his hands away from his gut and then put them back to his gut.

Again, in his unhurried Kentucky drawl, the sergeant said, "I'm not a gonna tell ya again. Hands all the way out, spread eagle. Do it now." The old man looked into the eyes of the sergeant and saw no pity, nor any give. He moved his hands and arms as instructed.

The sergeant said to one of his men, "Search him, and then cuff him." Two other guns and two knives were found on the old man along with his wallet and a small bag of gold coins.

"Get me a medic, Goddamn you!" The old man spit the words out through painfully clenched teeth.

The sergeant just stood and looked at him as his corporal read out what he had found in his pockets and wallet. The old man continued to curse and demand medical treatment, citing everything from Kentucky law to the Geneva Convention. The other two men had reported there did not appear to be any more hostiles in the area. They also believed they had found the man's brand new truck. Two sets of new truck keys were laying in the pile of the man's belongings.

The sergeant sent one man with keys to verify it was his truck before squatting down on his heels next to the old man. He thought briefly how the old man could have been his grandpa, but then decided he was probably too mean to have fathered children.

The sergeant reached into his medical kit and pulled out a plastic wrapped syringe and showed it to the man. "Mister, this here is my own personal morphine shot, you know in case some asshole like you was to shoot me and leave me laying there to die. Now when we got one of them Taliban idiots over in the Sandbox, we usually turned them over to the Afghan soldiers to get everything they knew. I got to watch a couple of times and they were pretty good at squeezing 'em. Far as I'm concerned, you're no better than one of them and maybe worse, 'cause you weren't even told we were invaders. Now the only thing standin' between you and this here morphine and a medic is telling me who paid you to do this."

The old man closed his eyes for a couple of seconds before muttering, "Fuckit, I ain't going to suffer for that sonofabitch. I might not live through this, but at least I can die knowing he'll get his. It was Tank Monahan who paid for this. That's his gold in the pouch. Hell, you can have it if you want." Gasping with pain, the old man continued, "He said something about the Fontaine people had hired him to hire us to get rid of a problem. That's all I know, now give me the damned drugs!"

The sergeant nodded, before asking, "When and where did he do this?"

"Goddammit, it was four days ago at the Pen and Pencil in Frankfort. Now please…" He drew out the last word with his agony.

The sergeant slit the old man's pants leg with his knife and gave him the shot of morphine, followed by putting on a pressure bandage. He then sat down on a nearby rock and began to dig for more details.

. . .

The White House
1700 Hours EST

Marc sat at his desk feeling like a zombie. He had grabbed three hours of sleep, early in the morning, before showering and coming back to the White House. He had been working with the President's speech writers when the news broke that the Kentucky Governor had been assassinated by what was believed to be paramilitary revolutionaries. Katherine had immediately reacted by demanding a portion of her speech be used to announce her ordered confiscation of all assault weapons and any semi-automatic weapon capable of shooting anything larger than a .22 caliber long rifle bullet. This would include semi-automatic handguns. Only police and military units were exempt from this confiscation, which would be coordinated by the Department of Homeland Security. The portion of the speech dealing with Walter's murder was to be downsized and emphasis was to be placed on the Governor's assassination.

Marc had heard whispers, conveyed through social media and mentioned as unconfirmed reports on the conservative news channel, that a surviving attacker had named a local man hired by the Regional Governor and even the Fontaine administration as being responsible for the assassination. The White House and favorable media outlets quickly condemned those reports. The surviving attacker had been taken into custody by DHS and had disappeared. DHS had also arrested the Commanding General of the Kentucky National Guard on suspicion of complicity to the murder. The usual requirement for a probable cause hearing had been waived under the State of Emergency by Regional Administrator Coyote Collins. Tensions were running high in Kentucky and throughout the heartland.

Marc had no chance to talk to Susan, who was spending almost every moment with the President. Events seemed to continue at an incredible pace, making it impossible to get ahead of them. He had stopped trying to write up explanations for the PEOs and instead simply disseminated them to the Press and the Congressional Record.

Thinking about the President's upcoming address to the nation, the sour feeling in the pit of his stomach seemed to grow. With everything going on in the rest of the world, it seemed that America was destined to go to war with herself.

CHAPTER 53
THE NEW YEAR - PLUS FORTY-FOUR DAYS

The Mike Broehm Residence
Outside of Cronin, Kentucky
2140 Hours EST

Mike was gathering himself to speak with his command staff and a few others in his family room following the President's address. Quite a few soft curses and comments clearly showed the contained outrage felt by all present. On the one hand, the President had actually apologized to the American people for the well-intentioned, but misguided actions of a few members of her administration. She even explained that the violent death of her husband, Walter had caused her to rely on inaccurate data when she made the decision to halt dissemination of what she was lead to believe was a staged video depicting his last moments. At this point her voice cracked, just a little, and a tear dripped down her cheek, as if she recalled the horror and was truly a devastated wife.

The President's demeanor changed when she described the attack on the Governor of Kentucky by what were believed to be militant revolutionaries. The DHS had quickly identified accomplices, to include the Commanding General of the Kentucky National Guard. All Kentucky National Guard members were ordered to remain in their barracks or training centers, with guard details from the active U.S. Army to be sent to each one.

The President had then announced a new PEO directing all Americans to turn in any automatic or semi-automatic weapons shooting munitions larger than a .22 caliber long rifle, to DHS collection centers. All of these weapons must be turned in within forty five days or offenders would be in violation of the PEO and would be arrested. This order included handguns. Only active military and police were exempt from this mandate.

At first, Mike didn't know what to say. He began by saying, "All right, this is not going to be the end of the world."

Just then Linda walked into the room. She had been to Frankfort, along with a member of Sean's security detail, to gather intelligence about the murder. With some relief, Mike said, "What can you tell us, Linda?"

Looking around the room at all the gloom and doom, Linda decided on a tried and true military briefing strategy. "Well, first Mike, I've got good news and bad news. Which do you want to hear first?"

"Why don't you give us the bad news first and we'll head uphill?"

"Okay, I heard the President's address on the radio on my way back from Frankfort. In fact I sat out in the car the past few minutes to finish it up. That stupid bitch just issued the opening salvo for what could be a very bloody civil war. Now for some good news, the Combat MP's helping out the Governor's detail were able to interrogate the guy responsible for staging the attack. He said that Tank Monahan had paid him a quarter million to do it and that Tank claimed the money came from the Regional Administrator's people. Probably Coyote's Chief of Staff. They paid in gold coins. A state judge has already signed the search and arrest warrants and the state police are out after Tank and the Chief of Staff right now. Also, in an unusual move, they are trying to get the whole story out on social media, but several of the social media moguls are taking down the sites almost as quickly as they can try to get them out."

Linda took a deep breath before continuing. "It is obvious that the DHS won't be using the National Guard to try to seize guns. They've been restricted to their barracks. It will take DHS a while to gather enough goons to begin trying to enforce the President's PEO. Frankly, I don't think the goons or even active military will be much interested in starting firefights with American citizens. If the orders do go out to the military, I would expect everything from a passive refusal to mass desertions. I think what we'll have to worry about most is the likelihood that DHS goons will target various areas, like this neighborhood, for plunder. After the last time, they'll most likely bring a lot more men and firepower. Again, the bad news is that there will be more of them with more firepower. The good news is they don't know how prepared we are nor how strong we are in leadership."

Saying this, she looked right at Mike. Everyone else turned to him as well and began a spontaneous cheer, to include comments like, "Yeah, Mike," and "We'll fight for Mike!"

Mike was completely humbled by the show of confidence and could feel the need inside of him to live up to their faith.

"I've been saying all along," Mike said, "if we stick together, we can get through anything."

Mike let things die down a little before asking Linda, "Now correct me if I'm wrong, but won't the arrest of Tank and the Coyote's Chief of Staff be viewed by the administration as some form of insurrection?"

This question sobered everyone quickly. Linda said, "Yes, Mike it very well could. But other than the DHS and its hired goons, I don't think she'll be able to successfully send anyone else out to enforce it. She and her advisors badly miscalculated the vast majority of the American people. She may be able to blow smoke up the ass of her most ardent supporters, but certainly not around here."

Linda's comment drew a suppressed smile and chuckle from Lauren and even a few of the men in the room.

Mike interjected, "Kentucky does have Ft. Knox and Ft. Campbell with lots of soldiers at each place. Won't they be tasked to help DHS?"

Sean said, "As it happens, I can answer that one. No, regular military troops are not considered to be suitable for that mission. Instead, they will want to use Special Forces operators to do that dirty work." Everyone in the room froze and gawked at Sean.

"Unfortunately, those resources aren't available to them quite yet." Sean just let the statement hang in the air and didn't clarify. Finally Mike decided to move on.

"Well, all right then," Mike said with resolution, "let's continue to plan for securing the neighborhood. I mean, we've already got a fence, right?" Again, there were chuckles all around. Mike had arranged with five of the small cattle farmers to bring their cows into the neighborhood. This had required the purchase and installation of an electric cattle fence completely encircling the neighborhood. It was made up of a single wire, strung about three feet above the ground and attached to spaced fence posts with electrical insulators on them. It would hold in cattle and maybe lazy horses, but nothing else. "How are the designs on the entrance gates?"

Rollie responded, "We've got all the lumber and hardware we'll need to build them, plus a few tricks I have in mind. We've also got two Bobcat front-end loaders to dig some fighting positions."

He gave Linda a small salute for that idea. "I've been waiting for a pretty day to get a crew out to get it done."

Mike just smiled and said, "Do ya suppose tomorrow will be a good day for that? A little bit of rain mixed with snow shouldn't slow you down none, now should it?"

"Sure thing, Mike. Tomorrow it is."

CHAPTER 54
THE NEW YEAR - PLUS FORTY-SIX DAYS

The Mountains of Southeastern Afghanistan
1600 Hours Local Time

Ahmed rode in the passenger seat of the old, bouncing Toyota Corolla with Hadi driving and Ali sitting in the back seat. Ali was wrapped up in full, black robes like a woman. On the seat next to him was a box covered in black cloth, shaped like a small casket. A large van trailed the Toyota loaded with fifteen men and their luggage. Hadi drove slowly, as was fitting for someone heading for a funeral. At this rate it would take several more hours to get to Kabul and their hotel, but it was also unlikely they would be stopped.

In the trunk was a quiet Cho, with shackles still on, that were now chained to a bolt through the floor. Ahmed had told him that when the martyrs were on their planes, he would be released. He had not decided whether he spoke the truth to Cho. No dishonor is earned if one lies to an Infidel anyway.

It was a struggle for Ahmed to contain his excitement. He was about to do something no one had done before. Once the Infidels were gone, the JOTP would be able to spread the word of the Prophet across the world.

Hadi had arranged to purchase plane tickets for each of the martyrs, departing in two days. Ahmed had wanted to send them out immediately upon his arrival in Kabul, but Hadi had convinced him to get the tickets and have an extra day in case anything came up to prevent efficient travel. They had been slowed by a washed out bridge, as it turned out. He would ensure the martyrs remained true as they boarded their airplanes to do their most important work.

. . .

Command Bunker
Outside of Beijing, China
1545 Hours Local Time

Song was miserable with an annoying cough that brought sharp pains in his cracked ribs and broken bones. His mood was brightened when Wong announced Lao's arrival. Song began with the usual polite pleasantries before turning to the upcoming invasion.

"Lao, the General Staff briefer just left an hour ago and reports the invasion can happen as early as two days from now. Is this information accurate?"

"Yes, General Secretary, it is." Lao made the declaration with some reservations, but he knew Song only wanted an answer to the basic question, when could they invade.

"Good." Song said this with both satisfaction and finality. "The invasion will commence at 0300 hours in three days."

Lao bowed and responded, "I would recommend, General Secretary that everyone is told to prepare for two days, and let my intelligence people assess whether there is too much advance warning preparations by our renegade republic."

Song responded, "Yes, see that it is done."

A painful coughing fit began as soon as the door closed behind Lao.

. . .

SOCOM Headquarters
1115 Hours EST

The analyst, a CWO3, or Chief Warrant Officer, grade 3, knocked on the Colonel's door before coming in and saluting in front of his desk. "Sir, I have that data you asked for regarding the JOTP." He then continued to stand at attention waiting for a response from the Colonel.

After only a few seconds, the Colonel looked up. "At ease, son. What have you got for me?"

He got up from his desk and motioned the CWO3 to follow him to the conference table nearby. The CWO3 quickly spread out maps of the target area on the table. "Sir, I've been able to locate human traffic at two locations in the target area that look very promising. Infrared imagery shows the usual pattern of guards stationed around what I believe are the main entrances to two cave complexes. Intel suggests that over the past three months, any patrols by the Afghan military are lead on a trail away from the area. Imagery also seems to show at least two major venting holes for what we believe are large generators at one of the sites. And here, Sir, is something very curious." He held up a grainy infrared photo. "You can see what looks like someone in a chemical suit that has been unzipped and is half hanging from his waist. The video showed him coming out of the cave and opening the suit quickly, before sitting down to smoke."

"Son," said the Colonel, "that just jumped this thing up to a top priority. Make up a dozen packets of this information and put it on a PowerPoint presentation. I want you ready to brief the operators[27] within 12 hours. And make sure they understand they need to be in chem/bio protective gear when they hit the targets. Got it?"

"Yes, Sir."

---

[27] "Operators" are titles given to Special Forces soldiers that carryout unconventional military missions.

CHAPTER 55
THE NEW YEAR - PLUS FORTY-EIGHT DAYS

Kabul, Afghanistan
1100 Hours Local Time

Ahmed rode next to Hadi, in the Toyota, feeling elated, exhausted and disappointed at the same time. He could tell no difference in Hadi, except for his small smile. His disappointment arose from his decision to release Cho, after the martyrs had all departed on their travels. He had enjoyed speaking with and learning from Cho about the world and how terribly the Infidels had ruined it. Men becoming women, women sleeping with women, men sleeping with men, and so much more. The world needed to be purged. Now, however he no longer had Cho's descriptions and theories to occupy his mind. He had been dropped off with almost all of the documents and money he carried when captured. He had said he would not contact his government and would find a hole somewhere in the world where he could wait out the chaos. Ahmed neither knew nor cared where he would go. His work for Allah was done.

Neither Ahmed nor Hadi had said anything since watching the fifteen enter the Kabul airport terminal in twos and threes and then dropping Cho off. Two hours earlier each martyr had received an injection from Ali. Men previously sent inside the terminal had called Hadi, as each group boarded their plane, on their trip to change the world. Each believed he would be well rewarded upon his glorious death, never realizing the horrible road of pain and suffering he now inescapably traveled and would inflict on innocent masses throughout the world.

Ali was sleeping in the back seat, next to the refrigerated container with the leftover vials of the new virus. The return back to the caves would only take five hours, driving at a reasonable rate of speed. Not too fast to attract attention, but much faster than that of a funeral procession. The two hour hike back to the cave complexes from the truck drop-off point would be much easier with their mission finally done.

"Hadi, the day after tomorrow you can move the wives and families of all of the fighters from their villages to the caves. The Americans will soon be too busy to bomb us." Both men chuckled.

Ahmed also decided he would, once again, take his second wife out of turn, possibly even twice, to celebrate.

• • • •

Special Forces A-Team 1
Mountains of Southeast Afghanistan
2300 Hours Local Time

The Special Forces A-team from 7th Special Forces Group had been in the vicinity of the second priority cave for over twelve hours. Between aerial imagery and their night vision equipment, the twelve operators believed they had pinpointed locations of four terrorist sentries. They had even seen the arrival of Ahmed and Hadi three hours earlier. Unknown to the operators, the vast majority of Ahmed's group, including a number of his personal security people, had remained behind in Kabul to visit with friends and relatives.

Each operator carried a suppressed .300 caliber Blackout rifle, similar to the old M-16 rifle used by American soldiers in the Vietnam War era, but with much more knockdown power. They also carried a suppressed .22 caliber pistol. With a suppressor, its shot was much closer to the quiet "spit" depicted in the movies than other, larger-caliber weapons. When the team leader gave the signal, the eight operators quietly killed the sentries with .22 caliber pistol shots to the head. No alarm was raised, so they moved on to the entrance of the cave, where two more dozing sentries were quietly dispatched.

The team leader made contact with the second A-team leader at the other site and prepared to enter the dark cave. At the same time, "Little Bird" small attack helicopters moved to provide direct air support, one at each location. SOCOM had denied use of heavily armed Apache helicopters, although one covert Blackhawk was twenty minutes away in case of the need for medivac. The requested A-10 close support aircraft and two or more Predator drones were also denied. Defense spending cuts had gutted all branches of the military, including SOCOM. They were literally having difficulty paying for fuel for any type of training.

With two operators designated to guard the cave entrance, the rest of the team moved into the tunnel. Each man's NVG, or night vision goggles, with infrared lights, illuminated the cave with eerie light that only they could see, as they moved forward quietly into the cave in single file. They were close enough to each other to communicate silently through touch. When the men came to an opening or branch of the tunnel, two men would quickly, but quietly, enter the unknown space to clear it of any threats. The rest waited quietly and provided over watch until the space was cleared. They would all then continue down the cave tunnel.

The fun began when the two man team entered the third chamber entrance they encountered and found six men sleeping in the darkened space. Unfortunately, two more men were standing; urinating in a pot near the door as the operators stepped in, causing them to scream. They were all cut down as they reached for AK-47s placed haphazardly around the room. It took less than six seconds before the lead operator shouted, "Clear left." The second operator responded "clear right," and both men left the cave to continue on down the tunnel behind the now-moving line of operators.

Just after the firing began in the chamber, the team leader, who had become the first man at the front of the line, could see a man holding an AK-47 rifle come charging out of a chamber a few feet down the tunnel. Instinct told the team leader this man might be important, so he shot him in the shoulder, knocking him to the ground. The man's rifle went flying down the tunnel. The team leader and his appointed partner quickly moved forward to secure the man as two more from the stack tossed a concussion grenade into the chamber the man had just left, before entering to clear it.

The remaining tunnel complex was cleared without serious incident, other than the operators being required to physically subdue three hysterical females.

• • •

Special Forces A-Team 2
Mountains of Southeast Afghanistan
2300 Hours Local Time

The second A-Team was not as fortunate as the first. Before one of the sentries died, he fired off a blast from his AK-47 rifle. The team had trained for this, so they quickly dispatched the remaining sentries, aiming with the night vision scopes on their rifles. They then moved tactically into the main entrance of the cave, meeting and killing two more sentries. Four more guards had been sleeping in an alcove just inside the cave. Each died with two shots to the heart and one to the head. One had a Chinese–made hand grenade in his hand, but he had forgotten to pull the pin to activate it.

Leaving two operators at the entrance for rear security, the rest entered the cave in a ten-man stack, each operator closely following the teammate in front of him. At each branch of the labyrinth that made up the cave complex, the team split apart, until soon there were five two-man teams clearing chambers dug into the cave sides as they went. Most of the chambers had food, water or other supplies, but no people. The lead operator and his partner rounded a corner in the cave tunnel to find themselves face to face with two crazed men in white lab coats and with what looked like empty, raised hands. When the operators paused and shouting in Arabic for them to stop, one of the men pulled out a pistol and shot the first operator in the leg. Reflexively, both operators released two short bursts of bullets into both men, driving them back down the tunnel, where they crumpled in a heap in the pool of bright light spilling from an actual doorway in the side of the passageway.

Light spilled out of doorway, causing the operators' NVGs or night vision goggles to become useless. When they flipped the NVGs up and out of the way, they squinted inside the room. It was brightly lit by LED lights and contained a modern laboratory. A lone figure stood by a refrigerated unit with a clear glass front, holding two flasks, one in each hand.

The first operator, with blood pumping out of the arterial wound in his leg, entered the room and ordered the man, in Arabic, to put down the flasks. The man looked at him calmly and said, in English, "Oh, no. You should put up your hands and beg for forgiveness from your God. But it won't matter anyway because we're all dead." He then hurled both of the flasks at the operators. While the flasks were in the air, both operators fired at the knees of the odd terrorist, having determined they needed to capture him alive. He fell to the ground screaming in pain. The flasks missed the operators, but smashed against the wall next to them, showering both men with liquid. Without a word, each man dropped to one knee and put on his gas mask. The injured operator then quickly applied his battle tourniquet and a pressure dressing to his leg.

The second operator moved to Ali and applied flex-cuffs[28] to Ali's wrists, securing them behind his back. He then placed tourniquets on each of his shattered legs.

Walking out into the corridor, the operator attempted to contact his team leader and was not surprised when the radio didn't work in the tunnel complex. He could hear no echoes of shots being fired, so he increased the volume on his gas mask voice box and shouted "Gas, bio!" He then took out two small flares from his pouch and placed them down the tunnel, one to each direction leading away from the doorway.

The team leader, Captain Charles Schneider, had encountered a mystery while clearing the furthest passageway. A heavy corrugated steel wall and padlocked steel door were blocking the passageway. He could see insulation poking out from the edges of where the steel met the rock wall. Beside the door were hung S.C.A.L.P. suits and gas masks. Schneider immediately held up his hand to stop his partner and began donning his gas mask. He thought about shooting off the lock when he spotted a key hanging from a metal screw next to the door. Opening the lock, he pulled the door open while his partner made a fast, tactical entry into the next chamber. Seeing the small figure huddled in robes on a wooden bench against the wall, the operator shouted in Arabic, "Show me your hands!"

The veiled woman looked up at the obvious soldiers and said in English, "What for, so you can rape me too?"

Both men stopped in surprise. Schneider then responded softly in English, "I'm sorry ma'am. We have to be sure you're no threat. We're U.S. soldiers. I'm a U.S. Army Captain. What's your name?"

The look in Julie's eyes said it all, to both operators. In less than three seconds her eyes went from disbelief, to wonder and joy to a flood of tears. She buried her face in her hands and sobbed uncontrollably. Through her fingers, the sergeant thought he heard her say, "Julie, Julie Carrithers." She hardly noticed as the sergeant apologized while he patted her down for weapons.

---

[28] Flexible nylon bands that effectively bind someone's hands.

When Julie's sobs subsided, she looked up at the gas masks of operators, tried to stand up, and fainted. Everything she had gone through over the past many months had built a wall in her mind. When hope had come through the door, her mind simply couldn't cope.

"My God," Schneider said, "poor kid's been through hell." He was about to take off his mask, when something told him not to. "I can smell death in here, even through my mask. Let's treat this as a chem/bio-weapons containment area until we can get the sniffers[29] in here. You stay here with her. I'll send someone back to help carry her out. Remember, she's probably contaminated."

---

[29] Sniffers refers to electronic testing machines designed to detect lethal chemicals or microbes.

CHAPTER 56
THE NEW YEAR - PLUS FORTY-EIGHT DAYS

SOCOM Headquarters
2200 Hours EST

The Colonel was sleeping on the spare cot in his office when a Warrant Officer came in to wake him. "Sir, we have our first Sitrep from the 5th Group A-team number two. There are technical issues with the communications satellite they're using and the air assets have had to return for refueling. Basically, Sir, they're out of touch for at least several hours."

The Colonel shook the cobwebs out of his head. He had been awake for thirty hours before grabbing three hours of sleep earlier this evening.

The Warrant Officer continued, "Sir, I have taken the liberty to type up a decoded, plain language version of the sitrep." He handed the single page to the Colonel.

TS/SCI/Team 2 reports that their target has been secured. One team member was wounded, but will recover. Twelve hostiles are dead. One hostile was captured and will be interrogated when he is medically stabilized. One female, believed to be a U.S. Citizen, was rescued and is currently unconscious. She will be questioned as soon as possible. A laboratory set up to handle biological agents was discovered along with what is believed to be nanotechnology equipment. Just before he was shot by operators, the living hostile spoke in English, saying, "You should raise your hands and ask forgiveness from your God. But it won't matter because we're all dead." He then threw two flasks of an unknown liquid at two operators, who shot him in both legs. Both operators being treated as bio-warfare casualties. The entire cave complex has been treated as a bio-warfare contaminated area. More to follow. End initial report.

"Dammit," muttered the Colonel. "We need to know if that stuff has been contained or if any got out before we got there."

"Sir," the Warrant Officer said softly, "that's a very good team on the ground there and I'm sure they're both aware of the potential and are working to get those answers for us. With your authorization, I'll have a drone sent back overhead with relay capabilities. It'll be at least three or four hours before it can get there. I'm more worried about the two operators who had the bio-agent thrown at them. If this stuff is contagious, they'll need to be quarantined."

The Colonel was now completely awake. "Yes, I agree. Send the appropriate directions that no one is to leave the vicinity of those caves until they have been medically checked and decontaminated. The decon gear was staged for this mission wasn't it?"

The Colonel's face fell when he saw the look on his subordinate's face. "Sir, the downsizing and budget cuts made it impossible to transport stored decon equipment for this mission. There wasn't time or resources to get it done. The closest suitable equipment is in Germany. I'll see that it is loaded and flying to Afghanistan within the next few hours." The Colonel could read the level of frustration of the Warrant Officer matched his own.

On sudden inspiration, the Colonel asked, "What about the medivac chopper? Can't that get signals out?" The Colonel's voice sounded hopeful.

"No, Sir. That chopper was attacked at its staging area by mortars and small arms fire. A reaction team has taken out the insurgents, but the chopper is grounded until parts can be flown in from Dubai."

"Do what you can, son." The Colonel sighed. "I just hope and pray that people won't die because of this. Oh, and on my authority, have two Apache's, an A-10 and a Predator dispatched to provide air support. The priority on this mission just climbed to the top." After giving that order, he lifted a special telephone and contacted the SOCOM Commanding General.

CHAPTER 57
THE NEW YEAR - PLUS FORTY-NINE DAYS

Special Forces A-Team 2
Mountains of Southeastern Afghanistan
1600 Hours Local Time

Captain Schneider was shaken awake by his Master Sergeant after a forty-five minute nap. "Sir, the girl, Julie Carrithers is awake. Sir, you need to hear this."

Schneider hurried from the chamber to near the mouth of the cave where Julie was sitting on a rock sipping coffee from a steel mug. She was telling the medic to leave her alone and that she better talk to someone who knew what was going on or everyone in the world would die.

"Miss," said the Captain, "I'm in command here. Are you feeling better?" He asked the question in a soft voice, expecting the same mousy demeanor he had encountered in the steel walled room. He was to be surprised.

"No Captain, I am not *feeling better!*" She emphasized the words with dripping sarcasm. "I've been held captive for close to a year, I've been gang raped, and finally was injected with some kind of germ that killed everyone else in the room where you found me, except me. Now I'm talking to a hulking freak of a creature in some kind of bad movie suit. Does that sound like someone that is feeling better to you?" Her glare and all of her pent up anger was directed at the calm man in camouflage chemical suit with a hood and gas mask.

Fortunately, for everyone, the Captain was the proud father of three teenage daughters. He responded in a muffled voice, "Sounds like you're feeling a lot better to me." He then stood there and waited until she stopped her next sputtering tirade and noticed the twinkle in his eye through the clear faceplate of the mask. She could even tell he was smiling.

"Goddamn you," she said, while at the same time fighting the urge to smile back at him. With a deep, calming breath, she said, "You guys better keep those suits on. The stuff these evil creatures have made is supposed to be the worst stuff the world has ever seen. Oh, and did I tell you they already sent fifteen of their so-called martyrs all over the world to spread this stuff? They think they will spread a plague commanded by their God to wipe out all the Infidels."

"Julie, honey," said the Captain with concern in his voice, "when did they send these martyrs out?"

"They left three days ago with them. I don't know if Ahmed or that son of Satan, Ali is back yet, but when they're back, it's because the martyrs are on their way." Quickly changing the subject, Julie continued, "Oh, and you know I'm blessed by God, don't you? They shot me up with the bug and even stuck me in the room with six other prisoners and I barely got sick. Four of the prisoners didn't even get shots of bugs, they just breathed it in. I heard Ali's two flunkies say Ali had made the Chinese bugs even better using nanotechnology. They would even kill the Chinese Infidels, despite their vaccine."

"Okay, Julie, this is really important, are you sure you heard them say Ali had gotten the bugs from the Chinese?" The concern on the Captain's face was obvious, even on top of everything else.

"Oh, yeah. You see, when they figured out I was immune to their nasty bug, they treated me like a lab rat. I'm not sure whether that's better than being treated like a whore, though." With that change of thought, Julie began to cry.

"I did everything the evil bitch told me to," she continued, "I taught them to speak English, I told them how to get through international customs, I even told them how to avoid attracting the attention of police. They were supposed to let me go after I did what they wanted. Instead, they handed me to the fifteen I had taught and they all took turns raping me. And laughing!" Her tears came in sobs. The Captain was next to her, holding her shoulders against his suit. Words were useless at this point.

After another ten minutes, the Captain let Julie know they were working on getting transportation out of there for her and asked Julie if she would share what she could with his intelligence sergeant. Through her sniffles, she said she would.

The hail of AK-47 bullets hit the walls of the cave mouth, throwing pieces of rock everywhere. Return fire was heard from somewhere outside as the perimeter security operators cut down the attackers. Waves of terrorists, who were returning from their two days in Kabul, advanced on the Americans. Over sixty terrorists, all of whom knew the area around the cave much better than did the operators, assaulted the cave mouth. Within minutes three operators were down with wounds, one of which was critical.

Julie was taken back into the tunnel, out of the line of fire, where in a calm voice, the intelligence sergeant continued his debriefing.

Outside the cave, operators had managed to drag their wounded team members into the cave, to receive attention from the medic. Other team members took up defensive positions. For the next thirty minutes they continued to beat back wave after wave of assaulting terrorists. Suddenly they were ordered to fall back to positions near the cave mouth. Quickly, they abandoned their tactically sound positions for new ones behind large boulders near the cave mouth. Firing at the carefully advancing terrorists continued until the area just outside their kill radius exploded. All around the area salvos of 30mm cannon fire blasted JOTP positions, missiles exploded and individuals trying to run away were cut down. In less than ten minutes, all firing stopped and the sounds of multiple Apache helicopters and an A-10 Warthog ground support airplane could be heard circling overhead. SOCOM had come through with reinforcements.

CHAPTER 58
THE NEW YEAR - PLUS FORTY-NINE DAYS

SOCOM Headquarters
0800 Hours EST

FLASH/IMMEDIATE

TS/SCI/Team 2 reports debrief of JOTP prisoner Julie Carrithers ((source)) revealed 15 (fifteen) jihadi martyrs were dispatched to several parts of the world after being infected with unknown bio-weapon. Source also heard from her captors that the JOTP received the bio-weapon from unknown Chinese sources before altering it through nanotechnology methods to increase potency and to defeat Chinese vaccinations. Source reports "Ali," the JOTP scientist handling the bio-weapon, spoke English and is believed to have received an advanced degree in the U.S. ((United States)). Source claims to have been "chosen by God" and given immunity to the bio-weapon. She also claims Ali was working on creating a vaccine from her blood, details of which may be contained in a laptop computer seized from Ali's sleeping chamber. Initial assessment is that source is credible. NOTE: Investigation incomplete. Arrangements for source's transport to CDC Atlanta delayed due her contaminated status.

Upon reading the Flash message, the Commanding Officer, SOCOM ordered the message be sent up the chain, Flash-Priority and picked up the secure phone and dialed the White House situation room. "Hello, son. This is the SOCOM Commander. I need to speak with whoever is in charge at the moment." After listening for a moment, he said, "Yes, I'll hold.

"Situation Room, this is John." The voice on the phone sounded just like what he was. A political appointee whose main purpose was to insure none of the President's wishes or policies were impacted by rash acts by people less in tune with political realities.

"Well, hello, John." The General drew out the greeting while wondering exactly to whom he was speaking. "This is General Johnson, the SOCOM Commanding Officer, are you in charge over there? And exactly, who are you?"

"I told you, General. This is John. That's all you need to know. Now do you have something interesting to tell me or are you wasting my time?"

"I called to advise you, John, fifteen highly contagious terrorists are currently flying to several parts of the world, presumably including the United States, and you, John, may want to get off your politically appointed, lazy ass and start doing something about it. Is that interesting enough for you?" By now, the General was shouting into the phone.

"That sounds like bullshit to me, General. How do you know this?"

"Some of my people raided a terrorist complex in Afghanistan yesterday evening. One of the cave complexes had a laboratory inside where bio-weapons were apparently being made. A rescued prisoner told my operators about the JOTP plans in detail. I can read the preliminary FLASH message they sent out if you like."

"You do that, General."

After reading the Flash message to John, the General waited for further questions. "General, first I want to know if this source has been thoroughly vetted. Has she?"

"No, John, she has not. There has been no time. My people on the ground have been doing this sort of thing for a long time and they believe her."

John cut the General off. "Second, she says the Chinese gave this bio-weapon to a terrorist group? Are you kidding me? That on its face is clearly in the bullshit category. Next, she says she's chosen by God to be immune to this bio-weapon? You're taking the word of a religious nut? Where are the other bodies of test victims? Hell, General, there are so many holes in this I can't believe you're taking it seriously! Let me tell you what we're not going to do, is to react in any way to this unverified, fantastical story and make a laughing stock of this administration. Anything else, General?"

The General looked at the phone in utter disbelief. Softly, in a voice even John understood was deadly serious, the General said, "John, if intelligence that my people believe true is, in fact, true, and my country is hit with a devastating bio-weapon, I will personally come to Washington, D.C., stand before the TV cameras and identify you as the man who had the last chance to stop it all. You disgust me." The General hung up the phone. He hoped and prayed that John, whoever he was, would manage to relieve him of his command. That would mean John had been right. In his gut, he knew that wasn't the case.

Two hours later, when the FLASH message came into the situation room, John was waiting for it. He tore off the paper copy, wrote "Handled" on it and placed it in the bin to be filed. The electronic copy was redirected to a file that did not require any action. Across the intelligence community, after a quick call to the Situation Room, most other agencies handled the FLASH message the same way. Those that did not were instructed by the Director of National Intelligence and Secretary of Defense to table the issue pending more concrete information. John was sure that the President wanted nothing pointing at the Chinese at this point in time. Especially something that amounted to an act of war. The Fontaine administration's emasculation of the U.S. intelligence capability was now complete.

CHAPTER 59
THE NEW YEAR - PLUS FORTY-NINE DAYS

Outside of Cronin, Kentucky
0825 Hours EST

Mike was worried. A standoff had occurred at the front gate of the neighborhood between two of the security teams and a group of about thirty rough, grizzled men wearing Homeland Security jackets and carrying some serious firearms. The new gates had been locked when a convoy arrived an hour earlier. When their truck had attempted to break through the gates, spikes had erupted from a concealed trench in the pavement and punctured both front tires of the two lead vehicles, effectively blocking the roadway. On each side of the gate were two, staggered, newly built, bulletproof bunkers, each manned by five members of the security team. They had over watch duty to the team leader, who was at the gate talking with the leader of the Homeland Security group. When the DHS leader had shouted to two men to take the team leader, both nests of security men had locked and loaded their rifles and pointed them at the DHS team leader. Both groups had backed off for the time being and a runner had been sent for Mike.

Watching the standoff from a distance, Mike softly discussed the situation with Linda, who was telling him, "Mike, if you let them into the neighborhood, you've acceded to their authority. I'm telling you, it's best if you stop them right where they are."

"Linda, what if one of those fools shoots one of my friends? It could start off a war."

"Look at me, Mike." Her voice was soft, but had steel in it. "It's important that you understand this. They are not your friends, now. They are your security people and subordinates. You need to think of them and treat them that way. They know and all of us know what we're in for and they know the danger.

Volunteers, every one of them. They trust me, but they trust you more. You need to show the same level of trust in them."

After a moment's thought, Mike nodded at her wisdom and said, "Okay, I see what you're saying."

Linda nodded with satisfaction at Mike's quick understanding and acceptance of a leadership concept that is missed by most. It reinforced her intuition that he was, in fact, a natural leader and a quick learner. He was just a little rough around the edges.

"Mike," Linda said, "I've been here before. Resolve and a firm hand will work, even if a few rounds are fired. I've told everyone something unusual for me. I told them not to shoot to kill unless they absolutely have to. If taking out an arm or leg will do, then they are to do that. You know those thugs don't have the same restrictions or even care one way or the other, but that's what will keep us on the right side."

Two hours later, power was cut to the entire neighborhood. It wasn't known to Mike and the others until later in the day, but power had failed throughout the area as well, due to lack of money for maintenance and the Fontaine administrations having shut down all coal fired power plants in the country. Fifteen minutes after that the DHS force leader shouted over a loudspeaker, "Who's in charge there? I want to talk to the man in charge!"

Per SOP[30] the security team leader shouted back, "I'm in charge right now. If you want to parley, you can talk to me. From there."

This response didn't please the DHS force leader at all. He had already tried to send some men around the sides of the entrance to flank the security team only to find more security people down each side of the neighborhood. One of the dumber DHS guys had tried to step over the electrified cattle wire fence, only to be struck in the flank with a pellet gun. That was directly followed by a young woman telling him, conversationally, that he was staring at the barrel of her other rifle, which was a .243 caliber varmint rifle. Her shot groups at 100 yards were less than an inch, so she figured she could remove one of his testicles with the first shot. After all, he was a lot closer than 100 yards. He promptly moved back across the cattle fence and went back to report that side was well defended by several men with what looked like fully automatic rifles, and they were behind cover.

Repeated calls by the DHS force leader to the Kentucky State Police for backup resulted in being told no one was available at that time. The National Guard was confined to their barracks, so they were not available. Four hours

---

[30] SOP – Standard Operating Procedures

later, the DHS force drove away, leaving the two trucks with punctured tires where they were at the neighborhood entrance.

Just after dark Linda arranged to have one of Sean's security team operators out with the security team, along with his night vision goggles. The operator provided training for two of the shift security team on the NVGs' operation and how to effectively patrol the perimeter of the neighborhood. He was pleasantly surprised to learn the security team had three night vision scopes available, but they were all either first or second generation and therefore less effective than his.

At the community shelter, Mike had gathered the residents of the neighborhood to let everyone know what had happened and what they should expect. His talk was not of the rabble-rousing variety, but instead it focused on what everyone had built and how criminals were trying to take advantage of the emergency to steal from honest citizens. "Let no one here be deceived. Their sole purpose is to come into our homes and take what they want to give to someone else. They call it "redistribution," and they don't recognize your right to provide for your family, as it says in the Constitution. If we let them past the gates, they will steal and pillage anything of value they can find. They will ransack homes, one at a time, just hoping for an excuse to drag away anyone who resists. The State Police won't help these thugs steal from us. Nor will the National Guard. Therefore, we shouldn't let them do so either. Now that isn't saying we are openly at war with these thugs or anyone. Let's just say we're preventing them from making a serious mistake, all the while protecting our individual ability to feed our own. Now, I know we don't have power right now, but it'll probably come back on and off for a while. Those with generators, please look out for your neighbors. Together, we can and we will get through this. What do you say? Will we get through this?" The group responded with a loud cheer.

Linda wasn't sure if it was the words Mike used, or just the way he said them, but virtually everyone in the crowd was nodding their heads and several were shouting out encouragement toward Mike, as he spoke. She had seen video tape of inspiring speakers like Martin Luther King, Jr., Ronald Reagan, and even President John F. Kennedy during his visit to Berlin, Germany on June 26, 1963. During that speech President Kennedy had said, "Ich bin ein Berliner,"[31] thereby declaring to the world his solidarity with the West German people. This evening, watching Mike, was the first time she had personally witnessed someone with that caliber of personal charisma.

---

[31] Ich bin ein Berliner – meaning I am a Berliner, or man of Berlin. A quote from a speech by President John F. Kennedy while visiting Berlin, Germany as the Soviet Union built a wall around the free Western part of Berlin.

Everyone departed the meeting feeling both uplifted and empowered. Even without electricity, they would protect their homes and families from all comers and get through the crisis. With Mike to lead them, they would not fail.

• • •

Special Forces A-Team 2
Mountains of Southeastern Afghanistan
2000 Hours Local Time

Captain Schneider accompanied Julie, along with his intelligence Sergeant, to the chamber where the medic had stabilized Ali until he could be airlifted to a hospital in Kabul. Schneider softly asked Julie, "Are you sure you're up to this?"

"Oh, yes," she said earnestly, "I want to help you identify and castrate each and every one of these devils. Can I borrow your knife? Just for a minute?"

While shaking his head no, Schneider couldn't help but admire Julie's spunk.

Walking into the chamber, Julie immediately focused on the man lying on a blanket with an I.V. drip going into his arm. "That's him. He's even worse than Mengele." She then walked boldly over to the man, who looked up at her in a morphine haze. She took off the rubber glove from her hand and slapped him strongly across the face. "My name is Julie, you vermin." Julie said this in English while looking into his startled eyes.

Schneider was smiling as he grabbed her by both arms and pulled her away from him.

"Captain, his name is Ali. I think he's some kind of relative, maybe a brother to the boss in this camp named Ahmed, maybe the brother of Ahmed's real bitch of a wife named Jasmine. God, how I hate that bitch. Ahmed used her to torture me into helping them. Oh, and I hope I just infected the swine. Too bad your men didn't blow his balls off instead of his knees. Where did you guys find him?"

Julie's wandering questions were hard to follow, but after a moment's thought the Captain said, "They found him in the lab and shot him when he threw two flasks at them. He then said they were all dead. Do you know what he meant?"

"My guess is there were live germs in the flask and everyone in the room breathed them in. That means your men are going to die and you might as well kill this swine." She paused for a moment before saying, "No, I mean you should make sure he lives for at least the next five days. It takes about a day and a half for symptoms to start showing, followed by two days of agony as he dies."

Looking at Ali across the room, and again in English said, "Heh, asshole! My hand is covered in the bugs you created, so your oozing ass is going to die!" With a big smile, she continued, "Remember, my name is Julie!"

The Captain quickly dragged Julie out of the chamber as the medic and another operator worked to bring the enraged and struggling Ali under control. The Captain asked Julie, "Didn't you wash your hand before being suited up?"

"Only one of them. I made sure the other had blood and crud from one of the poor victims, just for an occasion like this."

• • •

Special Forces A-Team 1
Mountains of Southeastern Afghanistan
2130 Hours Local Time

Julie stumbled off the Blackhawk helicopter into the waiting arms of Captain Schneider. She was now completely encased in a S.C.A.L.P. suit with a filter mask covering everything but her eyes. Schneider led her to the opening of the cave complex, where he was met by the Team 1 Captain and his intelligence Sergeant. Everyone entered the cave complex while the Blackhawk shut down its engines.

The Team I intelligence Sergeant asked Schneider, "So this is the amazing little lady you told us about, Cap?"

Julie was in no mood to be ignored. "My name is Julie and I want you to cut the balls off of two people tonight. I'll let you know who when I see them." Two of the three men were clearly shocked by her statement.

"Well then," the intelligence Sergeant said, "let's show you some of the terrorists and maybe you can help us sort them out." He then led the small group into the first of four chambers. Lying on the floor was Ahmed, with a bandaged shoulder and his arms and feet secured by flex cuffs. The Team 2 Captain later chided himself for not anticipating and preventing Julie from walking quickly to Ahmed, removing her glove, and slapping him across the face.

In Arabic, Julie said, "There, you swine, you now have the plague so you'll be an oozing ball of puss when you die, too! And by the way, my name is Julie. Remember that on your way to hell." The vehemence in her voice cut through even the horror Ahmed felt.

Julie then looked at the soldiers and said, "This is Ahmed, the fanatic that runs this place. He doesn't speak English and he has very little education, but everyone here is scared to death of him and seems to think he's leading them to heaven."

When Julie walked into the next chamber, she identified Jasmine as the brains behind Ahmed. "She's Ahmed's wife and the one who said I should be taken. She then tortured me until I had to help train their martyrs. Watch her carefully, she'll kill you if she can, and she is very, very clever, for one so stupid."

The next chamber held Ahmed's older wife. "She knows nothing," said Julie. "Ahmed only keeps her as a favor to his Imam."

In the last chamber a very young, teenage girl, who was very pregnant, sat crying. The operator guarding her told them she had not answered any questions and only cried. Julie walked to her, placed a gloved hand on her shoulder and softly asked in Arabic, "Who are you, little one?"

At Julie's touch and the sound of her voice, the girl raised her eyes and glared at Julie. "I am the third wife of the greatest man in the world. This child," pointing to her stomach, "and my children will bring the true faith to the whole world!"

Julie shook her head and said, "You are wrong little one. Your husband has only brought death to the world. Maybe even to you and your child. I hope you live to see all the evil he has done." She then looked at the Captain and said in English, "There's your answer. Ahmed's third wife. They even corrupted someone as young as this. Truly Satan has taken them all."

CHAPTER 60
THE NEW YEAR - PLUS FIFTY DAYS

Command Bunker
Outside of Beijing, China
1845 Hours Local Time

Song sat at his desk in his bunker intently watching the large screen on the wall. On it was displayed a bird's eye view of the PLA's main Command Room located less than one hundred meters from his own Command bunker. Both were connected by a wide, well-lit tunnel through which dozens of golf cart-like electric vehicles whizzed back and forth along smooth, concrete floors. The screen displayed data, diagrams and photos depicting the PLA's massive invasion of Formosa.

The invasion had begun at 3:00 a.m. that morning, although Lao's sources indicated the PLA had actually begun launching missiles toward the rebel island just after 2:00 a.m. local time. The EMP generators had struck on time at 3:00 a.m., immobilizing roughly 75 percent of the island's high tech defenses. American supplied missile defenses had been mostly neutralized, however the island army shore defenses seemed to have an uncanny ability to shoot down missiles as they crossed the straight from the mainland. Intelligence was unsure whether this was due to operational radars or tremendous hand/eye coordination by the anti-missile defense gun batteries.

After eight hours of massive missile and artillery barrages into the island, the rebels and their defensive systems continued to fight back. The air campaign had not gone well. Attempts to use the new EMP weapon against enemy aircraft had proven to be ineffectual. Flying older model American F-16 and F-14 fighter aircraft had turned out to be a benefit, as they all had older, hardened electronics that were less susceptible to the new EMP weapon. The island Air Force level of competency also proved to be far greater than anticipated, with over half of the invasion supporting PRC fighters and bombers having been shot down by enemy fighters. Attempts to bomb the hardened island military airfields had been mostly unsuccessful.

Despite all of the setbacks, the PLA Army had launched an amphibious assault of the island from across the straight and from a flotilla of landing craft attacking from the ocean to the East. With very heavy casualties exceeding sixty percent, the PLA had established beachheads on both sides of the island and were prepared to expand them when PLA fighter aircraft could regain at least a reasonable amount of air superiority. Island ground support aircraft were making progress very difficult at both beachheads. The invasion was helped tremendously by sabotage by PRC agents working within the island infrastructure. Power was cut throughout the island within the first few minutes of the attack. Water lines and telecommunications, including some military communications, were disrupted across more than half of the island. Although on its highest level of alert, the island military did not appear to know when or where the attack would take place.

Through coordination with Wong, Song managed to take two thirty minute catnaps throughout the day. For the most part, he did not interfere with the PLA General's running of the attack. On two occasions only, he had contacted the Commanding General and made a suggestion. Each time the General had sounded as though he were considering whether it was a good one, before thanking Song and ordering the necessary changes. Song knew this pause was mostly a face-saving gesture on the part of the General, as Song was clearly the Chinese version of "Commander in Chief," over the PLA.

Despite very heavy losses, Song believed the rebel island forces would be breaking within the next forty-eight hours. Intelligence and Chen had both indicated the American President was keeping their military forces out of the area.

· · · · ·

White House Situation Room
0800 Hours EST

Katherine paced the floor behind the busy staff working to develop a clear picture of what was happening in Taiwan. She had nothing to contribute and was there only at the suggestion of her Chief of Staff. After two hours, she ordered Secretary of Defense Hathaway to advise her if there were any major changes and to prepare a briefing for the staff at 10:00 a.m. She then stalked back to her office, almost totally numb. It had only been the day before yesterday when she had planted that stupid horn-dog of a husband in Arlington National Cemetery, during a nationally televised day of mourning. For some reason, it surprised her that she actually had trouble sleeping the night before the state funeral. His death effectively removed the club held over her head by the Chinese regarding those tapes. It had been a real plus that it was the Chinese-born maid that murdered him. Katherine had worked very hard to conceal her identity. All anyone could tell from the social media videos was that the woman in the back seat of Walter's campaign limo was oriental. Well, let the Chinese worry the whore from Walter's trysts had been the one to kill him. That should insure they'll avoid using the damning video tapes.

Although she was utterly exhausted, with a migraine threatening to split her head wide open, she didn't think she could take a nap, even a short one. After checking with Susan to insure all of her appointments for the day had been canceled, she decided to at least lie on her couch and try to relax for a few minutes.

Susan closed the door of Katherine's office and rushed out to make excuses for the hundreds of politicians and dignitaries that demanded to speak with the President.

Katherine walked into the conference room at 10:05 a.m. to find almost all of her Cabinet members present, along with their primary assistants. Burt had to coordinate and prioritize those in attendance, as there were far more in attendance than usual.

Most Cabinet members had been avoiding the White House since Katherine declared the State of Emergency.

Standing in front of the Presidential podium, Katherine looked out over everyone in the room before asking everyone to take their seats. It still gave her a minor thrill to see others standing, awaiting her commands. Susan had coordinated with Marc and his office to prepare a quick statement for her to make, before turning the floor over to SECDEF Hathaway.

Without preamble, Katherine said, "I will get right to it. Secretary Hathaway will be providing a briefing on the current situation. Many in the lying press have said I am too afraid to live up to this country's treaties with Taiwan and come to their aid. The fact of the matter is that the only treaty in effect is the Taiwan Relations Act (TRS) of 1979. Many don't know that this Act followed this country's decision to cut ties with Taiwan, abrogate the U.S.-Republic of China (Taiwan) Mutual Defense Treaty, and establish relations with the People's Republic of China. Essentially, both my legal team and I believe we have no legal obligation to defend Taiwan and I will not spend a drop of American treasure to declare war on China."

Continuing, with an afterthought Katherine said, "Or American blood, either." The muttering around the room followed, however no one wanted to incur the President's wrath by openly commenting or questioning her decision.

Marc Baxter had felt fortunate that Susan had prevailed on the President to order her Ambassador to the United Nations Ambassador to call an immediate Security Council meeting. During this meeting the United States lodged a strong protest and attempted to condemn the PRC's hostile actions. The condemnation failed when both the PRC and Russia failed to support it. Marc was inwardly revolted by Katherine's failure to stand by the Taiwanese government in their time of crisis. He also knew every U.S. ally in the world was rethinking whether a possible alliance with China might be more reliable than the one they had with the United States.

Turning to her Secretary of Defense, Katherine said, "Mr. Hathaway, please brief us on the current situation."

SECDEF Hathaway said, "Thank you, Madam President." He then turned on a large screen viewer on the wall. "At just after 1:00 p.m. yesterday, Washington time, and 2:00 a.m. Beijing time, The People's Republic of China began launching missiles at what they view as the rebel-held island of Formosa, which we know as Taiwan. No warning was given and this was an unprovoked, aggressive attack."

With a deep breath, Hathaway began to scroll through PowerPoint presentation, made up of several classified military maps and some photographs obtained from the world press. "Initial damage estimates indicate tremendous military and civilian deaths. We have no access to Taiwanese military or government information due to those channels of communication having been cut by Taiwan. This is presumably in response to our refusal to enter the battle. The President of Taiwan answered our request for information by this cryptic message: 'No talk now, busy." Much of our satellite imagery and other resources have been jammed by PRC installations along the East Coast of the PRC. Except for a few deep cover sources, with special communications equipment, we're not able to get much more information than is available to the press, which is where many of these photographs came from." The frustration dripped from Hathaway's clipped, precise report.

"What we do know," Hathaway continued, "is that the PRC has landed invasion forces on the East and West coast of Taiwan and have established beachheads. From extremely sensitive intercepts of some PRC radio traffic, our analysts believe the PRC suffered very heavy losses of over fifty percent of their invasion force and sixty percent of their deployed air force. The Taiwanese Air Force appears to be kicking ass, despite their somewhat antiquated and badly outnumbered equipment. The few PRC stealth aircraft, both fighters and bombers, have suffered even higher losses. My analysts are not able to determine how the Taiwanese are able to be so successful against those targets. A new EMP weapon has been deployed targeting the Taiwanese defenses, however for a reason unknown to the PLA, its affect has been much more limited than was anticipated. If the PRC continues their all-out offensive and is willing to endure the horrific losses currently being experienced, we estimate the Taiwanese defenses will fall within forty-eight hours." Turning to Katherine, Hathaway said, "Madam President, PRC losses are approaching one hundred thousand soldiers, sailors and airmen right now. In two days, that figure could be twice that number. Civilian losses are estimated as being four times that."

The Cabinet and staff were completely silent. A few in the room were stunned by the enormity of the carnage. Far too many seemed to shrug off the numbers as just that, numbers. Marc pretended to be intently reading through notes in his notebook. In fact, he was trying to dam the flood of tears that threatened to leak out onto his cheeks at the tremendous loss of life.

Katherine chose this moment to rise from her chair and said, "Keep me informed. Baxter, Burt make sure my speech for this evening is ready for my review by 1:00 p.m. and that the writer gets it right." She walked from the room leaving a dispirited pall of murmuring in her wake.

CHAPTER 61
THE NEW YEAR - PLUS FIFTY DAYS

The White House
1235 Hours EST

Burt bustled into Marc's office looking, and obviously feeling, disheveled. "Marc," he said quickly, "have you seen the crap the President's favorite speech writer just put out? If she wants open rebellion this shit will definitely get it. My God. You've got to fix this!"

Marc sat looking at Burt for several seconds before answering. "Burt, you're aware what he wrote for her was done using notes she gave him. She gave him marching orders, point by point. She essentially wrote the speech, Burt. What do you want me to do?"

"Fix it, Wonderboy!" Burt shouted at Marc, not in anger but in total exasperation.

"How am I supposed to do that, Burt?" Marc's tone was less than respectful to the White House Chief of Staff.

"Hell, I don't know, Marc." Burt's tone had turned to near anguish. "Maybe you can just re-write it and leave out the worst parts about rounding up revolutionaries that are actively destabilizing the country and threatening her government. At least get rid of the "my government," part.

"Burt, do you really think that'll fly?"

"Listen," Burt said this quietly, leaning over Marc's desk to come within only a few inches from his face, "if we can't fix this, her Presidency will be the first since the Civil War to shoot its own citizens in the streets. I've been getting reports from DHS that their people have already been fired upon by groups of citizens. Somehow it's been kept off the major news networks, but there'll really be an uproar when she informs the country that social media will be censored for the duration of the emergency. Even the liberal geeks will cry blood murder about that!"

Burt almost strangled on his words in order to keep them from carrying outside of Marc's office. "Marc, I'm haunted by the prospect of a military coup, if this shit keeps up. Please do something!"

"Burt," Marc asked again, "what do you want me to do?"

"Like I said, re-write it. Let her change it back if she wants to. Please do what you can to save this country. Will you?" The pleading in his eyes and voice were enough to convince Marc to at least make an effort.

"Okay, Burt. I'll do what I can. You'll have to handle her at 1:00 p.m. however. I can't get it done till at least 2:00."

"Done. And thanks, Marc."

Marc spent the next hour re-writing Katherine's speech, toning down the rhetoric and making her outrageous proclamations at least seem reasonable. For each one, he cited the unrest in the country and threats from abroad as justification. He was beyond exhausted when he finished it.

When Burt picked up Marc's draft of the President's Speech, he wrote across the top, "Polished by Marc Baxter," in his own handwriting. He had done everything he could do.

. . .

The Mike Broehm Residence
Outside of Cronin, Kentucky
1610 Hours EST

"Peter, while we're waiting for Sean and Linda, what can you tell us about what's happening in DC and on the other side of the world?" Mike asked the question calmly, while, Rollie, Fred, Jim Webb, Lauren, Onie, three security team leaders and two of Sean's security operators sat in his family room. With his generator running, the 4:00 p.m. news had just come on, with the lead story being the invasion of Taiwan by the PRC and the reaction nation-wide at the Fontaine administration's lack of response. Mike had cut the sound on the TV just before he had spoken to Peter.

"Mike, I wish I had more information, but that seems to be in really short supply these days. Most of what I have comes from the press, and we all know how reliable those Fontaine toadies have been lately." An ironic chuckle rose from most who were present. "We know the PRC has wanted to recapture Taiwan, who they view as nothing but a rebel province, since World War II. Until this President, the PRC was pretty sure the full might of the U.S. Navy would be brought to bear on any attempted invasion. The Chinese people are nothing, if not patient. It was clear the Fontaine administration was not going to lift a finger to help Taiwan, as evidenced by U.S. Naval forces having been completely withdrawn from the area. Japan has formally complained to the U.S. State Department and has reportedly begun a rapid program to build nuclear weapons as a deterrent."

Linda and Sean chose that moment to make their appearance. "Sorry we're late," Linda said in a serious tone, "but something that may be important just came up. Oh, Mike, you might want to turn up the volume," as she pointed at the television.

This just in, the Centers for Disease Control has just issued a statement that is highlighted on your screen. It says, "Reports have been received of a particularly virulent virus that has appeared simultaneously in at least fifteen states. Health officials are advising caution in treating those affected."

The commentators of the local news both paused to look at each other before one said, *"That sounds awfully ominous, don't you think?"* The other commentator agreed, before diverting to a sports story.

"Okay, Mike, you can kill the sound," Linda said. With a deep breath she looked around the room and continued, "This stuff is very highly classified, but I really don't think that will matter much longer. By the authority of the SOCOM Commander, SOCOM forces have just been informed that a group of Afghan terrorists, the same bastards that captured me and caused Sean to lose his leg, sent fifteen infected martyrs out into the world to spread a nanotechnology enhanced virus that is extremely contagious and is spread through the air. Operators from the 7th Special Forces Group hit their camp three days ago. The martyrs had already boarded planes to spread the virus to the planet a few days earlier. The martyrs are believed to have traveled throughout at least Europe and the U.S., but possibly all over the world. A surviving American prisoner and test subject provided this information to the operators and the SOCOM commander ran it up the chain to the Situation Room where nothing has been done. The

SOCOM commander believes that in light of information he received from the CDC, this weaponized virus, by that I mean a deadly virus that is far more virulent than even Ebola, is currently spreading around the world, and there's not a damned thing we can do about it."

Around the room were faces mixed with disbelief, horror and everything in between.

Rollie was the first to get over the initial shock and ask, "So some political son-of-a-bitch in the Situation Room had the only chance to stop or at least mitigate this, and they chose not to?"

Linda nodded her head sadly, "The communication to the field from the Situation Room was very explicit, saying the operators and SOCOM should stand down until all of the allegations made by the surviving prisoner could be verified. It wasn't even brought to the attention of the President."

Mike seized the opportunity to ask, "Sean, Linda, what can we do?"

Sean sank onto a stool before saying, "This is the worst case scenario, especially with what the CDC is announcing. I've been thinking about what we should do on the way over here. We need to seal off the neighborhood and stop all coming and going. We also need to quarantine everyone to their homes as much as possible. Travel outside of a sealed environment should only happen with chem/bio protective equipment like a S.C.A.L.P. suit, or something like it, and a gas mask with hood. If this stuff is airborne, the best thing we could do is to seal up our homes with duct tape and the like, and hunker down for a couple of months to let the sun kill off whatever virus cells are floating around in the air. With everyone scavenging right now, and with the power out, that might prove very difficult to convince people they need to just stay closed up in their home. Because of the possibility that someone may have already come in contact with the virus, we better not call another neighborhood meeting. Maybe write up a simple, one page explanation? I can have one of my guys deliver this flyer to each home in the neighborhood. I know we've got emergency power and the equipment to produce the letter if you'll give us the appropriate wording. If this thing is going to sweep the country, it'll be on the news within the next day or two, before everything begins to shut down. Mike, we better be prepared for that to happen as early as the next twenty-four hours."

Linda looked at Sean and asked, "Sounds like my security people are going to need to continue to man the perimeter, what about them?"

"Mike, do you know if anyone in the neighborhood has a gas mask?"

Mike chuckled at Sean's question. "Oh, I'd say about twenty-five percent or more have one or more gas masks. But something that occurs to me is don't you need to decontaminate the whole outfit before you can strip and be around other people? You can't just live in the mask and suit can you? How would you eat and drink?"

Linda answered that one. "Of course, you need to be able to decon, which will be very difficult in cold weather, without running water and electricity."

The rest of the evening the group hammered out the details of a plan to deal with the situation. No one was happy about it, but Mike finally bid everyone good evening feeling like they were protected as well as possible. As Peter was about to leave, Mike asked him to hang back.

"Peter, do you think it's time for me and Lauren to move over to your place?" A strange look came into Peter's eye and he paused, before saying, "How about tomorrow afternoon, Mike? I need to take care of some things first. Okay?"

The whole tone caught Mike by surprise, but he nodded his head and said, "Okay, maybe you can just come over and let me know sometime tomorrow afternoon?"

"Will do, Mike." With that, Peter quickly walked out Mike's back door.

"Wonder what that's all about," Mike thought to himself as he walked outside for more firewood.

CHAPTER 62
THE NEW YEAR - PLUS FIFTY-EIGHT DAYS

Command Bunker
Outside of Beijing, China
2015 Hours Local Time

General Hu lay prostrate on the floor in front of Song's desk, having just been thrown there by two of Lao's larger security agents. Lao was standing behind him and off to one side.

"General Secretary," Lao said softly, "here is the man responsible, as you commanded."

Song merely glared at Hu's quivering head pressed firmly against the floor. His hands were banded behind his back and his fingers were clearly swelling. After several minutes of silence, Song said in a soft, deadly voice, "Tell me what you have done, Hu. Tell me all of it. Leave nothing out."

"General Secretary," Hu said in a whiney voice, "I did everything Minister Lao asked me to do. I created the virus, developed a vaccine, manufactured the vaccine and had the real vaccine sent to those he identified to me as critical to China, while sending only a flu vaccine to those that were not critical. That is all I have done, General Secretary." He kept his head pressed against the floor throughout the explanation.

Song directed his stare at Lao. "Is this correct, Lao?"

Lao, too bowed his head to Song. "He did not tell me that the vaccine would fail to work, General Secretary."

From the floor, Hu wailed, "It did work, General Secretary! I tested it on myself after the three of us received our vaccination. The virus has changed! It is more virulent that the one I created! My scientists are working very hard to determine what has been done. It is only a matter of time before they can decipher the code of the virus and create a vaccine."

"Remove this thing that may have just killed China from my presence, Lao. Have his deputy brought to me."

Lao opened the door and his two security agents drug Hu from the room. On the way out Song said, "Do not permanently damage him before I know he has no more value."

With the door closing, Lao himself went down onto the floor. "General Secretary, our sources say the American Special Forces raided the JOTP camp and laboratory ten days ago. They found the laboratory and an American female, who survived exposure to the virus. She informed them fifteen terrorists had been sent all over the world with a nanotechnology enhanced virus. If that is correct, Hu's stolen virus was somehow manipulated by nanotechnology to make our vaccine worthless. We should be safe in this bunker, however unless Hu's people can develop a vaccine very quickly, we will suffer the same devastating fate as the rest of the world. Every day the number of people afflicted by the virus grows geometrically. My people estimate that sixteen million currently suffer from the virus, of which well over ninety percent will die. Before they die, they will continue to infect everyone around them, who will travel and infect more. So many infected bodies are scattered throughout China that it will be many months or more before the air carried by the wind will no longer carry the virus." Lao remained on the floor breathing heavily.

"General Secretary, I request permission to leave this secure bunker and spend what time remains to me with my wife and surviving family members. I do not deserve to survive this disaster."

Song looked at Lao and said, "I received a call from the American President who told me almost the same story you just did. She said the survivor rescued in Afghanistan had heard her captors say the virus came from China, but that the terrorists had brought in a scientist trained in America who altered the virus through sophisticated nanotechnology methods. Several of the infected terrorists were sent to China, as well as to the rest of the world. Whether we wanted to or not, the scourge of mankind on this planet has been arrested, at least temporarily. We shall see if the virus makes its way into this bunker, or if we will form the nucleus of a new world."

Song was looking at the ceiling of his office as he made this pronouncement to Lao. For his part, Lao tried not to shiver with the chills his body felt. When it became apparent what had happened, he had gone home to his wife and discovered she was dying from the virus. He held her closely, injecting her with painkillers until she passed to join her ancestors. He had bathed himself with fluids leaking from her dying body and had insured to covertly touch several objects in Song's office. Bringing the same death to Song was to be his last and most just accomplishment.

. . .

The Presidential Emergency Operations Center (PEOC)
Beneath the East Wing of the White House
0930 Hours EST

Katherine sat behind her desk in what was referred to as the nuclear bunker reading reports arranged in a neat stack by Susan. The one that had held her attention the most was the one from a Special Forces Captain Charles Schneider. It had several typos in it, but provided a pretty good picture of what had happened. After having read the report just after midnight, she had picked up the secure telephone and had contacted Chinese General Secretary Song. It had taken over two hours before he came to the phone, but it was worth it. She had previously read the reports of the virus' indiscriminate infection of whomever it touched in China, including the military and civilian elite. That tracked with what Captain Schneider reported. It was particularly gratifying to inform Song that his bloody invasion of Taiwan had been a complete waste of time and blood, as the virus his country had developed would kill almost everyone on both sides. She further informed Song that she would be broadcasting to the world that the virus originated in a Chinese laboratory and that a vaccine had been made and distributed only to those deemed important in China. A simple, uneducated terrorist in Afghanistan had stolen the virus and, with the help of a scientist related to the terrorist, the virus had been altered, leaving the Chinese vaccine worthless. The Afghan terrorist had then sent martyrs infected with the virus out into the world to kill as many Infidels as possible, including some to China. All of this was made possible by Chinese General Secretary Song. She ended the call by telling Song, "You have fucked us all, including yourself." She hadn't known how prophetic her words would prove to be.

The other part of Captain Schneider's reporting that was so interesting was the American prisoner, Julie's story. In direct defiance of instructions from a man named "John" in the White House situation room, SOCOM had covertly arranged to bring Julie, and samples of the virus, back to the Centers for Disease Control and Prevention (CDC) main laboratories in Atlanta, Georgia. Captain Schneider had accompanied her and had written his report while remaining at the CDC. In addition to the antibodies found to be in Julie's blood, the terrorist scientist had made remarkable progress in developing a vaccine to the altered, more potent virus, using his expertise in nanotechnology areas. All of his notes were found on his laptop computer, which had also been brought with Julie to Atlanta. Precious hours were saved because he had written all of his notes in English. Despite the virus having penetrated many of the laboratories at the CDC and infecting several of their scientists, they believed it had been contained. Also, progress was being made toward formulating the vaccine. Two possible strains of vaccine had been identified as being at least partially effective against the virus. Testing was ongoing using CDC staff to take care of co-workers afflicted with the virus. They should know if either of them might be effective within about four days and a limited production run of the vaccine would be started.

Katherine found almost gallows humor in thinking that her information about the virus and progress in creating a vaccine had come from one of the disloyal, murderous cretins in the military. She was their Commander-in-Chief, so they owed her that loyalty, even if she didn't want them in her home.

It had taken Burt only ten minutes to identify John in the Situation Room and have him interviewed by Secret Service security. He had cracked after only twenty minutes of interrogation. His demand to have his attorney present was denied based upon Katherine's Emergency Declaration. After confessing, John had then whined continuously about only trying to protect the President from all the "China bashers," that kept trying to foment revolt in the country.

Katherine's tirade to Susan and Burt about the incompetence that surrounded her had lasted for over fifteen minutes. Half way through it, Burt decided it was far past time to implement his exit strategy. He would tell his assistant he needed to go home briefly to get his wife and some clothes. When he got there, he would ditch his Secret Service transport, load his wife, two cats, his illegal pistol and some food into his SUV and strike out for the little lodge in West Virginia where they occasionally spent a get-a-way weekend. He'd be sure to take an extra gas mask to protect his wife and hope the cats would survive any exposure to the virus.

CHAPTER 63
THE NEW YEAR - PLUS SIXTY DAYS

Peter Worthington's Residence
Outside Cronin, Kentucky
1800 Hours EST

Mike felt amazed and blessed to be sitting down to the table with Lauren, Peter and Liz, and the two incredible young ladies, Lisa and Suzie. When he and Lauren had arrived at Peter's house more than a week ago, Peter had introduced them to Lisa and Suzie with the admonition, "Here are two young ladies that are under my care and protection. Their presence here is to be kept completely confidential until such time as they decide that is no longer necessary. From the looks of things, that may come sooner rather than later. Until then, please ask them no questions and just know that they are family friends of mine that can be trusted completely. Are you both okay with that?"

Although surprised, both Mike and Lauren had nodded their heads yes. Mike said nothing about recalling that Lisa was probably the daughter of Peter's FBI friend, Hugh McIntyre. Since then, Mike had gleaned that both girls were in the genius category of intelligence, with educations involving at least one doctorate. Both were also incredibly bored, although Suzie did seem to enjoy peppering him with questions concerning American history, political theory and the Founding Fathers of the United States. It was quite obvious Suzie was Chinese, which only added to the mystery of how she ended up at Peter's home. In assessing Suzie and her questions, Mike could see that for most professors, she would have been very intimidating. Fortunately, Mike had some understanding and a great appreciation for those that were mentally gifted and did not try to either keep up with her nor did he discount his own lifetime of experiences.

Instead, he tried to steer her in useful directions, the kind he wished he had the time to pursue himself.

Mike recalled it had taken six more days before the Fontaine administration announced to the world that the Chinese government had created a deadly virus, only to have it stolen and altered by Afghan terrorists, who had unleashed it on the world. She tried to sound reassuring that promising efforts were underway at laboratories around the world, the administration recommended everyone stay in their homes for at least a one week period, to avoid spreading the virus further. The lack of power and running water that plagued everyone nationwide would be hardships that must be endured rather than to become infected by venturing out. Mike considered these directions to be "too little, too late."

With the collapse of the power grid, the country had fallen into anarchy somewhat akin to the horror films about the zombie apocalypse, only this time the zombies were either starving people searching for food and water, those infected with the virus, or both. No power meant no heat, no cooling and no running water. Hospitals and medical centers had been completely overwhelmed, with a majority of their staffs succumbing to the virus. Wherever people gathered, the virus found fertile ground to expand its circle of death. Communications were relegated to either those fortunate enough to have a generator, an alternative power source, battery powered radios and ham radios. TV and regular radio stations had gone off the air the day after the administration's announcement. Virtually every communication outlet's staffs either refused to come in or had become victims of the rapidly spreading virus. Panic had erupted, however it had lasted only a couple of days as frightened people huddled in their cold homes.

Linda and Sean's security team, along with a dozen of the neighborhood security members with protective gear, had taken over guard and patrol duties. So far warning shots had been sufficient to drive off the few cars and people on foot that tried to enter the neighborhood gates. Twice, residents of the neighborhood had to be restrained and prevented from trying to smuggle in relatives or friends. Two days earlier, in Mike's name Linda had canvassed each house in the neighborhood for their status, number of people in the home, if they had enough food and water, and whether anyone in the house was sick. Of the 250 homes in the neighborhood, less than half had even responded to Linda's knock. The rest had no sign of life either in or around the home. Six of the residents had reported having at least one person sick in the house, causing Linda to mark the outside of the home with spray paint, similar to what they had done in Europe during the Black Death.

Most of the other homes Linda visited reported having enough food and water to last at least a month. Everyone was starved for news, so she shared what she could, with an emphasis on staying indoors and allowing no one to enter. Of course communicating had been challenging. The batteries on her gas mask voice box had died, but she was able to make herself understood most of the time. These visits prompted Mike to begin sending out a one-page newsletter, Scotch-taped to the window and delivered by a bio-protected security person to each home every other day.

After reporting this information to Mike, Linda returned to Sean's home, where she and the other operators had jury-rigged a decontamination tent just outside of the back door. He could even see a foot peddle that pumped clean, cold water from a cistern, which she used to wash off her mask and chem/bio suit. It wasn't perfect, but was much better than nothing. It would at least work until the cistern was empty.

Inside the home Sean was waiting to greet her. His hug and kiss felt like it washed the entire fate of the world from her shoulders. "Anything new over the wires?" She asked the question while anticipating more bad news.

Sean said, "SOCOM headquarters seems to be falling like most of the rest of the military. Their staff is down to twenty percent, with no officers left. I'm not sure how much longer they will continue to function. This damned bug seems to be unstoppable."

Linda gave him another big hug and looked into his eyes with determination.

"Mister, you need to focus. What do you want to see right here right now?"

With a wan chuckle, Sean smiled and said, "You're right, honey. I want to see everyone here that I care about weathering this storm and building a better world. One not based on hate, greed and the belief that it's okay to take what someone else made or built."

"That's my big guy. Now, does your mom have anything made for dinner? The MRE's fill the hole, but I love her cooking." Her smile was infectious, so both trooped into the kitchen to see what was available. Even though there were enough military field rations to feed all of them for a year or more, Sean's mom had begun filling their basement with long-term food supplies when Sean was only a small boy. Her system of food rotation had been a masterpiece, even if he did eat a lot of canned food past its expiration date. Somehow, she always made sure it was tasty and filling.

Sean sighed wistfully, as they walked into the kitchen, "Man, I miss bread."

Linda punched him playfully in the side, "It's full of gluten, you dullard. You know your mom only keeps good stuff."

Both Sean and Linda suddenly froze and sniffed the air. Wafting into their nostrils was the unmistakable smell of dinner rolls. "Mom?" Sean drew out the question in his amazement. "Where did you find whatever is smelling so wonderful?"

"All you do is work, work, work. You never look in freezer," she said in her accented voice. So long you keep giving me electricity; we can work on eating up everything in freezer and fridge."

Sean looked at Linda with a question in his eyes. She responded, "Yesterday, one of your sergeants told me the two-five hundred gallon tanks of propane should last at least six months, if we only operate it six hours per day. The filter for the air intake in the house should remove any of the nasty bugs that might be floating around outside." Her face turned back into a look of concern. "It's too bad we can't use the wood stove. But bringing wood inside is just too dangerous, since it might be carrying the virus."

CHAPTER 64
THE NEW YEAR - PLUS SEVENTY DAYS

The Presidential Emergency Operations Center (PEOC)
Beneath the East Wing of the White House
1830 Hours EST

Katherine sat in her small office in the PEOC sipping on a glass of fine scotch from one of four bottles that Susan had found in Walter's bedroom suite upstairs. It had required Katherine's stern order for the Secret Service security personnel to allow Susan out of the PEOC for this very important mission, and only accompanied by one of the security folks. The entire building above had been completely unguarded for at least the past twenty-four hours as the surviving White House staff had either gotten sick or abandoned their post as the country literally fell apart. Both Susan and her guard had worn gas masks. When Susan found the four bottles of scotch, she gave one to her security escort and, after washing the exterior of the bottles thoroughly, carried them into Katherine's office.

Throughout the country, all public services had collapsed. No electric power, no running water, and virtually no trucks or cars on the roads as survivors huddled in buildings they hoped would protect them from the insidious bug that no one could see. The few ham and private radio signals flying around the atmosphere described death and what was universally called the apocalypse. The few military units still functioning operated in full chem/bio gear, but struggled to keep things from being contaminated by the virus. They encountered death wherever they went.

"Susan, dear, the CDC says they will be able to send me 1,500 doses of vaccine tomorrow. I need you to make a list of top 1,250 people that are critical to government continuity. And Susan, make sure they are all politically reliable. You know what I mean? Can you do that for me?"

Susan was completely horrified at what she had just heard, but no more so than what she had witnessed over the past several weeks. Katherine had seemed to be losing touch with reality. Two foiled military coups were attempted by generals who felt Katherine was leading everyone to destruction. Other, more politically active generals had stopped the attempts, but they had rattled Katherine badly. The friendly press had, fortunately, refused to report the coup attempts or the few street protests that happened after Katherine's last address. Homeland Security had squashed the protests quickly and brutally, using techniques reminiscent of those used by the Bolsheviks prior to WWII, minus the mounted sabre charges. All news reporting had ceased two days after Katherine's last public address.

Susan and Marc had been part of the essential staff brought into the PEOC. Twice the number of people were jammed into the PEOC than it was designed to house. With Burt's disappearance, Katherine had designated Marc as her acting Chief of Staff and her communications director, while Susan delivered some, if not all of Katherine's edicts to the rest of the staff. Almost as soon as everyone was directed to the PEOC Towanda had been bound and gagged by the security staff for her constant loud and outrageous demands. After three days she requested to leave. Katherine had willingly granted that request. Most of the rest of the leadership in the government had gone to either the Capital building or the Pentagon, where the virus had penetrated and had begun to infect those inside. With news outlets down, the only information available was coming in from the military, which was itself, being decimated.

• • • •

Home outside of Frankfort, Kentucky
2045 Hours EST

Kerry DuBois sat in the basement, wrapped in a blanket, sipping on a can of beer. By candlelight he watched Tank and Blondi wrap up the body of the old lady that owned the place inside of three large garbage bags. They then lifted the body, Blondi grabbing the shoulders and Tank grabbing the feet, to carry her up the stairs. They dropped the body in a closet near the door and quickly when back down the stairs, closing the door behind them.

Tank looked at Blondi before popping open a beer for himself. "You sure the prepper you worked with won't be coming back to see his mom? Hell, he set this place up like a bomb shelter!"

Blondi shook his head, "No, he was one of the first in the newsroom to get sick and some other fools rushed him to the hospital. I'm just glad I gave him a ride to his mom's once. Arrogant asshole was always telling everyone that we should prepare for the end of the world. Guess he was right, and I'm damned glad he did the preparing!"

"Kerry?" Tank asked. "How long do you figure we should hunker down here?"

Kerry rubbed his stubbly chin for a few seconds before saying, "Well, according to Coyote's Chief of Staff, this shit could stick around in the air for at least a couple of weeks, and probably a couple of months. At least until the dead people decompose and the sun kills all the airborne spores. Looks like we're gonna' run out of beer long before that. Seems to be a lot of food, but I'm gonna' get real tired of using and smellin' the crap bucket over there."

Blondi showed an evil smile, and said, "You can always go on up the stairs and just use the great outdoors." All three men laughed at that, before taking another swig of beer.

"Tank, how'd you stay out of jail, after you took out the Governor and all?" Kerry's question was asked in a tone of admiration.

"I got me a few hidey holes here and about. Unfortunately, none of them have the kind of stocks this here place has. How'd you know it was me?" His expression on his face had turned threatening.

"Chapman found out through his sources in the KSP." Kerry was wary now, as it sunk in that Tank might consider him a threat to turn him in. "Don't matter now, though. Ain't gonna be any more police or maybe even any more people." None of the men had any comment to that.

. . .

Outside of Cronin, Kentucky
1015 Hours

Linda sat in Peter's family room talking to Mike, with everyone else listening intently. Her report had been short and concise. "Only sixty homes have someone living in them and two of them contained people sick with some type of illness, although not necessarily the virus. It was reported through military communications that the President continued to monitor things and issue orders from an undisclosed location, but realistically, nothing has been done. The country would be in complete anarchy, except almost everyone left is too afraid to leave their homes or shelters. Wherever the military people go, they find death. Those that the virus hasn't killed seem to have died through exposure, lack of clean water or simply giving up. The military estimate is that over fifty percent of the country's population has already died, with that number being much higher on the coasts and major urban centers. They keep promising that a vaccine for the virus is coming, but there has been nothing yet and pretty soon there won't be any medical people to even administer it."

With a deep breath, Linda continued, "Now for some good news." Almost everyone registered surprise. "The CDC has successfully made a limited run to produce what they believe is an effective vaccine. That's supposed to be all hush, hush, but considering, I don't think that matters to this group. I don't know when it might be available, but at least there is one. Some more good news is that so far, the survivors in the neighborhood seem to be holding up pretty well. Mike, all of your suggestions for preparing for disaster seem to have gone a long way toward making that happen."

Mike nodded, "Thanks, Linda. If I may, let's have another positive prayer right now for all of us, and particularly for all of humanity." With that Mike lead everyone in a prayer worthy of a cathedral. Su Ling listened with rapt attention, trying to understand both how his words moved everyone, including herself, and why they seemed to be so effective.

CHAPTER 65
THE NEW YEAR - PLUS SEVENTY-TWO DAYS

The White House PEOC
1500 Hours EST

Marc felt almost claustrophobic in the white jumpsuit with hood and the gas mask, as he stood outside of the PEOC. The day before a Marine Major had gotten off of Marine One, which had landed on the front lawn of the White House. The Major had delivered two padded Pelican heavy duty suitcases and a large, thick plastic bag to the PEOC. Inside, Marc knew, was possibly the hope for the country and even mankind. He had been surprised that neither Susan nor the President had come out of the President's office to receive the vaccine. Instead, a message from Susan directed Marc to make sure the 136 people in the PEOC received the vaccine immediately, and that the rest, all but 250 doses, were to be delivered to the Pentagon the following morning. Marc had just returned from personally making that delivery, as directed.

While waiting for security to open the outer door to the PEOC, Marc had a funny feeling in his gut. He hadn't seen Susan for over two days, as she seemed to be cloistered with the President. Something was happening, but he didn't know what.

When the PEOC outer door opened, he was stopped by a hand, palm up, in his direction. A booted foot kicked out a smaller Pelican suitcase, followed by a grocery-sized plastic bag and an envelope. The door was then closed in his face. In shock, he leaned over to pick up the envelope in his gloved hand. It had his name on it, in Susan's flowing script. When he opened it, he found her personal letter to him.

My Dearest Marc,

For the entire time that I've known you, you have been my life saver. A voice of reason in our crazy world, a shoulder to cry on, a man to hold me close, and the most special person in my life. It is now time for you to leave this nuthouse and go forth and, as you always wanted to, save the world. The President and I are both sick, probably with the virus. She is delirious now, but I was able to get her to sign the enclosed order a few minutes ago. You are to order Marine One to take you to the safest place you can think of, and give these 250 vaccine doses to those you believe best deserve them.

The CDC had some type of accident before they were able to vaccinate more than a handful of their own personnel. The vaccine doses you carry are the last that will likely be available. There is a girl named Julie Carrithers that seems to have a natural immunity to the virus. She is at the CDC in the company of Special Forces Captain Schneider.

I'm sorry to be rambling on, but think my fever is getting worse. Please think kindly of me. I always just wanted to make things better for everyone. Now GET OUT OF HERE! NOW!

All my Love,
Susan

Marc tried to wipe the tears from his eyes, only to find the gas mask in the way. He opened the second folded piece of paper in the envelope and found it to be a PEO directing the Commander of Marine One to take him to the confidential destination provided by Marc Baxter. It had the Presidential Seal on it. Marc folded it back, and put it back into the envelope. Susan's letter was placed in the outer pocket of his white jumpsuit. He then stumbled back up the stairs, into the White House and out to the waiting Marine One.

The Major looked over the PEO carefully, before saying, "You Baxter?" When Marc bobbed his head up and down, he asked, "Where to?"

Marc mentally kicked himself for not having given that question a lot more thought. Out of nowhere, which he later attributed to divine providence, came the image of his sister Lauren into his mind. "Take me to Kentucky, a place in Central Kentucky outside of Cronin. Just head for Lexington and I'll give you directions from there."

The Major looked doubtfully into Marc's mask, seeing the streaming tears, but finally said, "Okay, get in and strap up. Should take a little less than three hours."

Marc looked at the White House and downtown Washington, D.C. as the chopper lifted away and began flying away to the West. The flood of emotion was dampened by the numbness brought on by extreme fatigue. He was asleep within fifteen minutes of departure.

CHAPTER 66
THE NEW YEAR - PLUS SEVENTY-TWO DAYS

Outside of Cronin, Kentucky
1745 Hours EST

Marine One circled the neighborhood as twilight began to fall. It took a couple of minutes searching before the Major decided to land next to the neighborhood shelter. As he circled the shelter 500 feet in the air, he shouted over the intercom, "Baxter, there are men with gas masks and guns out there waiting for you. Still want me to set you down?"

Marc looked out the window and saw at least six men, all armed with what looked like M-16s taking cover around their intended landing zone. "Yes, please. These guys won't be taking any shots at you so long as you don't shoot at them."

All Marc heard on the intercom was a grunt as Marine One descended. One of the crewmen had Marc unbelted and on his way out the door within seconds of touchdown. As Marc looked back, another crewman was handing him the Pelican case, plastic bag and envelope. No sooner had the exchange been made then the large chopper rose into the air and flew quickly away to the East.

Marc stood in the open grass by the shelter as two apparent soldiers in full chem/bio gear approached him with weapons raised. With the absence of the helicopter noise, he could clearly hear them shouting through their masks, "Show me your hands!" Marc set down the case and plastic bag and raised his hands. One of the two men approached, while the other kept his rifle trained on Marc's chest.

The man approaching said, "Who the hell are you?"

Marc initially felt the urge to be flippant, but instead decided simplicity was best in this case. "I'm Marc Baxter. I'm looking for my sister, Lauren. She and

Mike live right over there." He motioned with one of his two raised hands at their house.

The one soldier quickly looked at the covering man and said, "This guy claims to be Mike's brother-in-law. If he's delivered by Marine One, I'd bet he probably is." With that the second soldier lowered his rifle and both approached Marc. "You just come from Washington?"

"Yes. Is my sister okay? All I hear about these days is death."

"Follow me. And please do only what I tell you to do." Seeing Marc bend over to take the Pelican case, the man said, "I'll get that. By the way, what's the likelihood these things are contaminated with the virus?"

Marc paused for a beat, before saying, "Probably pretty good. They need to be decontaminated, but their contents are pretty important. Please handle them carefully, okay? Oh, who's in charge here?"

"That would be Mike. Mike Broehm. You'll be seeing your brother-in-law shortly. I hope he's happy to see you, because anyone else trying to get into the neighborhood gets shot."

When Marc looked carefully at the man, he did not detect any humor in his eye.

It was over an hour later before a raw skinned Marc Baxter, with a shaved head, was led into Peter's glass walled greenhouse, in a bathrobe, slippers and a filter mask. The two operators had stripped and scrubbed him with soap and brushes better than a surgeon scrubs his hands before surgery. Looking at him through the glass window of the house were Marc, Lauren and several others that he didn't know.

"Oh, my baby brother! I'm just so happy you're alive!" Lauren gushed over the microphone that went to speakers in the greenhouse.

Mike moved to the mic and said, "Heh, Marc, I'm really sorry about the whole decon and quarantine thing, but with all the people this bug has killed, we can't be too careful. Are you okay? How did you get here? What can you tell us about what's going on?"

Marc looked around warily and mumbled about how he was just happy to be away from Washington. Mike picked up on the problem immediately and said, "Marc, just so that you know, everyone here has a need to know everything you can tell us. I won't keep secrets from them. Can you at least tell me what's in the case you brought?"

Marc stood with bowed head for a while before looking up and saying, "Mike, please. Can just you and I talk for a few minutes? You can decide after that who needs to know what."

Mike turned to the others in the window and said, "Would you guys excuse us for a little bit. I promise, I'll share all the juiciest parts later."

Everyone but Lauren turned and walked away. Interestingly, Mike could hear Suzie ask, "Is he single?" He had seen no indication she had an interest in anyone of the opposite sex since he had met her, until now.

Marc then said, "Lauren, you know I love you like a sister, but can I talk to Mike alone? Please?"

Although shocked and more than a little offended, Lauren walked away as well.

CHAPTER 67
THE NEW YEAR - PLUS SEVENTY-TWO DAYS

Outside of Cronin, Kentucky
2000 Hours EST

Mike looked sternly at Marc before saying, "All right, Marc. What's so damned important that it needs all of this?"

With a deep breath, Marc asked, "Do you know the history and origin of this deadly plague?"

Mike surprised him by saying, "Yes, actually, I do. Two of the people you just sent away are Special Forces officers that were briefed about the terrorists who unleashed this stuff and that it came from the Chinese originally. What else can you tell me?"

"Mike, someone with a natural immunity to this virus was rescued in Afghanistan and was taken to the CDC. The CDC claims to have concocted a vaccine, based on this girl's blood and the work done by the terrorist that created this stuff. Mike, I've been given a dose of vaccine. In that Pelican case, I have 250 more doses of the vaccine. Some kind of accident happened at CDC after the vaccine was made and it is likely no more vaccine was produced. I don't know. Regardless, I have 250 doses and 250 syringes to administer them. Besides you and Lauren, I don't know who to give them to. This is probably life and death stuff, Mike. If I can stay with you, I'd really like you to decide who gets those doses. Please?"

Of all the things that had happened over the past several months, this one hit Mike the hardest. He also now understood why Marc wanted a private conversation with him. "Is that all that can't be shared with the others, Marc?"

"Yes, Mike. It is. Oh, who's the Asian girl? My God, but she's beautiful!"

At that Mike smiled and said, "That's Suzie. Careful, she's brilliant and you'll get to meet her later." Mike then shouted for everyone to come back and the next two hours were filled with information sharing, sad stories and many funny ones. Marc didn't try to hide his disgust with what the President had done and only claimed that he did his best to mitigate the worst of her policies.

Late that night, Mike sat with Linda and Sean in Peter's big pickup truck in the garage. They had been discussing Mike's decision of who should get the vaccine. The first fifty or so were easy, being close friends, family and security people. After that it became more difficult. At one point, Mike asked both Linda and Sean if they would take up the burden and decide. Both adamantly refused.

Mike," Sean said, "like it or not, you're in charge here. You are the only one who can make the decision that everyone will accept as being completely unbiased and fair. Brutal as the decision is, you also need to take into account who will help lead the human race going forward. Buddy, I trust you'll make the right decision." Linda nodded her agreement. Everything having been aired, both got out of the truck, leaving Mike to the longest night of his life.

THE END, BOOK 2

APPENDIX A: CHARACTERS

I. KENTUCKY

Mike Broehm (Pronounced Brame and rhymes with frame)
Mike is an outwardly simple man who lives in a nice subdivision in Kentucky. He is married to Lauren, has two grown children and suffers from a weight problem, along with high blood pressure and pre-diabetes. He works as a research biochemist at a local university.

Lauren Broehm
Mike's wife. Lauren's parents had died in a tractor trailer/car accident when she was in college. Lauren was 18 at the time and her brother Marc was only 6. Lauren had helped her aunt raise Marc and was later appointed as Marc's guardian.

Kerry DuBois
Kerry lives in Mike's neighborhood and works for state government in the transportation cabinet. His background includes a bachelor's in Social Engineering from UC Berkley.

Jim Carson
Jim is one of Mike's hunting buddies and a CPA and economist.

Fred Callahan
Fred is one of the few black men living in Mike Broehm's neighborhood and is Chief of Police in the nearby town of Cronin. Fred's Korean-born wife is named Penny. His son is Sean Callahan.

Sean Callahan

Sean is a Major in the U.S. Army Special Forces Command (SOCOM), commander of a Green Beret company and is the son of Fred Callahan.

Onie Lisle

Onie is the widowed wife of retired KSP State Trooper Jim Lisle and mother of four grown sons and three grown daughters. She becomes Mike Broehms's go-to person to handle neighborhood relations and general, non-security related organization.

Linda Sharpe

First Lieutenant Linda Sharpe is a Team Leader in Sean Callahan's Special Forces (Green Berets) Company. She leads an "A" Team of operators in the field. She's the orphan of two Army parents and just missed being on the US Olympic swim team.

Rollie McDermott

Rollie is another of Mike's hunting buddies and a builder who can build or fix anything.

Peter Worthington

Peter is a university professor of mechanical and environmental engineering. In his mid-50s he is recognized leader in meeting environmental standards for exotic metals mining, through which he has become wealthy. His land is connected to Mike Broehm's land. He is married to Elizabeth, who is a good personal friend of Lauren Broehm.

Jim Webb

Jim is a semi-retired electrician who lives in Mike Broehm's neighborhood. He is a life-long member of the IBEW (International Brotherhood of Electrical Workers).

Freddy Dobson

Freddy is Kerry DuBois' crony and the son of a wealthy East Coast family.

John Chapman

John is Kerry DuBois' crony and a former community organizer from Louisville, Kentucky who had been brought on by the previous governor to be his Lieutenant Governor. John is well wired with the unions throughout the state and was instrumental in organizing the get-out-the-vote effort to get elected. He convinced the Governor to pardon his friend and money man Jerry 'the Tank' Monahan for the minor drug transgressions for which he was convicted 15 years earlier. His brother-in-law is General Steven Thompson, Commander of the Army National Guard in Kentucky.

Jerry 'the Tank' Monahan

Tank is from the mountains of Eastern Kentucky. He accumulated a great deal of wealth from extortion activities targeting the coal companies back in the 1970s. He branched out into marijuana sales before being arrested by federal and state agents. Tank owns the Pen and Ink Saloon in Frankfort, through a shell company, where he has a private office and meeting room, including a very private entrance to an underground garage.

Mickey Blondiac

Mickey, known as "Blondi," is a DuBois crony and the political commentator for the largest paper in Central Kentucky. He publishes a weekly column called *Blondi's Corner.*

Scott Shelby

Scott is a financial advisor who left Wall Street, after his heart attack at the age of 32, and opened up a small financial firm in the town of Cronin. He handles Peter Worthington's portfolio.

II. WASHINGTON

President Katherine (with a "K") Fontaine.
Katherine Fontaine is the ambitious wife (and attorney) of former Senator and former Vice President Walter Fontaine – and a former liberal/moderate Senator from California.

W. Allen Kidd
Director of the Federal Bureau of Investigation (FBI).

General Steven K. Taylor
Chairman of the Joint Chiefs of Staff

Walter Fontaine
Former Vice President, Walter left the Vice Presidency with a strong belief he never wanted to be President, a stance which was not popular with his wife Katherine.

Su Ling
Su is a both very attractive and beautifully accomplished in her ability to meet the needs of a man. She was trained at the MSS *Charm* School located outside of Shanghai.

Sung Hong
SU Ling's MSS handler in Washington.

Don Stetson
Stetson was Katherine Fontaine's campaign manager.

Susan Cassel
Susan is an attorney and personal assistant to Katherine.

Marc Baxter
Marc is a Columbia trained Journalism graduate and New York Times Junior Political Editor who joined Katherine Fontaine's campaign and then became a

primary assistant to Presidential Press Secretary Marjorie Klein. Marc is also the younger brother of Laura Broehm.

John Butler
Marc Baxter's administrative assistant in the White House Press Office.

General Roger Tignor
General Tignor is Katherine Fontaine's Director of National Intelligence. Tignor is an Air Force General and one of the brightest minds in the military who was tagged by Katherine to be Director of National Intelligence. He is in charge of all U.S. government intelligence collection.

Towanda Jefferson
Towanda is a Georgetown University School of Journalism graduate who is forced upon Marjorie as her deputy by Katherine's need to placate wealthy donor Eli Fredericks.

Burton Combs
Katherine Fontaine's Chief of Staff. He was a Senator who was recruited by Katherine right after she was elected President.

Bradley Pittson
Director of the CIA.

Donald Clayborn
Director of the NSA.

David Cummin
Secretary of State under Katherine Fontaine. A holdover from the previous administration, he ends up staying due to his personal patriotism.

Seth Goldberg
Secretary of the Treasury under Katherine Fontaine.

Dmitriy Roskov

Roskov is Director of Homeland Security, a former Chicago Police Commissioner and political hack who plays the political game well, and has both backbone and character.

Carlton Hathaway

Secretary of Defense in the new Fontaine administration. He was previously the Administrator of the United States Environmental Protection Agency (EPA).

Lisa McIntyre

Lisa is a graduate student at American University in Washington, DC studying a dual track of Chemistry and Biology. Lisa is the daughter of Hugh McIntyre.

Hugh McIntyre

Hugh is a Unit Chief in the Counterterrorism Section of FBIHQ.

Eli Fredericks

Fredericks is a graduate of Princeton. He is an extremely wealthy man who has made billions through hedge funds and government contracts directed to minority contractors. He is a frequent visitor to the White House and the primary donor for Katherine's campaign.

John Levy

Levy is the lead agent for Walter Fontaine's protection detail. He is financially strapped or he would have quit the detail and possibly the Secret Service all together, due to the stresses and annoyances he endures from Walter.

III. PEOPLES REPUBLIC OF CHINA

General Hu Sengai

Hu is the General responsible for the PRC's "Special Warfare" arsenal, to include nuclear, biological and chemical weapons.

Song Ren

Song is the Chinese Premier and General Secretary of the Communist Party in China. It places him at the head of the Chinese government. He is obsessed with retaking control of the Chinese renegade province known in the West as Taiwan or Republic of China and formerly as Formosa.

General Lao Tung

Lao is the head of the PRC Ministry of State Security (PRC version of the Russian KGB). Lao has the ear of Song and is the perfect balance between being a spy master, an economist and a politician.

Wong Jie

Song's Secretary and de Facto Chief of Staff.

Major Cho Chong

Cho is the bright, up and coming MSS officer sent by Lao to meet with Ahmed. Cho is fluent in 8 languages, including Arabic.

Gong Xi

Foreign Minister, People's Republic of China. Gong does what Song and Lao tell him to do.

Chen Wen

Chen is a major industrialist in the People's Republic of China. He is a billionaire who has gotten wealthy by knowing the right people within the Politburo and supplying military material to the PLA.

Ching Kai

Chen Wen's assistant that conveys confidential directions to high-ranking officials and business people. He towers over most at just over two meters (6'6") tall.

Wu Chin

Wu is Chen Wen's clandestine contact with Eli Fredericks, usually in Washington, DC.

IV. Afghanistan

Ahmed al-Rasheed
Ahmed is the undisputed leader of Jihadists of the Prophet (JOTP), a radical Muslim group loosely affiliated with al-Qaida and ISIS (Islamic State). He second wife is Jasmine and he has been recruited by Cho for future actions.

Abdullah Muhammad
Abdullah is close confidant of al-Rasheed.

Ali al-Hadiz
Ali is the brother of Ahmed's second wife Jasmine and the rising star within the family. Ali just graduated from the University of Kentucky - School of Pharmacy, with a PhD.

Julie Carrithers
An American, Arabic speaking aid girl that had been kidnapped and imprisoned by the JOTP for purposes of teaching Ahmed's martyrs enough English and other skills to allow them to be able to travel throughout the world.

Captain Charles Schneider
Special Forces "A" Team leader, Team 2, 7th Special Forces Group with a mission in the mountains of Southeastern Afghanistan.

APPENDIX B: FORTY-FIVE GOALS OF COMMUNISM

Congressional Record--Appendix, pp. A34-A35 January 10, 1963
Current Communist Goals
EXTENSION OF REMARKS OF
HON. A. S. HERLONG, JR. OF FLORIDA
IN THE HOUSE OF REPRESENTATIVES
Thursday, January 10, 1963

Mr. HERLONG. Mr. Speaker, Mrs. Patricia Nordman of De Land, Fla., is an ardent and articulate opponent of communism, and until recently published the De Land Courier, which she dedicated to the purpose of alerting the public to the dangers of communism in America.

At Mrs. Nordman's request, I include in the RECORD, under unanimous consent, the following "Current Communist Goals," which she identifies as an excerpt from "The Naked Communist," by Cleon Skousen:

[From "The Naked Communist," by Cleon Skousen]
CURRENT COMMUNIST GOALS

U.S. acceptance of coexistence as the only alternative to atomic war.

U.S. willingness to capitulate in preference to engaging in atomic war.

Develop the illusion that total disarmament [by] the United States would be a demonstration of moral strength.

Permit free trade between all nations regardless of Communist affiliation and regardless of whether or not items could be used for war.

Extension of long-term loans to Russia and Soviet satellites.

Provide American aid to all nations regardless of Communist domination.

Grant recognition of Red China. Admission of Red China to the U.N.

Set up East and West Germany as separate states in spite of Khrushchev's promise in 1955 to settle the German question by free elections under supervision of the U.N.

Prolong the conferences to ban atomic tests because the United States has agreed to suspend tests as long as negotiations are in progress.

Allow all Soviet satellites individual representation in the U.N.

Promote the U.N. as the only hope for mankind. If its charter is rewritten, demand that it be set up as a one-world government with its own independent armed forces. (Some Communist leaders believe the world can be taken over as easily by the U.N. as by Moscow. Sometimes these two centers compete with each other as they are now doing in the Congo.)

Resist any attempt to outlaw the Communist Party.

Do away with all loyalty oaths.

Continue giving Russia access to the U.S. Patent Office.

Capture one or both of the political parties in the United States.

Use technical decisions of the courts to weaken basic American institutions by claiming their activities violate civil rights.

Get control of the schools. Use them as transmission belts for socialism and current Communist propaganda. Soften the curriculum. Get control of teachers' associations. Put the party line in textbooks.

Gain control of all student newspapers.

Use student riots to foment public protests against programs or organizations which are under Communist attack.

Infiltrate the press. Get control of book-review assignments, editorial writing, and policymaking positions.

Gain control of key positions in radio, TV, and motion pictures.

Continue discrediting American culture by degrading all forms of artistic expression. An American Communist cell was told to "eliminate all good sculpture from parks and buildings, substitute shapeless, awkward and meaningless forms."

Control art critics and directors of art museums. "Our plan is to promote ugliness, repulsive, meaningless art."

Eliminate all laws governing obscenity by calling them "censorship" and a violation of free speech and free press.

Break down cultural standards of morality by promoting pornography and obscenity in books, magazines, motion pictures, radio, and TV.

Present homosexuality, degeneracy and promiscuity as "normal, natural, and healthy."

Infiltrate the churches and replace revealed religion with "social" religion. Discredit the Bible and emphasize the need for intellectual maturity which does not need a "religious crutch."

Eliminate prayer or any phase of religious expression in the schools on the ground that it violates the principle of "separation of church and state."

Discredit the American Constitution by calling it inadequate, old-fashioned, out of step with modern needs, a hindrance to cooperation between nations on a worldwide basis.

Discredit the American Founding Fathers. Present them as selfish aristocrats who had no concern for the "common man."

Belittle all forms of American culture and discourage the teaching of American history on the ground that it was only a minor part of the "big picture." Give more emphasis to Russian history since the Communists took over.

Support any socialist movement to give centralized control over any part of the culture-education, social agencies, welfare programs, mental health clinics, etc.

Eliminate all laws or procedures which interfere with the operation of the Communist apparatus.

Eliminate the House Committee on Un-American Activities.

Discredit and eventually dismantle the FBI.

Infiltrate and gain control of more unions.

Infiltrate and gain control of big business.

Transfer some of the powers of arrest from the police to social agencies. Treat all behavioral problems as psychiatric disorders which no one but psychiatrists can understand [or treat].

Dominate the psychiatric profession and use mental health laws as a means of gaining coercive control over those who oppose Communist goals.

Discredit the family as an institution. Encourage promiscuity and easy divorce.

Emphasize the need to raise children away from the negative influence of parents. Attribute prejudices, mental blocks and retarding of children to suppressive influence of parents.

Create the impression that violence and insurrection are legitimate aspects of the American tradition; that students and special-interest groups should rise up and use ["]united force["] to solve economic, political or social problems.

Overthrow all colonial governments before native populations are ready for self-government.

Internationalize the Panama Canal.

Repeal the Connally reservation so the United States cannot prevent the World Court from seizing jurisdiction [over domestic problems. Give the World Court jurisdiction] over nations and individuals alike.

APPENDIX C:
EXCERPT FROM PRESIDENTIAL EXECUTIVE ORDER 13603

Excerpt from Presidential Executive Order 13603, issued March 16, 2012.

Sec. 201. Priorities and Allocations Authorities. (a) The authority of the President conferred by section 101 of the Act, 50 U.S.C. App. 2071, to require acceptance and priority performance of contracts or orders (other than contracts of employment) to promote the national defense over performance of any other contracts or orders, and to allocate materials, services, and facilities as deemed necessary or appropriate to promote the national defense, is delegated to the following agency heads: the Secretary of Agriculture with respect to food resources, food resource facilities, livestock resources, veterinary resources, plant health resources, and the domestic distribution of farm equipment and commercial fertilizer; the Secretary of Energy with respect to all forms of energy; the Secretary of Health and Human Services with respect to health resources; the Secretary of Transportation with respect to all forms of civil transportation; the Secretary of Defense with respect to water resources; and the Secretary of Commerce with respect to all other materials, services, and facilities, including construction materials.

APPENDIX D: TERMS AND DEFINITIONS

Charm School
Special school located outside of Shanghai, China where young women and a few young men are trained to exert sexual and psychological influence over others, usually men. This school is operated by the MSS.

DNI – Director of National Intelligence
The Director of National Intelligence (DNI) is the U.S. government official – subject to the authority, direction, and control of the President – to advise the President and other agencies about intelligence matters related to national security. He or she also serves as head of the sixteen-member U.S. Intelligence Community.

EMP – Electo-magnetic pulse
An EMP is a surge of energy that can be caused by a solar flare, high level nuclear detonation or other mechanical means. It will burn up and render inoperable most electronic devices or circuits.

FEMA – Federal Emergency Management Authority
The Federal Emergency Management Agency (FEMA) is an agency of the United States Department of Homeland Security, initially created by Presidential Reorganization Plan No. 3 of 1978 and implemented by two Executive Orders on April 1, 1979. This organization coordinates the federal response to emergencies of all kinds, including hurricanes, tornados, floods and other catastrophic events affecting large numbers of people.

Formosa – also known as Taiwan
This island off the coast of Fujian Province, People's Republic of China (PRC) is also known as the Republic of China. Following World War II, the Communist insurgency defeated the Nationalist Chinese government, the remnants of which

fled to the island of Taiwan and nearby islands. Under a democratic, capitalistic government Taiwan has flourished economically while the PRC remained closed until the early 1970s. The PRC Communist Party views Taiwan as a break-away province that will be eventually returned to the Chinese empire.

HRT – Hostage Rescue Team
The FBI Hostage Rescue Team (HRT) is the counter-terrorism and hostage rescue unit of the FBI. Its mission is to rescue American citizens and allies who are held hostage by hostile forces, usually terrorists and/or criminals.

Intel – Intelligence
Intel is the description for a group or agency that collects secret information or "Intelligence" about an enemy or area. Intel is the collected information used by decision-makers to form actions and policies.

JOTP – Jihadists of the Prophet
The JOTP is the Afghan terrorist group lead by Ahmed al-Rasheed.

MSS – Ministry of State Security
The Ministry of State Security (MSS) is the intelligence and security agency of the People's Republic of China (nonmilitary area of interests), responsible for counter-intelligence, foreign intelligence and political security. It is headquartered near the Ministry of Public Security of the People's Republic of China in Beijing. It has responsibilities that are roughly equivalent to the old Soviet KGB and a combination of the FBI and CIA and is an organ of the Chinese Communist Party.

Nanotechnology
Nanotechnology ("nanotech") is manipulation of matter on an atomic, molecular, and supramolecular scale.[32]

Operators
Special Forces Operator is the title and description for those soldiers who carry out Special Forces operations or missions in the field.

---

[32] Wikipedia

PLA – People's Liberation Army

The Chinese People's Liberation Army (PLA) is the official name of the armed forces of the People's Republic of China. It is under the complete control of the Communist Party of China (CPC).

Posse Comitatus Act

The Posse Comitatus Act, 18 U.S. Code, Section 1385, prevents the military from enforcing civil laws in the United States, except in a declared emergency.

Proletariat Revolution

A proletarian revolution is a social revolution in which the working class attempts to overthrow the bourgeoisie. Proletarian revolutions are generally advocated by socialists, communists, and most anarchists.[33]

RPG – Rocket Propelled Grenade

A Soviet designed shoulder-fired anti-tank weapon somewhat similar to a bazooka. It fires a grenade, powered by a small rocket. The grenade is made of a shape charge capable of penetrating light armor or building walls and spraying hot metal fragments after penetration occurs.

SOCOM – Special Operations Command

USSOCOM synchronizes the planning of special operations and provides SOF (Special Operations Forces) to support persistent, networked and distributed GCC operations in order to protect and advance our Nation's interests.[34]

SVR

The Foreign Intelligence Service of the Russian Federation (Russian: Служба вне́шней разве́дки, tr.Sluzhbavneshneyrazvedki is Russia's external intelligence agency, mainly for civilian affairs.[44] It is roughly equivalent to the CIA.

SWE – Secure Working Environment

---

[33] Wikipedia

[34] United States Special Operations Command Website [44] Wikipedia

A space or office which is specifically designed to protect classified or sensitive information from access by hostile entities.

VA – Veteran's Administration
The U.S. Federal Government's agency responsible for administration of benefits earned by military veterans.

APPENDIX E: TAIWAN RELATIONS ACT (TRA) OF 1979

The TRA was passed in 1979 in direct response to President Jimmy Carter's unilateral declaration to vacate a 1954 mutual defense treaty with the Republic of China (ROC), currently located on the island of Taiwan. That treaty had been ratified by the United States Senate. Court challenges to President Carter's executive actions were unsuccessful. In support of President Carter, the U.S. Congress passed a watered-down version of an original bill meant to provide more security for this now-orphaned Pacific Rim ally.

TRA Sections 2 and 3 contain the key provisions with respect to military defense of Taiwan. Section 2 declares as a matter of U.S. policy that the U.S. expects the "future of Taiwan will be determined by peaceful means," that "any effort to determine the future of Taiwan by other than peaceful means, including by boycotts or embargoes, [is] a threat to the peace and security of the Western Pacific area", and "to maintain the capacity of the United States to resist any resort to force or other forms of coercion that would jeopardize the security, or the social or economic system, of the people on Taiwan."

Section 3 implements this policy by requiring that the U.S. government "make available to Taiwan such defense articles and defense services in such quantity as may be necessary to enable Taiwan to maintain a sufficient self-defense capability." It further requires the President "to inform the Congress promptly of any threat to the security or the social or economic system of the people on Taiwan and any danger to the interests of the United States arising therefrom." Finally, the TRA requires the "President and the Congress shall determine, in accordance with constitutional processes, appropriate action by the United States in response to any such danger."

On its face, the TRA appears to only require the U.S. to sell defensive materials to allow Taiwan to maintain self-defense and for the President to inform Congress of any threat to the security of Taiwan. If China launched a military assault, the President is only legally obligated to "determine, in accordance with constitutional processes, appropriate action." This requirement is for executive-legislative consultations and hardly seems like an obligation, "to intervene if China launched an armed strike on Taiwan."

Since the Carter presidency, Taiwan has lobbied very hard within the halls of the U.S. Congress and the White House to maintain good relations with the U.S. They have also maintained a very capable defensive military presence on the island as a deterrent to PRC aggressions. They are acutely aware that legally, the TRA is not much of a security guarantee at all. However, the TRA should also not be dismissed as legally inconsequential with respect to U.S. obligations. After all, other U.S. defense guarantees in the region are not much more robust than the TRA.

ABOUT THE AUTHOR

Originally from Louisville, Kentucky, the author is a graduate of Indiana University and Salmon P. Chase College of Law. Following a short stint as a rural attorney, he joined the Federal Bureau of Investigation (FBI) as a Special Agent. After his first assignment to the Green Bay, Wisconsin FBI office, he was transferred to the New York City Field Office where the next ten years were spent identifying, investigating, recruiting and operating foreign spies. This work continued for another 18 years after his transfer to the FBI office in Central Kentucky. His work also included a major case involving a corrupt public official. During his 31 years in the FBI, the author served as an undercover agent, SWAT operator, division assistant legal counsel, pilot, Strategic Partnership Program coordinator, Weapons of Mass Destruction coordinator, Domestic and Internal Terrorism coordinator and Airport Liaison agent, among other duties. The author is married with one son and lives in Central Kentucky. Hobbies include motorcycling, golf, racquetball, flying single engine airplanes, travel and membership in the American Legion.

Note from the Author

Word-of-mouth is crucial for any author to succeed. If you enjoyed *The Final Proclamation*, please leave a review online—anywhere you are able. Even if it's just a sentence or two. It would make all the difference and would be very much appreciated.

Thanks!
Carlton James

Thank you so much for reading one of **Carlton James's** novels.
If you enjoyed the experience, please check out our recommended
title for your next great read!

The First Coronation

"Although clearly fiction, certain passages bare striking
similarities to recent events and readers will want to prepare
for what may soon come."
-Arlynn McMahon, author of *Train Like You Fly*

View other Black Rose Writing titles at
www.blackrosewriting.com/books and use promo code
PRINT to receive a **20% discount** when purchasing.